KINGS OF JUPITER

Ink and Lyrics Duet
Book One

Nacole Stayton

*For all the women who grew up with daddy issues.
My hope is that you find a man you don't have to beg to love
you ... or in this case, three.*

My Neck, My Back- Elle King
Don't Fear the Reaper- Blue Oyster Cult
Rise Above It- I Prevail
All the Things I Hate About You- Huddy
Bloody Valentine- Machine Gun Kelly
Toxic Energy- Blackbear & The Used
Pillowtalk- Zayn
You and Me- Lifehouse
Anti-Hero- Taylor Swift

I'm thrilled for you to meet the band members of the Kings of Jupiter. Though, before I make any introductions, I think it's only appropriate to offer a friendly warning for those readers who are fainthearted.

This story broaches topics that might be triggering to read, such as infant loss, death, drugs, cussing, and toe-curling kinks—voyeurism, consensual-non-consent, and degradation. This book is a male-female-male-male romance. Usually, this genre is dubbed as reverse harem, but it's now widely known as *why choose*. This means that our heroine tattooist has multiple love interests and part-ners. *All aboard the polyamorous train.* Swords do cross, and it is delicious. If you choose to forge on—and I hope you do —you have been warned.

If you have zero interest in meeting Mazen Wilde, Oliver Collins, or Cannon Rhodes, I urge you to choose a *cleaner* novel of mine to read—hint: *Beauty in Chaos*. Because labeling the members of this band as anything remotely close to *clean* would make me a liar. Unless we're talking about their last bill of health, if you catch my drift.

If you're still reading this—*winks*—you're my type of bibliophile, and I think we're going to become fast friends.

Rock on,

Nacole

THE VIBRATOR DILEMMA

SOPHIA

"WHOEVER THOUGHT it was a smart idea to make a vibrator with a USB charger must have had a dick between their thighs," I huff, annoyed, through gritted teeth. The white cord, clutched like a rosary in my hand, dangles limply as I talk to myself like a certified lunatic.

Leave it to me to wake up from a glorious dream, where I stumbled onto private property, looking desperate for harbor and a hot shower. Only to find a man, built from grace, with rivulets of sweat clinging to his form as he stacked firewood.

When our eyes locked, wanton need passed between us for a solid minute before he spoke with a tantalizing grin. "What are you doing—besides me?"

I woke too early, irritable and unsatisfied.

An exacerbated sigh leaves my mouth as my mind wanders idly seconds after I tethered my dead wand to the wall. I sit cross-legged, waiting, watching as the fluorescent-pink light blinks excruciating slow. There's no penance offered by the charging wand, which will take forever to charge to full capacity. A mix of arousal and irritation radiate through me.

The wooden floor's unforgiving firmness adds to my body's discomfort as I sit on my bedroom floor rug.

It's as if the universe is taunting me for being horny and decides to toss a tight-lipped sneer in my direction before mocking me with a, "Simmer down now," to my overactive libido in a voice that reminds me of Fran Drescher from *The Nanny*.

A morning orgasm puts the *good* in good morning. If you try to tell me a killer orgasm isn't the absolute biggest euphoria ever, you're a fucking liar. And news flash: I don't tolerate liars just as much as I don't favor dead vibrators.

There isn't a use for either.

The thought of *not* having a convulsing, toe-curling, hand-clutching-my-bedsheets orgasm this morning has me contemplating crawling back under my covers, calling in to work, and sleeping until the sun rises again tomorrow. I need a redo. I'm pissed off, and nothing—and I mean, *nothing*—but riding the wave of pure bliss is going to quench this festering exasperation.

Since this is a no-judgment zone and women love to get off just as much as men do, I'm convinced we should devise a committee on outlawing the production of non-battery-operated sexy toys and pitch it to the makers of this stupid pink wand, which is uselessly resting on my floor, roped to an outlet. *Women unite*. Sure, the subject is a little taboo. So is selling worn underwear on the internet. People do that every day and are paving the way for entrepreneurship in today's society. Along with jarred farts—a topic not up for discussion.

I guess if you're still carrying cigarette holders and using hair rollers, masturbation is a dirty little secret that might be too touchy of a topic for you to consider verbalizing out loud. You'd rather do the deed behind a closed door, apply fresh lipstick, flatten your pantsuit, and pretend that nothing sinful ever happened. Sister, no one is going to judge you for admitting to handling your business and partaking in the big M-word. It's 2024. Miley is, dare I say it, normal, and Elton John finally retired. There are far bigger fish to fry than caring about who masturbates and who doesn't.

Sexuality is just as much a part of me as my right arm, and I know I'm not alone in this. As a tattooist, I literally need *said* arm so I can work, keep a roof over my head, and afford to eat. Subtly isn't my style. I'm airing my dirty laundry out on the line for the world to see because, trust me, no one wants to be around me without my morning coffee or orgasm.

I recognize I've lost my wits when a plea escapes my lips. "Come on." I shoot daggers at the wand. "Charge, you little bastard."

The throb between my legs rouses with a desperate need for release and causes my nipples to grow taut. Their hardness rubs against the thin fabric of my T-shirt. This feeling right here is precisely why I know that nipple piercings aren't for me. Lacey, my younger sister, has hers done and is adamant that her sensation is still intact. That's just not a chance I'm willing to take. The way my shirt feathers over my skin, dusting against my raised flesh, is enough to drive me mad. I feel the sudden urge to clench my legs together.

The tension in my room is palpable, a dense fog of despair.

Is masturbating with your hand still a thing these days? I contemplate kicking it old school.

I'd been hostage to my little bullet for years before it gave out on me and the wire broke, separating the small metal piece from its controller. Lacey had gifted me this pink apparatus for my birthday last year, swearing that it came with rave reviews and was life-changing.

The world is flipping me the bird for some unknown reason today. That's it. I'm going to one-star this sucker. See how you like that, big sex-toy manufacturer. Your marketing campaign can kiss my ass.

Changing batteries I could deal with. I have an entire drawer full of double-A and triple-A batteries, dedicated to pleasuring myself and keeping my mood placated. This stupid wand is going to ruin my day before it's really even begun.

I'll add *plug in my vibrator* to my mental checklist of things I do before I leave my house next time.

- *Unplug my hair straightener. Check.*
- *Turn my plants toward the windowsill. Check.*
- *Plug in my vibrator. Check.*
- *Lock the door. Check.*

I'm like a feral lioness, waiting to be mated, as I circle around a boulder, just begging for the big bad lion to come derail me. I keep waiting and waiting and waiting, and no lion shows up. Not even a hyena ambles by. At this rate, I'd even take the one that laughs nonstop to put me out of my misery. The torture of waiting is maddening.

Welcome to the land of Orgasmic Bliss. Population: zero. Thanks to my vibrator dilemma.

"Fuck this," I exhale.

I decide the light that repeatedly flashes over and over has taunted me enough and elect to shower and get ready for the day to keep my mind occupied while the device charges. By the off chance my gadget is charged when I'm done, I'll be able to send myself off this morning with a little extra pep in my step before I'm due in the studio.

Hell hath no fury like a woman who couldn't come before noon.

Water cascades out of the showerhead, and I crank it open, full speed. I like my water like I like my men. Scorching hot. When the temperature is searing enough to steam the entire bathroom, I finally peel off my pajamas, which consist of an ancient, threadbare Jimi Hendrix T-shirt that I found at a consignment shop for two dollars and my infamous blue monkey pajama pants that Lacey tells me she can see my ass through every time I wear them. The material is so thin from years of wearing them that I couldn't even cut them up and have one decent rag. I refuse to throw them away, and I swear on Tupac Shakur's grave—if he's really even dead, and that's a steep *if*—if Lacey takes it upon herself to trash them, I will tattoo her forehead while she sleeps.

When I hit play on my phone's music app, Elle King's live version of "My Neck, My Back" croons from the speaker sitting on my tiny vanity. Her insinuating lyrics and fog from the shower fill the bathroom in a spiritual mixture that only makes the ache between my thighs worsen as the time passes. Redirecting my thoughts, I busy myself by doing an everything shower.

A solid forty-minutes later, I step out of the stall. I perform my usual morning ritual and skin prep and then blow-dry my hair. I grab my brown-tinted pencil as the door to my puny en suite bathroom swings open, welcoming a gust of cool air at the exact same time a song ends.

"Smile, sis," Lacey calls out, her voice purposely seductive. "Show me those scandalous, pouty lips you flaunt around that beg to be wrapped around a cock," my younger sister by two years prompts, earning a justifiable eye roll and headshake.

She has zero tact or modesty as she struts through the threshold of my bathroom, sputtering her usual nonsense, not caring in the slightest that I could have been naked. She's a no-boundaries kind of woman. I don't think she's ever put one up herself or didn't make it her life's mission to cross one laid down.

In a black bra, pushing her cleavage up—which clearly doesn't need help lifting—Lacey is the epitome of a smokeshow. Hence the fact that her clothes—when she does decide to wear them—melt on her curves, accentuating the sway of her runway-model hips. I tease her relentlessly that she'd be a better fit in the nudist colony a couple of miles down the road.

Welcome to Florida.

Where Lacey is confident in her skin, attire, neon-pink hair, and colorful tattoos covering her flawless skin, I'm the ordinary sibling. With my dirty-red hair and ivory skin that's only been under a tattoo gun once.

After making it through my apprenticeship with only one small rose tattoo on my shoulder blade, which just so happens to be my middle name, I almost started my solo career as a tattoo virgin. I understand the irony of a tattoo artist not covered in ink from head to toe. I'm not opposed to getting more if something feels right or a design calls out to me. I don't pass judgment on those who sit in my chair, asking for something idiotic, like a burned slice of toast. *You do you*—a personal motto that quickly became a mantra during my career.

Right now, my only concern is attempting to decipher the shit-eating grin on my sister's face. I whirl toward her, unfinished brows in a deep V. Panic written on my face.

Capping my pencil, I huff, "Why are you taking pictures of me? I don't even have my eyebrows on yet."

"Because"—she sounds out every syllable—"I'm fully invested in your love life like a good sister, and I'm making you a dating profile." Her words jumble together as she quickly spits them out.

"Like hell you are. Get out! I need to get ready, and by the looks of it, so do you." I eye her profile, which consists of said skimpy bra and a thong that looks like it's about to cut her in half, leaving little to the imagination.

Lacey's curvier than I am and audacious in her appearance. I'm often envious of her full figure. I have good style—don't get me wrong. Between us, we have more pairs of heels than a department store. I've always felt a smidgen insecure, comparing my body to her feminine curves.

"You've been in a dry spell since the tool Joe—Josh—Jacob—" She doesn't make eye contact with me as she scrolls through the images she just took on her phone.

"Joel. Don't act like you don't remember his name." *I wish I could forget his name.* My eyes burn with fire at her audacity to bark in on my sex life. It's not warranted. The last thing I need is Lacey playing matchmaker. "Don't you remember what happened the last time you set me up on a blind date?"

Her left eyelid twitches—her tell—and I know she does. "He stole my shoes!"

"So ... what I'm hearing is that you think he had good taste." It's not a question.

"He was a certified creep in every aspect, and you know it. I don't trust your judgment when it comes to men. You need to leave this alone.

"Anyway"—she bores easily at my warning and barrels through—"back to Joel. I could have called him Dick Face or Limp Dick Joel. How about Joel Missed-the-Hole Howard? I *was* being nice. Sophia Rose Lozier, you're long overdue for a good pounding. This"—she waves her hand dramatically, like she's warding off a swarm of gnats—"negative aura is clouding our apartment. I keep having to crack the window in the kitchen just to let out your bad juju. A cataclysmic orgasm should help with that."

"I don't need a man to make me come." I clench my brow pencil in one hand and put the other on my hip as my breath comes out simmering with anger. I blame my attitude on my lack of orgasm that Lacey is droning on about. But I'm not about to let that truth slip.

"Hate to break it to you, sis, but that statement is precisely why you need a man." The haughty rebuke she lets out hits me like a smack to my face. "No orgasm or coffee yet, and you're ready to commit homicide."

"Were you listening at my door with a glass or something?"

"Don't flatter yourself. This isn't one of those raunchy, taboo romance books you read. The evidence is on the charger."

I peer through the bathroom door at my lifeless wand.

"It's *dead*, dead," I confess, shamefully averting my attention back to the mirror in front of me, foolishly coloring in my eyebrow with a gamut of pent-up energy soaring through my veins.

Lacey shrugs like that's *not* the most drear news she's heard all morning. "So, use mine."

The offer leaves my stomach churning with bile.

"You're repulsive."

Our eyes meet in a standoff. Hers etched with bright mockery.

"Don't act like you didn't consider sneaking into my room and grabbing a functional toy."

I offer a sidelong glance of absolute disbelief as my pitch holds a rasp of authority and disgust. "Have you used my wand before *without* my knowledge?" A shudder of humiliation runs down the back of my neck the longer it takes her to form an answer, which is all the answer I need and suspected.

"I'd have the decency to ask, Soph. I mean, I'd want to know it was sanitized. Unless it was an emergency." The self-satisfied face she makes taunts me.

"What exactly constitutes an orgasm emergency?" My fleeting embarrassment morphs into infuriation at lightning speed.

"A dead wand." Her shoulders rise.

The perpetual merriment in Lacey's tone turns my skin a deep crimson.

"I'm going to unalive you ... you dirty bitch. The next time you come snooping through my drawers, you're going to be sorry. Count your days, roomie." My openly amused threat falls flat.

Planting her body on the edge of the bed, she taunts, "What are you going to do, buy a safe for your silicone collection?"

"Don't tempt me." I give her a smile and nod dubiously, ending our gentle spar. "I can't even with you right now, Lace. You're ... never mind. Get dressed. We have to be downstairs in twenty minutes. Piper texted that she has the flu and won't be in to open."

Wrinkling her nose, Lacey glances up, nodding her head, and mutters, "Yes, boss."

2

INK EMPORIUM

SOPHIA

DEVON, our security guard, leans in through my office door. His yard-wide physique and towering stance fill the entire entrance. I fully acknowledge that it's illegal to hire someone based on appearance, but in an all-female tattoo studio, I knew the safety of both my staff and clientele was almost as paramount as the art we created. Thus, the first male who applied and interviewed and could also be a stunt double for The Hulk was hired on the spot.

Devon's been a lifesaver a time or two when a couple of catty friends started pulling out hair extensions. He even bagged a blonde offender's weave and gave it to her before instructing her to never set foot in our shop again.

What a gentleman.

"You're unusually temperamental this evening," he comments before leaning back against the doorframe, his eyes trained on me in an observant manner that makes me feel judged.

I feign offense, rolling my eyes. "Why do you say that?"

He appears to think twice before answering, and his split-second hesitation gives me a moment to drink him in. Devon's jawline is almost as flawless as the rest of his rich mocha complexion. I'm envious of a man. I'm not the least bit ashamed to admit it either. I wish my skin looked as soft and hydrated as his does. Genetics, he claims, but he's not fooling anyone.

Letting my irritability overflow, I throw my hands up in the I'm-waiting motion that people do as I urge him to answer me.

"Boss lady, you've been pounding that stapler like it personally offended you for the last five minutes. Either you strongly have an aversion to paper clips, or you have something on your mind."

I lean back further in my office chair, allowing it to swallow me whole. The tension in my shoulders spreads, coursing down my back muscles. Sitting in this exact spot for hours will do that to a person. I beg the discomfort to supernaturally dispel and sulk further into myself when it doesn't.

When we opened this fine establishment, we were hell-bent on being the best tattoo studio in Tampa. With aspirations and balls the size of the Atlantic, Lacey and I have created a lucrative business that's been featured in several tattoo magazines and on television a handful of times. Getting tattooed by me or one of my elite colleagues is a hot commodity in our community. That might sound snooty to some. It's the truth, a celebrated reality, and it's why we're always booked.

I expected the business to blossom, especially when Lacey took an interest in piercing after she graduated. Since we started offering both services, our days have only gotten longer and our pocketbooks fatter. What I didn't expect was having to be tied to my desk, pushing paperwork all day, every day, instead of in my chair with my gun in my hand and a client's flesh at my disposal.

Between fulfilling my administrative duties and my lack of orgasm this morning, my mood is bleaker than someone who just wrecked their new car as soon as they pulled off the lot. Lifting my chin, I open my mouth to feed Devon a lie to assure him that I'm fine just as Lacey slides under his outreached arm.

"You in the mood to tattoo tonight?" she asks casually, her pink hair glowing under the fluorescent light in my office, making it resemble glass.

The animation on my face when she asks, paired with my stamina from earlier, is like a lightning bolt to my veins. Lacey just saved my soul from the decrepit pits of book-keeping hell, and she doesn't even know it.

Fuck you, QuickBooks.

"I could use the distraction." A smile tips my mouth. "What do you got for me?" My face now splitting into a wide grin, I'm unable to hide my enthusiasm.

Lacey's lips twist into a pessimistic smile. "Walk-ins."

My least favorite. They're usually young college kids with virgin skin who bitch and complain the whole time or tourists who want a symbol of their vacation etched into their flesh, smaller than a quarter.

"How many?"

She's quick to reply, "Three."

I glance at the clock on the wall to see it reads six o'clock. The shop opens at noon and closes at one o'clock in the morning on both Friday and Saturday. I have plenty of time. Patience, on the other hand, to sit with three people who didn't even have the decency to call ahead or book an appointment online is another story.

"Are they inked already?"

Lacey dips her chin. "From what I can see, there's no visible skin to even draw a stick figure on. They said they'd make it worth your while, and they're willing to pay triple your hourly rate per person."

"Come again?" I query, stunned.

"They don't look like your average frat boys from the shore who found us on Yelp. Make 'em put their money where their mouth is, sissy." She looks up at Devon and winks.

God, she's a flirt.

This is just what I needed tonight after dealing with a mountain of paperwork. I long to feel that invigorating euphoria that inking gives me. It calls to me from the depths of my soul, like a monster that can't be tamed or housed in the dark any longer.

Greeting her with the merciless curve of a half smile, I mumble, "Skin is skin."

"Skin is skin," she retorts.

Three tattoos should fill a couple of hours and hopefully put me in a better frame of mind until I get home. *That forsaken wand had better be charged by then.*

"Get their paperwork ready. I'll be out shortly. I need to print these checks, then get them addressed. Piper has my index cards on her desk. Use one as a template."

"Who do you think made Piper that example? I'm not an invalid. I got you. Come on, Devon. Our high rollers brought their own security. You'll have someone to chat with for a few hours at least."

Who brings security to get a tattoo?

Before I can inquire further, Lacey and Devon make a beeline to the front of the shop, leaving me with questions that can be put on hold until I finish printing these pesky checks. I've considered hiring a shop manager to do the mundane tasks I clearly despise, which would allow me the space to create and do what I'm good at.

Making art.

Tattooing.

Being around people.

I just can't pull the trigger for some reason. I like being in charge. Even though the weight of the world feels like it's on my shoulders, I know things are done timely and to my liking because I'm the one completing the tasks. This is *my* shop. I have a reputation to uphold. Lacey is co-owner in name only. It was my blood, sweat, money, and tears that opened the doors.

Knowing I have an awaiting client provides much-needed motivation not to get into another fight with my stapler. It takes less than twenty minutes to print, address, and stuff the mail. I slide the small stack of crisp white envelopes into my tote and scurry into the bathroom inside my office. Dabbing a little perfume from my shelf above the towel rack on my neck, I run my hands through my loosely curled hair. There's nothing worse than continuously having to blow whisps of hair out of your eyes when you are mere centimeters from a client's face.

Thinking of it, I decide to give my mouth a rinse with mouthwash while I'm in here, just in case there's any lingering aroma from the club sandwich I had earlier for lunch.

"The first client's in your room." Lacey peeks in, her wealth of pink locks dangling over her shoulders.

"Almost done." I wipe my hands on my formfitting black leather pants. "You already put her in my office?"

"Your client is a he, not a she, and *he* insisted on a little privacy. Your index card, ma'am," she says as her slender fingers extend the white paper in front of me, her brow rising a fraction. "Have fun with this one." Without missing a beat, she leaves just as quickly as she came.

"You're fucking kidding me." I give a half laugh, half eye roll simultaneously as I offer a middle-finger salute to the universe that is edging me ever so slowly today.

My office is adjacent to my tattoo room. Other than Lacey's piercing room, it's the only other private space in the suite. The rest of the staff has cubical-shaped spaces near the front of the building. Rose and Lace Ink Emporium employs three other tattooists. Each were sought out and scouted, bringing something diverse to the table.

Our fine-line lady is Khloe. Her specialty is creating dainty pieces with precise details. Maxine is our traditional artist. She has a heavy hand and an even harder heart. I don't think I've seen her even so much as grin since she was hired. She's a total badass, and men come in flocks to get tattooed by her, favoring her infamous no-nonsense attitude. Novalie is our kick-ass cartoonist—from Disney characters to anything that calls for 3-D design. She is our newest hire and hasn't disappointed me once since her first day. Bringing a lot of older clients from her previous shop has kept her book full.

Then, there's me. A jack-of-all-trades. I favor all aspects of tattooing and have a newfound appreciation for bold colors lately. It's a good thing I lean on the versatile side because of what's written on my index card. Nothing says easily adaptable like tattooing a stranger's dick.

Ready to feel the vibration of my gun in my palm, I swing open my office door with a buoyant feeling in my chest. My jaw hits the stained pink concrete floor under my shoe when I take in the sight in front of me.

The image of his erect, jutting cock gains my attention

first, for obvious reasons. Second, I notice the expanse of his body as he lies on my tattoo table with his pants around his ankles, the curve of his cupped hand sliding up and down his shaft in a steady tempo.

It's going to be a long night, no pun intended.

Damn my stupid libido and my dead wand.

3

TENTACLE BOY

OLIVER

I'VE COME to cherish the quiet. Being on the road with a group of guys nonstop for years will have you chasing solitude quicker than an addict after their next fix. There's a freedom this empty tattoo room provides that I haven't experienced in a while.

When you're forced to watch porn with AirPods in for years, like a curious teenager scared to get caught, you learn to stroke your dick in silence. Which is why I'm lying against the cream-colored faux leather table, pants around my ankles, openly stroking my shaft, feeling like a free man. The faint sound of my palm rubbing against my cock echoes in the small space.

Memories resurface from a hard-core porn I watched the other night on the bus somewhere between Louisiana and home. Each vivid image that flashes by causes my hold to tighten around my shaft, and I pump it and pump it and pump it.

It was some erotic shit that was on another level, even

for Cannon. Who had to have overheard the commentary from his bunk across from mine when my pod tumbled off the bunk and he picked it up, reaching across the small walkway to return it to me.

I vaguely recall him whispering, "Sick bastard," from behind his drawn shade before I slid it back into my ear.

Anyway, this dude fucked this lady's pussy with a loaded gun. If that isn't the most insane game of Russian roulette you've ever heard of, color me shocked. The fantasy of thrusting a loaded pistol into a woman's pussy urges my wrist to move just as the sound of the door rasps open, disrupting my stroke.

Second to the sound of the door opening, a high-pitched female's voice cuts through the silence.

"What. The. Fuck?" A shrill comes from the doorway sounding like a roar of thunder in a summer storm. Bold. Assertive. Out of nowhere. The revolt laced in her tone pulls my attention away from my throbbing appendage.

"Are you here to lend me a hand?"

Half a smile crosses my face as the female's shoes plod against the floor in a heated stampede. Oh, *stilettos*. I'd know their sweet sound a mile away.

The female's abrupt appearance doesn't throw me off-kilter. Instead, it entices me to slide my hand up and down my shaft with slower, more provocative strokes. If the onlooker who just swung open the door and came barreling in with metaphorical guns blazing wants a show, she should know I'm a professional performer, and a show she will get.

"Chill out with the handy. There're a couple of things we need to discuss before I even agree to do this tattoo," a feathery voice says from behind me.

"I take it you're Sophia then." *Handy patrol.* I crane my

neck to the side to meet the eyes of the female who caught me beating my meat like a teenager in the shower.

"In the flesh," she says moving further into the room.

The soft material of a small towel is tossed onto my lap with force. The cloth floats across my lower abdomen, tenting my raging boner like a makeshift fort. My dick is rock hard from just thinking about the gun video.

Mission accomplished.

"What's there to discuss? I want my dick tattooed. You're a tattoo artist. Two plus two makes four."

"It's not every day someone walks in and decides to get his penis tattooed."

I contemplate for a moment, then add with an exhale, "I read online that you can't have a flaccid dick; it makes it near impossible to tattoo. I'm not about to stretch it around a soda can. I got it hard for you. Problem solved. Seems simple enough to me. Unless the tattoo comes with a free— what'd you call it? Handy?" I grunt at her expense. "I'm stealing that term, by the way. Thank you."

My cock twitches. Thankfully, he's a friendly dude, never met a stranger he didn't like.

The sharp edge of her amusement fills the room. "I'd watch your mouth. I'm about to have needles penetrating your dick repeatedly. If I agree to this, you might not want to get on my bad side."

"Fair enough." I roll over onto my side, my eyesight abandoning their spot on the ceiling, and deadpan, "You win."

Never in my wildest dreams could I have conjured up a more beautiful woman to hold my cock in her hand and insert a hundred tiny needles at once. If I had a kink for pain, you'd better believe I'd be shooting down the ceiling tiles with a load right now.

In my line of work, one can never be more careful where women are concerned. I did my research online and found this swanky little studio that read *all-female artists*. I knew this was the shop where I'd finally get my long-awaited penis tattoo. The studio's slogan did me in—*We bring grown men to their knees.*

As if I had an epiphany, I contemplate climbing off the table and kneeling in front of the siren in front of me. Even with my pants around my ankles and everything from my navel down on display, my heart thrums in a steady rhythm against my rib cage. There isn't an ounce of doubt about the studio's hundreds of five-star reviews online now.

I get it. I so fucking get it.

The slim waist of the female perched in front of me is leaning against a steel stand behind her with her arms crossed over her chest. Her stature resembles a petite hour-glass that's been delicately curved and blown from hand.

My eyes slowly make their way up from her agile thighs, like a snake on a prowl for his next meal. The woman before me is much younger than I imagined the owner of a thriving business would be. I saw the headshots of the owners who work here on the shop's website. Like I said, I did my research. But her ... I must've been high off my ass that night because, surely, I would have remembered *her*.

The website listed the owner as a woman named Sophia Rose Lozier, and I'm staring right at her. Correction: gawking.

Her regal features cause my exposed shaft to twitch of its own accord as I gulp, allowing my eyes to melt into the softness of her exposed peach-tinted skin. They travel over the mounds of her jutting breasts, fashioned tightly in a bright teal bodice; down her legs, covered in faux leather pants; and back up, landing on her delicate face. The red-gold strands of her hair gleam in the fluorescent lighting above us. It casts a copper glow on her silken mass of waves hanging over her ivory shoulders. There are two thick pieces of blonde framing her face, adding an edge to the innocence of the rest of her outward appearance. A few freckles pepper the hollow of her neck. I feel pulled to count every one of them and memorize their pattern, like a constellation of stars.

I narrow in on her, my eyes ablaze, mouth dry. I'm too enthralled by her presence to notice when she opens her mouth, ending my blatant visual appraisal.

"What brought you in?" Her voice, laced with attitude, is deceptively harsh in contrast to her angelic, innocent face.

She should come with a danger sign. The purity that engulfs her is how she lures sorry bastards such as me into her web before cocooning us and engulfing our essence without a blink of her eye. I can feel myself sinking into the depths of her quicksand.

The malice lingering in her question takes me off guard. I break my trance, incline my head downward, and nod to the tented cloth before glancing back up and rewarding her with my disarmingly poised charm, meant to break her grimace.

"Isn't it obvious?"

"I mean, what brought you *specifically* to Rose and Lace Ink Emporium? How'd you hear about us?"

Twirling a copper piece of hair around her finger, the act screaming virtuous, she waits for my answer. If it wasn't for the cat-eye slits in her eyes, I'd be fooled.

This woman is a man-eater. I call her bluff in my mind.

My brain and my body wage war because, right now, I'd give my left ball to be on her menu for dinner. After being on the road for so long, having women lining up and begging to suck you off, you get fairly good at reading others. From the emerald of her eyes, a rich contrast to her pink cheeks with hints of pale gold undertones, this woman is a temptress hidden in plain sight—mark my words.

Call me a gemologist because this woman is a gem.

"In my line of work ..."

My irises meet her jade ones, holding her captive. I tempt the siren with my allure, trying to even the playing field, knowing damn well that her beauty is as composed as an elegant sculpture made from scratch.

"Things get rowdy pretty quickly. I figured an all-female studio wouldn't attract a lot of female clientele. Less women littering your waiting area works in my favor."

My brass-colored eyes meet hers, and I analyze her reaction as she ponders on what I said and surveys me shrewdly. The savage intensity of her glare has my cock convulsing under her blatant scrutiny.

"That makes absolutely no sense. Are you drunk? High alcohol levels increase bleeding. I won't tattoo you if you've been drinking. Come clean."

If I ever want to come, it's by her hands. Or mouth or ...

She halts, as if choosing her words carefully, and a bemused look lands on my face. Hoping she doesn't recognize *me*, I tilt my head in the opposite direction. Mazen told me to wear sunglasses and a hat. I hate when that fucker is right.

"Not an ounce of booze this evening. Pinkie swear." Unwrapping my hand from my shaft, I hold it out to her, wiggling my pinkie finger.

"Whatever," she replies coolly before swatting at my hand.

The sudden aloofness that rolls off her doesn't pair with someone who just realized *who* I am. I regard her quizzically for a beat, trying to decipher if she's hiding her excitement from uncovering my identity while simultaneously analyzing what female her age doesn't know *who* I am.

My ego deflates as she lowers onto a stool, turns away, preparing her tabletop, leaving me to struggle with the lack of my popularity.

"Enough chitchat. Let's get this show on the road."

There it is. A pun. I knew she had to have recognized me.

"I have a couple more clients after you."

She holds up the white index card the girl with pink hair in the receptionist area wrote my information on. I used a fake name and identification card.

"So, you want me to tattoo a jellyfish on your fanny flicker?"

"Yep." I pop the last letter for good measure. "Then, I'll have the baddest sea monster to ever exist ... in my pants."

"Pump the brakes, tentacle boy. This is a first for me. On a penis at least. Realistic or more cartoonish vibes?"

"Open to suggestions. I've always wanted a jellyfish. What better state to get it in than Florida? Put your creative take on it."

"I take it, you're not from around here then?"

I lean back to my original position with my head facing the ceiling and take a deep breath. I'm on the verge of being discovered. I can feel it in my bones.

I evade the truth, not wanting to raise any red flags—unless, of course, she is pretending to be coy. "Just passing through." With sharp eyes, I watch for any sign of recognition of who I am to dance across her face.

I'm used to women throwing their cotton-soaked panties at me onstage. The indifference of her attitude from her sitting in a room with someone of my fame leaves me feeling torn between wanting to blurt out my real identity and getting lost in the persona of the naive male client who stumbled upon her studio.

"Very well." She disregards me like she has more important things to discuss.

A fleeting feeling I'm not used to stirs in my chest. I find it a little offbeat that I *want* her to ask where I'm from and what my story is.

"First things first. I prefer free hand to stenciling. I'll draw it out, and then if you like it, we'll move forward and outline."

I offer a nod of understanding.

"Since you're giving me leeway with the design, this might be my favorite tattoo of the night. Just don't go telling the buddies you came with. I like all my clients to leave feeling special."

The small smile she finally offers makes an explosive current of electricity race through my veins, in search of an outlet. The outlet is my rock-hard dick, and, fuck, do I want to take this woman over this bed.

"Let's talk about aftercare," she says, her voice calling to my wayward thoughts. "Then, I'll need a few more minutes to finish getting my supplies ready and start. Sound good?"

Things would sound even better if you were screaming my name.

There's no way I'm going to get through this tattoo with the drop-dead vixen sitting before me and not make a mess in her hands. It's an impossible feat. Just the thought of her holding my shaft, paired with the distant smell of wildflowers and citrus, leaves me feeling smug enough to shoot my shot. I swallow it down due to the nagging feeling and suspicion that she'd rather be doing anything else in the entire world, including raking leaves in a tornado, than having to hold my dick for an hour.

Deciding to accept the dull ache from her disinterest, I strum my fingers against the skin of my bare stomach, playing a riff on my makeshift guitar, willing the ceiling to fall on me and put me out of my misery. The humiliation of my desire wraps around my sack like a vise since the level of excitement on *her* face is as bland as mashed potatoes without butter. I try to force my mind on anything other than the woman I now know as Sophia in an attempt to keep myself from acting like a sixteen-year-old boy who just found his dad's dirty magazine stash under the bathroom counter.

"Fire away." I count the exposed rafters on the ceiling, masking my scorned pride that she still doesn't recognize me.

Isn't this what we want though? To come to a studio, or anywhere, where our fame doesn't make us stand out like a sore thumb.

"Colors?"

"You pick." I chew my bottom lip, stealing another glance as she nods with a youthful glow at my indecisiveness.

I wish our label would allow our creativity to soar like I'm allowing hers. It's been years since we had that sort of freedom. Nowadays, we're almost like prisoners to our art.

"Sex sells. No one gives a shit about your tortured youth. Men don't listen to your music. Statistics show that women are streaming your music, and they want to hear songs that leave their panties dripping," Rodney—who we've dubbed Little Dick Rodney, the head of our label at Near Death Records—says in my head.

I swear he has it out for us. Yet we're the reason he

drives around in a sweet whip and lives in a gated subdivision.

Twisting at her waist apprehensively, Sophia who've I've already been referring to as Soph in my mind, clears her throat and once again grounds me with her question. "Size?"

I catch her eyes fall toward my cock.

Thank fuck. It seems like I've finally struck a nerve. Her wide-eyed appraisal confirms it. My shrunken pride couldn't take another second of her stone-cold exterior. I chalk her widened gape up as a win.

"I want the jellyfish's tentacles to wrap around my shaft, like it's holding my dick, squeezing it. Size doesn't matter. As you can see, you're working with a thick canvas."

I hear her quick intake of breath and tuck the newfound satisfaction that I have gotten under her skin in the back of my mind, knowing that the thought of that sound, her sharp breath, will help keep me erect for the duration of my tattoo and days following.

Seemingly pensive, she offers another grin before punching me in the gut with her iron-sized fist. "I hope you got laid recently because you'll need to refrain from any kind of sexual activity for the next six weeks while this—"

"Sea monster," I finish her sentence.

Soph freezes, too stunned to retort.

"I was going to say, while this tattoo heals."

"I'm going to permanently have a jellyfish on my dick. It'll be known as a sea monster from here on out, and six weeks is like an eternity for someone with my ... stamina. Is there any wiggle room with that rule?"

"No, there's not. Unless you want the jellyfish not to heal properly and resemble a ... glob of algae. You're welcome to go knock your rocks in the hall bathroom while I finish prepping if you don't think you can refrain for six weeks."

I weigh her suggestion, my teeth biting down on my bottom lip, before rocketing off the table, nearly colliding with her petite frame resting on her stool in front of me.

Fuck. What is it about this chick that has my pulse quickening? She's stunning, but it's more than that. Maybe it's the fact that she's not pawning over me or throwing herself at me that has my balls drawing closer to my body. Her indifference toward me is hot as fuck. She seems like a chick that has a backbone and her shit together.

That's got to be why I've never wanted another woman as much as I do Soph. No other conquest has mirrored the enthrallment I feel toward her. There's something ... refreshing, alluring about being a stranger in her eyes.

"It's really a stipulation?"

She slides a small clear bag over her tattoo gun with expert precision. "Absolutely. Anything involving friction over the area has to be eliminated." Her words lack any tenderness, stinging my heart like the tentacles I desire to be etched into my skin.

Reaching forward, Soph's ungloved hand pats my knee heartily before driving a knife into my heart. "That includes masturbation and oral, babe."

My demise comes from the term of endearment that seeps from her blush-painted mouth.

"Fuck. Shit. Fuck." I was too preoccupied researching how bad penis tattoos hurt and if it had to be hard or not that I didn't even consider the so-called aftercare. My hand finds my head and pulls on several strands of hair before sliding down to cup the back of my neck.

She looks up through long, wispy lashes. "Backing out?" It sounds more like a statement than a question.

I roll my neck, feeling irritable by the onslaught of news. "Not a chance. I'm here. Let's do this thing." There's a cold edge as the words roll off my tongue, and I gesture to my still-exposed cock. "I'm ready when you are."

"It's a showboater tattoo. You know that, right?" She raises her eyebrows with the bid of her two cents. "You don't seem like the type of guy who has to lure women into his bed with promises of seeing the most realistic jellyfish outside an aquarium or from the actual sea." She subtly sounds out her next words. "And to be honest, you don't come across as a man who refrains from sex often."

The astonishment of her gibe is paired with the heavy sarcasm in her featherily voice.

"What kind of man do I look like?"

A hint of skepticism dances across her face before it's replaced with a museful glare, like she's deciding very carefully how to answer. "You allude sex appeal. But you also don't give me creepy vibes. That's all. Don't read too much into it."

Cocking my head, I'm keenly aware that the air around us has shifted. "It's a fair assumption that you *are* reading into it. Do explain what kind of man you think I am though."

"You're really going to make me say it, aren't you?" She laughs. The warm sound waves farewell to her hard exterior. The sound goes straight to my balls. "You're easily the most attractive guy that's ever sat in my chair. You have an aura that's ... I don't know. I guess you seem ... authentic and brutally honest. You've had your dick out for"—she glances at the clock on the wall—"a long time and not once have you appeared bashful."

"What's there to be bashful about? I have a nice-sized dick."

She offers a knowing grin before rolling her eyes and tucking a loose strand of hair behind her ear.

Fuck me.

Her earlobes are lined with small gold hoops. Suddenly, I'm an earlobe fan.

"Shut up. It's a reassuring trait that not many have anymore. I like people who are raw and—"

"Have massive dicks?" I ask, fully knowing that she's referring to the authenticity she claims I encompass and not the size of my manhood. "Fuck, what kind of suitors are pounding down your door? Come here." I hold open my arms, gesturing her toward me. "I offer free hugs to women who have been cursed with a history of riding small dicks." A laugh escapes me. "Shit, I don't even think it's physically possible to even ride a small one. You probably more or less just have to rock back and forth, don't you?"

The sweet-sounding laugh she lets out before saying, "Your charm is dwindling by the second," is euphoric.

"I'm sorry, continue." I cross my arms, eyes glued to hers, extending my undivided attention.

"Aside from looking at me like you want to eat me alive and interrupting me, I appreciate your honesty. I, too, don't like secrecy or beating around the bush. Honesty is my middle name. There. Are you happy now?" She looks pleased when she finishes, holding her composure like a blanket wrapped around her shoulders.

"Do you have a bush for me to beat around? Body hair isn't my jam, but call me Tarzan, baby because I'll swing through your jungle any day."

Annoyance replaces the intrigue on her face.

"You want my truth?" I pause and hold her glare, which earns me a faint nod of her head. "I would very much like the privilege of eating you, bush or not. I'll make it work."

Starting up my invisible chain saw, I mock, "I'd rather listen to that sweet laugh even more though."

That earns me another bout of her laughter.

"Wow, and a smooth talker. I think your string of honesty just went out the window if you're really claiming you'd rather listen to me laugh than eat my ... never mind."

"I have a way with words," I confess, baring a little of my soul. "Let's get back to the *you allude sex appeal* comment."

"You don't come across as a guy who fishes for compliments." Her words, thick as honey, bruise my ego.

Bunching my brows, I offer a skeptical look. "Do you always judge a book by its cover?"

For seconds, we sit in a staring match, tossing riveting glares across the ring until her resolve melts under my penetrating look. Conquering Soph just became my favorite pastime.

Crossing her arms pointedly, she offers a reply. "When I feel like I know what the inside is about, yes, I guess."

"Can you read me?" My voice is low, intentionally seductive.

She takes a beat before answering. "I'm a read-the-end-of-the-book-first and search-for-the-spoilers-of-a-movie kind of girl. I don't like surprises or not being in control, and I don't like being taken off guard. Reading people is my specialty. Lucky for you, I'm not in the fortune-telling mood tonight. I'm in the mood to get lost to the sound of my gun making you bleed. Let's get started, tentacle boy, and then I'll try to read you."

Her unexpected response leaves my head spinning. I can't help but question what idiot left this precious girl scorned to her core that she doesn't enjoy the thrill of the ride. I toss aside any notion I had about her being brokenhearted from the memory of the Ghost of Small Appendage Past. This girl has been scorned, and it wasn't by the size of a former lover's cock, rather his heart or lack thereof. From the sound of her anguished voice, she's been burned before.

The inner turmoil of her confession, paired with my own assumptions, sends me reeling. My basic nature is to weave together truth through my own eyes, creating my own version of it. Lyrically speaking, of course. I am a story-teller. I debate on jotting these feelings down in my phone. The rawness in her admission sparks my inspiration, which comes to a grinding halt as her leather-clad knee gently brushes my leg. She extends her hand, planting it palm down on my thigh.

The words of our tour manager, Nick, mesh with the source of the quote Harvey MacKay once said. *"Ideas without action are worthless."*

My mind falters at the innocence of her gesture right about the same time my dick springs back to life, spurring a brilliant idea with it.

My middle name is action. It's actually Reid, but fuck it.

4

LAB RESULTS

OLIVER

"WE SHOULD FUCK. I MEAN ..." *Shit. Did I just proposition my tattoo artist for a quick fuck? Yes. Yes, I did.*

I'm going to ruin this before I can even get the idea out there.

"I'd love to take my time with you, cherish every part of the glorious body I know you have under that outfit. I know we're in a time crunch, but if I won't be able to get off for six weeks, I need to ... get off. Preferably in a woman ... you, not my own hand. Before you get all sterilized and gloved up, consider helping a man out?" Any personal restraint I had goes out the window, along with the notion Soph had about me being a gentleman, as I finish my sentence without taking a breath.

As soon as my offer hits the air, an abrupt change of temperature in the room ignites, sweltering not only the small room, but both of its inhabitants too.

We're easily pushing hazmat territory.

I'd happily die now if it was by being suffocated with her legs wrapped around my head.

Here lies Oliver Collins. Death by consumption of ... pussy.

Soph gapes, stunned by my straightforwardness for a second before gathering her wits. Backbone back in place, she shrieks, "You're shitting me, right? This has got to be a joke."

Her words say one thing, but the fitful tremble in her voice is enough to tell me she's considering my offer. I peep down just in time to see her thighs push together. I watch as her eyes dart around the room cautiously, like she's looking for a hidden camera.

"Lacey, you can come out now." Soph stirs uneasily on her stool, exhaling an enraged huff. "If she put you up to this or swiped right—whatever the hell that even means— come clean. Tell me how much she paid you." Demand edges her words. "I'll double it if you just leave. The stupid bitch has really hit a new low this time." She hangs her head and rubs her temple.

Raw emotion filters across her face, and a knot forms in my stomach. I'm baffled by her deceptive composure and abrupt change in attitude. Confusion lingers between us thicker than my offer to elicit a sexual advancement from her. She said I wasn't a creep, and here I am, asking her to let me screw her. Like that isn't creepy as hell.

Shit.

"I'm not sure who Lacey is." I shrug and then try to ebb the rage harboring in her adorable little frame with another truth. "No one paid me to be here either. I've had a dick tattoo on my bucket list for a long time. Who wants a big, burly-ass man with a buzz cut holding your shaft while tattooing it? Not this dude."

I hope I'm not crossing a line when I reach out and gently raise her chin up with the pad of my thumb, forcing her to look at me directly.

"I'd scouted every state we were in until I came across an ad for your studio online. You're gorgeous, and from the reviews I read, you've got mad talent. Now that I'm here though, I might not have thought this through all the way. I'd much rather have Ben the biker holding a gun with a hundred needles in it, aimed at my dick, than sit here under your gaze, on the verge of erupting like a volcano."

"I can't even with her. She really fucking overstepped this time." The peach of her skin darkens into a murderous red as her face pulls into a tight grimace. "I'm only going to say this once. Put your junk away and get out of my studio. I'm going to wring Lacey's neck until it snaps off like a dandelion, and unless blood play is a kink of yours, I'd rather not have an audience."

How in the actual fuck does this literal angel know anything about blood play?

"Are you surprised I'd want to fuck you? Have you looked in the mirror recently?"

The rage wound tight in her gracefully carved brows reduces at my compliment. I continue trying my hand at calming her down and extinguishing her desire to commit murder. Knowing she can hold her own is one thing. I don't think she has the backbone for prison though. That would certainly bring the press and paparazzi barreling through the doors, and I, for one, don't have time for that shit.

"Soph …" I grab ahold of her refined wrist with a strong hold. My long, slender fingers could easily wrap around her wrist two times over. "I don't honestly think jumpsuit orange is your color, and I am a paying client. This lady … Lacey or whoever, didn't bribe me. I just happen to have a rather abundant sex drive. I won't last six weeks without sex. There's no way."

The bitter battle to coax her back to reality with my admission leaves me vulnerable.

"I didn't mean to come off so straightforward."

Her watchful gaze draws me in like a magnet, and the curiosity in her eyes throttles my core, encouraging me only further.

"If you'd let me, I'd love to bend you over this table, raise your hands above your head, forcing you to submit, and pound what I imagine is a sweet little snatch in those pants. Until our cum mixes and runs down your legs."

If I wasn't holding on to her wrist, I wouldn't notice how my words penetrate her resolve by the way her spine goes rigid, like she's standing at attention and I'm the drillmaster.

I wish I could order her to her knees and fuck her face like the Tasmanian devil without worry of gag reflexes and time.

"Lacey is my sister at the front desk. The girl with pink hair." An undiluted laugh slips passed her pouty lips. The sweet chorus unlocks something primal inside me.

I chuckle back realizing who she is referring to, and then diminish her worries. "Lacey definitely did not pay me to proposition you with sex. You'd be doing me a favor."

A faint twinkle of inquisitiveness comes to light in her eyes.

"If I don't get off once or twice a day, I'm a drag to be around, and no one wants a guy on sta—" My steadfast determination to get into this woman's pants should be a virtue. "Listen, I'm going to be real with you, Soph. Arguably the most genuine I've ever been with a stranger. You have to swear you won't spill my secret though. I'm only telling you this so you'll can the look of being pranked and possibly reconsider my offer of letting me discard these cute, formfitting little pants."

Sweeping her eyes over my face, the tight line of her mouth breaks. "You'd be surprised by the deep, dark confessions people tell their tattoo artist during a session. It's like people assume I'm here to offer them penance, like a priest. Nothing you say will surprise me—"

"I'm a rock star." The truth rolls off my tongue like I guzzled a gallon of truth serum.

The moment realization crosses her face, she arches one of her eyebrows.

"And Pamela Anderson is my mom," she croons sarcastically.

I don't miss a beat. "The resemblance is uncanny." With the tip of my head, I motion to my wallet lying at the foot of the table. Using the prop to my advantage, I dare her, knowing that the truth lies inside. "Open it."

There isn't a glint of hesitation before she reaches for my wallet with greedy hands. She peers down, examining my driver's license, and her eyes widen. "You know, it's illegal to forge documents like consent forms with fake identification, Scotty Girth or should I say Mr. Oliver Collins?"

I take notice of the way her mouth parts when she sternly calls me by my *real* name. My balls constrict, air gets stuck in my throat, and I inch back toward her body, as if a gravitational pull caught me in its orbit.

My name on her lips is a shock to my system. I'm used to staying incognito as Scotty Girth. Go ahead; laugh it up. Get it out of your system now. I drew the last name from a damn red Solo cup. It's what I've been stuck with for years. I'm as much Girth as I am Collins at this point.

"Oliver Collins, as in lead guitarist for Kings of Jupiter," I confess through parted lips.

I half expect Soph to ask for an autograph on her chest, like every other female I've ever encountered. I'm mistaken wholly when she divulges an indifference that leaves me drowning in a flood-tide sensation.

"Your name doesn't ring a bell. Sorry, bud." Seemingly uninterested at my declaration, she tosses my wallet aside, oblivious to the stack of one-hundred-dollar bills folded tidily inside.

Her lack of interest feels oddly similar to being dared to put my dick in a blender. Both devastating.

Punch to my fucking gut.

Ego deflated.

"Now, who's playing who?" I don't accept her reserved response.

There's no way this woman—or any other woman in Tampa, our hometown—doesn't know who we are. I might be barking up the wrong tree, but our band members' faces are on a billboard directly outside her studio.

"I'm *not* playing." Soph eyes me, trying to place my face that's undeniably in one of the tabloid magazines sitting in her waiting room. "I have no idea who that band is."

Her naiveness is a giant turn-on for some reason. Typically, women are clawing at one another just to get a better view of me or my best friends onstage. Her ignorance of who I am has me going from exasperation to thrilled in a nanosecond.

This might be fun after all.

"For all I know, Kings of Jupiter could be one of those indie folk groups that are paving the way for aspiring musicians on social media. No hate. Just not my style. Sorry."

"Do I look like I'm in a folk group?"

"No. But Scotty Girth, your repulsive pseudo name sounds like he's a mechanic at his stepdad's body shop."

"Fairly accurate assessment. I can see it. Girth's Garage." I drink up her amusement at my idiocy.

"Let's assume you're telling the truth and I give you the benefit of the doubt by taking your word that my sister didn't hire you to lure me into bed. The rest of it though is pretty … far-fetched."

"Lacey the receptionist, correct?" Gathering facts like an arsenal, I smile, comfortable in my skin, although still exposed during our untimely heart-to-heart.

"Our usual receptionist, Piper, called in sick today. Lacey's the lead piercer and co-owner of this establishment. *Rose and Lace.* She's my kid sister."

I take notice of the widening of her mossy globes as they flutter with pride.

"I dig it. I'm glad we're clearing the air here, so I'm going to go ahead and ask, why would your sister hire someone to screw you? You don't look like the kind of woman who has trouble getting laid."

"Here we are, judging a book by its cover again." Her hands circle her waist.

"I'm in awe of the complete badass business owner you are, but I'm here with a limp appendage, and apparently, you need to get laid as well. So, the clock is ticking on a decision."

"Lacey was droning on and on this morning about this *dry spell* I've been in. The little brat went as far as making a dating profile for me, like I can't get laid on my own. Her intrusiveness knows no bounds. I just … no one has seemed interested me in a while. Maybe I haven't been interested in anyone. Whatever the reason, you trusted me with your big secret." Her tangent ends as the leafy color of her eyes darkens like a forest in the night. "It's only fair I confess one too."

The ardor in her tone surprises me.

Through hooded lashes, she unleashes a truth that has my balls tightening. "I haven't been fucked in weeks, and … I'm going to explode if I don't get off soon. Spontaneous combustion style."

All the air in my lungs evaporates in a haste, and I wither under her declaration like a deflating helium balloon. I've died and gone to hell with her confession. Even Satan himself is shaken by the fallen angel's wayward disclosure. Beads of sweat form across my shoulder blades as the stunning redhead in front of me spouts on about not being properly banged in weeks. I don't have it in me to continue with her chitchat. My resolve faded with her *I haven't been fucked in weeks* line.

"Today's been the worst day ever," she explains, her tone defeated.

I half hear her because my mind is still blown.

"My wand died. Lacey was making fun of me. I loathe QuickBooks."

Under normal circumstances, I'd find her rambling adorable, but my breath is still lodged in my throat, and I can't form any coherent thoughts.

"At this point, screwing a stranger who I'll never have to see again is more appealing than sailing the sea on an all-inclusive yacht with the cast of *Magic Mike*. I am in a bit of a rut." Exhaling, she shakes her head. "She was right. I'm pathetic. So, I'll help you," she announces, sounding purposefully sincere and *serious*.

My dick springs back to life in anticipation, and my eyes are glued on her full, blush-colored mouth. Women in the music industry often have the same juicy, plump lips as Soph's. Except with her, I can bet a million dollars that they're a God-given feature and not injected with fillers.

This innocence she wears, although alluring, is a front.

Called that one.

The redhead before me is a vixen in disguise. I find it unsettling that I *want* to know more about her and how she landed in this dry spell. More importantly, I want to drag her to pound town and bury my aching cock in her sweet spot. The latter taking precedence right now.

"Define your definition of helping."

"I'll have sex with you."

"Are you clean?" I kick off my shoes, jeans falling to the floor, without waiting for her answer in a fruitful attempt to get naked as fast as possible.

"Yes." Her deprived eyes hover over my most prized body part.

I give my favorite muscle a little flex, which causes her eyes to widen—not in horror, but rather raw, unleashed desire.

Attaboy.

"I am too." I scroll on my phone, locating the document saved in my photo album, and shove the screen toward her. "Look."

"What kind of psycho has lab results saved on his cell phone?"

"Not a psycho, baby, just a man who enjoys sex and doesn't have time to waste when a woman as breathtaking as you sobs about not being properly screwed. Everything's digital these days."

Needy hands move to hold her body, as I climb off the table and slide her frame in front of my own. The tender skim of her breasts across my chest has me panting like a dog.

"I need to hear you say it, Soph. If you want me to end

that dry spell and fuck your sweet little cunt, I need to hear you say it. Use your words—preferably fast."

If anything, in the music industry, I've learned there's a fine line between consent and implied consent. I might play dumb and wear the mask like a second skin. I'm not a fool, and I don't ever want to be on the end of a vacillating implication that could ruin my career while I'm in my prime.

"You have my permission, Ollie. I want this. I *need* this." The way she hums my nickname without even being told sends a shot of desire through me at a steady pace. "Fuck me senseless."

Those three little words will be burned into my memory until the day I die.

"Slide down your pants." My cock juts forward, begging to be buried in her perfectly sculpted body, molded for my pleasure. "I know we're pushing for time here. Lie on your back. I've been dying to smell your sweet scent."

5

SMOOTH AS BUTTER

SOPHIA

HE'S PRACTICALLY SALIVATING as he watches me climb on the table with a predatory stare. There isn't a submissive bone in my body. I'm too headstrong to allow any man to boss me around.

Damn if the way he orders me to lie down so he can smell me has me begging for him to take the reins, urging him never to return them. Perhaps my fervor is due to all the porn I've been watching as of late. Do you know that it fundamentally changes your brain?

Recovering my thoughts, I scoot to the edge of the table, like he asked. The position leaves me exposed and a little queasy in the pap-smear-stirrup kind of way. Oliver saunters closer, desire etched onto his gloriously handsome features.

"Good girl." He praises my obedience, mouth hovering mere inches from my sex. Warmth assaults my core with his breathy exhale. "Fuck. Your pussy is an irresistible display. A work of art in itself."

Oliver is smooth as butter.

And suddenly, I vow to start the keto diet because, hell ... his filthy words, open appraisal, and toffee-colored eyes, which seem to have glossed over like a volcanic rock on the verge of eruption, have me melting.

I usually don't get nervy before hookups. The danger is sometimes a part of the allure. Not knowing someone and not being able to fully trust them to keep you safe. Just the thought of endangerment leaves me trying to clench my legs together. Oliver pushes them apart, snaking his hands, both covered in ink, down my thighs before settling at the crease of my legs. A thrill of arousal and a soft moan later, I'm ready to kiss any apprehension about our involvement away.

"I ... I don't ... I'm not taking off my top."

The voracity in his tawny gaze, paired with the slow way he licks his lips, preparing for a feast, leaves me writhing. Adding a little pressure with each palm, he looks up at me, eyes slowly roaming over my exposed legs.

"I didn't peg you as a woman who shies away from showing off this exquisite body."

The faint scar lining my stomach from hip to hip lingers in the forefront of my mind.

"It's not that at all. It's ... this top is ... too hard to get undone, and this needs to be quick." *Good recovery.*

The pulsing knot from this morning that never got unwound tightens in my core, threatening to untether and begging for a release of its tension. This is my reckoning for not being a responsible woman. Failure at keeping my wand fully charged has led me to this moment. I'm weak and horny.

"I don't want the coldness from the table taking my attention away from you rubbing my clit if you're going to devour me like I hope you are," I add for safe measure, not wanting to let my body's insecurity paint me like a prude.

Yep. The porn has changed the wavelengths in my brain.

"Marry me?"

The good-natured question causes my heart to beat in an insubordinate rhythm in my chest.

"How have we *never* met before? Actually, hold that thought. We'll come back to it. Settle in, Soph."

With a quick intake of breath, I rest my back on the table. I'm not even fully situated when the warmth of his tongue slides between my crease, beckoning entrance. A primitive, wanton shiver of delight spreads my legs, my core like a welcome mat.

Hello, leave your clothes at the door.

There's not an ounce of intimacy in the way his rough hands hold me open. His touch is raw, unguarded. Needy. It's a death grip, and he's a starving man, my slit the only thing that can satisfy his famishment.

He sucks. I quiver.

He nibbles. I moan.

My heart is hammering as my core tightens in ecstasy. My fingers fly to his tousled, blond-tipped hair, digging into his scalp, clawing in desperation. His leisurely licks turn feral. Pair his devastating appearance with his edge of hipsterness, and I lose myself in the ecstasy of Oliver's skillful tongue with each quaking lap.

In seconds, I'm diving off a cliff, free-falling as he dips a second finger into my arousal with one skillful move. My world spins dangerously fast. Arching my back, I push my core closer to his delicately carved mouth—a silent plea for more. As if he anticipated my involuntary greed, his face is there, pushing into my folds with an unleashed fervor I've only ever witnessed on the internet.

Biting the inside of my cheek, I choke back a sob, riding Oliver's face like he's a roller coaster. I'm buckled in, enjoying my all-access pass.

The wand gods must've heard my prayers and felt sorry for me.

Praise you.

There's no other explanation for this mind-boggling man with exotic ethnic features and a perfectly sculpted nose. There's an air of mystery in his beautifully thick brows, and I *never* want to exit this ride.

With every stroke of his expert tongue, I come unhinged, closer to release. He eats my core like a ravaged animal that's been caged for far too long.

The rapture starts in my toes. I'm clenching the table, nails biting into the cool material as I hang on for dear life. I'm fearful that my nails are going to pierce through the faux leather.

Fuck it, I think to myself, knowing there's a nail salon down the street.

My harsh breaths turn into a pant moments before an off The Richter scale tremor surges through me. A blistering moan escapes me mere seconds before I see stars and come undone by the abundantly competent stranger who drinks me up.

"Fu ... fuck." My limbs go slack as I'm lulled into my euphoria from the high that his expert tongue gave me. I feel rejuvenated. Alive.

"Shh, we don't want company." His eyes drift over my body, and he shoots a mischievous wink before he flicks my clitoris like he's ringing a bell, acknowledging his work here is done. "You cannot imagine how good you taste," he murmurs with a pleased sigh.

We lock eyes. The hold magnetic.

"I didn't come here tonight prepared to get laid though, sweet thing. Are you on the pill?"

Although his question is valid, my heart starts to race at another truth slipping past my mouth this evening. Not wanting to kill the mood, I muster up the nerve to say, "I'm on the Depo shot. It's good for five years, and I already told you that I'm clean."

"You're a *literal* angel."

He settles into one of the chairs resting adjacent to my tattoo table. The sight of him caressing his shaft and the bold stare on his unflawed face stoke a gently growing fire between us. The prolonged eagerness of what's to come is almost unbearable.

"Come sit on my dick and milk it, pretty girl. Take every last drop."

I've never been happier to not *be lactose intolerant.*

There's an air of demand hanging between us. It beckons me like a crook of a finger, and the unmistakable buoyancy in my stride has Oliver sweeping me into his arms, like I'm as weightless as a feather. His strong hands bite into my waist and hold me suspended over his thick erection, which is poised at my entrance. I squirm in anticipation and tilt my core down.

"You're needy, aren't you?" he asks, spacing his words evenly before he lowers me an inch closer to his shaft.

I'm hovering over him, wet and withering with a searing need to be sated.

The thrill of my arousal coats his head as he ever so slightly—and cruelly—rubs it along my entrance with a move that seems practiced.

"Tell me what you want, Soph." His velvet-edged voice fills the small space of my tattoo room like a symphony. "I need to hear you say it, baby. I *want* to hear you beg for it. I don't fuck slow. I take what I need, and with you, I want to take it all."

My sexuality has never been dormant. Cowering isn't in my nature, and I'm not afraid to ask for what in the bedroom or in this case, my studio. Passion bursts through my veins.

"I want you to fuck me so hard and so deep that I feel you next week."

In a sudden movement that leaves my toes curling in my stilettos, Oliver spears me with his thick cock, filling me to the hilt. There's no grace period. Just pure, heated passion as our bodies connect, his groin and mine. Having made a vow to myself when I came into this industry that my personal and professional lives would stay detached at all costs. I learned my lesson when I broke it once before Oliver—aka Mr. Rock Star—sweet-talked me into this little rendezvous. The magnitude of our joined bodies is not lost on me. I've broken my golden rule of not mixing business with pleasure for the second time in my career.

As his eyes capture mine, moments before his head falls back and his breathing becomes labored, thoughts of how fucked up this is abandon me completely, and I allow myself to get lost in the unadulterated ardor that pulses between us. The consequences of this electrifying moment can be dealt with later.

The next thirty minutes bring me to a brink of pleasure that I know I won't easily forget. This pivotal moment with Oliver leaves me at an impasse. How in the hell am I supposed to get back to work and tattoo this man after this?

We pant in unison, trying to collect our breath and bearings. My limbs are gooey, and my aching core is thoroughly satisfied as Oliver pulls out of me and leans forward to kiss my cheek.

"Thank you," he draws out as he grabs the towel that I threw at him earlier and grips it in his clutch. "How's that for ending your dry spell?"

"Solid six." I rate his performance.

"How many times did you come in less than thirty minutes? Two, three? It's a nine, and you know it."

"Should I be offended you don't think it was a ten?" I brush a red strand of hair off my cheek. My core still resting on his lap.

"It would have been a ten if you'd removed your shirt so I could see those perky tits as you bounced on my dick."

I bite back the words *next time*, knowing damn well that this can never happen again, and settle with, "Fair enough."

If postcoital bliss is real, I'm going to be chasing this exhilaration until I'm old and senile. Retelling this story to the nurse's aide who Lacey pays to change my diaper. The intense fervor of this evening is going to be hard to beat for all future suitors. Almost as sure as knowing that when Lacey finds out what debauchery just went down right under her nose, she'll have me writing an explicit essay, not sparing any details.

Never in a million lifetimes could I have expected to be greeted with such a handsome man when I walked into my quaint little tattoo room this evening. Even with his cock jutting out from his molded hips, his face is what drew me in. His sizeable manhood a close second. I was a goner before I even took a step in the room.

Standing on shaky legs, I decide to get to know my client in a less intimate way. "What instrument do you play in this little band of yours?" I shake my head remembering he already told me. His pounding must've caused my brain to short circuit momentarily. "Guitar, right?"

"Ouch, should I be offended you don't think I'm the lead singer?"

From the contrast in his olive skin that glows as luminous as a field of oats under the sun's rays to his unruly hair, this Adonis of a man has my heart palpating and my skin sticky with a layer of sweat.

"The way your fingers ..." I clear my throat.

"That was just a sample of what these fingers can do. Trust me." He helps me off his lap. "Let me clean you up, and then we can get started on my tattoo." Oliver drops to his knees and gently pushes my body so that my butt is now perched against the table. He kisses the soft spot directly over my sex before he tenderly uses the towel to wipe away the remnants of our quickie.

With a quick intake of breath, I start to say something just as the door to my room swings open. A cool wisp of air across my exposed midriff comes with a stunned and wide-eyed Lacey.

"Now, I know what was taking so long. I'm going to let your friends know that, ugh, it's going to be a little longer." Lacey's mouth hangs agape a little too long.

"You can go now." I make a dismissive gesture.

She tilts her head to one side and giggles. The sound makes her seem ten years younger. "Right, um ... damn. I never get this lucky."

"Lacey, out. Now." I excuse her once again before swiveling my head back to Oliver's watchful glare.

The exultation of my climax comes crashing down with Lacey's presence. I swallow instant regret. Reality is like a bitch slap to my face and suddenly I'm immobile. Torn by guilt and disappointment. The misery of the only other night I broke my treasured rule haunts me. The inner voice in my head rings loud and clear, tormenting me for succumbing to desire again and forfeiting any restraint I had carefully cultivated. The old wound of despair showers me with emptiness, just like I felt the morning I woke up after the best night of my life in an abandoned hotel room. I swore then, promising myself to never ever fall for the lustful eyes of a client again.

"All clean," Oliver chimes. The warmth of his smile does little to ease my self-induced affliction. "You ready to get started on this epic jellyfish?"

"Yep. Let me hit the ladies' room real quick." I excuse myself to the bathroom across the hall, mentally kicking my own ass for being so naive and horny.

Hopefully, he's telling the truth about being a rock star, which means he will for sure hightail it out of town and I won't ever have to hear from him or see him again.

6

PROPOSITION

SOPHIA

THE USUAL BANTER and chitchat I generally dole out during a session is gone. Screwing your client before tattooing his junk doesn't leave much in the way of conversation. The sound of my machine thrumming pairs well with the words of Blue Öyster Cult's "(Don't Fear) The Reaper" as it fills the room and keeps my mind occupied.

"You like the classics?" Oliver asks, full of adoration, looking both smitten and relaxed, awaiting my answer.

I nod, having lost my voice and backbone, apparently.

"I'm an old-school rock lover myself. Music is no different from the type of art you create."

Looking up to steal a glance, I find myself locked on his moss-colored globes, observing me intently. "How do you figure?"

"Musicians bleed onstage. Every show we play, we're praised for our outburst of emotion. It makes our shows authentic. The passion helps captivate our audience. We're performers; creating is our lifeline."

"And that relates to tattooing how? My clients bleed under my gun."

"The creating part. Art, in any way that it's expressed, is liberating. You don't sing onstage; your words don't become concrete in someone's memory, but *your* art is on their skin forever, tethering them to a moment in time, just like performing music does. We both create core memories; only your art is permanently etched on someone's skin."

I let his comparison resonate while I continue creating.

"That's why I love classic rock. They just made music to simply ... create. Because a need had festered inside of them. Do you think that people like Bob Marley gave two shits about marketing? Hell no. He had to make music to stay alive. Anything we do should be with enough passion that we'd physically perish without it. Creating. Fucking. It's all fueled my passion."

It's not every day that words escape me. I'm a vocal person. Right now, I don't feel like anything I say can back up his explanation. Sometimes, saying nothing is enough. This is one of those times.

Time elapses as I get lost in my work. Every so often, doing my due diligence, I check in on him. Shoot me, okay? He's too pretty not to admire. His comparison is nothing short than a regal compliment to the art of tattooing. Plus, I'm a woman, which means even though I have practiced separating sex and emotion, Oliver is devastatingly handsome, and I can't help but appreciate his profile.

I'm almost done shading the last tentacle when he stretches his arms over his head and lets out an audible sigh. Penis tattoos are brutal. Not only is it one of the most sensitive areas on a man's body, but the skin is also thin. Fragile. Oliver's eyes have been shut since I started his outline, he even stopped talking about his passion for music. Dude hasn't even flinched under my heavy hand. If I didn't just ride said appendage, I'd think it was a prosthetic. Kudos to him for taking it like a beast.

"I'm man enough to admit, this shit hurts. I'm glad you're almost done."

He is human after all, I think to myself. I was starting to wonder if I'd screwed a robot.

Feeling like I'm as unreadable as a dead tablet, I whisper, "Me too," before nodding through my smoke screen of sensations.

I feel like I'm walking a tight rope and I'm stuck in the middle. Torn between continuing to chastise myself for falling under his spell or just accept the wave of lust he's cast over me and taking this...moment for what it is...fleeting.

"Am I that bad of company? Shit. Was it the sex?" The hint of worry in his tone warms my cold exterior. He hoists himself upward, leaning back on his elbows, concern etched on his sun-kissed face.

Looks like we're taking a break. My foot falls to the side of my machine's footswitch. I use the time out to stretch my back purposely avoiding his gaze.

My thoughts form like a knot inside the pit of my stomach. He thinks the sex is the reason for my palpable awkwardness. I drop my lashes quickly to hide my dismay. "No, it's not that."

"Then, what is it?" He folds his arms behind his neck, elbows pointing in my direction, as his face pinches. "You regret what happened. I couldn't pass up the opportunity. You're hot as sin. Sorry if I sprung this on you. Truly."

A rock star with the self-confidence of a preadolescent male sounds like the commencement of a joke.

I dip my tattoo gun into the small colander of light-blue

ink in preparation of finishing his tattoo before I say, "I particularly liked the act of what we did and I think my vocals made it clear." I give a coy smile, reassuring him before I rip off the Band-Aid. Feeling deflated that my reserve has caused Oliver to second-guess his sexual competence, I breathe in quickly and exhale the truth. "I have this rule that I never fraternize with clients, and I ... I'm just upset that I—"

"Broke your rule."

My cheeks burn like charcoal in a grill as he calls me out, stating the obvious, and a faint smile dances over his sculpted lips. Turning my attention back to the reason he's in my studio, I make a couple strokes across his skin with my gun.

"Aren't rules made to be broken, Soph?" I like the way he purrs my shortened name.

I can feel my eyes brimming with tears. I'm on the brink of losing it. Add humiliation to my list of failures tonight.

His eyes caress mine, a smile forms on his lips. "You can bet I'll remember you every time I see this jellyfish on my peen. Which will be often. He's my best friend. In all seriousness, I'm not sorry in the slightest that we screwed. I am sorry that you're already regretting it while I'm sitting here secretly glad you broke your rules and let yourself enjoy my company tonight. You needed that release, Sophia."

The sinful way my name drops from his mouth has me squeezing my legs together firmly on my stool, knowing that his mark there satisfied me only for a short while. I wouldn't call myself a sex fiend. I think having a healthy libido is normal.

The gentle way his eyes undress me, even as my heart is torn by my own foolish decision, leaves me feeling breathless again.

It's evident; Oliver is a man who knows what he wants and isn't afraid to go after it. Men like him sweat charm in droplets. Pair that with his fabricated story of this so-called band he claims to be in, and I'm drenched, wanting another sample of what he has to offer despite my nagging rule hovering above me like a rain cloud. Threatening to pour down on my parade.

Looks can be deceiving, and I play the sweet, innocent part like my sights are set on winning a Golden Globe. Right now, in his presence, as he looks over at me, I feel raw. Bare. It's not a feeling I'm used to. Usually, my clients are the ones who are vulnerable in my chair, telling me their life stories without shame.

"Thank you for—"

I cut him off, "Servicing you." A laugh escapes me, and I instantly scold myself for being so blunt. His presence makes me bold. Carefree.

"For helping ensure I take this fresh tattoo seriously and making sure that I abide by all your rules," he finishes.

"I'd say you're welcome"—I spray the bottle of green goodness onto a paper towel and hold his penis down as I wipe it with the towel—"but you did me a solid, too, even if I'm beating myself up for it now. I guess we're even."

I admire my finished product permanently on Oliver's shaft. Despite being distracted, I'm pleased with the result. I hope he is too.

"Is there anything else you're too prideful to ask for?"

The slow, sensual smile he offers holds me captive for a moment. As soon as his session is over, I'm searching this band he's supposedly in to see if this panty-melting smirk is plastered all over the internet.

Oliver's words hit the wall of my heart and ricochet off like it's dodging a bullet. He thinks I'm too prideful to ask for what I want, which couldn't be further from the truth. I know exactly how to ask for what I want—both inside the bedroom and out.

Deciding to prove him right, I blurt, "A hundred thousand dollars," as a joke before turning my chair away from him.

The sounds of him shuffling to climb off the table and pull up his pants stall seconds before I hear him mutter, "Sent," under his breath.

"What did you just send?" After my morning with Lacey snapping pictures of me in my towel, I'm on high alert.

"Sent a picture to my bandmates."

"You sent a dick pic to your friends?" I survey him with questioning eyes.

"Sure did, Fireball. You'll meet them shortly."

"Fireball? Really? How much more cliché can you get?"

"It suits you. The red hair. Spunky attitude. Not to mention, you taste like sin. You're like a shot of whiskey to my bloodstream. It's not cliché at all."

"Whatever." I laugh, knowing he's about to hit the road, along with his juvenile pet name. "Let me wrap that before you slide your pants up."

He hoists himself back up on my table, and I wrap a thin piece of Saniderm around his fresh ink.

Sliding off my gloves and discarding them in the trash can, I give him the okay to stand. "Now, you can get dressed."

Drawing my attention back to my workstation, I begin to prep my space for my next client. Who I can only presume also came with fake identification. Wealth has a way of making people careless with their money.

I face him once again. "Is my next client in your band also?"

Shell-shocked, he leans back and traces his bottom lip with the pad of his thumb. "You've really never heard of us?"

"Honestly, no. I'm not really into boy bands. I grew out of that stage by the time Justin went solo."

"We're the furthest thing from a boy band." His powerful hand grips my chin, challenging me to look into his eyes. He leans forward and places a chaste kiss as light as a breeze welcomed in the summer against my lips. "I know my checking account number by heart."

His conciliatory voice causes me to falter, and I drop my gun against the metal table with a loud thud.

"What would you use a hundred grand on?"

I'm met with a smile that sends my pulse racing once again.

With my lip still quivering from his sudden change in subject, I inhale deeply and allow my confidence to spiral upward, admitting something I've only verbalized out loud a handful of times. "I want to expand and open a second location."

Knowing that I'll never see him again, I feel no burdensome chains connecting us. I continue to spill my plans to the stranger before me. "I watched self-help videos and did a lot of the renovations myself. Other than the electricity and plumbing, Rose and Lace was literally built from my blood, sweat, and many, many tears. Not to mention bottles of wine that were indulged in during the renovation."

"You should be proud of this place. It looks like it's a well-oiled establishment." His clear, observant eyes tell me he means what he says. "What if I could make your dream of a second location a reality?"

The what-if game has never been my favorite.

Oliver's question is a well of uncertainty. A raw cut of meat dangling in front of a lion. How could he turn my dream into a reality?

I carelessly approach the topic. "How's that? I just told you I don't like relying on anyone, including—excuse me for this—random men with penis tattoos. I never want to have to be indebted to anyone or owe anyone anything. Which is why we'll keep saving until we can fund our expansion ourselves. Thanks though."

There is a glint of wonder in his eyes. "You'd fuck a stranger, but not do business with one? And this jellyfish is epic. The artist is a creative genius. I know where she works if you want to hire her for your own tats. You know to cover some of your virgin skin."

The flattery adds to his lure, which is short-lived as I eye him with a precarious squint.

I obviously didn't screw my head on tight enough this morning because my heart and mind aren't on the same page. Why I'm even entertaining this idea is beyond me. I should collect the money for his tattoo and kick him to the curb.

Except I don't.

Words spill from my mouth before I know I've said them. "What does having sex with you have to do with expanding my business?"

He settles back into his position on my table, his long legs slack. "Hold tight, I'm getting to that. Follow along, Fireball. Everything started when we went on our first tour. Hell, we weren't even headlining then, but we were so high on hope that one day we would be that we made a pact right then and there after hearing Mazen's crazy idea. At the time, we all had flawless, untainted skin and jumped at the idea to look more the part. Rock stars ooze sex appeal and are usually tatted. Who wants to watch a band perform who looks like they'd be better suited in a church choir? Mazen, our lead singer, was the one who introduced the idea to us about getting a tattoo in every city we stopped at. After we did our opening tour and started to establish our band in the industry, we got our band's logo tattooed on our backs in Chicago. Then, time went on, and we kept the tradition going. Kings of Jupiter blew up, and before we knew it, we couldn't just walk out in public anymore and had to start sneaking into back entrances of tattoo shops."

Chicago. It seems like a lifetime ago that Lacey and I fled our home.

"That's a gnarly idea." I sit and revel in his open adoration for his friends and the band. "I've heard of people getting tattoos in every city they travel in before. Your little twist of getting inked while on tour is pretty cool. Art is always more meaningful when there's a story behind it."

"I've been throwing around the idea of hiring a personal tattoo artist for the guys and me for some time now. We need someone qualified and without strings to go on tour with us and tattoo us in the luxury of our own tour buses. We wouldn't have to do so much research and hire extra security guards just to escort us to studios anymore. Scotty Girth, my alter ego, could take a break. If you came on tour with us, you could be our personal tattoo artist and give our crew some peace of mind. You'd alleviate a lot of stress."

"Why not just stop getting tattooed in every city if it causes such a headache? You're clearly not lacking in ink nowadays. No one in their right might would peg you as a choir boy."

His demeanor grows serious. "Are you superstitious?"

"Not particularly. I mean, I don't think so. Why?"

"Musicians are a lot like athletes. Except it's not dirty socks we wear on game days that keep our mojo strong. It's traditions, like Cannon licking his drumsticks and then throwing them into the crowd after every show or Mazen ripping his shirt in half, shredding it, and then tossing the pieces into the front row like a snake who just shed his skin. Post-show tattoos are our reward. Second to pussy, of course. Getting inked has become our release. A way to unwind and a remembrance of our journey. Not fulfilling our ritual would be like forgetting our prized socks before a big game."

"Let me get this straight. You're offering me to go on tour with you and your band—which might or might not be make-believe since I've never heard of your band before—and in exchange, you'd just cut me a check for one hundred thousand dollars? If this doesn't sound like a scam—"

"I'm a lot of things, Fireball. A scam artist isn't one of them." He winks, and liquid instantly pools in my panties. "And I'm not swindling you either. I'll have our attorney draft up a contract if that would make you feel better about my offer. I am serious though. I saw your portfolio online. You're talented, and I think you'd be a great asset to our team. From the sounds of it, you have aspirations that are a little out of reach. I can make your vision a reality."

My face is blank. I'm both amazed and stunned. I don't know how to respond.

"You don't have to answer me now. Think over it. Talk to your sister and shoot me a text." He jots down a number on the index card from Lacey resting on my table. "I'll send in someone else from the band. Maybe you'll believe me then." He strides to the door and then looks over his shoulder. "Oh, and don't think on this offer for too long. We leave for Europe in two days."

When he shuts the door behind him, I let out a breath I didn't realize I was holding and run my hands through my thick crop of hair. "Holy fucking shitballs." Using the index card with Oliver's name and number on it, I fan myself.

Not only did I just break my golden rule of not frolicking with a client, but I'm also actually contemplating his proposition.

Several minutes pass before I work up the courage to open my door. Lacey's voice echoes from down the hall. She's laughing, probably plotting a way earn some extra cash by running a brothel instead of a reputable tattoo studio after witnessing Oliver on his knees in front of me.

I fall back into character, attention focused on prepping my workstation as I will the universe to do me a solid. By letting this whole band thing be a giant lie. Anything would be better than falling for another musician. I've met my quota for one lifetime.

7

ROSELLA

MAZEN

MY BEST FRIEND waltzes down the hallway with a smile on his face, the gold in his eyes flashing with fire. The absence of agony in his gait has me questioning if he really went through with his long—no pun intended—awaited penis tattoo. If my eyes weren't blistering from the abhorrent image of his dick as proof on my phone, there'd be no way in hell I would believe him.

"Comrade." He plops down next to me on the sturdy couch in the waiting area and winces. I smile at the fact that he's finally showing a little discomfort. "She's all yours."

I stand up, stretching my back. "Lucky me."

He was in the room for-fucking-ever, and I'm stiff as shit from sitting on this hard couch that was made for anything but comfort.

"I could have lived without seeing your junk," I add with a steel edge in my voice.

"Don't kid yourself. I know you already made it your screensaver," Ollie sneers, his amusement disturbing.

"Murphy wanted proof that I went through with it. Since his lame ass isn't here, I sent it to the group chat."

I eye him intentionally as he pats my shoulder, and a subtle look of amusement flashes across his face.

"I highly doubt the proof he wanted was an up-close-and-personal picture of your puny dick. And need I remind you? I. Am. Not. Murphy. I didn't need or want proof." I slide my phone into my pocket and return his gesture by reaching forward and patting him on his shoulder. "Cut Murphy some slack. Let him enjoy his engagement and have some dignity, man. You should have done it at a different angle, knowing we'd have to zoom in on that shrimp-sized appendage you call a cock."

His body stiffens like I struck him with the back of my hand before he adds by way of grumbling, "He's messing things up, man." The tinge of complaint in his voice betrays his ardor.

I give him a sideways look, my eyes muttering, *Shut up and grow a sack.*

"You heard he bought his own tour bus, didn't you? He's bringing *her* along," his gruff voice rasps.

It's something we've all been holding hostage in our minds since Murphy, our bass guitarist, announced that he purchased his own bus a few weeks ago and dropped the news that his fiancée would be joining us on the next leg of our European tour.

Holding the white index card I filled out, I exhale. "As long as Vanna remains cool and doesn't turn into a bridezilla and their upcoming nuptials don't cause a rift in the band, I couldn't care less what those two lovebirds choose to do or how they choose to get to our shows. One less body on the bus means more room, man. I call dibs on the bedroom. I'm getting too old to climb onto the top bunk." Running my hand through my hair in a cupped motion, I surprise even myself with the solemn-filled statement, making me sound more like a man pushing thirty and less like a hard-core rocker.

"I might believe those words if they weren't said by the king of hitting it and quitting it." Throwing back his head, Ollie lets out a hearty bellow of laughter.

If the outburst wasn't at my expense, I'd laugh at the sound of his cackle alone.

Cannon Rhodes, our drummer, who is sitting next to Ollie, is too immersed in the book he's reading on his phone to give his own opinion on the subject. His silence gives Ollie free rein.

"I'm judging him for the woman he's choosing to legally bind himself to, not the fact that he found one pussy he's willing to devour for the rest of his miserable life. Marriage means no takebacks."

"Just because she turned you down in high school isn't a reason to hold a ten-plus-year grudge. If I remember correctly, you screwed her cousin who was visiting from Asia at *her* birthday party and then tried to hit on her."

He lets out a grunt, casually offering a dismissive shrug.

Oliver Collins is our band's guitarist and resident comedian. Even when we were younger, he was always the one trying to make us laugh. That undiluted humor he had back then has only magnified and gotten more daring with age. The fucker has a strange morally gray sense of humor that edges on darkness.

I take a quick glance around the dimly lit waiting room that has an array of dark pink and grays of different shades littered everywhere. I offer him a low, throaty laugh of my own and watch Ashton, the head of our security team, and crew outside the window, blowing out a puff of smoke into the darkening sky. The absence of any other customers is a reassuring sight. It means we don't have to hide our true identities if we don't want to. Yet we still filled out our information with our pseudonyms. It was second nature at this point.

"What ink did you choose?" Ollie asks me as he mindlessly flips through a magazine in front of him, not looking up to gauge my reaction.

I smirk, knowing that he's been waiting years to get his infamous sea-monster tattoo. "I'm feeling something Floridian. I think I'm going with a jellyfish."

Pushing his buttons is my favorite hobby, second to getting my dick sucked.

There's no better feeling in the world than grabbing a female's head, accepting the power she gives you by kneeling at your feet like a peasant, and then fucking her sweet little mouth as she chokes on your cock. I can almost hear the sound of gagging and feel the wetness the motion brings.

Fuck, I'm getting a semi.

Adjusting myself, I retreat back a step as he sets the magazine down on the table.

"You bastard. You would. Whatever." He glances over at Cannon, diverting his gaze from mine. "Soph probably has the stencil still out if you're serious. You might be able to catch her in time."

My feet become glued to the concrete floor below, as if a torch melted my boots into a heap of rubber. "Come again?"

"You never fucking listen to shit I say. I told you all of ten times already. Her name is Soph."

"Selective hearing." My shoulders tense. "What's her full name?"

"Sophia Lozier. I dubbed her Fireball. She's a sexy little

redhead. Where the hell is Ashton?" His gaze dances around the room like he just noticed the absence of our closest ally.

His wavering attention causes him to miss my deer-in-headlight look.

There's no way. I regain my composure.

"Outside smoking. He got all pissy when he pulled his vape out, and that fiery one over there with pink hair"—I motion to the reception desk—"said she'd flog him if he smoked in her shop. The scary part is, she didn't even bat an eye. I wouldn't put it past her to have a riding crop behind the cash register. There's a screw loose in that one."

"No shit." He nods. "Lacey's harmless though."

My brows tighten when he raises his hand and offers her a small wave with the flick of his wrist.

Their unusual exchange is off-putting. Leave it to Oliver to make friends wherever he goes. This bastard has a way with women. They flock to him like gnats. I usually blame it on his Mediterranean features that he wears like a badge of honor. Not in this case. Lacey looks like she packs one hell of a punch. Which means Ollie isn't her type. He's a golden retriever. There's a reason he and Jupiter, our bands twelve-year-old-Husky and live-in mascot are thick as thieves. It takes a dog to know one.

Women flock to me too. Just for different reasons.

As the lead singer of our band, I'm used to being the center of attention. I can't count how many times I've woken up in a cold sweat with the chants of "Mazen" being yelled by a mob of fans.

At the start of our careers, I reveled in it. Can you blame me? From performing in Cannon's parents' garage to performing on a stage in front of thousands of women—most topless—screaming our names, I became the epitome of a rock star. And fucking enjoyed all the perks that our fame brought us.

I've snorted a line off a stripper's ass crack and ridden off on a just-released motorcycle for free just so the brand could use my image on their advertisement. If that isn't the life, I don't know what is. The privileges our lifestyle has provided are endless and … lonely. I wouldn't dare repeat that to Oliver, Cannon, or Murphy though. Not in a million fucking years.

"Go on, you tattoo-stealing jackass, before Soph tosses the stencil away. Oh, and, Maz?" His eyes go wide, and he winces as he palms the center of his pants. "I wouldn't suggest getting a dick tat tonight. Did you know you can't have sex for six weeks?"

"Did you *not* know, is the better question?"

He stares at me blankly.

"You stupid fuck." A laugh escapes me. "I can't believe you went through with it. Your bunk is across from mine, dude. I see and hear everything. There's no way you can refrain for that long."

He raises one of his fluffy, dark brows, like he does onstage, and as innocently as a child who snuck a cookie before dinner, he spaces his words evenly. "I. Got. Mine."

He gives a slow wink, and all the blood in my body simmers to a steady boil.

He had sex with *our* tattoo artist.

The confession that slides through his teeth isn't meant to be boastful. Ollie has always had a swagger and charm about him that leaves women weak and needy in his presence. He's the ultimate wingman. Being an avid dog lover alone makes him a pussy magnet. The bastard literally has the face of Jupiter, our damn dog, tattooed on his forearm. I love Jupiter too. But Ollie's commitment and adoration are a little extreme and on the verge of obsession though.

No doubt he approaches woman with, *Do you have any pets?*

Hook, line, and sinker.

That thought should make me laugh. I don't feel any humor bellowing within, following his declaration. Only madness. Knowing this small yet significant information about my best friend and *Soph* feels like a bucket of ice-cold water being doused over my head.

"Soph got hers too. Don't worry. I'm not a pig. The sound of her release will keep me sated for weeks. Six weeks. Hopefully."

The aloofness of his behavior is like a chain tightening around my spine. Immobile by his confession, I stare at the neon sign hanging above the reception desk seconds before fate slaps me across the face. My cheek stings.

Rose and Lace Ink Emporium ...

Sophia *Rose.*

After all this time searching for *her*, have I finally found *my* Sophia?

My *Rosella.*

The simple name belongs to a delicate flower that sprouted in my past a long, long time ago. The young tattoo apprentice who stole my tattoo virginity and my heart in one of the most passionate nights of my life has haunted me for nearly a decade.

After searching aimlessly for years, I finally succumbed to the fact that finding her was a dream just out of reach. She became my pot of gold. When Ollie picked this place, for the first time ... ever, I refrained from looking at the shop's website. After scouring images of the artist in every tattoo studio, in every single city we stopped in, seeking her out for years, I had finally given up, succumbing to the reality of never seeing her again or finding her.

There are some people or instances in life that resonate deep within someone, marking their soul or damning it. For whatever reason that's too far-fetched or impossible to explain, that was what my Rosella was to me. A fleeting memory of a night that's held my heart and memory captive for nearly a decade.

Only my best friend doesn't know who she is to me because I've kept that night in Chicago hidden behind a vault belonging to me and only me. I didn't want her memory to be tarnished by my friend's brash remarks. That night has remained unsullied for years.

Until now.

Fuck. I pull at the dark hair on top of my head, gripping it painfully hard in a dire attempt to rein myself back in. I don't handle emotion well. Never have. Thank my sperm donor for that little fact.

Music has always been my outlet. Allowing my feelings to bleed onto paper, forming lyrics, is the extent of my emotional capacity. There's no way this is happening—that we've landed in *her* tattoo studio this evening. That would be too cruel, right?

Sophia hooked up with my best friend.

Mi fa arrabbiare. Makes me angry.

The Italian blood flowing through my veins is easily tamed until my anger soars. I swallow down my heritage, severing any tether to my father with forceful breaths.

A shadow of annoyance crosses my face as I glance back in Ollie's direction and my dark eyes lock with his. I'm not a jealous man. Eons of touring with your best friends and fucking countless communal partners has eliminated all jealousy between us. This girl—now woman—is different.

Knowing that my closest friend just screwed her—while I was sitting down the hallway, no less, oblivious—makes me want to choke the living shit out of him.

I should do just that. For claiming someone who belongs to me.

Guitarists are a dime a dozen, and a man's heart can only take so much. Even if it's been lying dormant for nearly ten goddamn years.

Il suo comportamento è snervante. His behavior is unnerving.

Without a backward glance, I saunter down the hallway. I need to see for myself if it's really *her*.

A ghost of my past.

The woman who became my muse.

My feet feel like they're anchored by chains as I walk down the small hallway with a twinge of envy guiding my every step. He got to touch her in the most intimate way possible, like I meant nothing to her. Her memory has been my salvation. A tether to a part of me that has long faded. A version of her lives in every song I've written. For a small fragment of time, she was a crutch, a dream.

Now, she's my best friend's whore.

I deadpan when I see the silhouette of a woman with deep red hair sitting on a stool, her back facing the door. Despite the chains clanging against the floor, tied to my ankles, she doesn't hear me as I approach. I use the time to drink her in.

Without realizing it, I gulp, appreciating what time and age have done to the contour of her body. From the plump ass that bows into a waist so puny that I could fit both hands around it and brush each fingertip to the deft tattoo of a rose on her exposed shoulder blade. She's still a paradox. A tattoo artist with only one tattoo marring her skin.

I clench my mouth tighter at the identifying marker. Its sight sends my heart constricting. My pulse throbs so quickly that I can feel the rush of blood pounding against my eardrums.

The beat is unnerving at best.

Performing for thousands of people every night has left me immune to pesky butterflies or jitters. I perform best under sweltering lights and swarms of fans chanting, yelling, going feral. The stage is my sacred place. When I'm in my element, I'm untouchable. This feeling of ... I can't name what exactly, it's lodged in my throat. I've only felt the unnatural serenity that encompasses me as I stand, watching her, once before while not onstage. It was the night I claimed Sophia's soul and gave her mine on a golden platter. Imagine the irony when I had to leave her, naked and alone, to embark on our first tour that following morning.

My heart stopped beating on that dreary Chicago dawn and turned to stone in the years I spent searching for her. The elusive tattooist who had left her mark on both my skin and soul.

Apprehension isn't in my nature. Not even my brain is in control of me now. I'm running purely on hope. It's an odd feeling that doesn't settle well. My stare drills into her, and a sudden wave of nerves takes me under like a riptide. My body thrashes violently against the water that holds me under, threatening to suffocate me. Accepting my fate, I open my mouth and allow the salty water to fill my lungs. I'd willingly take being dragged down to the ocean's abyss if it meant an eternity of cherishing her body in the afterlife.

Will she remember me?

I've fought through years of searching for her, and here she sits, with warm red waves cascading down her back. She doesn't need to turn around for me to know that it really is her. I vividly remember those locks being wrapped around my fist as I impaled her over and over.

Ten years ago, I walked away from the one woman in the universe who saw me for *me*.

Mazen Wilde.

The guy with demons, which seemed to be erased with a sultry glance from a stranger at a bar. Not the disappointment of a son whose father threatened to disown him. Not the up-and-coming rock star that the world was getting ready to meet.

Just the sorry bastard who stumbled into the right place at the wrong time.

8

AMNESIA

MAZEN

"YOU'RE GIVING off Dahmer vibes. Don't just stand there. Come in and have a seat."

The redhead's timbre breaks the through the torment of my thoughts. Even with her snarky assertiveness, her influence lures me forward. Like a siren calling to her victims, enticing them with her glamour. Except I fell under her spell once and it cost me everything.

With a gamut of emotions, I pass the threshold of the doorframe into her domain, unease tethered around my spine. I take a seat on the table adjacent to her. Sophia swivels on her stool to face me, and red waves of thick hair dance at her midline.

I wait for her to look up, wanting to gauge her reaction to seeing me after so much time has passed. A heaviness in my stomach, like an anchor dropping to the depths of the ocean, pulls me under when she holds out her hand, not caring enough to look up at her awaiting client.

"Index card, please."

A swift and disturbing thought flashes before me. *What if she doesn't recognize me?* It might be for the best, considering she was just with my best friend. The girl I met that night, the one who captured me with one glance, might be long gone. Too much time has passed. *I've changed too.* I'm no longer the naive boy I was then. I'm a man now.

A livid one.

"Toxic Energy" by Blackbear and The Used plays like an anthem in my head as my heart rages against my rib cage when her green eyes, nearly dark as a forest, rise to meet mine. She lowers them, raking me in from head to toe in a blunt assessment.

She's not even trying to hide it.

I hold my breath, waiting for the glimmer in those jade eyes to spark with an indication that she recognizes me. Her gaze holds mine, and for a fleeting moment, I think that this is it. She *does* recognize me.

It's short-lived as she tosses her head to the side, a bemused scoff on her face as she examines my index card with my fake persona. Her eyebrows quirk upward. "You don't peg me as a Keith."

I seethe, nose flaring.

"Cut the shit. Your buddy already told me your secret."

"He told you I like eating dry cereal?" I feign offense, plastering on a smile that hides my ... disappointment. "That dirty dog really threw me under the bus with that one."

A simple yet extravagant smirk spreads across her face, causing her red-stained lips to thin. "I'm guessing you're either Mazen or Cannon. Which one is it?"

Damnit, Ollie. He'd rat after one night in a jail cell.

"Cannon," I murmur, watching intently as she bites down on her smooth lip. "You caught me."

"Try again." Holding up her phone, she pushes it toward my face. "I searched the name of your band as to see if your little friend *Scotty Girth* was who he said he was. Looks like *Oliver* does have an honest bone in his body after all."

"If you knew who I was, why'd you ask?"

Confusion bunches her brows. She ignores my question altogether and stares at the index card before tossing it in the garbage. "It says you want a palm tree."

"When in Florida."

"Right. That's exactly what Ollie said."

"Ollie." I scoff at her use of his nickname. "It looks like you guys got close in the span of a couple of hours."

She offers me a casual, dismissive nod. It's a gesture she seems to have mastered.

"The least favorite part of my job is meaningless chitchat."

The starkness in her tone bites against my heart. It's a clear indication that she doesn't recognize me. Why would she? It's been years. The guy she met vanished that morning anyway.

The recognition that I've harbored feelings for a ghost doesn't sit well with me. That, paired with Sophia's stand-offishness attitude and absence of memory of the best night of my life, causes a stir of emotions to twist like a hurricane in my chest.

Years' worth of pent-up angst left me rifling every tattoo studio across the globe in search of my mysterious one-night stand, leave me hovering between wrath and an ache so deep that it will unquestionably scar.

"What's the best part of your job?" I square my shoulders, not hiding the anger racing through my veins. I lean forward and whisper into her red wealth of hair that smells tangy like citrus, "Letting strangers into your pants while you're on the clock?"

Uncaged resentment dances in my words like venom, causing her spine to go immediately rigid.

Sophia's sage sandy eyes slit like a cat ready to attack. Her voice catches in her throat, she flounders. The hooded eyes that once beckoned me widen in disgust as she musters up all of her courage in her petite frame.

Unleashing white-hot anger, she bellows from her lungs, "Who do you think you are, talking to me like that? Get the fuck out of my studio."

The potency in her voice is unmistakable.

The pair of eyes boring into me quickly turn into three sets as Oliver and the receptionist, who I now know as Lacey, come to a grinding halt in the doorway. Their combined glares silently ask what all the commotion is about.

How can she not remember me? Sure, I've aged. Time took me from a boy to a man. The main difference is, my once-virgin skin is now covered in sprawling ink, like I'm a walking coloring book. She's changed, too, though, but I remember her delicately carved face. It isn't hard to forget since it's been tattooed on my heart.

"What happened?" Ollie breaks the silence. A wave of ferocity travels through the room as the syllables leave his mouth.

Thoughts evade me as Sophia's hand skates across my cheekbone. The sound of her palm hitting my cheek reverberates in the small room, bouncing off the walls. I smile inside, knowing that the fierce girl I once bedded is still in there. Even though her cold eyes reflect a sheen of hatred in them.

Fuck this shit. *She's* the one who forgot me and made a

habit of fucking strangers. It's not lost on me that our first encounter started the exact same way—with limbs and mouths mingling.

Rein it in, Maz. She doesn't even remember you, for Christ's sake!

I want to punish her for forgetting me.

For not seeking me out.

For screwing *my* best friend.

In the end, it's Sophia who punishes me. A long awaited retaliation for my leaving her that morning without a good-bye. Now, I'm left to pick up the pieces of my shredded heart, so marred that I don't know if even I can piece them back together this time.

"Vaffanculo." Fuck off. I stand, hastily brushing past Ollie, desperate to put some space between us.

Exiting the building in a rush, I slide into the blacked-out SUV parked outside and jerk my notebook open, almost ripping it in the process. The pen in my hand scribbles down words before I even comprehend what I'm writing. A few moments pass before Cannon swings open the back door and silently slides in beside me.

"I don't want to talk about it." I grit my teeth, my pen dangerously close to snapping in my hand.

His quiet and nonintrusive character is one of his best qualities. He doesn't pry, like Oliver does, and he doesn't encourage me to talk about my feelings, like Murphy. He just lets me ... be. It's probably why he and I get along so well. Cannon is complex. The big guy dwarfs over us in size and strength. His stature aside, he's the softest-spoken person in our group—when he actually chooses to speak, that is.

He's the band's drummer, but his talent and what he brings to the table don't require any words. Cannon is an melophile. Music is his passion, not the words we string together. He loves the melody and can play any instrument from just watching someone and observing them. I don't think he even knows the words to any of our songs, and it's his fucking job to know them. Nevertheless, he performs every night without issue.

We've forged our companionship through silence over the years. I'm thankful for his understanding that I need solitude, to get lost in my thoughts for a while. Accepting this, he slides out his wireless earbuds, places them in his ears, and then lays his cell phone gently on my lap.

Having a conversation with someone else's words ... lyrics ... is something that he can do. It's something we've all been doing for years. Expressing ourselves through lyrics is the only therapy we've clung to throughout the years. Which is why when I grab his cell phone, shuffle through the music app on his phone, and choose a song that depicts what I'm feeling, I know Cannon will understand the message loud and clear.

I hit play, and "Rise Above It" by I Prevail blares from his AirPods. Handing his phone back to him, I say, "Take us back to the hotel. Ollie can find his own way home," to our driver as I sink into the leather seat.

Cannon mimics my movement, leaning his head back, and offers me a reprieve that only solitude can.

The best art is often born from misery of any kind. Despair, divorce, death. Any of the big *D*s usually does the trick. It doesn't matter what genre of music someone is drawn to; getting lost in someone else's story is powerful.

Turning pain into music is what got me into this industry. Our first number one hit, "Heart on Fire," was a clear indication that agony sells.

She came in like a siren
Seduction coursing through her veins
A sweet whimper from her lips
Whispering my name

Blinded by her touch
Her kiss
I knew I'd never be the same

She set my heart on fire
Burning with desire

I wrote it the morning I left Sophia lying naked, filled with my cum, sprawled across her hotel bed. The only goodbye she got was a simple note, written on the hotel's stationery, and yet I blame her for my broken heart in some warped, fucked-up way.

Old sorrows threaten to resurface, prompting my hand, and I scribble words across the small notebook I carry everywhere I go. Cannon silently nods his head, getting lost in a song, and I get lost in mine.

Writing is my outlet. A way to make sense of the thoughts that run erratically in my head, threatening to drive me insane. There isn't a day that passes where I don't jot something down. Even a single word. It's never my purpose for my thoughts to turn into hits. Sometimes, it just pans out that way.

We don't even make it onto the interstate before my page is full of words that bled from my soul, along with the recollection of Sophia's face as my words cut her like a knife.

One night shared between strangers
Two souls bared
Cheap whiskey, red wine, two bodies
intertwined
Goodbye never came
Like a knife to my heart, your absence tore
me apart
I'm tired of shouting out your name
Brokenhearted, torn to shreds, your ghost is
all that's left

A coldhearted monster remains, born from
guilt and from shame
Your memory is the reason for my paranoia
I summon your memory in my sleep
I still recall your name
The feel of your body next to me
It haunts me in the day and taunts me in
my dreams
I wish I could forget your memory
Fuck the ghost of our past
A love destined for greatness never meant
to last

You don't remember me, and I can't
forget you
I wish I had amnesia

WHEN OLLIE finally strolled into our shared suite, wearing a smug-looking grin, I knew he was up to no good. True to his fashion, he dropped a bomb on us bigger than any the nitwit had ever done to date. He detailed his offer to Sophia Lozier to become our live-in tattoo artist, and a strained scowl took up residence on my face, followed by a mass of obscenities.

Said scowl must still be present this morning based on the pleading of his hooded eyes.

"Morning," he skips his usual banter. Odd. "I need a favor."

"Fresh out of them."

Inhaling a puff of smoke, my lungs expand from the fat joint that Cannon must've rolled and left on my nightstand this morning. He never pried or asked why I got into the car without a tattoo. I didn't figure he would. He's like that. The present he left for me this morning speaks volumes.

"Come on man. This isn't something I can send Ashton or anyone else to do. I need your help."

"I'm not your little errand boy," I say as I fight for air.

"Can you go get Soph while I take Jupiter to the vet?"

"I'm waiting for the punch line of this joke."

"Dude, come on. I'll owe you." His brows draw inward.

"You want her on the bus? Go fetch her yourself."

"She's not a dog." He sloshes around the iced coffee in his hand. The sound grates on my nerves. "I'm busy, and I need your help."

I was pissed when I went to sleep last night and woke

up in the same mindset. My head throbs as I try to steer my thoughts away from deciphering why Oliver stayed at Rose and Lace after it was clear Cannon and I were leaving. There's safety in numbers, and we always travel as a group. Last night was an exception since he apparently stayed behind to coddle his new plaything.

"Go easy on the reefer, pal. It's not even ten o'clock, and you already smell like an ashtray." Ollie huffs before pulling a green hoodie over his head, sinking onto the hotel couch beside me.

Our pooch, Jupiter—a white-and-black husky—jumps on his lap and snorts a heavy, content exhale.

Traitor.

"You hate going to random studios and getting mobbed by fans just as much as we all do. I did us all a solid, Maz. Are you mad that I came up with a solution? Or is it that you didn't meet *her* first? From my perspective, it's that I tasted her before you. She seems like a cool chick. I'll ask her if she's down to be shared when you retrieve her and bring her here."

My longest friend in the universe has no fucking clue that once upon a time, I had dibs, although fleeting, and what a glorious thing it was. I'm not nearly as high as I need to be for that confession. I groan in protest, smothering myself with a throw pillow to add to my dramatics.

Coming up for air, I exhale. "Sophia doesn't seem like the sharing type."

The unrelenting bastard continues, "I wouldn't have pegged her as the type to bone a stranger either, yet my thoroughly satisfied dick says otherwise. Enough about pussy. Listen, we'll have our own professional tattoo artist with us for this leg of the tour."

Jupiter nudges his hand, and he rubs his fluffy head.

The dog is almost as much of an attention-seeking whore as Oliver.

"Instead of finding random studios, Soph can just learn about the culture in the places we stop and sketch something up in the comfort of our own tour bus. And ..."

There's always an *and* with Ollie. This fucker can justify just about anything. It's like his personal talent. If music fails him, at least he has a backup career as a car salesman.

I'm on defense, ready to rebut whatever excuse he has when he opens his mouth.

"Jupiter has his annual vet appointment while we're in town today, and he can't miss it. I think the vet we took him to in Amsterdam misdiagnosed him. His ear is still red and looks swollen. I bet money that it's infected, and if it is, that rent-a-vet is going to wish he'd never met me."

I pat the cherry out with my thumb and pointer finger before laying my roach on the table and pulling my hood over my head. Nothing beats a morning high. Maybe a morning blow job. That's a moot point since I'm surrounded by men. I need to find someone to fuck Sophia's memory from my own. I add it to my to-do list for the day.

"Let Cannon or Murphy take Jupiter to the vet."

"What the hell else do you have planned today other than getting stoned and napping?" The potency in his tone irks me enough that my buzz starts to fade.

Folding my arms across my chest, I lean back on the couch, extend my legs, and rest them on the coffee table in front of me. Jupiter shifts his enormous body and nestles his head on my lap.

"Well, Mother, if you insist on knowing every detail of my day, I was also going to order sushi and take a bubble bath in that giant-ass Jacuzzi tub in my bathroom. It sounds like you've forgotten, but we're going back on tour tomorrow. I need to stockpile all the peace and quiet I can get before I'm crammed in a bus with you and Cannon."

"You could get engaged, like Murphy. That earned him his own tour bus." He shrugs before standing and securing the black leash in his hand to Jupiter's collar, giving our dog a gentle pull.

"I'd rather die than be tied down to one pussy for the rest of my life." Monotony scares me.

"Never say never. Get your ass up, swallow your pride, apologize to Soph for talking to her like she was one of your groupie whores, and go retrieve our tattoo artist." He shuffles to the door, irritation dripping behind him.

"Why don't you invite Dr. Cangelosi on tour with us too?" I ask, referring to the vet we've used every time we're home for years. "Then, you'll know Jupiter has the best care around. Since you're making a habit of inviting people to tour with us and all."

"Be careful what you wish for, nimrod." With his hand on the door to the hotel, he gives me one final plea over his shoulder. "Muster up some decency and be nice. You really hurt her feelings last night. I know it's not in your nature, but she seems like a cool chick."

"Since when did you start to care about any female's feelings?"

"Since *we*"—he emphasizes *we*—"hired one."

Ignoring the badgering voice murmuring in my head, telling me to hold my ground, I nod, acknowledging Oliver's request, and send him off with a forced smile.

Sophia's memory already ruined me once. That one night caused a perpetual reel in my head, haunting me for some unknown reason without ceasing. Women have come and mostly gone, yet her stupid fucking memory has stayed, ingrained in my brain. I'll be damned if she gets the opportunity a second time to make another lasting mark in my life. If I were standing in front of a mirror, I'd see the gunmetal of my eyes inflame subtly at the thought of combat—I'm sure of it.

She claimed I hurt *her* feelings.

She fucking flayed mine.

There's nothing I love more than edging a woman. Leaving her panting, begging, and only when I decide that it's time, coaxing all the fire out of her. Nothing will make me happier than punishing Sophia for forgetting me and what we shared. I know she felt it too. Anyone with a soul would have.

She's going to wish she remembered the innocent person I was because the rock star I turned into doesn't give two shits about connection or feelings.

I'm going to make her beg for me.

Or beg to leave.

Vengeance is the best medicine, and I'm in dire need of being healed from this woman once and for all. I give her a week before she's crying and petitioning her sister to come fetch her.

Sparking up the remainder of my joint, I laugh, knowing that I'm too wicked for redemption and a little too sober for my delegated task.

9

KINGS OF JUPITER

SOPHIA

"EXPLAIN this to me again because I'm having a hard time wrapping my mind around the fact that you're just up and leaving. What do those jaw-dropping, panty-melting men who claim to be rock stars have on you?"

Lace's cheetah-print yoga pants cling to her full thighs as she sits with her legs tucked underneath her in a seemingly innocent pose.

Her eyes narrow. "Do you owe them money? Are you in some sort of trouble I don't know about? Are you being extorted?" She fires her questions off like this is an interrogation.

I half expect her to pull out a lie detector kit.

Lacey's pleads, "Blink once for no, twice for yes, just in case they have hidden cameras and you're scared for your life right now."

Every time I toss an article of clothing in my suitcase, she tosses one out. We do this dance a couple of times before I give in, letting out a grunt of exasperation that comes from the pit of my stomach.

"I've explained it umpteen times. Oliver Collins—"

"The one who claimed to be Scotty Girth?"

"Yes," I master the art of eye rolling. "His *real* name is Oliver Collins. He's the guitarist for the band Kings of Jupiter."

Fiddling with the zipper of my bag absentmindedly, she grumbles in dispute, "I knew he was lying about that name. No parents in their right mind would name a little boy something so"—her frame quivers—"cringeworthy. Whatever his pseudonym is, he's a stranger. I know we had a shitty upbringing, but even I remember stranger danger."

"His band has a cool tradition of getting tattooed in every city they perform in. He offered me one hundred thousand dollars if I follow them on tour. We don't make that kind of cash in six months in the shop, Lacey. All I have to do is play nice and be the band's personal tattoo artist for a short time, and the money is ours."

"Play nice. Mr. Girth, or *Oliver*," she purrs, "doesn't know who he just hired, does he?"

"Shut up. I. Am. Nice. When I want to be."

"You're a certified bitch"—she gestures from my head to my feet with a wave of her hand—"hidden under this glorious facade. I can't believe you didn't castrate the dark and gloomy one. If I ever see him, so help me."

My stomach rolls when I think about last night. "Screw him. He can kick rocks for all I care."

Leaning against my headboard, she shrugs and grabs a pillow, holding it against her stomach. "I don't know about this, sis. You've always been the responsible one. This screams irresponsible."

"It's insane. Certifiably so. Don't you think I know this?

It's also a crap ton of money to turn down. You don't have to look at me so judgmentally. It's not like he hired me as an escort. It's legit tattoo work. That. Is. It."

"Let me remind you that I walked in and saw you freshly fucked by said guitarist."

I smother a groan, sinking to the floor. The hardwood is cool against my legs. "You're right; this is a bad idea. A very bad idea. My stomach hurts—"

"That's probably because the milk you poured in your coffee this morning was old." Her smile is without humor. "Sorry. I should have dumped it out when I noticed the date. I got sidetracked by an episode of *Caught on Camera*. Did you know that show still airs? This lady caught her husband and their babysitter—"

"Focus," I snap. "Am I making a mistake?"

My senses are dizzy when I try to keep up with her. Skepticism furrows her beautifully shaped brows. The only redeeming quality my dad left us was the good genes of his eyebrows. At least one of his daughters got them.

"How do you know this isn't a scam? What if you go with them and they murder you or sell you to a sex trafficker while you're abroad? Have you ever even watched a gang-bang video? It can be brutal, and I know you're a feminist" —she holds her fist in the air above her head—"and all that jazz. I know you can hold your own, but gang bangs are intense, even for someone like me. I've been deflowered in every hole on my body, and when I watch those clips, I cringe a little at how callous those men can be."

Her whole face splits into a wide shit-eating grin. "That's a lie. If someone kidnapped me and threatened me with a gang-bang, I'd be drooling and naked in a nanosecond. My point is, these guys, with their fake names and bodybuilder bodies *are* complete strangers."

"You're absolutely right. They're also superstars who live in the public eye. Did you not notice the giant billboard outside the shop? I highly doubt they have a hidden agenda that doesn't get blasted on TMZ. Also ..." I pause, trying to find the right words to pair with Lacey's outlandish commentary. "You're seriously deranged, and you need to seek help while I'm gone."

Studying my sister's face, I say, "Oliver's lawyer emailed me over a contract and a nondisclosure agreement. It's not a scam."

From under a pile of clothes, I slide out a small stack of crisp papers, which I printed downstairs in my office before Lacey even opened her eyelids this morning, and hand them to her, pushing them into her chest. "It's all there. Look for yourself."

I dare her to call this opportunity a bluff after she reads the contract. The only gray area is how I'm going to steer clear of my attraction to Oliver Collins or any of his band-mates that ooze big-dick-energy.

Taking time to read over every page with more precision than she's ever done with our own business documents, she finally looks up; perpetual merriment is written across her dusty-rose cheeks. The heavy lashes that shadow her cheeks fly up, and she speaks in a rush of words, littered with enthusiasm in every syllable. "We can expand. Soph, this isn't a hoax, is it? It's real. Holy. Fucking. Shit. We won't have to eat packaged noodles anymore unless we want to."

With a sweatshirt draped in my hands, I stand and watch as understanding dances across her beautiful features. "It's real, and I'm going. I'm doing this for *us*. We will have the future we've always wanted. I'll make sure of it."

"You're always the one paving the way and protecting

me." Her lips tremble with the need to smile. "When Dad left—"

"I love you more than anything in this entire world, Lacey. I promised Mom I'd always take care of you. So, let me do this." I pull her into my embrace and feel when her defenses subside. I stand strong enough for the both of us. Like I always have and always will. "I'm your big sister. It's my job to protect you."

She sputters, "I just don't get why *you* get to travel the globe with three men who drip sex appeal and play instruments for a living."

"Four," I blurt, and she pushes away from my embrace with a raised brow. "There are actually four members in the band. One I haven't met yet. He's apparently engaged, and his fiancée is coming on tour with him, from what I gathered."

"Life is one big dildo, and I just keep getting fucked. Just to make this clear, you're telling me that you're going on a lavish eight-week vacation with *four* men, and I get stuck here, running our business? The universe hates me. Do you think it's karma? I swear I didn't know I'd screwed that guy's brother who took me to that swanky wedding last year until we were sitting in the church pew and his eyes widened to the size of a soccer ball."

"You screwed your date; his brother, who just so happened to be the groom at said wedding you were attending; and *their* father, all on separate occasions."

"It wasn't like it was a family orgy. I have more self-respect than that."

"Seriously, Lacey. This is definitely karma forcing you to atone."

Her face pales to a ghostly white. I know my sister well enough to know that it's not because she feels bad; it's because she got caught between a rock and a few hard dicks.

"I'll send you pictures every day. It'll be like you're with me. I just need you to promise me one thing while I'm gone."

"Anything. Just name it." Her touch is reassuring, it's like an acceptance of this wacky situation that I'm longing for.

I cover her hand with my own and set my shoulders. "I need you to keep Rose and Lace thriving. Without me there … it'll be a lot to work. You've never had to fill both roles. Never mind. I don't know what I was thinking. I can't leave. This was stupid to even entertain the idea."

Lacey holds a hand up to silence me. "I know the studio is *your* baby. You latched on to it like a mother hen, just like you did with me when Mom died."

I pay close attention to her aversion to mentioning our sperm donor.

"And with those damn plants that line our windowsills. The shop will be in good hands. I promise. I am co-owner after all. I guess if you're forcing me into adulthood, I can bitch up and take responsibility of our booming business too." She raises her chin proudly.

"Before you leave today, I expect to get the juicy details of last night—on what I stumbled in on and why you sent the one named Mazen off with his tail tucked so far up his ass that I could see it protruding from his mouth."

Having a conversation with Lacey is like trying to keep up with a hamster on one of those wheels that never stops spinning.

"Give me an hour to finish packing and shower. I promise to leave you with enough scandalous gossip to keep you reeling for a week."

"Deal." She tosses the contract onto the top of my mound of clothes and leaves me alone with my thoughts.

I love my sister something fierce. She's the only family I have left in this world. Is it bad to look forward to a couple of weeks without her though?

I quickly strip out of my clothes and walk to the bathroom. Showering and doing my hair are high on my priority list before I embark on a crammed tour bus with men that sing about beautiful women for a living. Thinking about it, I make a mental note to grab my vibrator and stupid USB charger before I leave. Going eight weeks without sex might be a new personal record for me. There's no way that I'm going to surrender to my desires again with a client and especially not with my new *boss*. Despite how quickly he had made my knees quiver, I painted a very firm line for him when I texted and agreed to his little proposition. You can bet my panties melting is a hard limit for me. *I will* not *have sex with a member of Kings of Jupiter again.*

I gather my arsenal of beauty supplies after my shower. I either wash my face with hand soap or layer on five serums. There's no in between. I apply a small amount of makeup to my clean face and blow-dry my hair.

Finally confident in my appearance, I stride back into my room and grab a sports bra from my dresser. It's like trying to fit into a toddler-sized leotard as I stretch and pull the elastic fabric in all directions.

I'm out of breath and disheveled. *Women deserve an Olympic medal for successfully climbing into one of these suckers*, I think to myself as I finish packing my suitcase.

LACEY'S JAW hits the floor when I fill her in on the earth-shattering orgasm Oliver gave me. Her eyes bulge with each minuscule fact I slide her way.

"I honestly didn't know you had it in you."

I nod in agreement while surveying our small living room. *I'm going to miss this place.*

"Tell me you're not wearing that stupid shirt though. No confident woman should embark on a tour bus with mouthwatering musicians who all resemble Harley-Davidson models wearing something as atrocious as that."

Glancing down at my shirt, unsure of which one I threw on, I see *Aloe there!* written in an adorable font across the chest.

"Don't be rude. It's cute. News flash: I want to stay off their radars. I already made a horrible mistake with Oliver. One that cannot happen again. So, if wearing yoga pants and T-shirts make me unattractive, so be it. That's the route I'm going."

"Your odds of staying celibate are about as slim as my waist."

I hate when she body-shames. "Your size is irrelevant."

"Says the runway-model big sister."

I roll my eyes at her very inaccurate description of me.

"Pint-sized runway model."

"What you need is water and a little more sunlight, honey." I can't help but laugh at myself. "You're like a plant, only with emotions."

"You know what emotions and I have in common?" She

takes a drink of lemonade and sets it back on the coffee table. "Nothing. Which is the same for plants and me. Unless, of course, you're comparing me to a cactus. I am prickly."

With a giddy laugh and amusement lacing my tone, I ask, "What did the food critic call the cactus pie?" I can't keep my hysteria in when a beat passes and she doesn't even attempt to guess the punch line. "A succulent meal."

"I can't with you. Please don't start with the dad jokes, or they'll kick your ass off that bus, and I'll have to come fetch you. Better idea: go heavy on the plant jokes."

The soft material of our worn cushion welcomes me as I lay my head back. "You know when I get nervous, I start rambling, and the jokes, they fly out. Speaking of flying, why did the airplane get called to the principal's office?"

Crickets.

"He had a bad altitude."

"Why can't you be normal and bite your nails or something when you're anxious? You're so strange."

I smile widely, like my dentist just claimed I have the best oral hygiene he's ever seen. "You're the one with pink hair and just confessed that you wanted to be involved in a gang bang. And you think I'm the *strange* one?"

Ignoring my comment, she presses on. "I'm still confused what happened with the brooding guy and why he got all riled up. What's his name again?"

"His real name or the one on his stupid fake ID?" I hedge.

"Real."

I press my lips together. "Mazen Wilde." His name comes out crisp and clear and tainted with disgust. "He insinuated I was a whore."

"If the shoe fits."

I scoff, "And you're one to judge?"

"Tit for tat. Tell your new pal Ollie that he's going to need a new lead singer. I'm going to unalive the current one." Heat steals her delicate features and hardens them. "Rock stars are honestly douchebags. No, men in general are. *They* can screw whoever *they* want, whenever *they* want and not get any flak for it. The moment a woman gives in and takes what she wants, she's labeled a whore. It's sexist and appalling."

"You should run for office." I offer her praise. "It was a onetime occurrence that I'd rather forget. Since he just hired me and all. Speaking of that, if I'm going to remain on the straight and narrow, I'll need my wand and charger. Hold that thought."

Hurrying to my room in a haste, I can't control a burst of laughter that escapes my lips as it ripples through me. I'm about to embark on a tour with four of the world's handsomest alternative rock band members, and all I can think of is packing my sex toy.

Oh, the irony.

10

ALOE THERE!

SOPHIA

"SOPH," Lacey bellows from the living room.

I can tell by the strain in her voice that she's still on edge about my leaving. I make a mental note to assure her once again that everything is going to be okay.

"Hold on," I hum dryly, annoyed mostly with myself for not learning from past mistakes. First, it was not charging my vibrator, and now, it's losing the damn cord itself.

My chest constricts as my eyes scout every surface in my bedroom, looking for the white wire. Tossing articles of clothing that I'm not packing onto the floor, I rifle through my discard pile.

"Come. Out. Here." She bites out every word, a strain evident in her tone, which echoes off the walls, traveling down our short hallway.

So impatient, that one.

Ignoring her, I fumble through my room like a madwoman, determined to find my little friend. Tossing my pillows on the floor, I huff when I notice the cord isn't under there, in its usual spot.

"Did I already pack it?" I whisper to myself.

I unzip my suitcase and quickly dive through it with zero luck. I contemplate yelling, *Marco*, and then realize that I'm an utter nutcase and I need to be committed to a psych ward.

Flinging out my hands in irritation, I lean over my bed and place both hands on the mattress in defeat. "Deep breaths. Where was it the last time you saw it?" I ask myself out loud, trying to trigger my memory.

It was in the wall, charging. I went to work, and then last night, I tossed it in my drawer.

I almost trip over my open suitcase as I round the mattress and swing my nightstand open. There, lying on top of random papers and junk, is my wand *and* charger.

"Yes. Yes! Thank you." I explode in merriment just as a male voice interrupts my conquest.

"Are you hugging a vibrator?" a husky voice that sounds like a hushed whisper asks from behind me.

My body jerks to attention as realization causes my skin to tingle.

The smug voice standing in my doorframe doesn't belong to Oliver, much to my dismay. It belongs to a certain lead singer that I've heard countless times over the radio since I was introduced to Kings of Jupiter only yesterday. It's like when you get a new car, one that you thought was super unique, and the moment you drive off the lot, your brand-spanking-new vehicle is suddenly everywhere and everyone you know drives one.

That's what the last day has been like for me.

Kings of Jupiter is *everywhere*. From the ads on my

social media accounts to their billboard that hasn't gotten taken down yet from their show in Tampa.

How did I never notice it before?

Their faces literally tower over my studio, staring down at each client as they walk into the shop with their panty-melting smirks that scream, *Sex is art.*

Determined not to reveal my abhorrence for him and give him any more fuel to hate me, I studiously avoid his presence, toss my device into my bag, and bend over to zip it in place. Mazen doesn't deserve my attention. Not after he spoke to me like … I was trash. Why women even find him remotely attractive is beyond me.

As far as I can see, Mazen Wilde doesn't have any qualities that matter in a person. Aside from his good looks, he's just another douchebag in a sea of men. I peek over my shoulder as I step into my bathroom to make sure I have all my belongings, only to find him casually leaning against my doorframe, like he's been in my room a million times.

If my mother were still around, he'd be the type of man she'd warn me about. Mazen Wilde screams mayhem. Dressed in ripped jeans and a black hoodie that reads *Make America Emo Again* in white lettering across his chest. He's a walking billboard. If I didn't know who he was from the research I'd done online like a possessed fan, I would have guessed he was a pro skateboarder or BMX rider. The whole vibe he gives off screams Ryan Sheckler, circa 2009. This is *Ryan* in his prime.

With a ripped body, covered in ink.

I hate to admit this, even to myself, but Mazen drips swagger. His essence is pure lust, rolling off him like rain on a windshield amid a storm. It's as much fascinating as it is nauseating. My eyes settle on his mouth, finally giving him an ounce of attention.

"What does your shirt say?" he requests in an amused tone.

A tone that reminds me that he's a lead singer to a freaking band that has accolades longer than a receipt from the drugstore. A tone that threatens to unglue my aversion of him.

Instead of answering him, in rebellion, I stretch the material over my breasts, holding each side with an outstretched hand. *Aloe there!*

Mazen's hazy-charcoal-colored eyes grow, openly amused, as mine grow wide with infuriation.

"Cannon's going to blow his load. The way to his heart is through herbs of multiple varieties. Cannabis to"—his brows bunch together in deep thought—"succulents. I think they're succulents that line the window of our bus. Anyway, he does not discriminate between green plants, if you catch my drift."

"What does Cannon play again?" I ask vaguely skimming through the band's roster in my head. I don't recall a lot of articles mentioning Cannon, much less his role in the band.

It doesn't surprise me though. Most of the knowledge I learned about Mazen was filled to the rim with rumors of debauchery and lewd behavior, like him getting shit-faced and snorting a line of nutmeg powder in an attempt to ride the hallucination wave—the articles words, not mine. I peer at Mazen, waiting for his answer, arms crossed. A small smile forms on the corner of my mouth when I think about the stupid headlines online that had his name scrolled in bold and the ones that fans left in the comments. Those were the good ones.

Mazen is more than Wilde. He's a trained pussy assassin.

Or the almost indistinguishable slogan, *Wet for Wilde.*

The one that left me making mental notes to talk to Oliver about rings clear in my head as I hold my ground with the culprit.

Lead singer's sister slain in auto accident. No charges have been filed.

"Drummer," Mazen says, drawing my attention to his mouth. "He's our drummer." He blows out an aggravated breath.

It seems like my question has offended him somehow, though he uses stern restraint on his expression.

Mazen Wilde isn't only the king of music. He's the king of this deceptively composed glare that seems to ward off ... people ... from seeing *him.* The real version. The haunted man under the mask the media has created. The man tossing out charisma and sweltering sex appeal that oozes from his lusciously plump lips like a trained professional. Said lips that I should not be ogling like I want to see how many licks it takes to get to his center.

Pull it together, Soph. He's a dick. *I wonder how big it is ...*

Lacey was right. I have been dick-deprived for too long. It's making me irrational.

Focusing on the silky, full, straight black hair of the man in front of me, I gather my composure while attempting to smother my naughty thoughts with a brick to the skull.

Mazen's rock-hard facial features soften. "You didn't get the chance to meet him. He's a big dude. Scary even."

Is he warning me off his giant, elusive drummer?

"He's harmless though and a big plant enthusiast, like I said. His mom owns a nursery. I've never seen him meet a plant he couldn't rehabilitate and coax back to life."

Great. Now, I have a hard-on for a forbidden, plant-loving drummer. One I obviously didn't have the pleasure of meeting yet because I had slapped Mazen in a haste and he stormed off, taking his little minions and security detail with him, including said succulent-saving botanical drummer.

"Watch out. I might steal *all* of your best friends." After my attempt at a jab, I laugh, then offer an olive-branch. "Kidding. I was just trying to *plant* a smile on your face."

"Oh, and she has jokes," he says softly, his eyes narrowing. "Even if they're on the corny side. Laughter is the soul's best medicine—or so I've been told. Murphy Miller, our bassist, is the insightful one in our bunch." He rolls his gunmetal eyes.

"Shouldn't it be, *Music is the soul's best medicine?* And here I thought, you claimed to be a musician."

Tucking his bottom lip with his teeth, he turns his attention from me as if he purposely doesn't want to continue our conversation. I watch him as he scans my bedroom with steady eyes, like he's taking it all in. I'm not rich by any means, but I make a decent living. His judgmental glare is sickening.

My defenses go up tenfold. "It's not Beverly Hills, but it's home."

"It's ... cozy."

Rude.

I'm about to tell him to fuck off when he adds under his breath, "We don't have the luxury of calling anywhere home anymore."

The small outpour of humanity he just willingly shared is startling. A play of emotion dances across his face as I study his profile. For a moment, I don't breathe as I drink in his truth.

A minute passes and then another.

"Go ahead and get your eye-fucking out of your system. It's the only fucking you and I will be partaking in, Rosella."

My body ignites rebelliously against my better judgement. Chill bumps race from my toes to the hair follicles on my scalp. For a split second, my mind betrays me, and a memory of a night long ago jolts to the forefront of my mind. A night that I've tried my best to camouflage, to forget, to erase. Even though I know that if I forget that night, I'll never forget the small pocket of joy that it brought me.

Rosella, I repeat in my mind, trying to jog the memory I've fought hard to repress.

A primitive feeling of grief washes over me and reminds me that *his* memory wasn't a hallucination. The evidence in the form of a small white note with the hotel's logo, where we met, with his scribble on it. I can recall bits and pieces of *him.* I remember he was sweet, a little timid, and a gentleman. Everything that Mazen isn't.

As if I were hypnotized, a desolate conscious thought races through me at the mention of this epithet, and an odd twinge weighs me down at the recollection. I haven't thought about that night or the tragedy that happened after in many, many years.

Bracing my spine and swallowing the sudden grief that clouds my vision, I force my lips to part, knowing that this ... guy in front of me makes my skin crawl.

He couldn't be further from the one who whispered, "Little Rose," in my ear as he claimed my body and set my soul ablaze.

No, Mazen Wilde is a tool from what I've gathered online, and so far in person, he isn't proving to be any better. My mind refuses to think otherwise.

"I'd rather fuck a silicone toy until the day I die than

stoop to the level of screwing you. It'd be like riding a corpse." He raises a brow in confusion, which only urges me to continue, "Since you're as close to evil incarnate as one can get. You know since you call people whores and ... and stupid *pet names* for no reason. I won't let you get under my skin."

I'm well aware I sound like I'm sixteen, hand on hip and all.

"Be careful. If you call out the devil, he just might come." The steel gray of his eyes turn to an obscure void as they roam my body from my feet to face.

Long gone is the free-spirited metaphorical skateboarder that sails through life without a care in the world. He's been replaced by the man standing before me with a rigid back made of steel, swathed in attitude and sin. A wave of apprehension quakes in my stomach. I might have wound the clock a little too tight.

"Are you even Italian?" I stir the pot.

He doesn't speak with a thick accent. At least not in the interviews I recently watched. When he said Rosella, it broke through. His voice was all melodic, lustful, and undiluted.

Men with accents are every woman's undoing. Prove me wrong.

A probing query dances in his smoldering irises. Unexpectedly, I feel like I'm stark naked, being assessed like a woman dancing in the red-light district by the smoldering depths of his appraising look. He quickly draws his reassessing gaze away as mine bore back into him while I try to gain the upper hand. I won't cower or back down even if I'm holding on to my fragile control like a rosary.

I'm the owner of an all-female tattoo studio. That hasn't been an easy feat, trust me. Mainly because men dominate the industry and aren't too keen on outsiders and less ecstatic with women stealing their thunder. I've worked hard to earn my reputation, and no male, rock star or not, is going to intimidate me.

Despite his hardened glare, I take a deep breath and square my shoulders once again. It seems to be a habit I'm quickly forming in his presence. He should know he can't get under my skin—even though he so is. I'm sure it's his attempt to scare me off so I don't go on tour with them. What else would it be?

"Get over yourself. You might have fooled the world with those puppy-dog eyes, smooth lyrics, and apparent hidden origin." Every atom in my body surges, giving me a rush of power and confidence. I answer him with easy defiance, ignoring the fact that I'm even allowing him to get a rise from me. "Not me though. I see you for who you are. A jerk, clad in black to ward off the world. You don't need to go all emo to repel me, buddy. Your personality did that all on its own. Where's Ollie anyway?"

"You screwed him once, and you're already calling him Ollie? A nickname I dubbed him twenty years ago."

"I didn't realize you were so ... old." I know he's not much older than I am. Despite that knowledge, I throw my words like stones at his stupidly handsome face. "What wrinkle cream do you use?"

Two can play this game.

The eager response he offers matches my structured hazing. "Pussy juice. It's plentiful when we're on the road. You'll see. I bet your new buddy Ollie would be more than willing to rope you in for a threesome with his favorite stagehands. He's sure fucked his way through them over the years, and when he's done, he just starts back at bitch number one."

I refuse to allow Mazen's cavalier words, which he tosses around like he's a praised Frisbee golfer, to get under my skin. Musicians have had women lusting over them since the beginning of time. In hockey, they're called puck bunnies; in baseball, they're commonly referred to as baseball Annies; and in the music industry, they're known as groupies. I refuse to become one. Despite his overwhelmingly good looks—what? I'm not Helen Keller, for Christ's sake. Luckily, I know that dangerous men usually play dangerous games, and I'm not at a point in my life where I'd willingly tango with the devil and plunge into the darkness of his enticement just because he's hotter than freshly laid asphalt.

I solemnly vow to never fall for a musician.

"What, no snarky comeback, *Rosella?*" There he goes with that damn name. "Cat got your tongue?"

I can see his game. He's pushing my buttons, trying to elicit something, anything, from me.

Before I have a chance to retort, he goads, "It's not the first or last time I've taken a woman's breath away. Get your bearings. I'll wait."

His arrogance knows no bounds, I think to myself when he leans against the doorframe in a way that screams he's trouble. Sin wrapped in a black foil package.

Knowing that looking usually turns to buying, I turn my eyes downward in an attempt to break the trance he's cast over us like a sheer mist. Time ceases for a moment, and so does my resolve.

Mazen Wilde is an asshole, I repeat in my head. *A beautiful asshole.*

He's most likely a masochist in the bedroom if his ego is an indication of his true nature. As hard as I try to ricochet his hateful energy back toward him, I come up short when he breaks the silence by humming my name.

"Sophia."

The silky sound that comes out instantly reminds me that he's a musician. Which, in turn, makes my neck desperate to be choked by his large hands like a microphone.

Why the ever-loving hell would I conjure up that image in my brain?

I steal a glance at said hands. The left one has letters written on his knuckles—the word *wild*, starting with his pointer finger. It's no doubt a plug at both his lifestyle and his last name.

Wilde.

Despite my better judgment, my line of vision flees from his hands, traveling upward. I peer through my thick lashes that I just got filled in, not knowing when I'd be able to get them done again while on tour, only to see a somber expression staring back at me.

Is he thinking about choking me too? Most likely in an I'm-going-to-unalive-you manner and less in a pretend-my-cock-is-a-sucker one.

Our eyes hold one another captive for a beat that lasts longer than socially acceptable. Our wordless exchange leaves me feeling a savage intensity that covers the air around us. My body betrays my mind, and a battle ignites within my chest. This is wrong on so many levels. I screwed his friend, his bandmate, just yesterday, and now, I'm daydreaming about the asshole who called me a whore.

I didn't really have time to notice him fully in my studio yesterday. Feeling as though time has been suspended, I eagerly observe Mazen's features with a curious longing. The mouth that just purred my name like a lifeline has a cynical twist to it. A black ring in his nose glistens off the light from my ceiling fan. I wonder if it's a prop, like the skull rings that hug his knuckles, or if the piercing is real.

Are nose rings on a man a newly discovered kink? I think to myself, musing on the idea.

That's the problem in show business. People often lose their true identity, and before they even recognize it, like a puff of air, poof, they're gone. Just look at what happened to Nikki Sixx.

Continuing my assessment, I notice his beardless jaw before taking in the small dimple in the bottom of his chin. It's cute, and it makes me wonder if he ever went through an ugly-teenager phase or if he's always been this striking. His cheekbones look like they've been delicately painted by Van Gogh himself. The exquisite landscape of his cheeks guides the line of my vision toward his neck. It just so happens to be covered in an array of ink. From the underside of his chin, dark artwork voyages toward his ears and downward into the collar of his sweatshirt. I've never found a man's neck striking before now. There isn't an inch of bare, uncolored skin.

My gaze moves over his broad shoulders, sweeps past his torso, and lands on his long legs. He towers over me like a spruce. Mazen has a commanding air of self-confidence that I wish I embodied.

Why are women's minds so warped? We're not programed to be attracted to ... men like Mazen. I blame it on the copious amounts of smut I devour. Spice is my favorite flavor. Romance novels are to blame for my curiosity in gang bangs and the way dirty, filthy words set my soul on fire. It's altered my brain matter. I shouldn't want to be choked and filled in every hole of my body at once. I shouldn't, but I do.

I make a mental note to download something vanilla from Nicholas Sparks as soon as our metaphorical sparring match concludes. Rejecting the absurd idea that Mazen's crude, tantalizing mouth is the reason for my sudden rise in body heat, I force myself to look away, to regain my composure, only to see Lacey standing behind him in the shadows.

"You're a dick. I'm sure you're well aware though." My come back feels weak.

My eyes meet her nutmeg ones, and a silent conversation ensues. *Put him out of his misery, sis.*

I choke back my shock when I register the small object in her hand. Even though I shouldn't be the least bit surprised that she owns a Taser. The thing about Lacey is, if she indicates she's going to do something, her plans never falter. Which is why Mazen Wilde is so completely screwed right now.

"I've been called much worse and by far prettier women." Taking an unhurried step toward me, he blocks the doorway. Unbeknownst to him, he's about to fall into a trap.

The big-dick energy he oozes comes off in waves that threaten to swallow me whole. I'm not a conceited woman, but I know I'm attractive. I'm my own cheerleader, and I refuse to allow the words that slide from his deceitfully carved lips to affect me again. Arching my eyebrow, I offer him an almost-apologetic smile before my body loses control, and I bellow, vibrating in laughter, as Lacey draws closer with stealth grace to his back, like he's a mouse she's been hunting for hours.

The joy in having your sister as your best friend is that you never have to fight your own battles—unless you want to, of course. Which, hello, who doesn't appreciate a good duo? I'm the levelheaded one in this duet. The reasonable one, the peacemaker. She's the pull-the-trigger, think-of-the-consequences-later one. Which is why I know that unleashing Lacey on Mazen is like unleashing a bull in a china shop. Even though I don't think he truly deserves what's about to happen, his words do sting a bit too harshly. My normal, rational thoughts go out the window. I nod in her direction, crossing my arms, and struggle to maintain my composure as the black device in her hand reaches his sweatshirt.

"You're not my type, *skater boy*. I'm going for a Landon Carter next." Lacey pounces on her prey before he has time to filter through a list of male leads in his internal Rolodex.

I see the moment abrupt clarity crosses Mazen's face, second to the loud crackling noise from Lacey's Taser. The sound echoes off the walls. My spitfire of a little sister sneers behind him seconds before his body folds like a pretzel. Mazen drops to the ground in a loud thud.

"I heard him imply you were a whore again, and he basically called you ugly. Evidently, rock stars don't have stellar vision insurance." Lacey's smile doesn't reach her eyes.

My sister is beautifully cunning. A force stronger than any hurricane we've weathered since moving to Florida. I realize then that Mazen motherfucking Wilde has met his match and has hopefully learned his lesson.

Rose and Lace aren't weak bitches.

The scene gives off major Thelma and Louise vibes, and frankly, I'm. Here. For. It.

11

TASER DISASTER

MAZEN

AN EXCRUCIATING JOLT shakes my brain like a screw in a jar.

Figlio di puttana. Motherfucker.

Throes of spasms rumble through my body as I hit the floor, all thoughts abandoning me. My mouth dries as I stare off into space with what I can only imagine is a faraway look while my body contorts with one final flop against the hardwood floor, like a fucking fish out of water.

Who knows how long I lie, stupefied into silence, before I come to?

The last thing I remember seeing was a spark of indefinable smugness in Sophia's eyes before the zap of what I can only assume now was a Taser was fired off against my back.

Misery melts into a blunt flicker of wrath that sets a wildfire ablaze in my chest. I'd be on a warpath if I could muster the strength to pull myself up. It's a futile attempt. With a tightened jaw, a raging fury wells inside of me. I succumb to the aftereffects of being Tased and close my eyes, trying to catch my breath. Thank fuck I now know I don't have an undiagnosed heart condition.

"You just Tased a celebrity." The alarm in Sophia's voice dances between disbelief and gratitude at her batshit-crazy sister's actions.

It's not lost on me that I'm on the floor, writhing in agony, a few steps away from Sophia, and her first thought isn't to check on me to make sure that, I don't know, I'm alive and still breathing. Rather, it's to have a discussion with the psycho who Tased me.

It goes to show that Ollie doesn't know this heartless woman at all. The truth is, I don't know *this* version of her. Too much time has elapsed to really remember the version I once liked, lost, and scoured the continent for.

"That I did," the Taser-wielding maniac acknowledges smugly. "I'll do it again if he doesn't learn to watch his mouth and talk to you like a lady. You're not a peasant or one of his bimbo groupies. I'm sure he's used to being the top dog in his *little* band. That shit doesn't fly in our shop or house. Take this one with you in case he tries to mouth off again while you're on the bus."

Remind me to sleep with one eye open.

Thundering footsteps echo down the hall and then come back, stopping where I see Sophia standing, her stupid-as-hell plant T-shirt bunched in her hand.

"I have an unopened one. Wasn't Oliver supposed to pick you up?"

"Something must've come up, I guess." Sophia's tone gives me the impression that she's trying to regain her composure.

Trust me, Little Rose, I didn't sign up to play chauffeur today. I was forced into it by your precious soon-to-be bank teller.

"Why do you have these anyway? Please tell me it's not some new kink you've discovered. I know you're a freak in the sheets, Lace, but this"—she pauses—"is a little over the top, even for you."

"I draw a hard line at forms of electric currents. We own an all-female tattoo studio," she says matter-of-factly. "Someone has to protect us."

"Isn't that what we pay Devon for?"

"Precisely," Lacey's voice hums in irritation at her sister's debriefing. "I don't like taking risks. We have to protect *our* female employees by any means necessary. Not to mention, what if those goons come look—"

"Stop. He could be listening. Wait, can he hear us?"

"I certainly hope so. I didn't want to kill the dude. Just put him in his place. Plus, cops get Tased all the time and live to tell the tale. It's part of their initiation or something to do with the academy. Orange is not my color. It'd clash with the pink hair, don't you think?" There's zero inflection in Lacey's tone.

"Right. He probably just lost consciousness. He hasn't moved though." Flowing hair falls around Sophia's face before she brushes the unruly strands away. "Don't tell me you have a gun stashed behind the cash register too." She lets out a stifled and an unsettled puff. "No way. I draw the line at firearms, Lacey."

"I never even said I had a gun there," her psycho sister retorts, and my body relaxes.

At least now, I know I'll avoid death today.

"You know I can read your face, right? It's telling me you're lying."

Huffing, Lacey taps her toes on the hardwood floor a little too close to my face, which is pressed against the cool wood. "I never said I had a gun. Because I don't have *a* gun. I have two."

"We don't have time for this conversation. Get rid of them. I don't want one falling into the wrong person's hands. Something stupid can happen."

Something stupid has already happened, I desperately want to add.

"Anyway, Oliver said they're all from here. Tampa's their hometown. I guess he had something to do. I don't really know. I'll text him."

Their casual conversation yo-yos from subject to subject. If my head wasn't already throbbing, the minimal attention span they share would sure do the trick.

"Have you ever heard of their band before?"

I can only assume Lacey shakes her head.

"I swear it's so odd that I've never once heard of them, and we've been in Tampa for almost a decade now. They're actually really popular. Won-awards popular."

"These days, everyone gets participation trophies, sis. The music industry is probably no different, and we've never heard of them because we like *real* music. Black Sabbath, Metallica, Alice in Chains. Rock that will stand the test of time. Those bands eat little alternative rock bands like Kings of Jupiter for breakfast."

If I could gather my energy, I'd spring up and put Lacey in her place. Kings of Jupiter is legit. Nothing irks me more than a person who claims that alternative rock isn't a *real* genre. Earth to the pink-haired psycho, Green Day and Linkin Park slayed the industry and paved the way for our genre years ago. I wonder, if Brian Burkheiser from I Prevail were standing right in front of her, would she have the gall to claim such bullshit?

Subgenres of music have spawned over the years and

influenced metal as a whole. Expanding it from the melodic, classic metalcore to grunge and even added influences from hip-hop and other prominent inspirations. I have a few choice words for Lacey that she would indisputably not consider ladylike.

I lie, unmoving, on my spot on the floor and disregard her ignorance for good music, knowing that *not* getting Tased again in this lifetime is better than correcting a dumb broad.

"Maybe he had some family to see before they left again," Sophia matter-of-factly declares—an excuse for his missing presence.

She couldn't be further from the truth. I. Am. Oliver's only family.

"Either way, I'm not going anywhere with this scumbag. Either Ollie shows up or Kings of Jupiter can find a new tattoo artist."

"Works for me. Who else was I going to do scary movie Sunday with if you actually left? Hey, you don't think he'll wake up and press charges for my Tasing him or anything, do you?"

"I would if I were him."

The soft sound of Sophia laughing almost has me jerking my lids open, wanting to bear witness to her amusement. The infectious sound calls out to me like a siren. Even if, simultaneously, I want to plow my fist through her wall since the reason for her laughter is the state I'm currently still in.

"I honestly think he'd be too afraid to admit to the world that he put himself in a position to be Tased in the first place, you know? All those tabloids say that he's the cold-hearted one in their band. I read in an article this morning that he's even a dick to his staff and road crew."

"I think he just met his match. Give me a minute to put this away, and I'll check our little Marilyn Manson wannabe."

A foot brushes by me as it steps over my body, and from the footsteps, it sounds like she's soaring down the hallway. The balls on these ... women are bigger than the Pacific Ocean by a long shot. They leave me lying on the floor like a discarded condom after a long night of debauchery for what seems like ten minutes or longer.

As time passes, my limbs feel stronger. I slide my cell phone from my pocket and decide to teach Lacey and Sophia a lesson by sending a quick text to Ashton, our security guard, who is waiting downstairs in his vehicle. It doesn't take longer than two minutes before the front door of their apartment swings open and my friend comes barreling in.

"On your knees," he bellows deeply from his lungs and reaches for the gun holster on his waist.

Mustering all my might, I drag my body up the wall and rest my head against it. I have a front-row seat for the performance Ash is about to put on.

A loud, ear-piercing scream travels up and out of Sophia's chest. Pure terror rings in her indignant shrill as she rambles, "What? Who? Lacey!"

The icy daggers of Lacey's glare tell me my cover is busted. "Stop screaming, Soph. I know him. Don't I, Ashton? He's their security guard."

I stand up fully and stretch my sore back.

"I wouldn't forget a handsome face like yours so soon."

"Gag me and put me out of my misery." My words are heavy with sarcasm.

Fuck Ollie and his stupid idea.

I need a favor, he said.

He's on my shit list now too.

"I'm sorry." Sophia's voice seems shakier than her exterior lets on as she meets my gaze and frowns.

The width of her eyes spans wider, and as much as I want to believe her apology because I think she sounds sincere enough, I could give two shits about feathering her with an ounce of kindness. This little stunt of theirs is about to be matched by a wretchedness that'll leave her begging for the simple jolt of a Taser. Making a mental vow to keep my guard up where she's concerned, I stride over to the first piece of furniture I see and plop down in it, allowing the worn cushion to suck me in like a cloud.

"As soon as I came in, she," he motions to Lacey, "was already crossing her arms in defiance. This one, on the other hand"—he signals to Sophia—"looks like she's going to piss her pants." He turns to address Sophia. "Red, if you're coming on tour with us, you'd better bring your big-girl panties. These dudes hazed me for two weeks when I was first hired before I gave them a taste of their own medicine and showed them who was boss."

"Go ahead; make yourself at home." Lacey rolls her eyes and sits on the edge of their coffee table.

Sophia's eyes land everywhere in the room, except on mine.

"I think we're far past pleasantries. Don't you? You. Fucking. Tased. Me." A picture frame shakes in the distance as I bite out every word.

At least my outburst finally gets Sophia's attention. Her head twirls toward me like she was slapped.

"What happened? You didn't say anything about getting Tased." Ashton rubs the coiled hair on his head.

"This one"—using my middle finger like a ruler, I point toward Lacey, who is perched on the coffee table like she doesn't have a care in the world—"tried teaching me a lesson and Tased me."

She shrugs casually, picking up a drink and taking a slurp. "He had it coming."

"What did you do?" Ashton has the audacity to ask me. His eyes falter when they meet mine. He's huge and intimidating as fuck, but not to me. He knows who signs his weekly paychecks. "It doesn't matter if you think he deserved it or not, you can't just Tase people. That's got to be against the law."

"He called her a whore for the second time, and we've only known him two days." Lacey's eyes bore into my profile.

The tension in the room is palpable.

Ashton shakes his head, hands in the air between us, before he stresses, "My mama didn't raise me to degrade women, Maz. Sorry."

And just like that, three sets of eyes flash icily toward my own, and suddenly, *I'm* at fault for this act of terrorism.

"You know what? My buzz has long worn off, and this is not how I wanted to spend my last day in town. I told Ollie he could've fetched his own piece of ass this morning." I pry my unsteady legs off the couch and take two strides to their front door. I mutter over my shoulder, "Go on; get it. I know you want to."

Running my hand through my dark wisps of hair, which are more than likely sticking straight up from my unexpected electrocution, I wait a beat for Ashton to pull out his cell phone and hand it to Lacey. No words are spoken as she grabs it, quickly programs in her number, and hands it back to him with a smile that says, *Fuck me later*.

My voice is harsh when my gaze falls on Sophia's. "I'll be seeing you again, Rosella. Unfortunately for me."

"I hate you," she spits out forcefully through gritted teeth. Her voice, loaded with bitter cold, only encourages me. "Don't call me that again."

If her threat had a taste, it'd taste like a wasabi-dipped lollipop, and I'm a wasabi supporter.

"And I *don't* give a single flying fuck."

She shudders.

"I'm not blind, *Sophia*, and I'm not stupid. I've been in this game for a long time. No one hates me. Even you. You just hate that you don't hate me. What you feel for me isn't hate. It's something else altogether. I'd bet you a million dollars, if I slid down those yoga pants, I'd expose you because I guarantee you're wet. Don't confuse hate with lust. Eight weeks is an awfully long time to lie to yourself."

Folding her arms across her chest like a child throwing a tantrum, Sophia throws up a wall of hatred. I take notice of the redness that blotches her skin, drawn brows taut in apprehension. She isn't the only one marred with anger. The pent-up madness of her not remembering me was like a ten-year-old wound being flayed open. The wrath that I feel right now, coated with anger and the urge to jog her memory about our one toe-curling evening we spent together in Chicago many moons ago, fades quickly, like summer rain on the beach. The resentment coursing through my veins now is blistering. I swear to fuck, if she so much as lets one word fall from her mouth, I'm going to explode.

"*If* I even go now—"

The bomb inside me detonates, and war descends upon us.

With a quick move, I hurl her onto the top of my shoulder blade. "Oh, you're going. If only so I can ruin you slowly over the next several weeks as payback for your sister's stunt. You can thank her for what's in store for you. Ashton, bags." I'm usually not callous toward him or any of our staff despite what the tabloids report. He's clearly chosen a side though. "There might be more downstairs in the studio with her equipment. We're leaving."

Sophia's petite build is weightless as she thrashes and kicks from her place on top of my shoulder. The futile attempt to free herself from my iron grasp is tiresome.

"Lacey, if you'll excuse us, your sister has a contract she needs to fulfill."

Much to my surprise, she doesn't object; instead, she gestures to the door.

"Seriously, sis, you're just going to let him manhandle me like a caveman? I raised you better than that."

Making a mental note on that one, I hold my head high and face the pink-haired assailant, readying myself for a battle.

Shock washes over me when she says, "Yep. That was so hot. I only wish it were me being dragged to God knows where with these two beautiful men. Have fun and be safe!"

There's a wistful longing in her expression, and I have the feeling that we'll be seeing her again, sooner rather than later. Too fucking bad I've already formed an opinion of her, and it isn't pretty.

Holding the door handle, I twist it with the flick of my wrist before calling out behind me, "I'll have Ashton text you the name of an app you can download. We have a tracker on our bus that our record label uses to track our whereabouts as a security measure. Download the app, and you can see where she is at all times. Satellites allow it to work across the globe. It used to piss me off. I guess it'll come in handy now."

"I'm not going to apologize for what I did." She holds her hand on her hip as the next round of thrashing from Sophia almost causes me to drop her.

Without warning, the hard palm of my hand lands on Sophia's thin yoga pants, and as I shut the door behind me, I swear I hear Lacey mumble, "Why couldn't they be addicted to piercings and not tattoos?"

12

SUSHI BOAT

SOPHIA

THE RIDE to the band's hotel, where we're crashing for the night, is insufferable for three reasons.

The first one is the giant elephant in the back seat.

Mazen is still seething—for lack of a better descriptor, like murderous. Despite the twenty-minute drive of complete and total silence, fumes continue to spew from his ears. Animosity lingers in the death glare he tries not to offer me but does when he thinks I'm not looking.

I want to tell him to let it go and to get over this hostility that hangs between us like a punching bag with its insides firing out through tiny holes. Aside from the recent Tasing incident, his hatred of me is unwarranted. We're strangers who have evidently gotten off on the wrong foot. I refrain from opening my mouth, making matters worse by adding to the fuel and creating a thicker tension between us.

Allowing him this ride of silence and reprieve is all I'm willing to offer. He's my new roommate, my new boss's best friend, and a wet dream for every woman with black manicured fingernails. I bite my tongue and swallow my words, knowing that I have to bide my time. It's not an easy feat. My refute gets lodged in the back of my throat.

I can't fault him for being furious at what transpired in my apartment. I take responsibility for Lacey's actions, although in my opinion, it was warranted. Mazen once again showed his true colors. She put him in his place, and now, he's sitting here, arms crossed, probably plotting his revenge.

To make matters worse, he refused to accept my apology. There's not much else that can be said. The damage is done. The line drawn. We're at an impasse neither of us is prepared to breach and surrender.

The second is the air of animosity Mazen keeps rubbing in by way of subliminal messages in the form of music. Huddy's "All the Things I Hate About You" blares over the speakers next. He must have a control on his phone or something because when the chorus hits, he turns the volume up, driving the memo home.

My intolerable sister continues her tirade of texts. A constant loop of GIFs of people getting spanked flashes on my screen. I'm going to lose it with this third strike. I contemplate opening my door and meeting a premature death.

The thought of his spur-of-the-moment punishment in the form of spanking causes me to shrivel in humiliation in my seat. That, and the fact that his cologne rubbed off on my shirt, so every time I inhale, I smell him. It's a spicy aroma that I want to detest but can't. I've never been spanked before today, not even as a child. Chastising Lacey for her incessant messages, I power down my phone, tossing it on the seat between us.

I watch out my window, considering how bad it would

hurt to hurl myself into oncoming traffic. A slew of buildings in varying shapes, sizes, and colors pass by the window as I peer out into the cityscape. Years ago, we settled in Tampa, claiming it as our new home, and in all that time, both Lacey and I have never taken the time to explore downtown and its bustling metropolis. We're outsiders in our own city.

"If you're going to screw everyone you meet on this tour, you might as well give Ashton a turn next." Mazen breaks the thick silence with his acid-dipped tongue. His eyes stay glued to his phone, not straying to even gauge my reaction.

I consider calling Oliver, telling him that I don't think this agreement is going to pan out like we both hoped. I'm not too prideful to tuck my tail and scurry back to the safeness of my sanctuary. For a split second, I contemplate ripping up our newly signed contract before the ink has even had time to dry.

The aloofness in which he talks about me like a ... Vegas Strip girl is almost as awful as being drenched with a bucket of frigid water over the dome. Any idea I contemplated about fleeing goes out the window. If he has something to prove, he can start with me.

"Is this what it's going to be like?"

"If you don't want to be treated like a hooker, you shouldn't act like one."

And the blows keep on coming.

"That's rich, coming from you. I read the tabloids online. They all drag your name through the mud. It's a good thing you're a decent singer because your personality and credibility are seriously lacking." An insensitive laugh pairs with my words. "And for the record, I'd rather paint my fingernails with a Q-tip before I worry about why you don't like me."

"Then, you're up-to-date, and you know *not* to get on my bad side." His tone offers a warning, though his words are as transparent as air.

No one who is really bad calls themselves out like that. Villains don't walk around with T-shirts that say they're villains, for Christ's sake. The title of being wicked is a stark contrast to the person underneath the forewarning.

"Is there even a good side?"

"No. And if you keep asking pointless fucking questions, you're going to find out the hard way."

He plays the part all too well as the band's front-line heartthrob when, in reality, he doesn't use his voice for good. The ardor that he was gifted is wasted because he's worse than scum. Worse than a pile of horse manure. He's a prick, dressed as the dark prince.

Which leads me to believe that at his core, there's more to the guy sitting next to me, seemingly unbothered by my relenting glare. I don't know why a sudden feeling of marvel claws at my spine. Maybe it's the sublime mix of spice and earth that wafts throughout the back seat, pulling me under his spell because of our proximity. Or maybe it's his amped-up warning that has me caving him like a groupie, another Kings of Jupiter admirer. Either way, I know nothing good can ever come from lowering my shield.

"Oh, go fuck yourself." I turn my body toward the window, effectively ending our heated exchange.

"There's that opposition again. It's quickly becoming a kink of mine."

The shock of his words hit me full force, and I know before he even finishes that I walked into this one.

"Why would I fuck myself when all I have to do is wait for my turn? It seems you're making your rounds. I'm bound to be on the schedule soon."

Anger erupts like lava from every pore in my body. I'm on the verge of being listed as a cold-blooded executioner on a true crime podcast when, like an answered prayer, the SUV comes to a sudden halt.

"Word to the wise: Cannon is stacked. I've seen him walk out of the shower on the bus, sans towel. If I were you, I'd work your way up to that stallion."

The hinges groan as Mazen swings his door open wider than necessary and then marches off, disappearing through a door that looks like it's intended for employees only.

"We only use the back entrances. Too often than not, fans linger out front," Ashton calls out from the lowered divider of the SUV, drawing all my attention toward him and away from the asshat I was sitting next to. "You'll get used to it."

"His attitude or utilizing back doors?"

"Both," Ashton quips. "Let me get your door."

"I don't think I'm going to get used to either, and I got it. Thank you though. I'll only be here for a short time." *Thankfully,* I refrain from voicing.

Sliding my belt bag over my chest, I square my shoulders while gifting him an impassive smile. Ashton hasn't done anything to earn my wrath. I backpedal into his good graces. One enemy on this tour is already more than I want. No need to add another.

"Don't want to get used to being treated like a queen."

He nods before grabbing my luggage from the trunk and then meets me at my door.

"Give him a chance. He'll come around to the idea of you being here."

"He has a higher chance of Lady Gaga sliding into his DMs than me forgiving him for being an asshole on multiple occasions now."

"Your sister did Tase him." The somberness of Ashton's voice is a reminder of the only valid reason for Mazen's resentment toward me.

"You're right. He might have just had a bad night's rest. Let's go catch up with him and offer to make him a lavender tea. I heard it helps with sleep. Then, maybe I can borrow his nail polish and only paint my pinkie nails pink, just like his." The enthusiasm in my tone is as flat as the heartbeat of a corpse.

"Oh. I would not go there if I were you. If you push him too far—"

"I want to push him off the rooftop of this damn hotel."

Ashton's intense brown eyes, ringed with thick black lashes that cause a bell of jealousy to ring in my chest, meet mine. "Don't go there, okay? The nail polish thing, I mean. It's not a topic to be discussed. He's an asshole to ... mostly everyone. Most of the time. But he's been dealt a shit hand. The devil wasn't born bad. His fall from grace sealed his fate." The layered warning from his soft but alarming timbre cause my thoughts to hoard, question after question.

My pulse beats at the base of my throat. Far-fetched scenarios and thoughts begin to unravel, my heart lurching madly in a frantic attempt to piece together the puzzle that is Mazen Wilde.

"I can almost hear the gears in that head of yours spinning. My last piece of advice, if you'll take it ..."

I glance up, my eyes urging him on.

"Make friends with his demons. It's better for everyone." He seals his message in the hard glare he offers.

My mouth snaps shut. Taking my silence as understanding, Ashton places his large palm on the center of my back and ushers me through the back entrance of the hotel.

Wordlessly, I stare ahead, walking beside him blindly,

trusting that he's not going to throw me to the wolves. After all, he just forewarned me about the biggest, gnarliest one I've ever met. The one who signs his paychecks.

I'm stunned by the bluntness of his counsel. His warning not to pry into what makes Mazen tick. It did little to heed my thoughts that now run rapid.

As we walk, I take in how the hotel staff quickly moves to the side of the hallway when we pass by. Carts are full to the brim with supplies and clean bedding, stacked in perfect, pristine order. Most avert their gazes, eyes falling on every object in the corridor but me.

I offer a demure smile to the only person who looks at me directly.

Ashton pulls on the back of my arm, our movement halting with his lax hold. "This is O'Neil. He'll be available for the evening should you need anything." The deep timbre of his voice is startling. It's apparent that the man standing beside me is now on duty. Long gone is the carefree version of himself who indulged in trivial banter with Mazen back in my apartment and the one who seemed to have my best interest in mind moments ago.

"Hello, O'Neil. It's a pleasure to meet you."

O'Neil juts out a white glove-covered hand. "The pleasure is all mine."

"You don't work for me, bud. I'm in the same boat as you are. So, I don't foresee I'll be needing you much this evening."

Ashton clears his throat as O'Neil's hard posture relaxes.

"Come. I'll show you to your floor." O'Neil holds out an elbow like he's offering to escort me into a ballroom.

The rehearsed movement reminds me that this isn't some measly hotel that has become my abode for the evening. This is a five-star hotel, fit for a king—or four band members who want to think their band's name is their entire identities.

O'Neil and I trail Ashton as he walks a few feet ahead of us, eyes skimming the hallway, alert. I can't help but smile a little on the inside. I mean, who wouldn't be a smidgen excited to live, if only for a short time, like a rock star? I plan to take full advantage of this lifestyle and its perks, no matter how fleeting it is.

Starting with one of those fancy sparkling waters swanky people drink. I'm suddenly feeling very, very parched as the elevator doors slide open, revealing a room more vast than anything I could have imagined. Past the thick metal doors of the elevator is a massive living space, larger than a football field. The room—if it can even be called a room—encased in nothing but windows from floor to ceiling, is breathtaking.

As I step off the elevator, I'm teleported into another realm. The space is otherworldly at best. O'Neil's presence alone should have been an indication of what was to come. I was not quiet expecting this ... picturesque space. The atmosphere around me changes as my eyes move from one decadent feature to the next. My feet cautiously step forward, planting me in this magazine cover of a room with my mouth agape, as I feel more than a little deficient.

This room alone can fit my entire apartment and tattoo studio inside five times over. *Lavish* and *ritzy* don't even come close to describing the sight in front of me. I thought fancy hotels like this were all made of marble, stone, and stark white décor. Posh. This suite is the complete opposite. It's warm, inviting me with a crook of its delicate finger into its lure.

So, this is how the other half live.

For a long moment, my pulse skitters alarmingly at the realization that I'm here, with a rock band, as their own personal tattoo artist. It's as if my brain is finally catching up with current events, and the realization hits me all at once.

Making hasty decisions isn't my style. The reckless sister is Lacey. Yet here I am, being guided through a suite by a damn butler into a massive bedroom that he claims is mine for the evening.

O'Neil mumbles information about how to reach him if I need anything and ends with, "Mr. Wilde, Mr. Collins, Mr. Rhodes, and Mr. Miller will be busy for the duration of the afternoon. Please make yourself comfortable. Don't hesitate to let me know if you need anything."

"What are they doing?"

His eyes grow, and he seems amused by my brashness. "It's not my place to ask questions, ma'am." He nods before shutting the bedroom door behind him, leaving me alone for the first time in two days.

I take a deep breath and peer around the room, needing a second to reorient myself.

How much does it cost for one night in this place?

Curiosity guides my cell phone from my pocket, and my fingers dance over my keys before hitting Search.

Fifty-five thousand dollars a night.

Mouth, meet the floor.

"I guess it could be worse." My voice holds a howl of excitement.

The magnetism of the space beckons, tantalizing me with the promise of relaxation as I stride to the massive en suite bathroom. Running my hand along every surface I pass on my leisurely stroll, I take in several different textures. There is a king-size bed sitting prominently in the center of the room that looks more like a piece of artwork to be admired than a bed. It's adorned with an array of diverse-shaped and -sized pillows, in distinctive hues of tan and brown, each one softer than the next. A giddy feeling skirts up my spine when I realize that this bed is all mine tonight. I can't wait to let its feathery down comforter wrap around me like a hug, and I anxiously count down to a reasonable time to turn in for the night.

While it's not my bed in my apartment, there's no doubt that this ... this lifestyle will do wonders for my aching back. Years of being hunched over a tattoo table have left me with terrible back pain I'm too young for. If there's one good thing that comes from this ... new job and arrangement, it's the swanky sleeping quarters for starters.

My senses pull me in every which way, like a volleyball match, as I inch toward the bathroom. This space is a lot to take in visually. Even more so is the quaint sound of music playing from a speaker somewhere in the room, and an aroma of fresh oranges wafts around me. My body is tense, and the spacious Jacuzzi tub is beckoning me toward its lap of luxury. I try to grasp that this is not a dream I conjured up when my phone chimes from the pocket of my elastic yoga pants and I slide it out.

Oliver's contact sprawls across my screen.

A fiery amber that burns in my chest toward him for not forewarning me he was sending his dick of a best friend to pick me up sits on my tongue, arsenal at the ready.

> Ollie: O'Neil said you're getting situated.
> Going to be stuck with our manager longer
> than expected.

> Me: Okay.

The insolence in my curt message is clear as a warm,

cloudless summer day in Tampa. While Oliver and I shared a moment of intimacy, we don't know one another at all. Not in the ways that matter anyway. I have no qualms about showing my true colors. Like Mazen has reminded me countless times, I'm here to do a job and nothing more.

> Ollie: Not accepting okay as a reply, Fireball.

He doesn't accept my reply. My expression grows thunderous. Oliver might be used to being in the spotlight, dazzling people with his charm and allure, but that doesn't work on me. Not when I've had a glance behind the veil already. His prize has already won, my pussy is now an afterthought. There's no need for pleasantries now, I guess.

> Me: Do you give all your employees a play-by-play of your schedule?

> Ollie: Nothing about this arrangement screams normal.

> Me: Define normal.

> Ollie: (eggplant emoji)

> Ollie: You're more than a hired hand, and you know it. I'm sorry for sending Maz to get you. I'll make it up to you when I see you later.

I don't need to see my reflection to know a deep blush dusts over my cheeks. When I don't reply fast enough, my phone chimes again. This time, his message leaves me yearning instead of seething. I sigh heavily, accepting the fact that this isn't a *normal* business transaction. Nothing about this situation is black and white. We crossed that line in my studio when I gave in to my irrational need to be fucked seven ways to Sunday. The recollection of our paired moment of weakness is burned into my memory.

> Ollie: Sending up a sushi boat for dinner.
> Enjoy the peace. It might be the last
> moment alone you have for a while.

My stomach growls at his last message. Skipping breakfast, aside from my iced coffee Lacey brought me, probably wasn't the smartest idea. Traveling the globe with a band of heartthrobs might prove to be an even worse idea. The verdict is still out.

Sushi is my love language.

I let my hunger outweigh my trepidation about this entire situation and decide not to bother with a reply. Keeping his attention away from his manager longer than necessary won't bode well. I don't want anything to ruin what is panning out to be a good thing before it even gets started. Even if my head and heart are warning me that this is a very bad idea.

My rumbling stomach and pussy are here for the ride.

Shaking my head as if to clear it, I continue my appraisal of the en suite in front of me. Much like the rest of the suite, it's warm and inviting. A woven basket on the counter grabs my attention. Nuzzled inside is a white robe, a bottle of champagne with one flute, and a box of fresh macaroons. The welcome gift has me grinning wider than it feels my cheeks will allow. I usually fill the caregiver role. It's an odd feeling to be on the receiving end. I snap a quick picture of the basket of goodies and fire it off to Lacey before I lock the bathroom door, discarding my clothes into a pool on the floor. My phone buzzes, almost bouncing off the counter in a pick-me-up gesture. Less than thirty seconds has elapsed, and she's already FaceTiming me.

"You'd better be answering from a tub that can fit an entire hockey team." She smiles in glee.

"What's up with your recent fascination with hockey?" I turn the camera around, steadying it toward the tub of running water.

"On a scale of meh to your panties are wet, how nice is the hotel?"

I stifle a laugh. "They're drenched."

"Dammit. I knew it. Those bastards are the real deal. And don't hate on hockey, baby girl. It's all the rage. What's sexier than grown-ass men beating the tar out of one another in the name of sports? A girl can get off on that kind of violence."

Pampering myself, I finally slide into the tub.

"I really wanted them to take you to some run-down motel that would have you screaming for the hills, tucking your tail, and running home. I have to admit, it is nice to see that smile on your face though. Is the robe behind you soft?"

I turn my head to look at the plush material lying on a chair. "The second-softest thing I've felt in my life. The first is the comforter on my bed in my room. And screw you." I toss my head back in laughter before sinking into the scalding water, bubbles rising as I fall lower into the sizzling abyss. "You would hope for the best and expect the worst."

"I'm a realist. What can I say? I'm glad I was wrong."

"Wrong about the lavish pad. The rest is still up for debate. Mazen is a total asshole."

"Usually, it's assholes who fuck the best. Give him a whirl while you're there."

"Please. I'd rather hump the armrest on our couch, thank you very much. He's a dick, and you're not glad; you're jealous."

Lacey's eyes twinkle in delight as I blow a handful of bubbles toward my phone.

"*Hello, jealousy, my old friend*," she belts, her mouth growing larger on my screen as she holds it up to her camera. "Who in the heck wouldn't be jealous?"

Like a flame to a fire, I add a smidgen of gasoline. "Oliver's supposed to be sending up a sushi boat for dinner." I watch as her eyes widen; her glare says she wants to sucker punch me in my tit.

"Dial it back a notch. Some of us measly peasants are having grilled cheese and canned soup for dinner." Her fiery eyes glow resentfully, and I see a shift in her glare the moment a plan grows roots. "Ya know what? I'm on my way. It's stupid for you to be put up in a hotel when you're sleeping in our own town. They could have just scooped you up in the morning on the way to the airport." Her phone shuffles as she stands, most likely looking for her shoes or keys.

It's my turn to deadpan. "In what, their oversize metal tour bus? Excuse me if I don't want to paint a giant X on our shop or home that says we travel with rock stars."

"I didn't think that through," she huffs. "I want to come over and spend one last evening with you. You can't eat that much sushi alone anyway. Please."

"The guys are stuck in a meeting with their manager. Working out tour logistics or something before we leave in the morning. They'll be back later, and I'm sure they will want their fill of the sushi they purchased."

Hope glimmers underneath her fawning lashes. "So, is that a yes or no?"

"I'm not alone." I hold a bottle of champagne up.

"You're a spoiled-rotten bitch, and it's only been a few hours with the Kings. Ping me your address, or I'm using your QuickEats account and ordering my own sushi boat and champagne."

Gulping down a bubbly swallow, I retort. "I can't just invite people to a notorious rock band's suite. I don't have that kind of pull."

"No, but you have a magic pussy, apparently."

I laugh into my flute.

"I'm your sister, and from where I'm sitting, it looks like you could get away with murder, and Oliver would hire someone to bury the body."

"You're delusion—"

"You're naive," she boasts, having won this round. "And poor because I just spent a fortune of your money on sushi since you're stingy and you won't let me come bask in the high-rise with you."

Finishing my flute, I pour another. "I'm changing my password, brat."

A few beats of silence pass.

"Squad goals," Lacey sighs.

We haven't used our sisterly slogan in forever. Being younger than me by two years and having a completely different build than mine left Lacey as a walking target in school. Our peers either hated her because they were jealous of her curves or they envied her because they knew their boyfriends all gawked in her direction when she walked by, her hourglass figure swaying and her bubble butt jutting out.

I vaguely remember how it started now, years later. She was whining about the opinion of some thin, shallow blonde who clearly needed to worry about her own cheeseburger intake and not my kid sister's. I told her those girls wished they were as cool and funny as she was. With mascara-stained cheeks, our mantra of squad goals took root. From there on out, we'd say our slogan, loud and proud, whenever one of us felt less than … fabulous.

Blood made us sisters.

Squad goals made us friends.

"Enjoy your dinner. It's the last one I'm funding. I'll call you tomorrow."

"Thank you." Her smile reaches her eyes, making her appear younger.

I'm taken back to another time. A time where I wore the badge of being someone's mother, a role I accepted without a second thought, long before my time. A pang settles in my chest as I sit in a hot bath, the porcelain probably costing more than my car, while she sits in our apartment alone.

"Hey, Lacey." I catch her before she disconnects the line. "I'm doing this for us … for you, baby sister. Everything I do, have done, and will do is for you. You know that, right? This money is about more than expanding."

"I know." She swallows down a mouthful of words that we refuse to give light to.

"Squad goals." I smile, setting my flute on the stand next to the bathtub.

"The only goal I have is to grow up and be half the woman that my big sister is." The line disconnects before her words have time to resonate.

13

ALL HAIL THE QUEEN

SOPHIA

I'M PERCHED on a velvety blue barstool, stuffing my face with the sea's delicacy, as Zayn's "Pillowtalk" blares from my cell phone, sitting on the counter next to me. My taste buds are high, soaring in delight after each bite that I take. I eat my fill until my stomach is swollen. Sushi will do that to you. Rather, rice, in all its refined glory, will.

Rimmed with black glasses, my eyes mimic the front door as it swings wide. Wiping my mouth with the hem of my crewneck sweater that has a dancing skeleton on it to rid my chin of any remnants of rice, I hobble off the stool, fidgeting with my loose fishtail braid.

Am I presentable enough to meet the rest of Oliver's friends?

Nope. Definitely not.

Do I care?

Yes.

Will I show it?

No.

There's no time to contemplate how my appearance looks when a flood of chaos plunges into the large living space adjacent to the kitchen. Six pairs of eyes come to a halt when they meet mine. This is the moment I've been dreading. Mazen has made sure to remind me of his stance where my newfound business deal with Oliver stands. I already feel like an intruder and have no doubt that after my formal introduction with the rest of the band, I'll feel even more like an outcast. A thin sheen of sweat coats my back.

Eight weeks. You can do anything for a short time. I give myself a silent pep talk.

I'm practically another one of the band's groupies, vying for their attention, as I stiffly raise my hand in the air—the universal symbol of awkward. "Sup." My demure wave is paired with the lamest hello I've ever let leave my lips in my entire existence, and it makes my eyes glower with disgust radiating inward.

The sixth pair of eyes warily watching me comes in a canine form. The wiry-haired hound takes off in a stampede of interest, heading directly toward the kitchen island I'm holding up with my side. Paws and exhilaration urge the large white-and-black hound forward, barreling toward me with record speed. I'm greeted a second later by a hefty husky, tail wagging enthusiastically.

"Look at you, big baby."

I take a knee, closing the gap between us, and the mutt sniffs my face, rubbing its slick nose across my cheek and dipping into my braid with a steadfast enthusiasm that only an adorable dog full of curiosity can muster.

"Jupiter," a scolding bellow calls out, making me keenly aware that this adorable and friendly pooch didn't twist open the hotel door with his paws alone.

Jupiter.

"It's fine. I love dogs. My sister would say more than people," I admit to the small, gathered group at the door. "Hi, Jupiter." I generously rub my hands over the dog's large head, fingers gliding through smooth, thick hair.

Another firm reprimand echoes as the owner calls the dog again. "Come."

"Dude, she said she didn't mind. Ease up." A voice I've memorized and the body it belongs to pushes through the crowd standing at the front door.

Oliver strides toward Jupiter and me, and it suddenly makes perfect sense.

"Kings of Jupiter, huh? So, you all own"—I look under the dog's fluffy belly for an answer—"him?"

"Brains and beauty." He winks before offering me the same hello I did him. "Sup. I'm glad your dinner came. Was it good? It looks fantastic. I'm starving." His gentle nudge and boyishly affectionate smile disarm my armor.

"What's left of it." I offer a friendly smile. "You haven't eaten?" My attention narrows on him, a dash of worry crosses my face.

Oliver smiles blandly. It doesn't reach his eyes before he's shaking his head. "Management cares about making money, not our well-being. Welcome to showbiz, baby." Oliver slides next to me and wraps an arm around my waist in an almost-possessive manner. "You smell like oranges. Did you enjoy your bath?"

"Very much so. Here." I slide over, leaving an empty barstool open next to me, watching to make sure I don't hit Jupiter's paw. "You ordered enough food to feed an army."

The lazy smile he freely gives, a stark contrast to his bad-boy persona that pairs Mazen's. "I was hoping there would be some left over."

Picking up a roll with my chopsticks, I hold it toward him. "This one was delicious."

Surprising me, he leans down and swallows the entire roll, his eyes never leaving mine, and moans. Jupiter's ears straighten, head tilting at the sound one of his owners makes. The thought of four men sharing responsibility of a dog makes me chuckle inside.

This pooch has a better lifestyle than I do.

Picking up another piece of sushi, Oliver holds it in front of his mouth, lips parting. "If I get to eat dinner with you every night, this tour might be the best yet."

My eyesight darts over his shoulder to the other three members of his band, and a petite woman with long black hair eyes me suspiciously at our exchange.

I hear ya, sister. I'm taken aback by his blunt flirtation too.

"I'm Sophia. Nice to meet you guys."

I arch away from his grasp, distancing myself—a silent reminder that this is a business transaction and nothing more. Only his grip tightens, his fingers holding on to the cloth of my shirt securely. The air around the two of us stirs, his pull is strong as I tilt my head, trying to assess his motive.

Oliver leans in, his nose a mere inch from my ear. "I'm sorry I couldn't pick you up earlier. Jupiter had a vet appointment. Maz told me what happened with your sister." The statement hangs heavy between us.

Was that what their meeting was about? Did Mazen inform their manager or label, whoever, that Oliver had invited me to tour with them? Did he make a police report about the Tasing?

Sensing my internal outpour of questions, he warns, "The *king* is in a bad, bad mood. Not right now, okay?"

I study Oliver's olive-skinned face, heeding the look in his eye, which tells me enough. They're begging me not to stoke the fire that is his best friend. Parking my curiosity, I chew the inside of my cheek while leaning into him further. He's the only person in my corner right now, and I'm going to need his friendly companionship if I'm going to outlast this evening and the next several thereafter.

The newly awakened comfort he brings helps my back straighten with my usual confidence back in place. I deliberately ignored Mazen when he called after Jupiter as the band entered the suite, which is hard to do with his fuck-me-now magnetism that is more potent than I want to shine a light on. After our morning escapade, when he was taken down like a sack of potatoes and then his sudden departure from the SUV, it's clear as mud that I'm enemy number one in his eyes. Whatever the reason for his dislike of this situation, or me in general, I'm here. The deal was signed and notarized.

A small glow of hope stirs within as the dark-haired woman, who appears to be around my age, prances over toward me, her smile warm. All thoughts of Mazen's lifeless sooty eyes disappear when she cuts the silence.

"Since Ollie's manners must've gotten caught behind the elevator door, allow me to introduce myself." She laughs. "I'm Vanna, Murphy's fiancée."

"It's nice to meet you. You're ... stunning," I blurt nervously.

The neutral shade of her skin tone, paired with the dark contrast of her lengthy hair and small stature, is adorable. She's like a miniature Goddess. I hope she's as friendly as she is beautiful.

I always wonder why musicians find normal-looking

woman to settle down with. It could be that they get sick and tired of being lusted after by silicone-looking creatures, created by plastic surgeons, or maybe having a real woman with curves and imperfections is a reminder that they're more than the music they create and the public persona they have to embody on the regular. It's a sad life, if you ask me. I'm not here to judge.

Vanna doesn't seem unnerved by my blatant comment, and a cheeky grin tilting her lips confirms as much before she says, "I think I'm going to like you. None of these fools ever have steady girlfriends. Being the only female on tour gets *very* boring. There's only so many sound checks a girl can take before wanting to blow her brains out. Thank you, by the way. You're a sight for sore eyes yourself."

Murphy Miller hit a foreign jackpot.

"Trust me on this. I've probably seen as many tits and asses as these fellas." Running her hand through her hair, she offers me a wink. "You have a natural beauty that people in this industry have long forgotten about. It's classy."

Her appraisal sets in, and I gape at the naked-women commentary. Fearful images of thongs and bras being tossed onstage, one landing on my head in the front row, clouds my thoughts.

"For starters, thank you." A demure laugh slips through my lips. "I appreciate it. And I'm a tattoo artist, remember? I've seen my fair share of the human anatomy." The irony weighs in my voice.

"So I've heard." Her eyes, bright with merriment, hold mine. "We've all seen the infamous sea monster of the south."

"You showed your dick tattoo to your bandmate's

fiancée? You really have no boundaries, do you?" I address Oliver, who isn't paying attention.

He's hunger-crazed and inhaling roll after roll of sushi before he glances over with a sheepishly deceptive look.

"You have no idea, Soph. You will though. You're stuck on a bus with us, where all is heard and very little is masked." His ominous statement hangs heavy until our eyes meet, and I see amusement dancing in his irises. "I didn't show her. Murphy added her to the group chat without asking. Hence her knowledge of said pic."

"The coloring is spectacular. I don't know why he's *so* proud though. I've seen bigger dicks on Yorkshire terriers."

A wave of hysteria surrounds us, and Vanna smiles proudly. It's apparent by the ballbusting that they're a tight-knit group.

"Yeah, we're definitely going to be friends." I nudge her side.

"Are you all done having a fucking moment, or is it safe to enter our suite now?"

I'd be able to spot the slight rasp of his voice on a bustling sidewalk in the city at this point. It sounds like it's been dragged through the rough terrain of a mountainside and then steeped in the warmest honeypot imaginable. His voice oozes sex appeal. It's easy to see why women on the web gush about him like he's our generation's Elvis.

The big bad wolf, who Oliver dubbed king, is furious. The comment leads me to believe that he's not only the lead singer and backbone of the band, but also the founder. Dodging the daggers he shoots at me should be an Olympic sport.

"Here's to hoping he pulls the stick out of his ass or it's going to be a long several weeks." I divert my gaze and whisper to myself, irked by Mazen's disapproval at my presence yet again.

"You're telling us. Why don't you just pack up and head back to your side of town then? I'll make it easy and send for a driver. Shit, I'll cover the tip too."

"Fuck off and drop it." Oliver sets his wooden chopsticks down with a shake of his head. "Go to bed or out. Fuck, hire an escort if you don't feel like leaving. I don't care at this point. We're not going through this again. Sophia is *my* guest. Back off and give her a little room to settle in."

"You're only thinking with your dick, Ollie." When Mazen raises his large hand, I brace for the impact, except he snaps in front of his friend's face before lowering his hand. "Wake up and smell the *roses*. You want a live-in tattoo artist? I'm down with it. It's not a half-bad idea. Anyone but her, man. She's no good for you or our band."

Heat rolls between them, anger flaring.

"She's right here," I retort. "If you have something to say, no need to beat around the bush, Mazen. I'm a big girl. Tell *me* how you feel or what I even did to piss you off in the first place." I huff out a puff of annoyance as he turns his hostile glare toward me, boldly intimidating.

As if he's been propelled by some invisible force, he closes the gap between us, brows set in a rigid line. The expression on his face swiftly moves from annoyance to a straight-up murderous glare.

"Your presence pisses me off, and that was before you and your insane sister Tased me. I. Don't. Want. You. Here. Bottom line: next time you spread your legs for a stranger—"

Our tempers echo as I step up to him, chest to chest. My glasses fog from the proximity of our mouths, our heated breathes mingling. He's crossing a line, and I won't let him disrespect me again. Even if it means causing a rift with my new boss and contract.

"*You* got yourself Tased by being a royal jackass, and yet here you are, continuing to push buttons that you shouldn't be pushing. If I'm not mistaken, it sounds like you're jealous. This is now the second time you've brought up who I screw."

"Jealous?" His voice is hard as a rock.

He closes the remaining distance between us. My body betrays me as my nipples pull taut when they graze against his hard chest.

"You could screw every fan at every concert we have, and I couldn't care less. I don't do loose pussy, and at the rate you're going, you'll need the best plastic surgeon Florida has to offer to sew that snatch up tight again."

My lips thin with irritation and disapproval of his idea that I'm a hazard to Oliver or his band as a whole. It doesn't sit well. Neither does his assumption of my tightness. In my five-foot-seven frame, anger ignites, and I feel like I'm six foot tall as we square off. Neither retreating. This might be futile, but men like Mazen are all bark and no bite. I've dealt with way scarier and intimidating people in my life than the rock star with a godlike ego standing before me.

"Don't you worry about the tightness of my pussy." I glance over toward Oliver, his mouth slack, but his shoulders tense. "It was tight enough to milk your best friend."

He doesn't blink as he barks out his reply, "You might have ridden Ollie hard enough to have him seeing stars, but make no mistake; you're just another pussy that's boarded our bus. You're not the first or last one we'll fuck and grow tired of. You'll be discarded at a truck stop soon enough—mark my words."

"It's a good thing I'm a tattoo artist and not another one

of your groupies then, isn't it? I have a purpose for being here that doesn't include flaunting my body around. So, let's make one thing clear: the ink is dry, *stronzo*." Jerk.

There's a flicker of something that dances between desire and hate in his eyes as he finally blinks and takes the first step away from our heated exchange.

The man who I assume is Murphy from the images I've seen online plops down on the couch. His identity is confirmed as he drags Vanna down with him and gives Oliver a pointed look.

"I was wondering how long you were going to let that shit play out."

Oliver's masculine laugh brings me back. "That was the hottest thing I've ever seen, and I can't even jerk off because of this damn jellyfish tattoo."

My chest rises and falls like I've run a marathon as I come down from my battle.

"In the two years Murphy and I have been together, no one—and I mean, no one—has put Mazen in his place like that." Vanna wraps her arms around Murphy's neck. His dark skin is a stark contrast to hers. "All hail the queen."

A chorus of amusement erupts just as a luminous shadow in the corner of the room grabs my attention. I shift uneasily as my eyes meet the last member of Kings of Jupiter. The cold warning of Cannon's thick stare is almost as vicious as Mazen's unnerving distaste for me. A melancholy scowl sweeps across his sharp features, and it's not until his brows bunch and he shakes his head, stalking toward the dark hallway, that defeat nags at my heart.

I tense as the slam of his door startles me. "I'm so sorry."

Shame knots in my stomach, and regret is painted on my face as I look back and peer around the open floor plan.

Eyes are glued to me, most likely due to the scene I just caused.

"I'm not usually so ... aggressive. He just brings out the worst in me. For the record, I didn't Tase him. Ask your security guy, Ashton."

I turn to face Oliver, whose eyes are still staring off into space. I'd give anything to know what he's thinking. Probably deciding to shred our contract with a kitchen knife or burn it.

"That is not how I wanted our first night to go."

"It's about how I thought it'd go." Murphy dips his chin.

"The king has met his match, ladies and gentlemen." Vanna's smile is triumphant.

Nuzzling Vanna's petite frame, Murphy casually changes the subject. "So, you feeling up to carving some skin tonight?"

"Don't threaten me with a good time." A soft hum of laughter leaves my lips at my animated reply. His question plants me back in reality and reminds me why I'm even here in the first place. My palms itch half in excitement to hold my gun, half in anticipation to stab a slew of needles into Mazen's skin. Too bad the holes will heal. "I just need to grab my suit—"

Thunderous footsteps and the unmistakable sound of doors opening and closing halt me seconds before Cannon —all six foot four inches of him, with his linebacker physique and icy-white hair that he seems to notoriously keep in a tight braid, looking like the Viking of my dreams— saunters into the living room with my black hard-shell suitcase wheeling behind him. Almost as if we conjured him into existence, I fight a stupefied gasp from escaping with my tongue at his sudden appearance.

It's not every day that someone of his … fame or grandeur caters to you.

"Thanks," I peep evenly despite the giggly-schoolgirl feeling that stirs in my chest.

While Mazen's hateful aura makes him unapproachable and a shitty human at best, I've come to know what to expect from him. Cannon Rhodes's presence is menacing.

He offers no reply other than the simple dip of his chin, sharp as glass, before settling onto the couch. Pleasantries be damned. I was warned he was a man of few words. Not reading too much into his reserve, I climb on the floor and unzip my bag, filled to the brim with equipment, and get to work on setting up a sterile field.

The band's conversation is light and airy as they taunt, tease, and laugh at what seems to be inside jokes from either their years of friendship or adventures on tour. I welcome the distraction, anything to keep me from being the center of attention. A couple of times, I glance up, curious about the silent brute taking up space in the vast room. While he's immersed in his phone, I witness him nod a few times to both Murphy and Oliver as he answers them without words. Finding it a little odd, I brush it off and settle on my small travel stool. I'm not here to judge or make friends. I'm here to serve one purpose and one purpose only.

"Who's going first?" I ready my hand on my tattoo gun and settle into my element.

"First to go is the first person who gets to crash. I'm beat." Murphy plops down on the chair in front of me.

"So, what are we doing tonight?"

Everyone but me laughs in unison, like they're all a part of an inside joke I'm not in on.

My brows rise as I glance around. "Did I miss something?"

It's Oliver's mouth that parts. "These fuckers are copy-cats and want jellyfish tattoos of their own. An original bunch they are."

"Your wish is my command." I shrug. "It really makes my job a lot easier, doesn't it?"

Vanna laughs, and it's my turn to offer her a wink. When I turn my attention back to Murphy, my eyes wander the small patches of exposed skin on his brown arms. There isn't much empty space to work with.

"Where are we putting it?"

Leaning back slightly, he raises the black shirt. Abs galore come into view. "Right here." He points to his side. "Smaller than your palm. Colors to match Ollie's."

His smirk is unmistakable before he reaches up, tying his loose dreads into a low ponytail. I mark my understanding with a nod and start to clean his skin. I don my gloves, and with the first step on my pedal, my gun's steady vibration is the only sound in the room.

A glow of happiness stirs inside as I lean over him, careful not to press my chest to his body in respect for my newfound friend, Vanna, and get lost in my own world. Transfixed is how I'd describe the feeling that tattooing is. With each drag of my gun, the needles become an extension of my mind, and his toned stomach is my canvas.

"Music?" I hear Oliver ask no one in particular. When no one suggests anything, he chooses, and the sound of "Night Moves" by Bob Seger starts to play. Its melody floats out of the surround-sound speakers as everyone settles in for a night of tattooing.

"How'd you get into tattooing?" Vanna asks after several minutes and songs later. "I think it's cool as a female to do this, and you're obviously talented." Her genuine curiosity summons my attention from the black outline in front of me.

Debating on where I start, I dip my gun into the coal-black ink cap and divert my attention back to what I was hired to do before offering a reply. "Drawing has been an escape for as long as I can remember. What better career to have than something that lights your soul on fire every time you do it?"

Murphy peels his eyes open, nodding in understanding. "That's deep. It's the same for me. We've been singing together—or playing together, I should say—since before we all hit puberty. It's a bonus that we earn a paycheck, getting to do what we love."

Captivated by his honesty, I open myself up a little. "Art was always an escape for me, an outlet. I guess it's a lot like being a musician or an author. Getting lost in the music, creating lyrics, or writing books that make people feel or dream. Being able to evoke that sort of emotion from someone with the strum of an instrument or the imaginary world an author's mind can conjure is liberating. When my sister and I moved to Tampa, I had the idea to open an all-female studio." I wipe his stomach with a saturated paper towel and then dip my gun again, not looking up as I speak. "I only employ women. That's a lie. My security officer is male—for obvious reasons. I'm proud of the business I've ... my sister and I have built, and we hope to expand. That's why I'm here."

It's then the tiny hairs on the back of my neck and arms rise, and I feel a fixed glare boring a hole through my chest. The line of Cannon's mouth tightens a fraction as my eyes rise, meeting his. I take notice of the enigmatic expression of ... marvel ... or a quick assessment of me ... that passes over his rigid features. I stop suddenly, releasing my foot from my pedal as something passes between us. I'm immobile by the conversation our eyes have, our mouths never moving. His eyes darken in a gentle but firm warning as he stands and strides out of the living room. His bulky body and brooding eyes disappear into the obscurity of the hallway before my trance is broken.

Out of the four members of the Kings of Jupiter, Cannon's stony mask holds the most secrets.

14

MOMMY ISSUES

SOPHIA

THE ADORABLE HUSKY I now know as Jupiter is lying next to the chair Murphy Miller rests in. The constant buzz of my tattoo gun lulled Murphy to sleep. Like a respectable guard dog keeping one of his masters safe, Jupiter keenly watches the room with an observant glare.

I'm half tempted to remove my gloves and give his furry head a pat in an attempt to assure him that I come in peace.

Animals are such intuitive creatures. I've always wanted a dog, a steady companion. It seems like the band hit the mutt jackpot with this furry canine.

Minutes after I cover Murphy's fresh ink, and slide down his T-shirt, he stirs. I'm greeted with an earnest smile. The sight is infectious. Aside from Oliver and maybe Ashton, who is also growing on me, I'm lacking in the friend department. Making this contract I blindly accepted seem more like a jail sentence than an adventure. I consider Murphy, Vanna, and the adorable husky conquests. Earning their friendships might be the only way I make it off the tour bus with a shard of sanity intact.

Murphy yawns and stretches his back into a deep arch. "You didn't wake me?"

"You looked like you could use a nap, and Vanna encouraged me not to. She seems like a good woman." Discarding my trash, I finally remove my gloves and stretch my fingers. "She said you wouldn't mind if I went ahead and covered the new ink."

"Don't get any ideas; she's taken."

I didn't think it was possible, but his mouth stretches wider, showcasing his dazzling smile. Out of everyone, aside from Ollie, Murphy seems like the most chill and laid-back member of the band. The friendly gleam in his eye tells me he's teasing, and my shoulders relax.

"It's all good. When you have as much ink as we all do, the big reveal isn't nearly as exciting as it once was."

I ponder his statement, understanding the validity in his words.

Murphy glances around the living room, void of everyone but a gently snoring Oliver.

"She retreated to the bedroom to shower and pack your bags." I solve the equation of his missing fiancée.

"Good deal. We're getting married next week." Noticing my confusion about the timeline, he quickly settles my nerves. "We'll be back in the States for our wedding, and then we'll head back overseas. Did Oliver not give you a schedule with our stops?"

"He sure didn't."

"I'll have one emailed to you." Rubbing the back of his neck, he opens his mouth, and a stampede of words rushes out hurriedly, as if he wants to get them out before Vanna exits their room. "Vanna's from Cambodia, and it's ...

frowned upon in her culture and by her very religious parents to have any tattoos. She doesn't care though and wants her first tat to be my initials. We want to get each other's initials tattooed on our ring fingers as a representation of our love. We'll take it to the grave. Had I had known about Ollie's idea of hiring you temporarily and roping you in, I could have planned this better. Since you're part of this circus on wheels now, would you be interested in doing it after our reception? I'll comp you for your time since it's not a part of Ollie's deal."

"That's dope. Count me in." I turn, looking over my shoulder to see Oliver sound asleep despite our unmuted conversation. "I don't need to be compensated. It'll be your wedding gift."

A snake of annoyance slithers up my spine for my not being in the loop and seemingly the only one in this suite without an itinerary. I chalk it up to their unexpected meeting that stole a large chunk of his attention today.

"Is this what being on tour is like all the time?"

"Honestly, yes. Mazen has mommy issues and is a dick most of the time. We've all known him long enough; we just ignore him. Don't take his *delightful* personality to heart. He'll either come around or he won't. Just do your thing."

"Cannon?" My question causes Murphy to still, apprehension budding between us.

"Cannon is complex. After almost two decades of friendship, I gave up trying to understand what makes him tick."

Dread wraps around me like a noose. His outpour of honesty shoves me from curious to alarmed.

"Well then, which schmuck do you suggest I grab next?"

"Everyone thinks Maz is the biggest asshole out of the

four of us. It's a warped story the media weaved after ... never mind. They just play the tortured-lead-singer card and play it well. It sells. So, I get it. The truth is, Cannon is a ballbuster, hidden in plain sight. He's fiercely loyal, he doesn't tolerate bullshit, and he's a good dude to have in your corner in a bar fight."

"And you've been in bar fights before?"

"Before we got signed, oh, yeah. The label sprang for security quickly after, so that shit doesn't fly now. Rags to riches and all."

"I wouldn't say anything about Cannon being easily hidden though. He looked ... looks like he hung up his championship belt from pro wrestling and decided on a whim that music would be his next hobby. Thanks for the ... insight. I'm honestly just here to do my job, bide my time, and collect my check."

"He's a lot of things; acting on a whim isn't one." His tone drips full of warning. "Cannon is methodical. He's the type that doesn't speak much, but when he does, you listen. There's no lesser evil between those two. My vote is grab Mazen and ink Cannon last. He's a bit of a night owl anyway. I'm here for the check too." He winks before strolling toward his soon-to-be bride.

Heeding his warning, I tenderly shake Oliver, too chickenshit to go knock on Mazen's room door and retrieve him myself.

"Take one for the team and go get your lead singer, please." I bat my eyelashes, earning a sheepish grin.

Heavy footsteps clog down the hall a few minutes later. I square my shoulders, preparing for battle. This feud is beyond childish. I silently plea with the universe for a do-over because whatever I did to land myself on Mazen's shit list and deserve his wrath must've been ... appalling.

The thick heel of his boot lands on the edge of my suit-case in a thump just as I finish prepping my area. Tension rumbles as Mazen sits on the chair adjacent to me. He's still in the same clothes he picked me up in this morning. I don't have a clue what he's been doing in his room for the last couple of hours. It obviously wasn't kicking off his shoes. The thought of him relaxing, calm and chill, with no scowl in sight makes me laugh at the mere image in my head. My split-second contemplation is cut short.

"You gonna tattoo or sit there in la-la land all night?"

"Do you have somewhere else you need to be?" I glance at the clock on the wall. It's far too late for a rational person to be going out.

"Yes." He doesn't offer another word as he sits in the chair and buries his hands in his thick black hair. His heavy foot remains stretched, resting on my bag.

"That case wasn't cheap. Move your foot, or you'll be buying me a replacement," I spit, anger flaring.

"These are Christian Louboutin, which also aren't cheap. Your bag is fine, and if I wanted, I could buy the entire company."

"Do you mind? Seriously. I need this suitcase to withstand the whole eight weeks."

"Do I mind ..." A hum of amusement leaves him in a loud exhale. The corded muscles under his shirt move with the deceptively sweet sound. "Do I mind creamer in my coffee? Rolling the window up on a summer night? Walking to dinner in the rain? Fucking without a condom? Yes, I do mind. I mind very much." Smug delight at getting under my skin shines in his unfathomably cool, glacier-like look.

Getting a rise out of me will declare him the champion of the game we're both determined to win. I can feel my retort building inside, clawing at my chest and rising in my throat. I'd like nothing more than to put his arrogant ass in its place. But I know that if I do, we'll be right back to square one, and he'll have missed his opportunity to get tattooed again. Biting back any cruel words, I ask him what he's getting. His answer is not a surprise. The whole gang was in on the sea-monster theme before I even unzipped my equipment bag tonight.

I don't ask him where he wants it placed. His hand reaches forward, palm resting in my lap. Using his right index finger, he gently taps on his left hand, indicating he wants it on the top of his hand. Nodding in understanding, I bite back my respect for his bravery. Top-of-the-hand tattoos are a bitch to heal since they're used daily, and the swelling is intense. I can't fight the curve of my mouth, knowing that he's going to be in pain for the next week.

He asked for it.

After I clean his hand and apply the stencil of the jelly-fish body to it, I'm at a loss as to where we're going to place the tentacles.

Reading my hesitation, Mazen croons in a tone not laced with the wrath I have been privy to in our short encounters, "Down my fingers."

An hour and a half later, my back screams in protest. I toss my garbage in the small can resting at my feet and curl my body in half, bending, stretching, pleading for its forgiveness of my neglect.

"You gonna to make it?"

"Do you care?" I reply curtly, knowing it would make Mazen's day if I threw in the towel before the driver even turned the bus's ignition over.

"I most certainly do care if you quit before my tattoo is finished. Buck up, *Rosella*."

Sighing with exasperation, I glove up and get back to

work, shading in the various colors he opted to use. I silently curse Oliver for leaving me out here alone with Mazen. I don't have a right to be upset though. This is what I was hired to do. Just because I loathe the man in front of me doesn't mean anything. Oliver must know his best friend is harmless; otherwise, he wouldn't be in his room, showering or doing whatever it is that's got his full attention.

"How long have you been tattooing?" Mazen cuts the silence in a low, silvery voice. The arch of his brow tells me he's truly interested and not just asking to get under my skin.

I ponder ignoring his question, which might only make the wedge between us grow.

"Awhile," I say, making the mistake of glancing up, eyes roaming the molded broadness of his shoulders until they land on the pale gold of his face.

His skin tone is much lighter than Oliver's, whose body appears to have been dipped in warm honey and laid out to bask in the sun's rays, and Murphy's molten-cocoa expanse.

The rich contrast of Mazen's skin magnifies the inky steel of his irises. A lock of silky, straight black hair falls to the side of his temple, like a crest. I'm not blind to his allure, although I wish I were. Studying his face for far longer than intended, I can see the Italian in him. While his skin is light, his hair, and heart are black.

My breath hitches as his unoccupied hand reaches out toward me. I take notice of the bright pink fingernail polish that is only painted on his pinkie nail. My eyes dart to his opposite hand. They're both painted pink. Odd.

It's a futile attempt to process why Mazen has two of his nails painted hot pink because he quickly moves said hand and curves it under my chin. Fingers brushing against my cheek, he tenderly guides my head back down, bringing my attention back to his stenciled hand as he all but says, *Get back to work.*

There's a warmth in the tender contact of his gesture that leaves me wishing he weren't so damn striking. I don't think my panties or my heart can live with a version of Mazen Wilde that's both cruel and intoxicating, all the while knowing there's another side to him that harbors a pinch of gentleness and sincerity. He's a villain, covered in a cloak of compassion, and nothing has ever sounded more dangerous and alluring in my entire life.

With the final twist of my wrist, Mazen's jellyfish tattoo is complete. The design is the same as his friends'. It's the placement that has me itching to take a picture for my portfolio.

With nothing to lose, I ask, "Would you care if I snapped a picture of it?" I feel my chance diminish with every second I'm met with silence. "Never mind. Let me get it wrapped, and you'll be free to hit the town or do whatever it is you have planned."

Lost in thought, he doesn't move as I bend to grab a piece of Saniderm.

"Take the picture. You know not to post it with any association to me or the band, right?"

"You have my word," I assure him. I quickly grab a few pictures before covering it and then sighing. "Good to go." I slide back on my shoes that I took off. "I'm going to get some air on the balcony and walk this stiffness off. Do you mind grabbing Cannon and telling him I'll be ready in ten minutes?"

I don't have to turn to know that he's staring at me. I can feel the heavy weight of his gaze piercing me with force. Deciding it's best not to encourage another confrontation this evening, I walk away without waiting for a reply.

Fresh air greets me as I slide open the double glass door. The city is alive tonight. Lights in the distance dance across buildings, as long as the eye can see. I've never given much thought to my adolescence and what I missed out on. Reminiscing doesn't change the past or the fact that I had to step up prematurely to care for my little sister. The word *responsible* should be etched across my shoulder blades like my last name.

Yawning, I peer into the vast city, bustling with life and promise. The realization of my desire to hang up my heavy burdens hits me full force. I accepted Oliver's proposition solely for the opportunity to open a second location and take on more responsibility. Sitting behind a desk, repeating the same tasks day after day, is maddening. Maybe I should approach my time away, fulfilling my side of this contract, with an open mind. Instead of stressing myself over the details of Lacey's day and how the shop is running without me, I go out on a limb and decide to trust her. Trust her to girl-boss the hell out of these next weeks and reign in my absence. Giving obligation the middle finger is so close I can feel it.

The sound of the sliding glass door pulls my attention, my eyes locking on Mazen as he stands in the doorframe.

His eyes look distant, deep in thought as he looks past me. "Cannon said he's not interested in any ink tonight."

"I thought it was part of your little tradition or something."

"It is."

"Color me confused then. Should I get Oliver?"

I can sense the irritability in his harsh breath as he exhales. "To tell him that his grown-ass friend doesn't want a tattoo?"

I wince at how stupid he makes me sound.

"Usually, we all get something," he says trying to make a point. "He must not be feeling it tonight. Or he's not feeling *you* doing it. It looks like someone else is more perturbed with your presence than I am."

The act of him shutting the door between us is like another wedge of clarity reinforcing his dislike for me.

Planting my heels on the balcony, I breathe in the humid Florida air as I sit and contemplate my decision to leave with the band tomorrow. A part of me feels foolish for continuing to consider going, knowing that two of the four members loathe me. Another part, the side that wants nothing more than to succeed and expand my business, tells me if something isn't hard to achieve, it's usually not worth the fight.

PEELING MY EYES OPEN, I'm met with a lush orange glow casting through the expansive windows lining the spacious bedroom. Momentarily, my eyes dart around the empty room, taking in my surroundings.

My conversation with Oliver last night drifts back to the forefront of my mind.

His voice was laced with apprehension as he walked me to my door down the suite's long hallway, my tattoo equipment in a black suitcase rolling behind him. "We already had the suite booked prior to meeting you and starting this."

At twenty-nine, I've slept in far worse places. Having my own bedroom in this giant suite, surrounded by four rock stars, isn't my definition of putting me out. I appreciate his concern. It's another reason why I know that he's more than just a pretty face and talented musician.

At his core, Oliver Collins is good. Even in the very short amount of time we've known each other, his noble nature and pure heart are evident by his actions. I assured him by placing a faint kiss on his cheek, a silent thank-you and gesture of reassurance that my sleeping arrangement was fine.

After locking the latch on my door, I brushed my teeth, generously applied under-eye serum—knowing that I'd wake up with puffy eyes after tattooing for hours into the evening and sparring with Mazen—then climbed into bed. It didn't take long before I drifted off into the abyss, dreaming about what was in store in the next eight weeks and requesting it wasn't more combat.

The warmth of the sun's rays' stream through the window, dancing over my skin, the rays like silky, outstretched fingers roaming my arms and face. Growing up in Chicago, I longed for the feeling of the sunshine on my face year-round. When Lacey and I fled, I knew where we'd end up. There was no question. The Sunshine State beckoned us with arms opened as vast as the ocean surrounding it.

Turning to my side, I look at the window, appreciating the view. Anticipation and hunger claw at my stomach, causing my feet to swing over the thick pillow-top mattress.

Day two of fifty-six.

15

BREAKFAST OF CHAMPIONS

MAZEN

"OH GOD. THAT MOUTH. HOLY SHIT." The blonde spread before me, laid out like a buffet of pink flesh, moans as ripples of pleasure pull her under.

Her fingers tangle in my hair as she grasps my strands for dear life. With each ambitious tug and brush of her silky skin against my cheek, my fervent tongue rewards her.

Exhibitionism isn't something I'm usually into. I like to fuck as much as the next person. I just don't need an audience to get off. Making a point to our new red-haired guest is the only thing on my agenda this morning.

The method of my madness is timed perfectly by a deep moan rumbling from the blonde's mouth, her plea of release coaxing the air around us. Her naked back arches against the marble countertop her body rests against just as a startled shriek whizzes out of the mouth of Oliver's new employee.

My Rosella.

"What ... what are you doing?" Sophia's eyes, rimmed with shock, dart between my parted mouth and the naked woman lying on our countertop. Second to the shock, something else flitters across her face, a far cry from horror.

Lust.

Marvel.

Jealousy.

Lips wet with Amber's ... April's ... Angel's ... the blonde's arousal, I lift my head, hovering an inch over her sex.

I bid Sophia a pointed look before jutting my chin down. "Eating breakfast."

Her audible gasp is a hundred times more satisfying than every whimper I've earned from the doe-eyed blonde privy to our exchange.

My lips slowly draw upward in a rewarding smirk. "Are you hungry?"

"Famished," she bites out, anger turning her exquisite features hostile.

I half expect her to scurry back to her bedroom, slam the door, and dial a cab. Wishful thinking on my part. Instead, she stills, seemingly lost in thought for a moment of suspended time.

A couple of seconds pass and that's all it takes to see a shift in her posture. Sophia gathers her bearings, her backbone straightens, and a fire ignites in her eyes, creating a shield of indifference at the scene in front of her.

"Coffee and a Danish will suffice though."

"You sure? This right here"—I rub my chin up and down the slit in the blonde's opening, earning another gulp from Sophia, coating it in the blonde's heavenly scent—"is the breakfast of champions."

Thank fuck she finally stumbled in the kitchen. My lips are chapped, and I could use a cup of coffee.

Standing up, I tower over the counter, now hovering where my guest's legs remain splayed open. Her core, ready and primed, glistens in the overhead light. The savory sight causes my jeans to tighten. I contemplate adding more theatrics by impaling her on my throbbing cock in one swift swoop just to provoke my red-haired adversary in front of me.

The woman before me has fulfilled her purpose. Her mission was accomplished when the unmistakable shock painted Sophia's fair cheeks, darkening them a shade or twelve.

My eyes lock on Sophia's when I lean down and whisper in the blonde's ear, "Go to my room. Second door on the right. I'll be a second."

I dip my chin toward the hallway, and she hops off the counter, the creamy expanse of her skin on full display.

Dammit. This broad's body is fire. It has me sucking in my bottom lip with appreciation of her physique.

"What's your game, Mazen?" Sophia stalks into the kitchen, hands clenched at her hips, ready for the battle I initiated.

When she closes the distance between us, I notice her jaw is clamped tightly. I'm fearful she might break a molar.

"Haven't I made it clear? I don't want you here."

"Oliver does," she counters. "You should know that I'm *very* competitive myself. Eating a girl out on the kitchen counter isn't going to scare me off. That's what Clorox wipes were made for." Taking a calculated step, she barges into my personal space. "You're going to have to try harder to run me off. Much harder, Mr. Wilde."

There's no hesitation in her eyes, only spite and a deep-rooted perseverance that I've elicited from her by provoking and poking the beast within her, willing it out to play. Her unrelenting gaze catches mine, then drifts to the kitchen island, where she openly stares at the spot my breakfast buffet of molten flesh was sprawled out.

"Are you done in here?" Opening the cabinet under the kitchen sink, she grabs a container of wipes. The staff really thought of everything. "Now that I know the kitchen is fair game, I can't wait to serve Oliver the same kind of breakfast. Only my juice is much, much sweeter. That I can assure you."

The threat in her tone is heavy. Its weight should sink my determination. Urging me to throw in the towel and abandon my game. It doesn't. Her words only encourage me, fueling the flame between us.

I'm glad Sophia didn't age into a Goody Two-shoes or a weak-ass woman. The girl ... young woman ... I met all those years ago embodied confidence. I would have never known she was just a tattoo apprentice if I hadn't had to sign a paper at the convention, acknowledging it. Sophia was just as alluring as her beauty and hid any trepidation she harbored well, confidence soaring like a seasoned artist. It was in Chicago that she took my tattoo virginity, became my first one-night stand, and was the first woman I ever nutted in without protection. I blame my stupid infatuation with her on that fact alone. A man forgets a lot of things. The first person he screws without a rubber is not one of them.

That triad marked me permanently in completely different ways.

I remind myself that I'm the narrator in this war I've waged, and her willingness to participate only boosts my desire to win. Mark my words—I will come out on top. The sweet victory will be mine when she prematurely decides to void her obligation with Oliver, fleeing our tour prematurely. Maybe then I can force her memory away and out of my life for good.

With hope for a future not plagued by my past, this is one game I refuse to lose.

The alternative isn't an option. There is no fucking way I'm going to be able to survive the next eight weeks, sharing *my* tour bus, *my* best friend, and dammit, *my* dog. Of course she had to be an avid animal lover. Sharing has never been my forte, and her presence isn't going to change that now.

"Help yourself." I gesture to the empty kitchen and take a wide step toward the hallway.

My opponent inches forward, fear abandoning her as she accepts her role in my game. I might be the king, but this woman has the backbone to checkmate me, becoming a queen. Upping the ante, she matches my steps, stopping directly in front of me.

Loose red waves cascade over her shoulder, hanging down her back. Her face is freshly washed. Her skin smells of something zesty. Placing the soft pad of her pointer finger in the center of my mouth, her faint touch slays me. I'll never give her the satisfaction of knowing that my knees weaken as she removes her finger from my lips, holds it up to her own, and slowly licks the pad with my blonde guest's arousal on it.

"My pussy definitely tastes much better."

Drugged by her action, I close my eyes, toss my neck back, and exhale a pent-up breath.

"Do you know if Oliver takes creamer in his coffee?" Her eyes glow, basking with the comprehension that she's in a better position to win this game than I am.

Fuck. Me. That was the hottest act of rebellion I'd ever seen.

I hope Angie ... Abigail ... whatever her name is, is still primed because I'm going to purge my anger by screwing her senseless. The broad might need to apply for disability when I get finished with her.

16

APHRODITE

CANNON

THE BUS—THE overcrowding and habitual chaos—is the only place that offers abundant comfort, allowing me to sleep. As a creature of habit, traveling to different cities, states, and countries is downright hell. I haven't been conditioned by our lifestyle like my brothers have. I envy them for their lighthearted nature and bigger-than-life personalities.

Mazen and Oliver are the embodiment of what an industry musician should be. Gaudy, entitled, often intolerable. They fit into the mold in both appearance and disposition, reveling in the attention of the paparazzi. They don't harbor secrets that threaten to expose them in ways that their flashy attitudes and open-book social media accounts don't already allot their followers a glimpse into. Secrets that plague their minds and keep their paranoia at an all-time high. As children and then throughout high school, they were the sociable pair in our group with Murphy and me in the background. His composed disposition sways close to my own.

We're both somewhat inactive in the eyes of our label. Stagnant players who refuse to parade for the cameras like mannequin soldiers built by their meaningless opinions of what artists should represent or look like. Hell, I've been threatened to be replaced for failing to give a single fuck about their rules and stipulations, but you can't have a band without a drummer and or a bass guitarist who founded said band. The label knows that Kings of Jupiter would cease if one of us decided to bow out. There'd be nothing left of us than a memory, their money tunnel drying up in our wake.

Murphy and I pride ourselves on not giving two shits about our label's nonchalant commentary and are just along for the ride, having made a pact with each other many years ago. Long before puberty and pussy graced us with familiarity. We accepted our ancillary roles, both contributing our talent and nothing more to the band. Raw, authentic passion for creating art ... music. We forged the industry as friends, and we'll be friends long after our fame has been cashed in.

Music is my salvation.

I don't play for our fans. That's a forced statement fed to the masses and backed by a label. Contrary to the bullshit most performers feed you, I play for myself. In fear of if I don't, I'll cease to exist.

Beating my sticks against my drum is release to the confined war that rages inside my mind on a daily basis.

The drama of last night threatened to invade my concentration, and I don't have a need for anything that causes my focus to shift from creating music. The festering ambition to flee the bickering and foreplay that has planted root between Mazen and Sophia was enough to send me retreating to the bus earlier than normal. Choosing to skip out on getting tattooed by her again, in fear of falling under the same spell that she cast over Oliver and Mazen.

Slipping out of hotels undetected to sleep on the tour bus and resurfacing the next morning have gotten easier with time. Today is no exception. The best part of exemplifying solitude is that even our security team keeps their distance, having learned not to question my habits. Ashton and his crew have come to an understanding and are tolerant of this arrangement. They don't hover, and I don't make them feel like insignificant rent-a-cops. Being built like a brick house and towering over the slew of them by a head or more earn some leeway where my safety is concerned. They can save their overbearing bullshit for the others. I don't need their protection.

The elevator chimes on the seventeenth floor before the doors slide open to reveal Ashton leaning against the wall. He hands me a warm cup of coffee, and in exchange, I offer him a dip of my chin before he opens the door to the suite and waves me through. In one abrupt step, I'm reminded again that Oliver struck a contract with his dick. The consequence of his action is the red-haired woman in lounge clothes, examining me with a quizzical squint.

As she leans against the counter, a ray of light gleams through the window, casting a golden crown on top of her wealth of hair hanging over her shoulders. Sophia's well-groomed appearance and the apricot color of her skin remind me of the goddess of beauty, love, and pleasure. Aphrodite doesn't hold a candle to the woman standing before me with sparkling eyes and lashes that sweep down across her cheekbones.

"Coffee?" Her mouth is a delicate, beaming bud wafting

in the wind. "Tea?" The animation of her face is over-whelming. Especially at this hour.

It's hard to tell if she's gifting me with kindness because I'm a member of the band or because that's just who she is. My mind is always guarded, congested with doubts of people's true intentions. In an industry where people care more about status, appearances, and designer brands than someone's feelings, I've learned to expect the worst in people so that there aren't any disturbing surprises when their true colors shine through.

At the swivel of my chin, she accepts my silence, taking a gulp from her cup. I watch with a curious glint in my own eyes as she lowers the mug and sets it on the counter.

She folds her arms across her chest, lips pursed. "You know you've dodged getting tattooed by me twice now?"

The magnetism of her innocent appeal pulls me toward her.

A slight gasp leaves her mouth as I inch closer, stopping far enough as not to invade her personal space. I incline my head and glance at the inside of my forearm, wordlessly giving her permission to fulfill the job she was hired to do. In a desperate attempt to hide her exhilaration, she bobs her head in understanding before telling me to get comfortable in the living room as she strides by toward her room. The faint citrus scent left in her wake teases me. I resist the urge to breathe it in.

Moments later, with her bag in tow, she sets up an improvised workspace. Not sparing any time, she cleans my forearm, applies the jellyfish stencil we all decided on getting, and fires up her gun. While she's in her element, I watch as her face contorts as she drags her machine down my skin in a practiced motion. I'm marginally aware of her nearness and the fact that she makes no attempt to hide her periodical glances. My pulse grows more rapid with every puncture of her gun. Her foot offers a soft caress against the pedal under it while I sit, silently protesting with the hammering in my chest caused by her faint touch.

I treat physical awareness and the appreciation of pleasure with slight hesitation, knowing that my tastes are anything but singular. There's an unexpected response from most people when they learn that I have zero inhibitions or limitations to where sex is concerned. Pleasure comes in many forms. Control. Adventure. Unease. My reluctancy and aversion to companionship has nothing to do with the carnal aspect. I love sex and the turbulence of freedom it offers me to explore my varying tastes and desires.

It's the perception of emotion that some find hard to separate from the act of sex that I have no intention of entertaining. The thought of being distracted, allowing myself to fall into a flood tide of passion that could leave my defenses weakened, is why I don't take chances when there's a possibility of feelings getting involved.

I can't devote my heart to somebody when I'm already faithful to the greatest love of my life. Music.

17

SECRET LANGUAGE

SOPHIA

THE SILENCE that hangs between us is devastating.

With each pointed question I ask only to be rejected, my nerves began to fray by his prolonged muteness. I normally consider myself a fairly accurate reader of people. Having to grow up and dive into adulthood much earlier than most, I learned a long time ago to watch people closely.

You can tell so much from someone based on their body language. Their intentions are clear as day if you stop and really look at someone's movements and behaviors. Reading between the lines they paint with a simple glance is almost as forthcoming as words themselves.

The complexity of Cannon's natural disposition is baffling at best. I can't read him. Honestly, I don't even know if I'll like what I see under the mask he's painted, thick and hard.

I faintly remember reading an article in some magazine that Lacey left lying around the studio. A quote by Stephen

Hawking rings loudly through the deafening silence. *"Quiet people have the loudest minds."*

With his generously full build, guarded Nordic-blue eyes that are so sharp that they could cut me in half with just a flutter of his ridiculously long lashes, and his discreet temperament, Cannon is a puzzle I want to piece together. Finding a common ground with both him and the other members of the band is important. Not only because we're going to be spending a lot of time together over the next eight weeks, but also because I pride myself on my work ethic. This is a job and one I don't take lightly, knowing the payoff is well worth the unsufferable silence of the man sitting before me.

Much like his friends and bandmates, he doesn't have much viable room on his sculpted forearm. My job of tattooing them all over the next several weeks will be abundantly harder because I'm going to have to size and resize my stenciling to fit the small areas of free space that's available to work with. Like anything life has thrown my way, I accept the challenge.

Seeming lost in thought, Cannon keeps his eyes closed for what feels like the better half of thirty minutes. With the stenciling of the small jellyfish now complete, I muster the nerve to try to push him into conversation again. A girl can only take so much rejection by one man.

Knowing he's not mute, I square my shoulders and forge a path I hope he's willing to meet me in the middle on and say, "Oliver mentioned you've been playing the drums since you were four. That's pretty cool." I start with an indisputable fact, trying to lure him into conversation.

When he doesn't respond, I try again. "I heard that you like plants. Mazen said your mother owns a greenery. Hey, what did the flower tell the taxi driver so he'd go faster?" It's not a surprise when he ignores my attempt to chit-chat once again, like I'm an annoying fruit fly. "Floret!"

Refusing my bait, Cannon changes the song on his phone. Suddenly, it occurs to me that he probably doesn't even know I'm talking to him if he's as immersed as he looks in the music bellowing from his phone. The suppressed sound leaking from his earbuds booms louder. I realize he's tuning me out on purpose as the volume increases. With an imaginary drumstick in hand, he plays the air, ignoring me fully.

Small talk isn't his forte. Noted.

I recall the degree of roughness in the sound of his masculine voice, which he used like an instrument, in an interview I saw him in when my curiosity got the better of me and I surrendered to curiosity. Searching Kings of Jupiter online to ensure Oliver wasn't a big, fat, delusional liar was a necessity and a major part of my decision to entertain his job offer before my contract slid into my email. Aside from countless music videos that appeared after my search, the most shocking one was a clip of an interview with Cannon, who had made a very large donation to fund a music program in a low-income district in the city.

Although his words were sparse during the segment, when he did speak, there was a deep articulation in each syllable. Like they were carefully crafted in his mind and released into the world only when he was ready. Each word was almost as jagged and cautionary as his outer appearance. With sprawling tattoos littered over the front of his neck, snaking up his jawline, and one scripted word over his eyebrow, he looked out of place on my screen, seated next to the polished interviewer in a pantsuit. Cannon is the embodiment of a mystery. His appearance is meant to ward people away from him, each tattoo and scowl on the hard lines of his face a written threat.

As the interviewer whirred about his hefty contribution and detailed the project he had funded, I remember how his ultra-marine eyes winced, as if he was pained by her admiration. Just like he is now. His free hand strums through the air, his imaginary drumstick a security tic. With each flick of his wrist, he tethers himself to the action. It might not be my presence that is making him uncomfortable, like the interviewer's did; it's my push for him to talk. It's like trying to get a shark to walk on dry land—an impossible feat.

It's then that I realize that he's more than just a drummer with a penance for charity. He didn't want the clout that she showered him with. The accolade she cloaked him in fell on deaf ears. All he wanted was to give underprivileged children an outlet. His label no doubt used it as a media tactic, earning him recognition that he didn't want. His monetary gift gave those kids battling silent wars, like he is, a way to speak without words. The solace of getting lost in music is the true present.

The man behind the hard exterior with his gruff voice and hatred for meaningless conversation uses music to convey himself. When words fail him, lyrics don't. He's wisely crafted his identity from a melody that only he can hear. He was uncomfortable voicing something so intimate. That I can understand.

I release the pressure of my foot on my pedal, my tattoo gun coming to a halt in my hand. If his body language is any indication, Cannon doesn't even notice that I'm no longer penetrating his skin. He's completely lost in the song ricocheting off his eardrums. For the life of me, I don't know why I'm trying to connect with someone who clearly isn't a fan of connection. I blame it on the nerve-racking silence that hangs between us, thicker than smog on an autumn morning, that lures me to remove one glove and clasp his phone. I know this is a gamble. Shaking off my nerves, I slide it from his lap, grasping it in my hand.

He jerks his head in my direction as his eyes widen, questioning my motive. Their sturdy glare promises punishment for the sudden interruption of the song he had playing. Holding up my gloved index finger on my other hand, I silently ask for a moment. When he doesn't yank the phone from my hand, I quickly scroll through his app filled with music in search of a conversation starter that involves no spoken words to come to pass. If I'm right about Cannon, like I think I am, I might make some headway with the brooding drummer before me.

Taking a page from Mazen's ways to get your point across without words, I find the band I'm looking for—Melrose Avenue—and choose their song "Through Hell" before pushing play.

The downward cast of his lashes, paired with the audible exhale of breath, is like praise to my ears, telling me I was right about him. Relief washes over me as he closes his eyes briefly.

Music is his secret language, and I just learned the chorus.

Time hangs between us like the deafening silence I've grown accustomed to as I finish his tattoo. Vanna's eyes sweep between Cannon and me when she walks into the shared living area. Turning my attention from the clear wrap on his arm, I hit pause on the song playing on his phone.

"Good morning," she says, addressing us both before flinging open a cabinet in the kitchen. Standing on her toes, her midriff exposed, she huffs when she can't reach a mug on the shelf due to her short stature. A sincere smile graces Cannon's mouth, showcasing beautifully straight teeth.

Holy hell. His dentist must be proud. That smile is ... breathtaking.

Cannon strides past the massive island and shocks me by reaching forward and tousling the dark hair on her head in a playful gesture that has me questioning everything I thought I knew about the man. If I had ovaries, they'd be shriveling up smaller than the size of a dried grape by his playful exchange. I watch in utter disbelief and astonishment as he grabs a mug for her, fills it with coffee, stirs in her creamer, and then offers the cup to her like a gift, sans the red bow.

"Thank you." She takes a sip. There isn't a glint of surprise on her face.

Natural Cannon has made his presence known, and now, I don't want to backtrack to only knowing the mute, grumpy version.

I've been trying to get on his good side all morning. All Vanna had to do was use her miniature human form to her advantage, and she earns a smile more genuine than anything I've ever seen. My lips thin in irritation, and a humph escapes my mouth.

Attempting to ease the disappointment pounding in my chest, I smooth a palm down my face. "Good morning, Vanna. I hope we didn't wake you with all the electrifying conversations we were having. This one ..." I motion to where Cannon is leaning against the counter in the most relaxed stance I've witnessed from him.

His tall build hovers over the both of us, legs crossed at the ankles. One hand is nestled in his jeans pocket, and the other lies atop the counter, his palm spread wide. If I didn't know any better, I would call his bluff. This unperturbed version of him is not on trend with the brooding drummer I had the pleasure of tattooing for over an hour.

"He's a real Chatty Cathy, isn't he?" The amusement in my voice falters as a sound erupts from Cannon's mouth that reverberates in my chest.

His chortle echoes throughout the open floor plan of the shared kitchen and living room, causing my sudden jealousy of Vanna to melt into a puddle where I stand. His eyes gloss over as he loses himself at my expense. It sounds like years of pent-up laughter bellow from his lungs. With each animated rise and fall of his chest, I gather that he's laughing *at* me, not *with* me.

"You're cruel." Vanna swats his chest. "You both need to get ready. Murphy is already in the shower. He said we need to be at the tarmac in less than an hour." Leaving us both with a smile and an eye roll, she strolls from the kitchen with her mug and a second one for her fiancé.

Satisfied with himself, Cannon's demure silence slides back into place. I peer up into his gleaming blue irises, rimmed with thick black lashes, and shake my head, accepting defeat. Like the plants his mother nurtures, I will win him over. Even if it means playing the little-sister role that Vanna has perfected.

Holding my hand on my hip, I can't help my bitterness from showing. "You laughed at that and didn't even appreciate my plant joke?"

I'm met with more silence. Accepting today as a wash in our rapport, I'm about to head back to my room to shower and pack when two large hands circle around my waist. A girlie sound bellows from my lips as I'm lifted into the air and placed on the countertop.

"Why didn't you wake me, beautiful?" Oliver's morning voice is throatier than normal.

Pairing his tone with his messy bedhead, bare chest, and the low-slung gray sweatpants that showcase the deep V dipping under the waistband, and I'm kicking myself in the shin for not barging into his room earlier.

Color me shocked when Cannon breaks his vow of silence. "She was busy." The deep, throaty sound of his voice wraps around my body and squeezes tightly.

Stunned by not only his bluntness, but also the vague way he implies more leaves me with an unwelcome frankness that lingers between the three of us. Oliver tilts his head toward me, a question rising with the shape of his brow.

"I was busy tattooing him. He strolled in the suite when I got up. Jellyfish for everyone. Now, if you'll both excuse me, Vanna said we're leaving in under an hour, and for a woman, that's not music to my ears."

WE FLOCK from the hotel's parking garage in several black SUVs. Hordes of fans hold signs on the street corner as we pass by. Oliver rolls down his window, waving enthusiastically at the crowd. Blowing a few kisses, he eats up their attention.

"You love this, don't you?"

"What's not to love about people screaming your name?"

I nod while sliding out my cell phone and fire off a quick message to Lacey to let her know that we're headed to the airport. After getting our itinerary in my email this morning, I forwarded it to her as both a safety measure and out of pure eagerness. I've never left the United States before, and here I am, on my way to the airport to fly across the globe to places like England, Spain, Sweden, and Portugal. It all still feels surreal.

"Was everything okay between you and Cannon this morning? The vibe was off."

Biting my bottom lip, I give him my full attention. A questioning gaze passes between us like an air-hockey puck.

"There was definitely a strange vibe lingering there. I think it follows him like a cloud. He's a modern-day Charlie Brown." I buckle my seat belt. "He's a little standoffish for starters. Murphy warned me, but ... I was not prepared for the epic silent treatment I got. At first, I thought I had morning breath despite brushing my teeth. He let me do his tattoo though, so I guess that's a step in the right direction. What's his story? I know his mom owns a greenery and he likes to smoke marijuana. There's got to be more to the big brute than that."

Oliver leans his head back against the black leather seat behind us. "There's not really a story to tell. He has two incredible parents." He scrubs his hands over his face not once, but twice before continuing, "Honestly, Cannon and Murphy have the stablest home life between the lot of us. His dad, Marcus, has over a million subscribers on his channel, where he posts videos for teen boys without father figures. He posts an episode every week on topics like how to properly fold a fitted sheet—"

"Wait, really? He can fold a fitted sheet? That's impressive."

"That's nothing. He has hundreds of videos out there. How to change a tire, balance a checkbook, tie a tie, boil noodles without them getting sticky and gooey. It's insane. He's a good man. Helped me out a lot, growing up." His face is stretched into a smile, but he looks anything but happy.

Our hands inch closer on the seat. Taking the initiative, I interlock our fingers and offer a small squeeze. The gesture is met with a tighter squeeze and a shoulder bump.

"How did ... Cannon become so guarded then?"

My intrusive nature knows no bounds. I don't know these people and haven't earned the right to ask such personal questions, yet I want to know. They're going to be my roommates for weeks. A little honesty and insight aren't too much to ask for.

For several seconds, silence hangs between us, heavy as sin. I sigh, not knowing if I'm going to be closed out again or not.

"It's not my business. Just forget I asked."

Letting go of my hand, Ollie squeezes my jean-clad thigh affectionately, eyes glued to where his hand strokes my leg before his gaze travels up to mine. It lingers there with hesitation. "He loved someone who couldn't reciprocate what he felt. I don't know if he—if anyone really—can come back fully after that kind of heartbreak."

Innately, I'm lost in his devastating revelation. *Who broke him? How could someone not love him?* Not that he screams *I'm a cuddler* or anything remotely close. Everyone deserves happiness.

"Sorry, I, um ... I wasn't expecting that. It's the first honest thing I've heard that makes complete sense. No wonder he's so closed off."

"I've been called a lot of things, Soph, but a liar isn't one of them. One thing you can count on is honesty from me. I don't beat around the bush. Even when it hurts, I tell the truth. That's what got me ..." He pauses, his expression growing tense. There's a hint of sadness in his tight-lipped frown, a musing of another time.

I look away at the sight of his strain and smooth my hair over my shoulder. My thoughts linger nervously as his inadvertent truth settles between us.

Keenly aware of Oliver's precarious squint, I try to keep composed, knowing exactly who the someone was that Cannon loved and lost. The person responsible for his gamut of bitterness that ate and chipped away at his confidence and left him doubtful of the world around him.

Oliver's eyes blaze into my mind. False innocence flashes imperiously as my eyes speculatively narrow in on him, and an unspoken truth bleeds into the air. The man who crushed Cannon in the worst possible way is looking right at me.

18

MILE-HIGH CLUB

OLIVER

I STUDY Soph's face for an extra beat.

Long enough to see realization flitter across her pallid face and disappointment set in, replacing her attraction toward me.

I survey her expression with a shimmering hope that her faith in me isn't fully lost, and I speak in a compassionate tone. "We don't have the time to go down memory lane right now."

I search her face, trying to reach into her thoughts.

Soph nods, and then her eyes widen like she just recalled something startling. "Where's Jupiter? I haven't seen him all morning. Does he have a nanny like those children of other famous people?"

Half in contempt, half concern for our dog's whereabouts, she looks up at me through a field of dark lashes, wanting an explanation.

"Do we look like the type of men who don't take care of our child?"

The sweet sound of her laughter fills the back seat as our vehicle comes to a stop.

"Mazen ducked in this morning and said he was taking him. If Jup's not with one of us, which is fucking rare because our trust doesn't extend far outside the four of us, he's with Ashton. He has a soft spot for our boy."

She extends a warm smile, offering a shared kindness that's almost foreign in my realm. Being in the limelight for as long as we have, I've forgotten that genuine people like Soph do exist. They're uncommon, but they're out there.

The vehicle's revving engine decelerates to a gentle hum as we gradually slow down and park at our destination. I open the door, and the humid air wafts around us.

Leaving the Sunshine State in the summer is like escaping a curse that's shadowed you your whole life. My favorite season is winter for no particular reason, aside from the cooler temperatures. Holidays never meant much to me, growing up. I didn't see snow for the first time until a couple of years ago.

We were headlining a show in Colorado at the time. Nick, our manager, got an alert that a winter weather advisory was issued. He announced it into our earpieces, and Mazen, being the drama queen that he is, stopped the show and ran off the stage. I remember the crowd going nuts. I tried to imagine what the scene before them looked like from their point of view. You paid for a ticket and waited through two opening acts, and when the band finally came on, their lead singer fled the stage.

What in the actual fuck? was probably what they were thinking.

A couple of security guards followed him, and when he returned, he had a ball of white in the palm of his hand. A snowball.

He threw it at me before he sauntered over to his mic stand and yelled, "Snow is my second favorite white powdery substance."

The crowd erupted, and we played our hearts out that night.

The next morning, the four of us spent the day making snowmen and having the roughest snowball fight known to man, enjoying something that we never could have at home.

Humid air and the sound of my name draw me from my stupor.

"Oliver," Soph falters briskly, panic lingering from her lips.

Instinctively, my eyes skirt around us, looking for what's set her on edge. My spine goes ramrod straight against my seat. I'm half expecting a rush of fans to ambush the vehicle; it wouldn't be the first time they slipped through security and took us off guard. The tarmac is empty, aside from our crew. I fall short, trying to make sense of what's startled her.

"What does Jupiter have in his mouth?" A faint tinge of amusement in her tone has me looking toward the plane.

I roll down the back window, a laugh escaping me, and I'm not at all surprised by what I find. Jupiter's sitting at the top of the airstairs with what appears from here to be a pair of black panties dangling from his snout. I survey the SUV next to me as Murphy and Vanna exit the back door, snapping it shut before laughter erupts.

Shouting sternly, Cannon slides out of the back seat of his ride and snaps his fingers impatiently. A pointed glare is shared between Jupiter and him. It says, *You're in deep shit.* With ears perked, Jupiter takes off down the metal steps at full speed, panties clenched in his teeth like a prized possession. He skids to a halt in front of Cannon, fluffy tail wagging eagerly before he sits. When he tilts his head to the side in his infamous what'd-I-do-Dad look, Cannon's brooding glower diminishes.

Cannon grabs the underwear from his mouth and slides them in his back pocket, aggravation set again on his jaw. "You're fucking disgusting." His large frame bends at the knees, and I swear I hear them pop in the distance. "I'll take used underwear over fishing a condom out of your throat this time." He rubs Jupiter's head, anger melting at every rub.

"Shall we?" I wave Soph out of the back seat, resting my palm at the small of her back.

"Are we not going to talk about the condom confession?"

I shake my head and shrug. "Nope."

"Are you not worried about what we're going to find in there since those panties most likely belong to someone already on board the plane?" Soph blinks up at me, a sweet, musing look dances across her cheeks.

"Nope." *Again.* I grab my backpack and her small purse from the seat and add, "You'll get used to the chaos. It comes with the territory."

A faint threat of confusion dances across her roused features.

"There's not much Mazen can do to surprise us anymore. He's done a lot of fucked-up shit over the years. We all have, if I'm being honest. Touring together for this long, nothing really surprises me anymore," I admit, vaguely knowing that her mind is reeling. I can see the wheels spinning. *This ought to be fun.*

"As long as Jupiter steers clear of stealing my panties, we're good." She elbows my side, her touch sending a ripple of awareness throughout my body.

Great. Now, I'm thinking about her underwear.

"I don't recall you having on underwear when we … were together."

She presents a cavalier shrug of her own. "It was laundry day."

"Laundry day is my new favorite day."

We walk toward the plane. Step by step, her stride gets shorter. There's hesitation in her gait. Has she changed her mind about coming with us?

"You good?" I place one foot on the airstairs, turning to catch her answer.

In a broken whisper, eyes wide with fear and unshed tears, she divulges, "I've never flown before."

Ashton talks into his cell phone a few steps behind us.

"You said you were a transplant to Tampa, right?"

She swallows. "We drove." Her voice trembles as she tips her head to the sun. Gold strands of hair flutter across her face. "Lacey and I drove to Florida when we moved here."

Apprehension is carved into her perfect features. I know she's second-guessing her decision to board the flight. I stop just shy of the metal stairs where we stand. Cannon eyes me cautiously, giving me a what's-the-problem glance. I hold up my hand, silently asking him for a moment. Murphy, Vanna, and he hang back at my request.

With a small distance between us, I reach forward to cup Soph's face, her chin quivers in my grip. "You're a tattoo gun–wielding badass. You had spunk running through your veins when we met and didn't take any shit from me. You're a fireball in a flawless miniature package, and this"—I motion behind me toward our private plane, then bend down to her eye level—"is just a mode of transportation. If you let fear rule, you'll miss seeing all that the world has to offer. Don't let it take hold of you and harness you in its hands. Gather the strength I believe lives inside you." I poke right at the nape of her neck. "And let me show you the world."

I sound like a fucking Disney prince. That's something I can live with.

The tenseness in her shoulders evaporates like a fog abandoning its hold on an autumn morning. Swallowing, I see the moment she finds her strength and voice.

"I understand why the absence of your love was such a devastating blow to Cannon now," Soph reasons in a gentle tone before looking over her shoulder, eyes traveling to meet his. The air thickens around us, not from the day's mugginess that clings to our skin, but from the loitering of unspoken confessions that Soph picked up on.

Though we're a healthy distance away, I follow her stare, only to witness his expression darken, an unreadable flash flittering across his face. Despite his hard exterior, I know Cannon Rhodes probably more than I'd like to admit. He's a wild card in many ways. Always has been. The rogue one of our crew. Never forthcoming in conversation, but always there when we need him. It took a long time to earn his trust as kids, and when we did, I broke it.

I shake off her iron grip, along with the clouded visions of my past, and turn to move past her. Alarm bells ring as she naively drudges up old fears and uncertainties. It's my turn to tremble. Taking the metal stairs two by two, I feel like an asshole, leaving Soph at the bottom of them.

The need to take a beat, to regroup my wayward thoughts alone, is short-lived when I hear, "Good morning, Ollie." Mazen's cheerful voice coats me with unease as my feet skid to a stop.

"Morning," I say with rapt attention.

I watch as Mazen slides a hand around the neck of the

very naked stewardess sitting on top of his lap. Circling his palm around the front of her throat, he slams into her roughly and then relaxes into the leather seat, giving her permission to set the pace.

"Get ready for the ride of your life," he mumbles before shooting me a wink.

A fucking wink.

Has he lost his mind?

Full tits on display, she bounces on his dick like a deranged fiend. His cock is her salvation.

"Did you get a prescription of Viagra that I don't know about? Seriously, man. I don't think you've had this much sex since we met those twins in Poland."

He snubs my question, plowing into the flight attendant.

There's a loud inhale from behind, indicating Soph decided to face her fear of flying. "Well, I guess we now know who the panties belong to."

The casual way she pokes fun at the sight in front of her, sliding in front of me with her small carry-on bag, tells me that she's going to fit in just fine. I knew she would.

"Is his favorite hobby sex?"

"Most definitely." Setting my bag down, I wave dismissively. "This isn't anything though. I think he's actually being respectful since you're a guest."

"Respectful of me?" She laughs innocently. "Don't you mean condom companies? He's keeping *them* in business."

19

HOMIE HOPPER

SOPHIA

EIGHT AND A HALF AGONIZING hours later, a giant roar sounds, causing my eyes to spring open. A second later, my body shifts frighteningly as the plane's acceleration pushes me against the surface of a ... bed.

I'm sprawled across a soft duvet, confusion dancing in my mind when I realize I'm not where I drifted off to sleep after it claimed me hours ago. I'm in an unfamiliar bed with a very familiar face staring back at me.

I bid Oliver a sheepish grin before I open and close my fist in rapid succession in an attempt to release the tension in my hands. Both are sore from white-knuckling the armrests in my seat when we took off. Riddled with dread at the long fight, I greedily accepted the freshly fornicated stewardess's offer of a glass of wine—or three—before sleep lulled me under.

Yawning, I state the obvious. "You carried me to bed."

"It was either that ..."

He reaches forward, grabbing my aching hand and placing his thumb in the center of it. In a small, circular motion, he begins massaging my palm with firm strokes. Tension starts to dissolve from his expert touch, and relief floods me.

"Or forcefully removing your fingernails that were close to being embedded in the armrests. I figured you'd be out of commission quicker than a pole dancer with a broken leg if I didn't save your hands."

"How noble of you."

A strange feeling flutters in my stomach. It's been a long time since someone has cared about my well-being, aside from my sister and my friend Knox. He was the only man who's meant more to me than just sex. The random thought of him sends a pang of sorrow to my chest. I shove it down, not having the emotional capacity to embark down that road today.

I try not to read too much into Ollie's remark, knowing that he's paying me to tattoo him and his friends. That's the extent of this trip and his impulsive comment. Without my moneymakers in prime condition, I'm no use to him.

"That feels amazing," I purr. As eager as I am to explore London, I don't dare move an inch, afraid that if I do, his kneading will cease. "Thank you, by the way. I didn't realize how exhausted I was. It's been a whirlwind."

"Fear and adrenaline will do that to you. When we booked our first large venue, I felt the same way. It was like a high, and I felt the rush before and after the gig ended. Nothing compares. I remember sleeping for sixteen hours straight then. It was like once we were done, my brain knew I needed rest."

He focuses his attention on my other hand, massaging the strain away before turning away and stretching his tan arms above his head, releasing his own pent-up stiffness. I can't help but notice the small sliver of skin exposed above his waist.

"Do you think we'll be able to visit Big Ben or see Buckingham Palace while we're here?"

Anticipation of his answer lures me upright, and I walk to the windowpane. My eyes sweep over the tarmac that is vacant, aside from a slew of waiting SUVs. When I received our itinerary, my mind automatically conjured up images of bustling airports and people scurrying like ants, trying to find their gates.

Up until this very moment, I don't think I fully accepted the future I'd agreed to for what it is. The uninhibited airstrip brings me back to reality, grounding me in a moment of reckoning.

I'm traveling with the members of Kings of Jupiter. Four men who are idolized, worshipped, and lusted after—both for their talents and sex appeal.

Sure, I read my contract, signed their nondisclosure agreement, and packed several weeks' worth of clothes in a suitcase, ready to embark on this adventure, knowing good and well what I was doing. It's going to take some time to get used to their status and what that means for their security and my own now.

This is a wake-up call.

Peering through the window, I spot Ashton opening a door on one of the SUVs waiting for us, and a handful of other security guards mimic his rehearsed move. I wonder how long Ashton has worked for the band. They seem close. At least he and Mazen did at my apartment.

I glance over my shoulder, remorse in my voice when my eyes meet Oliver's. "Never mind. Of course you can't go parading through the streets of London just to take me sightseeing. I'm sorry. I wasn't thinking."

His heavy footsteps thud against the floor. He nears me from behind. Oliver sweeps my tangled hair over my shoulder and rests his chin on it in a gesture that seems too intimate for our newfound acquaintance. Strangely, it feels natural.

For a moment, we stand there, looking out the window, watching as his crew does their jobs as effortlessly as breathing. Our luggage is handed off and loaded into the back of our designated SUVs, and then we get a glimpse of the furball, Jupiter, as he hops into the back seat of one of the vehicles.

That dog quite possibly lives the most lavish life of any animal on this planet.

Oliver takes my breath away with his gentleness as he leans in close enough so I can feel the subtle stubble on his cheek. I don't do long-term relationships. Hell ... I steer clear of any form of relationship unless it ends with fuck buddies. Honestly, I don't think he's the type of man that does the whole dating scene either. For a split second, a ripple of time, I wish that he were just an ordinary man who stumbled into my studio and not the mega star who stands behind me.

"I want to eat fish and chips with you out of a basket as we walk around the street, holding hands, roaming cobblestone nooks and secret pathways that no tourist before us has ever ventured on. Enjoy a cup of afternoon tea while sitting in Hatchards bookstore in Piccadilly after reading for hours. Spend a whole day exploring the impressive gardens London has to offer, spoiling your love of plants." His smile turns into a laugh. "I heard about the *Aloe there!* shirt." I blush as he continues, "Then, end our day in the Sky Garden at the top of the Walkie-Talkie building."

He spins me away from the window, and our eyes hold on to one another as we relish in the day that he painted so clearly for us.

"You make me *want* to do normal touristy things that have never appealed to me before. I've traveled the globe, and not once in my entire life have I ever longed to explore the cities we play in. Not as much as I do right now … with you."

As soon as the words spill from his lips, years of defenses I've built, like a moat around my heart, falter into a pile of rumble at our feet.

I want to clutch my chest, palm my heart for what can never happen, a pipe dream crushed before it even had a chance to flourish. Because at the end of the day, the beauty in his candor will fade. Reality will replace his reeling confession, and I'll be left cursing his profession and my stupid, cold, dead organ I call a heart.

I'm his employee now.

Nothing more. There can't be anything more. I've never wanted … *more*. I hate the idea of marriage. So, why do I feel this strange flutter in the pit of my stomach when he's around? I'm not a picket-fence woman or a Sunday-brunch kind of lady. Nothing about it is alluring to me.

I find thrill in waking up and not being able to find my underwear in a heap of mixed clothes and deciding to leave without them. I'm *that* girl. The noncommittal type. The one who wants to have laugh lines when she's much older and can sit back and laugh about the time she screwed twins at the same time. Call me a floozy. A homie hopper. Your opinion of me doesn't mean two shits. I want to live a full life and not be held down by social ideations of how a woman should act.

Yet Oliver has weaseled his way into my heart. No one has been able to penetrate my hard exterior since ...

I inhale, refocusing my thoughts as several heartbeats pass, and the sincerity in his voice lingers between us, a promise that can never be fulfilled.

In another life, I think to myself.

I'm envious of his description of what that perfect day would entail and a little sad that it will never come to fruition. Exploring the city with expectant curiosity, with Oliver as my tour guide sounds like something straight out of a romance novel.

Disappointment furrows my brows. I give him an earnest smile, trying to mask my frustration. I asked a thoughtless question. Not once considering it before it slipped out. None of them, not Mazen or Cannon or even Murphy, has the luxury of discovering hidden gems of happiness in the countries they visit, like Vanna and I do. Hell, even their security guard Ashton has freedom to explore when he's not working. Being a celebrity is both a blessing and a curse, I've come to realize.

My chest restricts in sorrow for Vanna. She's marrying Murphy in a week, for fuck's sake. Have they even been on a real date? Has he walked her into a crowded movie theater on a Friday night and not been spotted by a mob of fans before? Surely, they've been given the opportunity to fall in love properly.

Their profession affords them a lot of things, but normalcy is not one of those perks.

With a budding ache in my chest, I offer another sincere apology. "It sounds like we'd have a magical time together. Thanks for entertaining the idea."

"Don't, please." He cups my chin with the palm of his hand. "I love my job. Who gets to travel the world and live a dream that flourished before we even hit puberty? This job has given me financial security. Something that I couldn't have fathomed, growing up. We're musicians. We create art, tell stories, and a bonus ... we get paid for it. More money than I know what to do with, Soph. I've never really cared about the disadvantages of it before. Not until ... you." He pauses, appearing to push his words around the lump in his throat. I feel as if he's trying to convince himself rather than me of his contentment in his line of work. "I've never really cared or wanted to drink in the culture of any country we've been to. If I could do all these things and experience a place with you, I would."

"It's okay." I cover his hand with my own. "Vanna doesn't know it yet, but she's going to be my travel buddy. We might even get matching T-shirts."

My attempt to make light of the situation I brought on unknowingly falls flat as a deep line of sadness pains his striking face.

A split second later, he regroups, sliding a mask of indifference in place. I thought I'd noticed it last night when he showed me to my room. He's a caregiver who takes care of everyone but himself and his own needs, and it's starting to show. Even right now, as he tries to make me feel better, he puts my needs before his own.

"I might get jealous if you start spending all your time with Vanna." A sprawling smile contrasts nicely against his olive skin.

I raise my chin, wiggle my brows, and try to lighten the mood. "I'll see you every night after your show, when I get to jab a hundred needles into your skin."

"There's nothing wrong with liking a little pain," he counters, his voice low, almost seductive.

"Touché, Mr. Collins. Call me a sadist then because I enjoy inflicting it."

It's apparent now that there's more to Oliver than the flippant, fun-loving persona that he feeds the world on a spoon. The truth of my recognition is solidified by the faraway glare etched in his olive eyes. I see a lot of myself in the reflection of them. Someone who had to grow up long before intended. A natural protector, carrying the burden of the world on their shoulders in a desperate attempt at lessening the load for their loved ones. Even though he seems fiercely independent, being denied the simple pleasure of exploring the streets without an arsenal of bodyguards or disguise will only keep him sated for so long. At one point or another, Oliver will have to open his cage and let his gilded wings soar. He will have to choose to live for himself, putting his happiness before others ... his band, and demand the simple pleasure of living. Not just existing.

He'll have to learn to be selfish. In time, we all do.

Which is exactly what I choose to do when I stand on my toes, press my lips against his, and clutch the nape of his neck. Warmth radiates through my body when our mouths part. Without hesitancy, Oliver invites me in with one brush of his tongue against mine.

The first night we met in my studio, when we shared our bodies in a frantic act of frivolousness, our mouths remained dormant, aside from the filthy words that skid out through pleas and roaming hands. Kissing felt too intimate then. Having caved to our mutual lust and desire, we forged a business deal as we came down from the high of our shared lapse in judgment. There's nothing about this moment that feels propositional.

This kiss isn't a lapse in judgment being made; it's fueled by my desire to be greedy, taking what I want without thinking about the consequences, and I want Oliver Collins.

My mouth goes slack. A steady rhythm thrums, and I savor the feeling of satisfaction from him kissing me back. Feeling more turbulence right now than while the plane was flying, I get lost in his gentle touch, tingling under his fingertips. This is about me though. It might have started with my selfish desire, but kissing him has taken on a new meaning. I take on the role of the caregiver, coaxing him with an awakened flame inside me. All the while silently begging him to surrender to me. Asking Oliver to let me take care of him with each caress of our mouths. I'm totally entranced, like a breathless eighteen-year-old girl, and my senses leap to life by the sensual kiss that comes to an end mere seconds before Mazen's steel voice ruins it wholly.

"Keep the humping behind closed doors. Thanks."

I clear my throat, and my pulse quickens in anger. "Says the guy who was frolicking, for lack of a better word, with the flight attendant who served me breakfast and lunch today."

He doesn't flinch.

"Womanizer, lady killer, modern-day gigolo." I step into his personal space, crowding him. That gains the attention I want. "I refused to believe what the tabloids said about you. I don't know what to believe now. When I look at you, all I see is a lonely fool that uses sex as an escape." Pot calling the kettle black. *Meh.* He doesn't need to know that. "At least I'm not afraid to admit that I have Daddy issues.

"If you want to screw your way through London, Spain, wherever else this tour takes us, be my guest. Just have a little respect for the women you're with, and *you* keep it behind closed doors."

Hiding my heaving chest, I purse my lips as a brief shiver fires through my veins. My heart thuds in my chest, its rhythm haywire from his closeness. Even with Oliver next to me, being caged in by two handsome men is doing something to me. Something I fight like hell to shove down.

The moment Mazen opens his mouth, I chastise myself for the fleeting feeling of wanting *him* ... and Oliver ... together.

"What are you, twelve? You can say fucking." He growls with a taut jerk of his chin. "I'm happy to report she was an adequate server and lay." His voice grates on my nerves. It's a wonder people even pay to hear him in concert. Looking over my shoulder, he turns his attention to Oliver. "Next time, join me in partaking in the Mile-High Club, buddy. Maybe she won't be as cranky then."

Images of the three of us flying in more ways than one resurface.

Don't even go there.

The idea sounds like the start of a Taylor Swift song.

"Are you even considered a part of the Mile-High Club if you couldn't even keep your dick in your pants long enough for the plane to take off?" Oliver asks as he palms my shoulder.

A knot forms in my throat. Although his touch centers me, the dirty, filthy thoughts I have of them both naked in the bed I woke up in has my cheeks coloring under the heat of Mazen's steady, dagger-shooting glare.

Pushing past the both of them, I descend the airstairs and land on European soil for the first time. A breeze ruffles my hair.

It's not every day that you get the opportunity to travel

to another country. There's a gait in my step that I refuse to let Mazen and his spitefulness diminish. I swallow down the incessant urge to throttle him that only roars when he's around and decide that I won't allow him to wreck my time abroad.

I'll dodge him every chance I can.

THE STUNNING REGENCY townhouse Ashton guides us toward was converted into a hotel with individual rooms. It welcomes us with its sprawling windows and light-cream brick exterior. There is an English country feel throughout the inside that reminds me that we're not in the States anymore. My eyes rake it all in, dancing from one piece of beautiful fabric to another pattern. Its traditional grandeur makes me feel high-class, and for a moment, I drink it in and pretend that this lavish pad is coming out of my pocket.

The thought almost makes me laugh out loud. I can't wait to call Lacey and tell her all about the digs I get to call home for the next week. With two shows at every stop along their tour, Oliver explained that it gives fans more chances to secure tickets. He wasn't joking when he said their overseas fanbase was just as big as their American fanbase, if not bigger. Every single show had already been sold out for weeks before he and his friends stumbled into my tattoo shop.

Happenstance, I think to myself, *really did me a solid.*

After the house is secured and my bag is delivered, Oliver shows me to my assigned room. I'm ready for a hot shower and a nap when a thud startles me from the trance I've been in for the last several minutes.

This life they live, the band and even Vanna, it's a lot to take in. Coming from a middle-class—that's even being generous—family, I never once dreamed that I'd be standing here in London, surrounded by a famous rock band.

I answer the door, and Oliver is standing in the hall, a beanie on his head, looking very devious in his all-black attire. I almost laugh in his face before he tells me that he and the guys are headed for stage rehearsal in their venue and will be gone for a couple of hours. It didn't occur to me that singers and bands of all genres still practiced. I just assumed that performers in their genre didn't require a lot of rehearsal since screaming was ... natural and not a mastered artform. Boy, was I wrong.

ON THE RIDE *from the airport to our hotel, Oliver schooled me on just how much goes into the preparation of a large show. From practicing their instruments to their vocals. Their crew preparing the stage and readying it for different aspects, like smoke, fire, and everything else. He named off all of the individual pieces that make a concert flow smoothly, and my mind drifted, scolding me. I felt like an invalid and a little dumb for having this misconceived notion.*

"We have to pay our dues with hard work and practice, just like every other musician out there. Sure, we can throw in a sexy purr here and there that doesn't take much energy. It does its job, drawing someone in. It takes a lot of work to

string together a song, putting important emphasis on words that don't fry our throats and make us sound like we smoked a hundred packs of cigarettes. The gritty rock sound doesn't come natural to a lot of us. It's something we have to work toward."

I nodded, taking in his words like a child being chastised for not knowing basic multiplication as he continued giving me a lesson I hadn't asked for.

"Don't you ever wonder why most musicians are physically fit? Rock and metal are fucking demanding. We use a lot of energy, singing and performing. Between diaphragm exercises, learning new riffs in a song, there's a lot of work that goes into being number one. We don't just hang out all day in our hotels, getting blitzed, and then go onstage for a little fun. Well ..." He paused, offering a boyish grin. "I won't say that's never happened. Usually, we work our asses off and party afterward."

"That sounds challenging," I said, mimicking his own description, at a loss for what else to say.

"A lot of various techniques and vocal range go into our famous demonic screeches. Not everyone is professionally trained, like Axl Rose or Rob Halford. Some are self-taught, like Mazen. Yeah, he has a vocal coach now, but he didn't start off that way. We were true grunge metal heads playing in Cannon's parents' basement for a decade before we all considered making music as a possibility for us. Add in the mental preparation that goes into performing for thousands of people, and ... well, it's easy to see why Mazen is such a prick." The warmth of Ollie's smile reverberated in his voice.

Having just sat through Oliver's impromptu school of rock lesson, my interest piqued at the last part. "How do you prepare for that?"

A smirk he tried to hide flattened.

"Before the jellyfish," he said, and I knew what he was going to say before he finished, "tattoo. I'd fuck away my stress. Now"—he rubbed the back of his neck, tension coiling in his brows—"I don't know. I'll find another outlet. Maybe I'll work out."

The car pulled up to our hotel, ending my lesson. "I'll text you when I can. Go explore with Vanna. Do all the things we talked about."

He curled his index finger under my chin and rubbed a small circle under my bottom lip with the pad of his thumb. Then, opened the door, and climbed out before he disappeared into another vehicle with the band, leaving me half absorbed by his gentle touch and half excited to explore all London had to offer. I was a ball of jitters as I stared after him and finally climbed out of the backseat.

HOURS LATER, with a bag full of Harry Potter merchandise, a Paddington Bear stuffed animal, and several samples of English tea for Lacey, Vanna and I make it back to the house before the band does.

"That was a lot of fun." I drop to the couch, stomach queasy from the copious amounts of pastries we tasted during our excursion.

Even with our tagalong, Felix—a security guard dressed in street clothes that Vanna already knew well from previous encounters—we covered a lot of ground around the city today.

"I don't think I can walk another step. My bedroom is even too far. My feet are so sore. I might have to crawl there." I pretend I'm joking. In reality, I'd rather saw my feet off at the ankle with a rusty kitchen knife than actually have to walk to my room.

"I told you you'd be sorry before we left. You're the one who refused to believe me and wore those boots with wedges," Vanna teases while removing her comfortable, low-ankle running shoes.

"Fashion over comfort." I wince. "Lesson learned. I'm ordering sneakers tonight. I cannot do this again, and we have more to see."

Vanna plops down next to me, the cushion barely dipping, thanks to her small physique. Eyes glossed over in adoration, she beams. "Don't worry about it. There are perks to being engaged to a member of Kings of Jupiter," she raves while trying her hand at an English accent. The attempt falls flat and leaves my already-hurting stomach clenching tighter from laughter. "Seriously though, you'll have so many shoes here tomorrow; you can just take your pick."

I've never had any real girlfriends. The thought of forming bonds and having to check in with someone every couple of days is exhausting. Most of the time, I don't even reply back to Lacey when she texts. Often, our threads just consist of memes back and forth instead of an actual conversation. It never fails; when she's hungry, she always refers to the classic meme where hot dogs are being thrown at that guy's face.

Female friendships take a lot of time and energy to cultivate. I don't have an abundance of either now, nor did I while growing up.

When our mom died, our sperm donor went into a steady spiral, turning to the bottle as a reprieve from his grief and responsibilities. Namely being a father figure and providing for his children. I was forced by his absence to drop out of high school and get a job to make rent and keep us fed. Bussing tables kept a roof over our heads and our stomachs full.

In hindsight, it might be my fault for Lacey's unhealthy hot-dog obsession. They were cheap, easy to fix, and until recently, when heartburn reared its ugly head, a staple of our weekly menu.

It was a pretty low point in my life when I started hanging out with a couple of employees from the restaurant and by chance met Knox. By day, he was the dishwasher at the place I worked, and by night, he was a tattoo apprentice.

In any interview I've ever given, I've always voiced my appreciation to Knox. If it wasn't for him catching me drawing in the break room for a solid two months and offering to help hone my craft, I don't think I ever would have had the courage to show anyone my work. Much less make a career out of it.

Art has always been an escape. It started as small doodles in my notebooks and grew into a festering need to create to unwind my mind. Alcohol was our dad's scapegoat until it morphed into the harder stuff that eventually caused his own demise. Drawing became mine.

I can still remember the first time Lacey found my notebook. She droned on and on about how talented I was. I knew back then that it wasn't complete garbage, but I wasn't naive enough to believe that loving to create in any form could provide a paycheck. With a stable income as a goal, I obtained my GED when Lacey was old enough to go to middle school. Education was the key to success—or so the world told us. After I obtained my certificate, I enrolled in a couple of classes at the local community college, which took up most of my time, aside from working at the restaurant and raising my sister. I obtained an associate's degree in business, and the week after I graduated, I quit the restaurant and started my apprenticeship as a tattoo artist under Knox.

He taught me everything I know. I'll forever be indebted to him. The bond we grew runs deep. Just not in a romantic way—at least not on my end—but he's there in my heart nonetheless.

Between the budding empire Lacey and I built, as far as I'm concerned, I'm content where I am in life. Which leaves me in the hilarious predicament that my funeral will be like that video on TikTok where the casket slides down the stairs at rapid speed because there aren't enough friends in my life to carry it. It's slightly pathetic if I'm being honest. Maybe if Lacey bulks up and uses those dumbbells in her room for something other than a doorstop, she'll have enough muscle not to let me slide to my final resting spot when the time comes.

"I never indulge in the stuff the designers usually send over." Vanna's smooth voice pulls me back to our conversation. "I have morals and self-respect. They just haven't caught on yet that no one needs that many negligees in their carry-on bag. For you"—she bops my nose—"I can suffer through a breakfast with them though." Turning her attention to her phone, she fires off a quick message at lightning speed. "Done. Murphy's stylist said she will be here in the morning with some stuff for us to try on ... including tennis shoes. You're welcome." The wide grin she wears like a second skin suits her.

"If my feet could thank you, they would."

It's been nearly six hours since we arrived and took off to sightsee. Between our flight and my sore feet, all I want to do is shower and sleep. Vanna excuses herself to her room, and I do the same. When I settle on my bed, the chime from my phone draws my attention. I roll onto my stomach as my eyes roll, mimicking my body's movement.

There's a notification from the stupid dating app Lacey signed me up for—a new follower. I haven't given the app any thought, but the name *HempDaddy* has my finger hovering on his profile. I click it before burying my face in a pillow, silently cursing Lacey and her intolerable antics.

20

VIOLETS ARE BLUE

MAZEN

THE HIGH BEFORE a show is addictive.

I chase the sudden rush of adrenaline like one would the thrill of skydiving or dangerous lines of work, like firefighting. My line of work doesn't ever put me in the crossfire, unless you call hordes of people chasing you down an alleyway hazardous to your health. Oddly enough, it still lights me on fire from the inside out.

As a kid, I was the one in our house, always yelling, "Listen to this!" or, "Look at me!"

I've been performing in a sense since I was old enough to remember. As an adult and a paid musician, it's still the same. Except now, I have masses of people and employees vying for my attention.

My longing of needing to feel seen undoubtedly started within the walls of my childhood home. The only person who really paid attention to me then was my baby sister, Bethany.

When our manager, Nick, pounds on my dressing room

door, yelling we have five minutes to showtime, I revel in the blast of epinephrine to my brain. Nothing can compare to what this moment feels like. It wavers between a frenzy and pure exhilaration. The feeling isn't drug-induced, although I've tried to mimic this feeling more than a handful of times with several substances and really good weed.

My chest pounds, and my palms sweat, not in apprehension, but rather anticipation to be in my element. I almost feel like I'm a car, revving up my engine at a stoplight. I know that go time is nearing, and I have to pump my brakes to slow my racing heart.

Allowing myself to blanket reality, I push everything from my mind and solely focus on the present and my preshow ritual. It's the same one I've been doing for nearly a decade. Starting with twenty-five jumping jacks, fifty push-ups, and finishing with fifty sit-ups, just enough movement to get my blood pumping rapidly and my body amped up. I jump up and down, and thunder ricochets behind my rib cage. I take a deep breath, hold it, and redirect my energy, preparing to enter my sacred place—the stage.

It's the only place in the world that exists where I feel truly at peace, free. The voices in my head go silent. It's just me and my band rocking out and letting our souls catch fire. Our dynamic is powerful. Years of honing our craft as one rather than individual musicians have ensured that we're as in tune with one another as the instruments we play. Our mood and vibes feed off one another and are encouraged by our crowd.

Music is an open forum love letter. A declaration of promises beating simultaneously with a myriad of emotion and sounds. It's not just what I do; it's who I am. It's embedded in the depth of my soul, my own chorus dashing through my veins. In a language that flows through my soul,

I become immersed when I write or perform. Without music, I'm nothing. Just ask Lorenzo Wilde. He's tried to rid me of this passion for as long as I can remember, both with words and his fist.

Pushing thoughts of my dad as far away as I can, I focus my breathing the same way that an actor does. Most call us musicians. Truthfully, we're storytellers in disguise. I've been writing my own songs since the beginning. Hell, I've been jotting down lyrics since before I even knew what a melody was.

Songwriting is liberating. It's the only outlet that's kept me afloat in a life that's stolen much more from me than I care to bring to light. Music isn't just my passion; it's my lifeline. Kings of Jupiter means more to us than this wild world has given us. I know without the label, the money, and clout that we'd all still be making music together as a band.

The outside world ceases when we step onstage. We're sixteen years old, in Cannon's basement, playing our asses off. Strumming until our fingers bleed and our strings break.

My heart starts to pace as the sound of the roaring crowd calls to my soul, beckoning me to my rightful place on the stage. Everything around me is heightened. The noises of the audience, the fog in the air from the stage. Their energy fuels me; it feeds me and quenches my soul. Jumping up and down, I look to my left and then right at my brothers.

We're all here, ready to rock and fuck shit up.

WE PLAY our fucking hearts out. As our last song ends, my euphoria starts to wane, and the crowd dies down. I find myself floating back to reality, covered in a sheen of sweat and starving to death. Burning calories onstage from running around and the sweltering lights have me fucking spent. I wipe my face with the rag hanging out of the back pocket of my jeans. Our show went smoothly, as they usually do—unless you count the time we brought Jupiter onstage, and he pissed on Cannon's bass drum.

I usually don't scan the crowd much. After years of this, all the faces seem to blur. A tinge of disappointment covers me despite the way I try to shove it down forcefully because I did scan it tonight.

Fuck, I did more than scan it. I searched for *her*. I'm pathetic. I can't even stand her presence, and yet some part of me wanted her there. It's a foolish thought, but I figured if she heard me sing, the memory of our night would come rushing back into her mind.

She didn't come. Because she doesn't care. I hate that I do.

It sucks because we played a new song I had written. I claim I don't know why I wanted her to hear it, but I know why.

You stung me like a jellyfish ohh ohh
Your hands are toxic tentacles ohh ohh

I welcome their sting
I welcome their burn
I welcome the way your touch makes me yearn

*Out of all of the monsters in the big bad
sea, I'm begging you, baby, to keep
stinging me*

I should be relieved by her absence.

Triumphant.

It's what I've wanted since I realized who she was. Her company not only grudges up old feelings about that night, but it also strangely reminds me of ... Bethany. Another part of me, the part that remembers the night we shared so vividly, brings me to my knees, just thinking about it.

My sister's name alone has me swaying on my feet as I exit the stage, holding tightly to the rail as I make it to the last step and head straight for the greenroom. I lost two people that I cared for in the span of a year. One is impossible to bring back. The other ... doesn't remember me.

Another reason why it's best to push her away. I'm walking a tight line between wanting to shake our history back into her and wanting her to forget it altogether. I refuse to feel the pain I felt the morning I left her lying in my bed. In an act to preserve my own heart from shattering again, I must keep her at a distance. It's ironic that I'm the one who left without giving her a proper goodbye and it seems that I'm the only who has suffered from it.

Pushing Sophia away now, urging her to quit and go back home, where she belongs, is the only way to ensure that I won't crumble again. As bad as I want her to remember me, I'm not stupid enough to think I'll survive the wreckage that only she can cause me. I'm tough, but my armor was cracked beyond repair when my little sister died. I know I won't be able to endure losing someone else I care about.

Unless it's done by my hand again. I can control the outcome of this situation with Sophia. It's not only something I plan to do, but also something I will succeed at.

The door to the greenroom swings open just as the swivel of Sophia's gaze meets mine.

"I thought you were Vanna," she admits as her attention swivels back to the Kindle in her hand.

There isn't a care in the world written on her face. My existence means absolutely nothing to her.

Fury replaces all logical thoughts.

"Sorry to disappoint." I stagger to the bar in the corner of the room and grab the bottle of vodka I opened before the show started. When I take a swig, the burn warms my throat, taking the edge off the frantic feeling in my chest as I look Sophia over head to toe.

She's modest. Not like one of the females that squawk my name during shows. Sophia has an edge to her style that is poised with a flare of rage tucked away behind her charm. Time has certainly done her well.

While her waist is still slender, her breasts are fuller than I remember. Her cheekbones are more defined, and her sass has quadrupled. That's the biggest change, though it's not visible. I feel it the strongest. Unlike most women, aside from Vanna, who wait for us in our greenroom, she's fully clothed. The realization washes over me as my dick and brain wage a silent war.

I lean against the bar, watching her intently in this small pocket of peace that floats between us. I notice a visible flush on her cheeks. It piques my interest as I sip my vodka. Her eyes fill with a glow that sends a jolt of electricity through my body. I'm curious as to what she's reading that's stolen her attention. Being ignored is a foreign feeling, and I don't fucking care for it. Giving into my own curiosity, I close the distance between the bar and the couch, where she sits, legs crossed, her elbow on the armrest.

Sophia's attention flees from the device in her hand toward me, hovering for a nanosecond before her eyes search the dimly lit room. "Where's everyone else?"

I don't owe her an explanation. Words flow before I even realize I've said them. "The rest of the band went to the meet and greet."

"Okay." She averts her eyes to the door, narrowing them. "Don't leave them waiting then."

I slide onto the cushion next to her and kick my feet up on the table with a loud thud.

"What are you doing? Your fans paid for a meet and greet. It would be so shitty if the lead singer failed to make an appearance, don't you think? Or is that the allure? You don't care if your fans think you're rude."

"I don't give a shit about being rude or who thinks I am."

The closeness of our proximity is intoxicating.

Clutching her device in her hand, she leans to the opposite side of the couch. "That's painfully obvious."

Minutes pass.

I continue to watch her, oddly interested in what she's reading. Hell, she chose to sit in a room alone for hours while we played an epic show. Who claims to love music, comes on tour with a band, and then sits alone in the greenroom? That thought alone leaves me curious as to what she's reading, apparently so engrossed in it that her attention is glued to a damn device and not our stage.

"Are you going to just sit there and stare at me? I can meet you guys on the bus if you need time to unwind or whatever it is you do after a show."

"I usually get my dick sucked by a bitch or two to wind down. You offering?"

Pretending to gag as if sucking my dick is the most repulsive thing in the world, she rubs her distaste for me in further by adding, "Not by a long shot."

"*Le vecchie abitudini sono dure a morire.*" Old habits die hard. "You sucked Ollie's though." I use the moment to pull the e-reader from her hands.

The audible gasp and horror that accompany the sound is like a welcome mat into her mind. It's not what people are watching these days; it's all about what they're reading. Women are no exception. We did an interview after our book *Kings of Jupiter: Behind the Spotlight* was published, detailing the parts of our lives that were already swirling on the internet. Nothing new about us was brought to light. Nothing we hadn't already offered to the world. I remember the interviewer was dressed in a tight black shirt that left little to the imagination. Her silky blonde hair was curled, and it was apparent she wanted to drop to her knees and suck me off. She referred to books these days being porn for women, claiming that ladies don't watch porn; they read it. Remembering her statement and her luscious lips, urge my finger to scroll to the next page of Sophia's book.

"*Despite the slickness between my thighs, I hold on firmly to my resolve. Knowing that if it wavers, even the slightest bit, I'll be at his mercy ... all of their mercies. Because my body craves them all, separately and together.* "Is this what gets your panties wet?" My cock throbs in my pants.

Hoisting herself off the couch, cheeks redder than her hair, she shrieks, "Excuse me. That's none of your business."

"Roses are red, violets are blue, who knew one dick wouldn't be enough for you?" I chuckle nastily, knowing that my jab will elicit more anger while dodging her death glare.

Riling her up doesn't even come close to the maddening way her presence makes me feel. If I have to suffer, so does she.

She presses her hand against her breastbone in an attempt to regain her composure and the upper hand. "My sex life or reading material is none of your business." She turns into a parrot. "Give. Me. Back. My. Device."

"Rosella"—my accent comes out thick—"you made it my business when you screwed my guitarist. For someone who prides herself on being respected in the tattoo industry, you'd think you'd have higher morals. Who's next, Murphy? Since you're into sharing, are you going to weasel your way into their relationship now too?"

"Not that my career or ... anything about me constitutes an explanation to you. And you're out of your mind if you think that I would ever put a wedge between those two. Even if Vanna is a smokeshow."

I am here for a little girl-on-girl action.

"Morals are damned anyway," she huffs, settling back onto the couch, defeat on her face.

Her words weave a spell, and my thoughts flicker back to the night we shared. The night I became a man and awakened the beast inside me. He's been raging since. Unable to be tamed. Using women to fill a void that only one person could fill.

I SPOT *the woman who tattooed me earlier at the bar. She's changed out of her ripped jeans, worn sneakers, and black T-shirt. Her hair is no longer pinned up. It now cascades down*

her back, dipping into the curve of her waist. The black dress she wears accentuates her delicate frame. I plod over toward her, one mission in mind—to quench the desire she awoke in me when she inked my virgin skin at the convention.

She stops me with one look over. "I don't screw my clients."

"I'm not your client now, so what's stopping you?" I inch closer, closing the gap between us, not caring in the slightest as the bartender eyes me curiously from his position behind the bar.

"Morals." She sips her drink, glancing away.

"I can tell you're not a saint, Rosella. Morals are damned anyway."

"EARTH TO MAZEN." Sophia's voice slaps me in the face, drawing me back to reality.

I catch her glare, etched with concern as she furtively watches me.

"You drifted off to never-never land. Did you make friends with a ghost while you were there?"

"I don't have time for this." I toss her device onto the cushion and pull myself up.

"You ditched the meet and greet. Looks like you have plenty of time."

Sophia stands, looking all sorts of casual. It takes me a moment to regain my composure. Using my silence as weakness, she steps into my comfort zone. Drops of moisture from my performance still cling to my forehead. Damp strands of hair stick up in all directions as I run my hands through my hair.

"What do you want from me, Mazen?" she asks, her hand outstretched, landing on my forearm.

The action is solely to gain my attention. It doesn't stop the muscles in my body from tensing under her gentle touch. The warmth of her hand is like an iron grasp on my heart. As if her fingers were constricting the blood flow in my chest, I stand as still as a statue, refusing to turn away from her touch. A touch that I've yearned for, for far too long. I catch Sophia looking down at her hand, spread expansively over my arm. When she glances up to meet my gaze upon her, I slide my other arm around her waist, pulling her affectionately toward my chest.

I expect her to shake her head violently. To shove and push me away.

She doesn't do any of those things. Instead, she strains her back against my arm and lifts her head up to mine, her brows perked up in question.

"You want to know what I want from you?" I ask, mere inches from her mouth.

"Yes," she replies breathlessly. "I wouldn't have asked if I didn't want to know."

I reach up, cup her cheek, and tilt her head so that my mouth now hovers an inch above her ear and whisper, "I want you to leave." I can tell when my words resonate with her sharp intake of breath. "I want you to break your little contract with Oliver." I press my body closer; there's no more distance between us, and our hearts fight for dominance in their proximity. "More than anything, I want you to fucking remember."

Her voice trembles as she speaks. "Remember what?"

I take a step back and then two, pushing her away, all

the while wanting to keep her within arm's length. Her compelling green eyes bore into my cold ones.

"It doesn't matter." I regretfully shrug, my expression almost somber.

"It matters to me," she whispers as her eyes darken with emotion, like an invitation.

The depth of her eyes, like pools of desire, lure me to step closer toward her. I can smell her fresh citrus fragrance. I blink once, my glance sharpening and focusing on the ridges of her perfect, plump lips. I dip my chin, and our noses dance as I ask for access to her mouth.

My Rosella dominates me. Her beauty should be illegal; even more so, her empathetic nature should be outlawed. The idea of leaning forward and claiming her mouth once more sends my spirit roaring. I've been drifting along, killing useless time, counting down until this very moment.

This is so fucked. Disturbing in every way possible. She screwed my best friend. She doesn't remember me, and yet here I stand with my heart unlocked, dangling the key for her to take. Sophia's nearness, her concern for me, and my high from my performance all clutters together, kindling a fire of feelings in the usual place that beats for only music.

I take her roughly by the back of her neck, then relax my hand, holding her gently. She's weightless in my arms, just like I remember. The familiarity with our bodies leaves us both heaving out hard breaths. I lean forward, prepared to offer her a slow, tender kiss when she stops me with her hand.

"Please don't kiss me," she demands in a hushed whisper, but it's loud enough to cause torment in my already-fucked-up mind.

Closing the distance, I honor her wish by placing a tender kiss on her forehead. My movement causes a sharp intake of breath. And for a split second, I swear I see her remembrance of us and the intimacy of the night we shared dance in her darkened irises. The memory is searing a path, challenging her to remember.

Footsteps thunder down the hall, triggering our moment to end abruptly. My mouth is burning with fire that only Sophia's can extinguish. An awoken desire sings through my veins moments before Oliver's voice fills the greenroom, killing our vibe.

"Dude, where the hell have you been? Nick and Rodney are beyond pissed."

The friction from my molars grinding is a clear indication that I'm not drunk enough to deal with any of this.

Oliver's eyes dart back and forth between Sophia and me, hardening when I say, "She has a kink for orgies. You'd better watch out, Ollie. Your dick alone isn't enough to please *your* girl."

In a swift step, we're chest to chest, he and I.

Oliver opens and closes his mouth twice before settling on a stance and offering a warning. "That's enough." His voice rings with finality. "Go do a line, fuck a fan, anything that will occupy your time. You're done here."

"She and I aren't even close to being done, and you know it, Ollie."

My best friend falters for a split second before clenching his jaw, preparing for a war that we're both ready to battle in. I narrow my eyes, my back stiff by the blatant threat hanging from his tongue.

"If and when Soph voices that my dick isn't enough for her, it won't be yours filling that need. Trust me on that, Maz."

"We've shared a lot over the years, Ollie. Dreams. Secrets. Women. It's her call to make, and when she makes it, there won't be a fucking thing you can say that will stop me from having her."

"*Her* is right here." Sophia waves.

"What's mine is yours. That's always been your motto, right?"

Feeling lightheaded by rage, I narrow my eyes at him suspiciously. "You've never been one to beat around the bush, Collins. If you have something to say, don't be a little bitch about it. Say it."

"Nah. It's not the time or place."

Oliver might be the best man between us. I'll give credit where credit is due and take the insensitive road, paved with regret and rage that boils in my chest.

With a withering glance, I snap my mouth shut. The words I want to shout sit on my tongue, ready to plunge into him. I want to knock the smug look off my best friend's face and then tell him the truth about his sweet little Fireball. I want to offer him an in on a friendly wager. Betting that the thing that gets her panties soaked is taking her choices from her. I refrain saying anything about the woman he thinks he knows. The woman I fucked with unadulterated passion, over and over for an entire evening.

Pettiness gets the best of me. "I finally figured out why you and Sophia are so much alike. It's only taken me a week. Better late than never. You both only take and never give. That's why our buddy came to his senses. Isn't it? He knew you had nothing to give him but dick."

I aim to cut him deep. By the look of pure shock on his stubbled gapping jawline, I know I took my vengeance too far. It was a low blow. Realization of the pain I caused sinks in when Oliver's brows contort, and on an exhale, he saunters to the couch. Falling backward, he lets the cushion engulf him, eyes rimmed with surprise, glazed in fury.

We've never come to a blow like this one. Not in our entire friendship. *She's* ruining everything I care about. Everyone I care about.

Sophia stalks toward me, puffing out her chest. "You're a real piece of work." Her beauty, clouded by anger, is breathtaking. She beams in icy luminosity. "Sharing Ollie's … whatever the hell that was … is wrong on so many levels. But you knew that, didn't you? That's why you said it. To hurt him. Because you're hurt. You feel inadequate."

"Fuck this shit and fuck you both."

She doesn't budge. "You're just a sad little boy living in a wolf's body. Empty and alone, using words like a tool to gut those you pretend to care about. Just leave." She pushes at my chest. "Leave us alone. You ruined a perfectly good night, and by the looks of it, you're going to ruin a friendship just as well. Quit while you're ahead and show a little decency."

Her words snap something inside my chest, like a frayed rubber band.

"Decency was not kissing you senseless like your eyes begged me to do."

My response forbids any further argument. Rosella's face pales with anger as she stands, dumbfounded, sputtering a response.

Replying in a low, infuriated voice, she hums with finality, "Go to hell."

I refuse to tell her I already live there. It's my permanent address.

21

EPITOME OF LOVE

SOPHIA

MY RESOLVE IS DWINDLING.

Two shows, a trip on the oasis on wheels the band calls a tour bus that is almost as regal as the hotel we stayed in, and it's the end of the first week into my contract. My steadfastness is unraveling like a ball of yarn. Quick. With little to no effort. I'm surrounded by a group of men who are totally off-limits.

Especially now that Mazen Wilde called me out on the whole group-sex dream. I'd be lying if I said I didn't want him to kiss me that night after their first show. I'd also be lying if I said that the mere thought of Mazen and Oliver having words and then the three of us ripping each other's clothes off in a hot fit of passion didn't excite me.

It did. It does. A lot.

The men of Kings of Jupiter are stupidly beautiful, and they know it. And two of them know that I know it too. What a clusterfuck of a little predicament I'm in.

Lacey might have been on to something with the app

she signed me up for, KnockOnce. Though I will never admit that to her. I feel like I'm about to hump someone's leg, for Christ's sake.

Everyone's legs around me are safe for now, thanks to my innocent flirting with my anonymous acquaintance, HempDaddy. Which has quickly morphed into something else ... more depraved. Lines with my new friend have been blurred, like the miles of road we've spent on the tour bus. We've been messaging well into the evenings, sometimes all night, and oddly, his conversations have kept me sane. A healthy balance of twenty questions and phone sex without the actual images or phone chats.

That's how depraved I've become. I can come from texting.

Fuck. My. Life. I'm pathetic.

Whatever is going on between Oliver and me ... and Mazen and me ... blah. There is no Mazen Wilde and me. Regardless, my deep-rooted aversion to love is still firmly intact. I adore one ... and want to ride the other like he's a prized horse. I have needs that either of them can satisfy.

Needs that I aim to fulfill this weekend. Ollie's self-imposed celibacy means he's not able to help. Mazen's self-imposed jack-off personality lands him in the caution-tape zone.

As we land on American soil and I'm on the same continent as my mysterious texting companion, I'm going to accept his offer to meet up in person. My eyes roam over our thread of conversation on the app.

YESTERDAY

> HempDaddy: What's your dirtiest fantasy?
> Don't lie. I'll know.

TattooKitten: You first.

HempDaddy: I'm not scared.

TattooKitten: Quit stalling then.

HempDaddy: Railing a man while he's
railing a pussy.

TattooKitten: Wow.

HempDaddy: Good or bad wow?

TattooKitten: Good. I volunteer to be the
pussy in that meat duo.

HempDaddy: Your turn.

TattooKitten: What I'm about to admit …
might sound sick. You're a total stranger
who doesn't know my real name, so here
goes nothing.

HempDaddy: There's nothing sick about
human nature. Fuck anyone who tells you
otherwise.

TattooKitten: I have this fantasy of being
taken against my will.

HempDaddy: Keep going.

TattooKitten: I want someone to break into
my house and fake rape me.

TattooKitten: OMG, I sound like a creep. I
just want to be forced. I say no, but the
person knows I really mean yes.

TattooKitten: Forget it. This is stupid. We're
not teenagers, talking about what gets us
hot and bothered.

HempDaddy: The only thing I'm going to forget is you saying "fake rape." You want someone to dominate you against your will. It's called consensual non-consent. That's nothing to be ashamed of. How realistic would you want this little scene?

TattooKitten: I want it to be set up. Obviously. But I want there to be some authenticity to it.

HempDaddy: How authentic are you talkin'?

TattooKitten: I want someone to cover my mouth, deprive me of air, and fuck me from behind while I kick and scream and claw … and only when I'm about to explode with desire do I want him to expose himself to me.

HempDaddy: The app paired us because we both live in Tampa. Ya know?

TattooKitten: I saw that as well. Your point?

HempDaddy: My point is … watch your back, TattooKitten. I'm coming for you.

HempDaddy: There's nothing fake about my intentions …

TODAY

TattooKitten: Traveling for work. TTYS.

I fire off a quick message to … my friend. Hell, I don't know what to call him or this thing we're doing. *Sexting associate.*

I store my phone in my bag, ramming down my erotic rendezvous thoughts, and focus on the reason why we're fleeing London. I'm happy to be traveling back home to the States for more reasons than Murphy and Vanna's nuptials.

The off chance that HempDaddy will make good on his promise to meet is the reason for my smile right now.

Marriage is almost as appalling as tattooing an infinity symbol on an eighteen-year-old. There's nothing more unique than the most searched tattoo on the internet, said no tattoo artist ever. Tattooing fresh skin on barely legal females who get inked for all the wrong reasons is as exasperating as a marriage certificate. Two signatures on a sheet of paper doesn't mean shit. Sure, in theory, it's binding. I'll even go as far as saying that I understand the sentiment of it. But tie a bow on my head and call me a realist because it's a pointless concept.

Just like popcorn shrimp. Who in their right minds enjoys a tease like that? Why not just fry a whole piece of shrimp, something with—I don't know—actual substance? It's degrading to crustaceans everywhere.

Marriage is as futile as popcorn shrimp. I don't see what the point is when you can vow yourself to someone—mind, body, and soul—without the giant celebration. It's nothing more than a public declaration, a flag waved through the air, announcing your devotion to someone else. Pointless. Meaningless.

Regardless of my stance on popcorn shrimp and my known abhorrence of battery-operated vibrators, I loathe the idea of marriage even more. The notion of wanting to be tied to one person for the rest of your existence sounds ... dreadful, and that says a lot, coming from an avid reader. Don't flog me for admitting that. I adore getting lost in all types of genres of fiction, even romance. My lifelong adoration for fairy tales and happily ever afters—sans third-act breakups because that shit is so annoying—I believe to my core that love is not worth the eventual suffering it always brings.

My point is—and follow along because I am going somewhere with this—a marriage certificate, in the grand scheme of life, doesn't prevent relationships from ending. A thin sheet of paper from the courthouse can't ensure your heart will forever stay whole. Nothing can because we live in the *real* world and not a fictional universe, where the heroine and hero always make things work in the end. The harsh reality is that we're all jaded, flawed, and prisoners to impending misery.

Once the ink dries, it's as if the universe sells your soul to the highest bidder and marks you, ensuring a special kind of heartbreak is in store for each of us.

Lacey calls me a pessimist. I prefer to be labeled as a realist; refusing to sign up for that kind of pain, despair. I've done a good job of guarding my heart thus far. Don't get me wrong; I've fallen victim to lust more times than I can count on my hands and toes. I can get down with lust. It's love that sends my body into a giant convulsion—and not in a good way. It's wild ... reckless ... and in the end, it's always devastating.

Love makes people do stupid things, like making promises that no one can keep. Forever is an impossibility. A pipe dream. The promise declared when you sign your marriage certificate isn't yours to make. We don't control time any more than people control the weather; both are capable of ruining people's lives in different magnitudes.

There, I said it.

Giving voice to the truth is euphoric, I think to myself as I fiddle around in my seat on the plane and then secure my belt around my waist, buckling it as I keep my eyes averted from the beaming couple boarding the plane.

I'm as happy for Murphy and Vanna as one can be—while still getting to know them, that is. Sincerely wishing them the best in my mind, I attempt to tuck my thoughts away by focusing my attention on loosely braiding my hair. When Vanna passes my row, hand extended in front of her, entwined with her fiancé's, I curse myself for having such dreadful thoughts.

Their wedding is this weekend. Despite my aversion to marriage, I know I'll smile and clap when they share their first kiss as husband and wife. I'll hug them both and tell Vanna how gorgeous she looks, and you can bet your sweet ass that I'll enjoy a slice of their cake that probably cost more than a boat.

Momentary optimism aside, my wary thoughts resurface tenfold.

My mom and dad were the epitome of love. Solid. Their relationship had been built from years of friendship. As high school sweethearts, they had vowed their hearts to one another long before they signed on the dotted line, making their union legal. When death knocked on our front door, stealing her away from us like a captive of the night, their marriage certificate became nothing more than ash in the fire her absence left us with.

Life's tragedies are greedy. They swoop in, as unexpected as a summer storm, and steal something that can't be seen. Time. Every one of us thinks we're entitled to it. We look forward to it, count down to it, and wish it away without knowing that it's slipping through our grasp from the moment we take our first breath. Our lives revolve around a ticking clock. When tragedy strikes, time ceases for those impacted, yet the clock ticks forward. It doesn't stop moving. The world keeps spinning, and those around us, not impacted by devastation, continue living, blissfully unaware that someone else's world teetered off its axis.

When my mom died, a part of me died with her, as did the promises of time. I think the same is true for both Lacey and our dad. It was the summer after my sophomore year in high school. Any notion I had entertained about love vanished when her casket closed. When her earthly body was sealed inside, something inside of me clicked shut.

It's an image you can never erase. Seeing your parent, your idol, being lowered into the cold, hard ground. It hardens a person, which is exactly what happened.

Right then and there, as I stood with my feet planted on the lush green grass that had just been mowed around her newly dug plot and the breeze filtering across my shoulders, was the moment my heart turned to stone. Her death fundamentally changed the course of my life. It changed me. Hardened me. I was forced to wave goodbye to the exuberant girl I had been. In her place was a girl with questions that I'd never get the answers to.

How can love be endless when time dictates our happiness? Sure, you can love someone even after death, but it's not the same. Life isn't the same.

The day she died, my crimson-colored heart grew ten shades darker and has been dimming ever since.

The harsh truth—a truth I learned before I even started my period and adolescence welcomed me into its cultivating grip—is that pain is inevitable. It's an ominous thing that looms over us, waiting to strike when we least expect it. Pain doesn't always come by way of a sudden death, like it did when my mom's life was stolen without warning. It can come by anything that steals your joy, your reason for breathing. Rest assured that when pain comes, it's always swift, stealth, and always outside of our control.

At the age of seventeen, I had loved three people. My dad, mom, and my little sister, Lacey. They were the only people in my life who would ever hear that four-letter word from my mouth. To ensure I never felt an agony like losing my protector, my person, my beloved mother, I set up a perimeter around my heart, a safety measure of sorts, and took a vow to never give my heart to anyone ever, ever again. I faltered once and was quickly reminded that no man is ever worth the pain that comes from his absence.

I'm not fond of pain on an emotional level. Physical pain … in the bedroom … well, that's something that sets me free.

An inhibition fulfilled.

I attempt to swallow down my mom's memory and collect my thoughts.

Two huge shows back-to-back with thousands of screaming fans, demanding press appearances, and strict workout schedules have seemingly taken a toll on everyone besides Jupiter and me. The pooch and I have found common ground and bonded over our brisk walks down the streets of London. The first time Ashton let me walk him alone, I felt like I might have finally been accepted into the fold after all. Other than their love for music, Jupiter is the tangible being that binds them all together. My acceptance was short-lived when Mazen bitched Ashton out for taking it upon himself to give me approval to take the dog on a damn walk. A dog that doesn't belong to Ashton, as he was reminded of when reprimanded by Mazen.

I'm relieved when Oliver takes his place next to me on the plane. I attempt to do a better job of keeping the notion of marriage out of my mind. So, when Oliver hands one of his earbuds to me, I accept it greedily. I want to drown out my own thoughts, replace them with whatever song that he chooses, welcoming the distraction. I choose to resonate in the lyrics that he's feeling right now. Something I've learned over the last few days in London with the band is that music isn't only their job; it's their passion.

Both Cannon and Oliver use it as an outlet, a voice, a comfort. They've both lent me one of their earbuds during each of their tattoo sessions with me. Most of the time, they pick a song first, we listen, and then it's my turn to do the same. It was almost eerie the first time Oliver did it, as he followed Cannon's tattoo. We take turns, talking through songs and sitting in silence, as I tattoo for hours on end. The first time Cannon did it, I recognized the gesture for what it was.

Oliver winces, saying he has a raging migraine before he pulls the hood of his sweatshirt over his head. Instead of talking, like we normally do, he hits play and then closes his eyes. "Bloody Valentine" by Machine Gun Kelly booms from the earpiece, and my heart constricts as I try to understand the message he's trying to tell me from the lyrics playing between us.

We haven't once talked about Mazen's commentary following their first show. We pretend like nothing out of the ordinary was said. It's not like I hadn't already had an inkling that something was between Oliver and Cannon that far exceeded a typical friendship territory. It was reassuring when Mazen voiced and confirmed my suspicions, although I know his words were purposeful. He used them like a knife to cut Oliver, and he drew blood. I haven't been around long, but I know the cut was deep and unwarranted. He took a jab at his best friend because he was irritated by me. For whatever unknown reason or issue he has with me being here, it's starting to fester into his relationship with his bandmates.

Now, my presence seems to have also festered into … appeal. He made his intentions toward me crystal clear.

Eventually, the hum of the engine, paired with the midnight sky and dim lights throughout the plane, lull me to sleep. Oliver jostles me awake as the plane starts to descend. A layer of sweat covers the nape of my neck; instinctively, I feel like I could use a shower. I must've drifted off right after takeoff, plagued by the memory of my mom's laugh, her tight embrace, and the way she used to make stuffed French toast on every birthday or special occasion. The faint taste of cream cheese, sugar, and a hint of lemon juice lingers on my tongue.

I don't fault Murphy and Vanna for being in love, but I can't lie and say that their upcoming ceremony doesn't send me to a place that isn't good for my soul.

A place where marriage, time, and love are worth the pain. Although, in the pit of my stomach, I know that isn't true. True love is about as far-fetched as winning the lottery.

Except it's not a dream of mine at all.

The idea of it is my living nightmare.

22

GIORGIO ARMANI

SOPHIA

THE CHORUS TO "YOU AND ME" by Lifehouse hums through the humid summer night. Murphy and Vanna's guests, including me, rise from the chapel-style pew seating and stand, a blanket of stars above us. I've never heard of a night ceremony before, much less attended one. It helps that Murphy's parents own this place, built from love and family legacy.

Miller's Meadows, a local winery, has been passed down for a handful of generations, and it shows. From the luminous lights twinkling, to candles that have been sporadically placed on the lawn, to the small lanterns hanging off branches in the large oak trees that surround us, this place is well maintained and cared for. The sight is truly magical. If I wasn't so opposed to love, I might be smitten by their enchanting, well-designed ceremony.

At exactly eight o'clock on the dot, the song ends, and our attention is drawn from the back of the aisle, where the bride normally appears from, to the front, where Murphy stands. His stance is both confident and exuberant as he turns on the microphone in his hand.

"As you all know, my beautiful fiancée is Cambodian. Out of respect to my future in-laws and their culture"—he nods toward Vanna's parents, I assume, as looks of adoration well in their eyes when their gazes meet his—"it's important for us to uphold a few Cambodian traditions on our special day."

It's then I notice a small red string peeking from his cuffed arm.

"Under your seat, you'll find silk strings in different sizes. The bride and groom are known to wear these for at least three days to preserve good luck. I figured it couldn't hurt if everyone wore them." The throaty laugh that flows from him is overruled by the crowd's laughter bellowing into the evening air.

I watch in wonder as he hands the microphone to Mazen, who appears at his side. Mazen slides the mic into the back pocket of his black dress slacks, his eyes never leaving the aisleway, and makes his way back to the pew where we're all seated.

It's amazing what a tailored suit and hair gel can do. The four of them don't just look dapper, they are the epitome of dapper. From the smooth way Cannon's beard is combed, to the tie holder that is tied around Murphy's dreadlocks, keeping them pushed back out of his face. My eyes drift to Oliver, and a breath catches in my throat at the sight of him. Sitting there with his hair combed back, toned physique accentuated by his couture suit and excellent posture, one might assume he's a Giorgio Armani model, not a Grammy-winning musician.

I'm surprised to see him already looking at me when my eyes finally trail to his face.

Oliver sends a wink my way, and if I had ovaries, they'd surely tighten. I might have a serious abhorrence to love, but not sex. Definitely not sex. Sex I can do. Easily. Without feelings getting tangled up and involved. Which is why I ignore the sudden spur of nerves that constrict around my heart. The music starts again. Vanna appears in a gorgeous, fitted dress, looking every bit as exquisite as I knew she would today. She mentioned on the plane ride that it is customary in Cambodia for the bride and groom to greet each other with their palms together—a motion called Som Pas. As she nears her fiancé, she lifts her hands. Murphy mimics her movement, and they both bow ever so slightly.

Sitting in our pew atop a bed of lush green grass, I glance around noticing that their guest list includes members of the band's management, label, and several staff and crew members, as well as hordes of relatives and friends. The actual wedding party is nonexistent. When the guests started to be sat, Oliver ushered me to the second pew that said *reserved*. He guided me to our seats and let me sit before he sat next to me at the outside of the pew, closest to the aisle. Cannon took his position on my opposite side, and Mazen capped the end of our oak-stained pew.

Hushed whispers harmonized with the sound of shuttering as several cameras clicking went off around us, and I kept my head down, eyes glued to my fingernails.

When the music hums, I smile widely as Jupiter takes his rightful place at Murphy's side, wearing a red ribbon tied around his neck. Vanna's sister walks down the aisle first, a hostile scowl on her face present as she passes by our pew. Her eyes unsubtly keep drifting to our general area from her position in the front pew, undoubtedly toward Oliver, who seems to not notice her blatant wrath. Vanna filled me in on his and her sister's short-lived fling, which is how I know with certainty that her metaphorical daggers are not intended for me.

A surge of guilt for being seated next to the perpetrator causes me to shift slightly in my seat. The gold slit on my dress falls open, revealing the creamy expanse of my leg just as it collides with Cannon's dress pants. Our accidental touch causes him to freeze, his body becoming stiff next to me. I half expect him to turn into a gargoyle statue for the rest of the ceremony. Much to my surprise, he finally lets out a breath and resumes bouncing his leg in a seemingly uncomfortable tic.

We continue to sit and watch Murphy and Vanna declare their love for one another in front of their closest family members and friends. Under a magical blanket of stars, a full moon, and surrounded by people who support their unwavering bond, they recite their vows. Vulnerability in both of their shaky voices floods the air, thickening it with purpose, with the intent to bind two people together forever. There's a physical pull between them, almost electric, like a live wire on the verge of sparking. That's what the display of their love reminds me of. An explosion of sparks.

After they exchange vows and their nuptials are complete, Murphy takes his bride's face in his hands, leans down until his forehead rests against hers, and speaks softly to Vanna. I don't know what he says; no one does. I think that's what Murphy intends. A moment with his bride.

I watch in wonder as the words he whispers resonate on Vanna's delicate features, and she nods, looking up to her husband with glossy eyes and unshed tears, and then they kiss, sealing their fate and future. A tinge of guilt shoots through me, a spear to my own heart, as an invading feeling of remorse curses through my veins. I watch as their lips meet in the tenderest and most passionate kiss I've ever been privy to. Rational thoughts go haywire, and I immediately scold myself silently. Condemning my thoughts about love and marriage being a waste of time. Oliver's arm, although already draped behind me, wraps around my shoulders, and he squeezes me tightly. I feel the warmth of his touch; it radiates down my arms and warms my cold, guarded heart.

My jaded perception of wedding ceremonies is a tad skewed. Lacey and I, unapologetically, are addicted to trashy television. The more drama, the better, and if the show title starts with *The Real Housewives*, I can guarantee we've seen it and streamed it a thousand times. Sipping on boxed wine in our pajamas and snacking on popcorn or whatever concoction we come up with have seemed to have altered my brain chemistry because as the ceremony comes to an end, it's easily the most intimate thing I've ever witnessed both in person and on television.

As soon as the newlyweds saunter back down the aisle, a crowd of workers start moving pews and shifting tables to their liking. In record speed, a dance floor now becomes the focal point of the outdoor area, where people start to loiter, me included. I'm put out of my misery of standing like a creep, alone like a sore thumb, when Murphy comes to my aid and asks if I'm ready to give them their initial tattoos.

We saunter to a room, and I prepare my equipment. The prep takes longer than the actual tattooing since the initials I plan to tattoo on each of their ring fingers is smaller than a dime. Murphy slides both his and Vanna's wedding bands onto a necklace and secures it around his neck and then offers me a wad of cash, which I decline, before he whisks his bride away. I quickly clean up my makeshift studio and saunter back outside to enjoy the party and the free drinks since I'm officially off the clock.

The gold sequins of my dress shimmer under the moonlight where I stand, perched against a high table, clothed in a thin, sheer fabric. Music floats through the air in a melody that has guests swaying to the beat, losing themselves in the moment. I watch in wonder from my spot at the side of the dance floor, nestled against the table as I wait for the waiter to return with another glass of champagne. I'm not usually a big drinker. I don't like not being in control of myself. Considering how very attentive the staff has been this evening, I allow myself some freedom to relax and check my responsibility for the remainder of the evening.

With liquid courage running through my veins, I sway on my feet, making a mental note to ask more about Oliver's past with Cannon when nothing else is preoccupying us this evening.

Where is Oliver?

If this wedding has taught me anything, it's that the bond between Murphy, Oliver, Cannon, and Mazen runs deep. They're more than friends; they're family, and that family dynamic was assembled long before I boarded their tour bus. Although I don't feel like the total outcast I did even a couple days ago. My union with their lovable dog and Vanna has won me some brownie points. I still feel like I'm living in a foreign world, even with our feet once again on American soil.

My phone dings and vibrates in my palm. My eyes dart around the dance floor—looking for exactly what or who I'm not sure. I tap my index finger against my bottom lip, debating on opening the new message on the dating app that's taunting me because I feel like I'm going behind Oliver's back. Even though we've only had sex once and we've never once had a discussion about us. I don't even want an us. Do I? Shit, this is why feelings can never get involved in sex. This thrill of messaging a stranger, sharing my darkest, most intimate thoughts, is invigorating, and nothing remotely close to discussing our feelings is involved. Fantasies? Yes. Feelings? Hell to the no. I'm convinced Lacey knew what she was doing by installing the app on my cell and logging me in without my knowledge. I'll make sure to get her an extra Christmas gift this year as a thank-you from my famished sex drive.

HempDaddy: 121 Rocking Hill Ave. Room 34. Midnight. Check in at the front desk. A key will be waiting.

TattooKitten: A little presumptuous, aren't we? I told you I was traveling for work. What if I can't make it?

HempDaddy: I don't offer rain checks.

TattooKitten: I'll see what I can do.

HempDaddy: It'll be your loss.

TattooKitten: Before I agree to meet you, I have one question. What's with the screen name, Hemp Daddy? Are you a stoner or something?

HempDaddy: Stoner is such an old-school term. I have a job. I pay taxes, and I smoke some herb on occasion. So what?

TattooKitten: Just curious.

HempDaddy: I like plants too. Succulents mostly. They're easy to keep alive. I assume you like cats based on your alias.

> TattooKitten: Not at all. I loathe cats. I'll explain in person.

> HempDaddy: You're coming then?

> TattooKitten: You have a 50/50 chance, stoner boy.

> HempDaddy: Stoner daddy to you.

Moonlight shines down, raining a dim light over the celebration as a faint breeze dances along my shoulder blade. I can't tell if it's the wind or the stir of excitement in my gut that has my cheeks growing warm in anticipation of where the evening will end. With my hair pulled to the side, pinned with intricate bobby pins, a wisp of hair tickles my now crimson cheek. I was aiming for a classy but feminine touch and went a little heavy on my eye makeup. In theory, Lacey aided me, instructing every stroke of the black and gold shimmer I applied while on a video chat with her earlier.

I take another look across the dance floor, my eyes sweeping over the joyful faces of everyone in attendance, gauging if anyone is looking at me. Bellowing laughter flows like alcohol as people spin and spin with different stages of enthusiasm written on their faces.

I can't tell if it's my excitement for the clock to strike midnight or the sudden feeling of a tight grasp that snakes around my arm, causing chill bumps to form and spread over my body like a wildfire.

"Aren't you lovely? One might say you're more alluring than the bride herself," a thick Italian accent coos from behind me as the grip on my arm intensifies. "You're too beautiful to be a stagehand."

An inexplainable look of dread washes over me as I turn

on my heels and come face-to-face with a man with salt-and-pepper hair, looking to be in his late fifties, staring back at me. His coal-black eyes, shielded by thick, dark eyebrows, drink me in from head to toe like I'm naked, ripe for his taking. It takes every morsel in my being not to shriek from his repulsive glare. He ponders to himself, eyeing me up and down without an attempt to hide his perusal over my body.

"Ah. You must be the new stylist. I can see that." The whiff of strong cologne, laced with the hint of a lingering cigar scent, fills my senses, and I physically recoil.

Keeping my expression void of the heavy banging in my chest, I offer the man an unresponsive smile, one that says, *I'm not panicked by your crude assessment of my body.*

"I'm sorry, I thought you were my date." My heart hammers in my eyes, and I lean forward, ready to whisper again, but the words get caught in my throat.

"There you are, *my* Rosella." The heavy way his lips quip out the word *my* has me questioning Mazen's intentions.

My skin goes ablaze when he pulls me into his tight embrace forcefully. His muscular arm tightens, staking claim around me for some unknown reason. I start to open my mouth and refute the insane gesture of affection he's demanding before he dances a chaste kiss across my temple, causing my words to lodge in my throat. My heart freezes. Several beats must have skipped because I feel faint. Mazen turns his attention quickly to Cigar Man, bringing my gaze along with his. If looks could kill, the man before us would turn to ash and blow away in the wind.

"She does look beautiful, Dad. I'm a lucky man."

My spine violently stiffens, not solely from the identity of the man with a stark contrast to the one holding my body captive, but also because of Mazen's statement. *She does look beautiful.*

I'm on the verge of electrocution from the currents that Mazen's touch brings, robbing energy through my limbs as he holds me into him, pressing me into the curve of his front. In an attempt to shield me from the vile man who continues to eye-fuck me despite his own flesh and blood telling him that I'm off-limits. This vile man who has no issue dissing the bride while he's a guest at her wedding is Mazen's father. Their ill-mannered commentary is uncanny. My pulse leaps under his touch.

"Dad?" I side-eye Mazen, a clear question in my serious tone.

"Did I forget to tell you my dad would be here, baby?"

I clench my teeth, reining in a gasp as he closes the gap between us. He nuzzles his nose at the base of my ear before dropping his voice to a whisper. His voice is a low timbre when he hoarsely pleads, "Play along, please."

23

DADDY DEAREST

MAZEN

"LONDON WAS FASCINATING." She shakes her head, clearing it like she forgot I told her my father would be in attendance and she would be meeting him for the first time. "It must've slipped your mind. You've been preoccupied, killing it on tour, Teddy."

My fingers stab into her side when she utters the pathetic pet name. I give her a cut-the-shit-or-else glare.

Teddy.

My father demands our attention. "You must have my son confused, *bellissima*." Beautiful.

His eyes trail between Sophia and me, traveling south to where her slim, gold-covered body meets mine. I look back up and catch him rubbing his hand over his freshly shaven jaw before it clenches. His dark eyes hood as he continues his assessment, eyeing us both conspicuously, deep in thought.

"He's not soft, like a child's insignificant teddy bear. I raised him better than that. Wilde men are hard, strong."

There's an unmistakable grit in his tone. "That nickname is a humiliation, just like his little musical hobby."

"You're right, Mr. Wilde," she agrees, and a heaviness threatens to pull me under.

My father glances up from his appraisal of his watch and locks eyes with Sophia. His glare says, *I'm always right.* Positioning her gold-sequins-covered body in front of me, in a slow, seductive prowl, she backs the mound of her ass into my front, making herself an unpaid referee between my father and me.

When she presses into my core, the subtle movement has my hands darting to grab her hips to hold her steady and prevent any more friction from her cloth-covered ass with my already-bulging dick. I bite the inside of my cheek as a memory of our one shared night together threatens to take over. The callousness of her voice brings me back to our heated exchange.

"He's not soft." Her eyes dart from his back to mine as she looks over her shoulder to peer at me. "He's hard, so viciously hard, in *all* the places that matter to a woman." Sealing her statement, Sophia leans her head back to rest it on my collarbone, then grabs my hand and splays it across her lower abdomen before slowly swaying to the beat of the soft music wafting around us without offering him another word.

My father's posture stiffens. Years of honing his emotions, caging the beast that eats away at him, have been futile as he stares at Sophia. He's impressed, which isn't good.

Anything I've ever had for myself stood as a threat to this man. He's fractured beyond repair, just to spite me. The only thing he hasn't been able to rip from my hands, the only thing that I've done for myself without his name tied to it, is my career in music. He hates that I've accomplished something for myself without his aid.

I can hear these thoughts running as he barely keeps his annoyance in check. The loudest thought, the flittering movement of his eyes speaking for him, is envy. Sophia stood up to him—for me, no less—and threw him for a loop. The fucker revels in breaking people, exposing them, and does it all without ever getting his own hands dirty. He thinks it's a talent, something to be admired that people are willing to do his dirty work for him just to stay in his good graces. It makes me sick, as does the proximity of his thrust-out chest as it heaves with the anger he's attempting to keep at bay.

The bastard makes no attempt to hide the fact that he wants to reach forward and claim the woman swaying in my grasp, her body positioned in front of mine with force. He wants the coveted object in my arms simply because it appears to him that she's mine.

His fiery eyes scorch mine, demanding a rematch.

Sophia's body stills. Turning, she faces me. "I'm parched, baby," she hums in an emotion-rich voice, not using the ludicrous nickname she unwisely tossed around moments ago. "I'm going to the bar. Can I get you anything?"

Her acting skills are fucking riveting. I have half a mind to do a background check and see if she took theater. Dipping toward me, she brushes her warm lips against my mouth. Without warning, her mouth parts, and her tongue darts out and slides across my entire bottom lip in probably the loudest declaration of possession that I've ever experienced.

Holy. Fucking. Shit.

This girl deserves an Oscar.

She was right about one thing; I am hard and not because of the asshole who raised me. I don't know how I'm ever going to repay her for this. Hell, I don't even know why she's playing along. I've baited and been a downright dick to her all week, and then I tried to kiss her and fucked shit up even worse. She could have told me to piss off and left me to deal with him alone and been justified in doing so. But she didn't.

Why?

Recovering from her assault on my mouth, I turn my attention back to my sperm donor, who continues to appear unraveled by her outward flirtation and worship of me.

That's right, fucker; someone actually cares about me.

It's eating him up inside, uncoiling his perfectly wound exterior. The shell of his face cracks just a tad before his lips thin in a sure sign of his rising fury. Even if this little tryst between her and me is just a front, seeing him visibly tormented, shifting in his expensive tux like the cloth alone is causing him discomfort, is the biggest win I've had in a while.

As much as I want to continue with this charade—fuck, do I ever—a part of me knows flaunting Sophia around him isn't good. He's dangerous, and now, he's pissed from seeing me happy, adored by someone who isn't under his control. Parading her around him is only going to paint a giant target on her back.

"I'll come with you, Rosella." I swing my arm around her waist. "Nice seeing you, Dad. I'll catch up with you in another couple of years." I turn with my hand at Sophia's back, ready to walk away, when the shaky voice of a woman chimes from behind us.

"Mr. Wilde, can I please take your photo?"

I'm not surprised in the slightest when my father answers first, "Absolutely. Make sure you get my good side."

Like he has one of those.

"I'm sorry. I meant, Mazen and his date," the photographer states wryly.

I look toward Sophia. Her luminous eyes widen, and I silently ask for her permission. Getting photographed with me or any one of my bandmates will change things. Being in the public eye comes with trouble, usually not the good kind. I didn't ask her when I took matters into my own hands and claimed her as mine in front of my father. It was a knee-jerk reaction to seeing him standing there like a wolf, eyes roaming, neck pulsating, ready to pounce on her. A tether snapped, and I was at her side with a fabricated story.

Sophia nods slightly, accepting her fate, as if being photographed with me isn't going to turn her world upside down. The corner of my mouth slides into a smile as I turn to face the photographer and then my father. I pull her body close to mine, once again taking notice that the gold in her dress matches the thin line stitching alongside my tie.

Fake or not, I possessively wrap my hand around her waist and pretend that she's been by my side for a lot longer than she has.

"One, two, three," the woman with the camera mumbles before the shutter sounds.

I don't see the flash of the bright light resting at the top of her camera because as Sophia smiles at the photographer, I smile toward her, drinking in the beautiful woman beside me.

"Lorenzo." Mr. and Mrs. Miller—Murphy's parents— saunter over to where we're standing.

The way they call him by his first name sends a shiver of torment through me. Like most people in our circle, they don't know what lurks mere inches below the smile and web of lies he has weaved. Being a Governor will do that to someone. Make them forget about things that truly matter in their attempts to get to lie, steal, and fake it just to get to the top.

"So nice of you to come. I know with the recent election, you must be busy. We really appreciate you being here for our boy."

"I wouldn't miss the wedding of one of our children for anything in the world. After all, this one"—he nods to where I'm standing, Sophia still on my arm—"is all that I have left, and he's given me a run for my money. It wasn't long ago I forfeited the notion that he would ever settle down."

I fight the urge to swallow my own tongue. As I contemplate our move to excuse ourselves for those drinks we mentioned, my body becomes instantly on guard again when Sophia meets his glare, firing back at him like a grenade of spewing truth.

"I'd settle down right now if this one"—she playfully nudges me in the side, using his own words against him—"got down and asked."

The gruff sound of his voice counters icily, "He's not marriage material. You're delusional if you think you can change his mind."

Sophia is playing with fire and doesn't even recognize that her enemy is the devil himself, masked in Gucci and the tears of everyone who has ever went into battle against him.

"Rosella," I warn in a vain attempt to rein in the vixen next to me, "we wouldn't want to take the attention away from Murphy and Vanna this evening. We'll have time to discuss our future. I can promise you that." In more ways than one.

Understanding flitters across her ivory cheeks as she acknowledges my hint and excuses herself to the ladies' room. I'm thankful for her departure. I don't know how much fakeness is left to string together between me and my father. I use that term loosely.

A couple of tension-filled minutes later, Murphy's parents follow her lead and excuse themselves as well.

"Entertaining is hard work." Mrs. Miller's face creases into a sudden smile.

"I wouldn't know anything about that." I offer her a wink when I catch her eye.

"Cut the shit, son." Lorenzo Wilde, Florida's Governor, and elite asshole, seethes as soon as my friend's parents are out of sight and earshot. "I don't appreciate being made to look like a fool—in front of a crowd, no less. Why didn't you tell me you were seeing someone?"

He never once looks at me directly as he demands a snippet of my personal life, like I'd willingly share anything of importance with him. His eyes stay trained ahead, his attention being pulled elsewhere as he nods to people. Keeping up with appearances is his specialty. It always was. Even as our lives were sinking like a ship in the depth of the sea, all this bastard cared about was upholding our last name and saving face.

"What I do with my life is none of your business. You made that clear when you gave me the ultimatum of going on tour or going to college and following in your pathetic shadow."

Diverting his attention from the crowd, he finally turns to look me in the eyes. His face is bronzed by both the sun and the budding relics of vehemence. The uncanny resemblance in the irises staring back at me is like a punch to the face. Bethany took after our mother. Like a curse, I took after him.

"Was it too much to ask that my only son get a formal education and follow in my footsteps, making an—I don't know—actual career for himself?"

"You never asked. You demanded it, like always, and I did follow your footsteps once. Don't you remember? You do, don't you?" I step closer into his realm, anger fueling my every breath. "I wanted to be like you once, *Daddy dearest*. So much so that I took a life, on accident. You led my soul straight to hell on purpose. You didn't crash that car, but you put her in there with me. Her death isn't just my cross to bear. It's yours, too, and that's what kills you, isn't it? You were too busy kissing ass and securing votes in your little country club that you didn't realize I was drunk. Too drunk to drive." I open and close my mouth quickly, words failing to form at the memory of that night that changed the course of my life. I force myself to hold his glare, to keep his eyes trained on mine. "My soul will burn for eternity because of the choice you made, putting her into my car."

The sound of my walloping heart roars in my ears. He's to blame just as much as I am. Maybe even more. I wasn't in my right state of mind. He was. He willingly strapped her into my car. I swallow the hysteria that's beating down the last shred of willpower I have to not to pummel him in the jaw right here and right now.

"As far as I'm concerned you lost both of your children that night."

"Don't I know it?" He presses a fist against his mouth. "You won't let me forget that I failed you, her, our family." He's standing so close to my side now that I can feel the wetness of spit on my cheek as he grinds out his words, spoken in a hushed, suppressed tone, as to not bring us any unwanted attention. "You can't blame me ... hate me ... forever."

That's his specialty. Hiding things under the rug. *Her* memory one of them.

"Watch me." An arrogant laugh leaves my mouth. Its sound deceptive to the anger coursing through my veins faster than a bolt of lightning.

"I don't have to listen to this nonsense. You don't think I already hate myself, boy? I'm here, living in this town where her memory plagues me at every turn. Can't say the same for you. You ran off, joined your little band, and never looked back."

I shift on my feet, anger taking over my every thought.

"I came to offer congratulations to Murphy. I left a hefty wedding gift. I'm leaving now." He spins, turning his back on me, fleeing, avoiding the truth that haunts him, even when he's awake.

It's his signature move.

WHAT FEELS LIKE AN ETERNITY LATER, Sophia finds me, plopping down next to me at the bar. Her voice is a low cackle as she mumbles, "Hello, Teddy."

"How much have you had to drink?" I ask, my eyes never meeting hers, knowing that I've already made enough mistakes, provoking Satan's protégé. I guilted her into something that she should have steered far, far away from if she knew what was good for her.

"The answer is a mystery," she confesses, causing me to

turn in my stool just enough to see a soft light rippling across her pearl skin.

I reach forward, knowing that she's far too gone for me to scold. It's not fun being a dick to someone when they won't remember your callousness the next day.

"Why Teddy?" I ask, curiosity getting the best of me before I pick up a strand of hair that has fallen out of place and caress it gently between my thumb and index finger.

She shrugs, licking her lips. "You're the furthest thing from a teddy bear. *Cute and cuddly* is not how I'd describe you in the slightest, Mazen Wilde. It seemed funny in the moment."

My eyes stay trained on her mouth. An aching need to press my mouth to hers and force her to kiss me without him as an audience this time quivers in my chest and places further south.

The air between us thickens. I don't give a flying fuck where the bride or groom are; if Oliver is watching, ready to beat the hell out of me; or if a line of photographers is snapping hundreds of photos of us right now. All I care about is the way she stood up to my father for me like it was the easiest thing in the world. No one, not even my friends, has ever had the gall to stand up to Lorenzo Wilde.

Bethany did though. She would give him hell for treating me like I wasn't born from his flesh.

Fuck. Sophia is so much like her. Fierce. Relentless. Compassionate. Even more headstrong than my little sister was.

"There's nothing comical about that. I'm an excellent cuddler." I finally break the silence between us, going with an angle that not many get to see. "Would you laugh if I told you I like to be the little spoon?"

Taking a swig of the amber liquid in my cup, I miss her

facial reaction. The sound of her bursting into laughter hypnotizes me.

"Little spoon, really?" Her hand lands on my arm, outstretched on the bar top before us. Her touch scorches through my body, an electric shock, paired with a trace of seduction. "I would never have pegged you as the little spoon. You just keep surprising me." She diverts her attention to the lip gloss in her hand as she applies a thin layer on her lips, seemingly unaware of the power her touch has on me. "Your dad was giving off major Joe Pesci vibes, by the way." A bright flare of terror springs into her eyes.

It's my turn to laugh. The gruff sound that escapes funnels around us. The bartender looks at us like we've lost our minds, but I don't give his stare a second thought. We continue to laugh at my father's expense. If only he had stuck around to see it.

"Thank you." My mood takes an abrupt shift. "I ... hate him so fucking much."

"Why?" Stowing her lip gloss, she rights herself on the stool, turning in a sensuous path toward me.

My hands itch to gather her up, pull her warm body to my pulsing one, and fulfill the unsated need I've had since seeing her again. I want to bury my cock so deep into her wet fucking pussy, forcing her into an epiphany. I want to tuck her squirming body beneath mine, curving her into me, and leave her panting, chest heaving, writhing beneath me, until she admits she recognizes my face. And then, only then, when I'm certain she remembers me and our one night in Chicago, will I sink into her and fill her with the flood tide of sentiment I've had filtering through my body since I saw her again. I want our chorus to ring with the sweet agony of her moans as the creamy concave of her spine tingles from my touch.

I'm fully aware of her thigh brushing against my tailored pants. I exhale, knowing that these thoughts will remain mine and mine alone. As much as I want to shake her, revitalize her senses, and remind her of who I am and was to her, an indefinable feeling of assurance that our past has long been buried keeps me mute.

Sipping a lemon drop martini that magically appeared in front of her, she asks, "Why, Mazen?"

"He stole something from me," I admit, baring a piece of my soul, my truth.

When she folds her hands in her lap, I give her one last look before tipping my head back, finishing my drink and firing off a text to Ashton to pull the car around.

"Teddy," she coos softly.

Although the cynicism dripping from her mouth is amusing, it's the sincerity in which she says my pet name that leaves me breathless. I'm about to ask her about her acting skills when I glance over and see her immersed in a message on her phone. I glance at my own when an incoming text comes through from Ashton.

"What's got you blushing like you're about to take some-one's virginity?"

"What? I'm not. Why would you say that?"

"I'm only kidding, *Rosella*. Unless that's a kink of yours. I fear we're fresh out of virgins in our little powwow."

"I didn't know you could smile so much in one evening. You might want to consult a doctor about that. Your gloom-and-doom facade is slipping."

Climbing off the stool next to me, I watch as she sways. She never told me how many drinks she had. The way she has to steady herself, pocket her phone in her small clutch, and brush the palms of her hands down her gown before turning her attention back to me and patting me on my shoulder tells me that she's far past being left unattended.

"Where are you going? You're wasted. I'll text Ashton to get the car and I'll track down Oliver and tell him we're ready to go." I glance around, looking for my elusive best friend.

Oddly, Oliver's kept to himself since our run-in. He's usually the knight in shining armor in our fleet. Despite his hatred toward me right now for wanting what he thinks he's claimed as his, he's going to need to suck it up so he can handle his drunken tattooist tonight. I don't have the capacity not to strip her naked and fuck her into next week as a sincere thank-you for putting my father in his place.

Her smile falters as she bites her bottom lip and starts to sashay away. "The night is young. I'm just getting started. Do me a favor, Teddy." She peeks over her shoulder. "Tell Oliver to call me in the morning."

The young version of Sophia I knew has vanished. I can feel it in my bones. This version, the exquisite-as-sin adult is trouble.

The best fucking kind.

24

MUSIC TO MY EARS

CANNON

CANNON RHODES, *dark, brooding drummer for Kings of Jupiter.*

I'm the mysterious one that the media loves to speculate about. If they knew anything about me, my interest, or my particular desire to fuck both men and women into an oblivion, they'd have more to report about than why I never attend meet and greets or volunteer to make appearances.

At exactly midnight, the door of the hotel opens.

"Good girl," I hum under my breath.

I'm a simple man. I live to please and to be pleased. The promptness of my new lady friend's arrival is a special kind of foreplay for me. My yearning to be gratified is met by this one act.

I lick my lips in anticipation of meeting TattooKitten face-to-face. Knowing that she's standing in the same room as I am has me wanting to abandon my methodical plan and fuck her against the wall until she has an imprint of the frumpy wallpaper on her back. We've been messaging consistently for almost a week. It's been an opportune reprieve, thanks to the unending drama that this tour has been loitered with, since Oliver ambushed us by hiring a woman that Mazen despises.

Sophia's presence doesn't affect me in the slightest. It's Mazen who seems to have the biggest problem with her for some unknown reason that he refuses to talk about. Hell, she's beautiful in a natural way that most of the women begging to suck us off after our concerts severely lack.

I've seen more versions of silicone tits and bleach-blonde weaves to imprint my memory for years. Sophia's warm and radiant smile and the buzzing of laughter that seems to echo out of her brings a reassuring satisfaction to Oliver that I haven't seen in him in a long time. It's infectious. Something I know I'll never have since my tastes are ... diverse.

I peer through the dim light in the hotel room as my guest shuts the door gently, her palm pressing into the back of the wooden door. She hasn't turned around yet, reluctance set on her small shoulders. I imagine she's giving herself a mental pep talk.

She made it here and opened the door; the hard part is already done.

This week has been torture in the best imaginable way. TattooKitten's profile said she was from Tampa, which meant that if we were going to meet in person, it had to be this weekend while we were back stateside. I booked this room a couple of days ago with hope that she would accept my offer to meet in person. After sharing a smoke with Murphy and some of our road crew, I gave him my congratulations and dipped out.

The dark ambiance of the room calls to my soul, both empty and void. I glance around, noting the absence of decor. I quickly gathered up the hotel's decorative bowls and sconces when I arrived. My guest has a particular fantasy that I aim to appease tonight. Dropping a hefty penny to replace broken items isn't on my list to do tonight.

The filthy things that TattooKitten has admitted to me in our little bubble of secrecy has made my dick ramrod straight. I've refused to give in and fuck my fist, thinking of her. She's about to meet me, the version that's going to have her begging for release, not the famous rock star hiding behind a dating profile.

The woman is swathed in a skintight black dress, the expanse of her peach-tinted satin skin is on full display for my viewing. With my eyes now adjusted to the darkness surrounding me like a starless night, I take in all of her, including her hair that looks like a light auburn in the dimness. It covers her face like a veil.

I debated on demanding her to disclose her identity prior to meeting this evening. Refraining, I knew not knowing who was going to show up was half the fun. The thrill of the chase ends tonight. She wanted to surrender to the obscure, vile fantasy of being taken, used, and discarded. She wanted to be fucked by a ruthless man and filled in every hole against her will ...

Here I am, baby.

"Hello," the woman calls out, her voice slicing through the darkness.

My eyes hold her body in place, raking across her petite stature. They land on her delicately carved hips. I reach forward, my finger sliding sensuously over her bare arm, skimming down to her elbow. The air in the room shifts urbanity before I strike, winding a hand in her hair. She jerks away ... hard, turning from me. The quick, unexpected movement only causes me to reinforce my hold on her smooth locks. I slam my other hand against the cool wooden door in front of me. My pulse trembles with eagerness to fulfill her little fantasy.

"Hello." I lean into her back, pressing my center hard toward her ass and sigh into her ear.

Her body straightens, and her shoulders tense before I reach into the back pocket of my tailored tuxedo pants and slide out a black ski mask, securing it on my head before wrapping my free hand around the column of her exposed neck.

"You asked for this. Do you still want it?"

While there's nothing more I enjoy in this world than brutally fucking someone until he or she has lost all sense of reality, I'm not a monster. At least not one who would take someone against his or her will without prior consent.

"Yes." Her groan is music to my ears.

That's all the consent I need.

25

NO CLAIM

SOPHIA

TENTATIVELY, with nerves bundled in the pit of my stomach tighter than a corset, I open the door to the room number that was messaged to me and slide inside. With senses on overdrive, I shut the door, allowing the darkness to engulf me like a blanket or a body bag, which seems more accurate since this stranger very well could murder me tonight. The room is chilly, thanks to my attire. My heart races with a thrill and a tinge of trepidation. The absence of noise is disturbing.

"Hello," I mutter into what appears to be an empty room.

The lack of a returned greeting or acknowledgment sends a sinister chill racing up my spine. Rooted to the spot by the door, I turn my head slowly, and loose hairs fall around my face, shielding it. There's an outline of a man, the man I've come to meet ... to sleep with ... a mere inch away from me now.

On shaky legs, I inhale sharply as he finally speaks, breaking the soundless atmosphere. I practically pant yes when he asks, seeking permission for whatever it is he's about to do to me. That thought alone warms my icy body. He won't hurt me. Surely. Why would he ask permission if he was going to?

I deliberately take a step further into the darkness, stopping in the middle of the large room in front of what appears to be a red couch.

"Are you going to hurt me?"

He stalks closer, quietly. Electricity snaps like a band between us as he stands before me. Moving me into his caged arms, he firmly plants me on the top of the back of the couch. His eyes sulk for a split second before he challenges me in a deep voice that I want to ingrain as a core memory. It's so gruff that it's as if it's been dragged alongside sandpaper before it bellows from his lungs.

"Do you want me to hurt you?"

Smothering a groan, I nod.

My tacit consent sends the man before me into a thundering frenzy. In an instant, a rush of things happens all at once. One of his large hand circles around the front of my throat, and his fingers push into my skin roughly. His tight grasp pairs with the maddening throb in my underwear. The other hand hurriedly pulls the top of my dress down below my bra. A pocketknife magically appears, its metal glinting in the faint windowlight. He cuts the strap of material on my bra, causing it to spring open. My chest heaves, but not in fear or concern over my favorite lace push-up bra meeting its untimely death. There's nothing but a flood of arousal pooling between my legs by the crude act of *him* ... HempDaddy. I tilt my head up to his, staring into the darkness of his eyes, the rest of his face hidden behind a ski mask.

"Sophia?"

The sound of my name coming from the masked man before me sends my thoughts in overdrive and my hands folding in front of my bare chest.

My face flushes simultaneously to the scrambling of my brain as I wonder how this man knows my name. I'm immobile, a true terror now present in my gut.

"What did you just call me? How the hell do you know my real name?"

The hungry, lustful eyes that bored into me only moments ago jolt, morphing into something of indifference now as he stares back at me through the holes in his mask. An inexplicable glare of withdrawal mars his irises.

With teeth clenched, I wait for his answer, for a shred of explanation at his sudden change in demeanor.

I peer at him in wonder in the darkness before determination guides him to the wall. He flicks the switch, and light illuminates around us. In a movement that seems practiced, he drags the mask off his head and tosses it at me. I catch it with my hand, holding it for a second before looking up. My eyes meet his ... Cannon freaking Rhodes ... a moment before he opens his mouth with an agonized plea.

"I didn't know." He takes a step toward me. "I swear. Shit."

"Of course you didn't know. You couldn't have." A peal of laughter ripples from my parted mouth. "Lacey is going to die when she hears about this. I honestly cannot believe this. Fuck you, algorithms."

"Lacey?" His unfathomably sharp eyes assess me. "Algorithms?"

"My sister and the algorithms on the app for pairing us."

I run my hands over my face, thinking about how she's going to react to this insane disclosure before the cool breeze of my movement reminds me that Cannon cut my bra and I'm standing in front of him with my tits on full display. My nipples harden despite the predicament I'm in.

In one fell swoop, Cannon pulls his shirt over his head and motions for me to take it. "Put this on. I need you covered up."

"Thanks." I slide it over my head. The shirt dwarfs my body, hanging well past my kneecaps. "What now?" I chew the inside of my cheek. Uncertainty lingers between us. "Do I just leave? Pretend like this never happened? Do you block me on the app and move on to the next willing woman?"

Cannon's face turns to stone, his gaze unresponsive to my onslaught of questioning.

"Back to the silent treatment—noted."

My stride is wide as I head toward the hotel door, prepared to drive back to my apartment and wallow in a pint of ice cream and several glasses of wine. It's probably for the best. I'm already on the proclaimed king's bad side. I do not want to give Mazen more ammunition to loathe my existence.

A hand darts out, wrapping around my wrist, hindering my attempt to flee. My gaze travels over to meet Cannon's. A gleam of interest blazes in his lethal eyes. Under the lights, I notice that his chest, now bare since I'm wearing his shirt, is rippled with wide abs, stacked on top of one another. I drink in the expanse of his physique. Cannon's hard body goes beyond toned muscle structure and chiseled lines. It's something else entirely. Like a work of stone art. The beefy man in front of me has me salivating like I've been trained by Pavlov himself.

"What are you doing?"

"I'm leaving. What's it look like? I won't say a word about this ... whatever the hell we were just about to do," I quip.

It doesn't surprise me that he doesn't even incline his head. I'm taken off guard by his tightened grip on my wrist and the menacing way his eyes hood over.

I'm on the verge of exploding, a mixture of irritation and puzzlement lacing my tone. "Cannon, what do you want from me? Either use your words or let me go. It's been a long day. I'm tired, confused, and horny as hell."

"You ..." His stiff lips part.

The hard stone-like tone of my plea turns to rumble by his admission. A muscle quivers at his jaw, almost like it pains him to admit what he desires out loud. A beat of silence loiters between us, thick with questions, hunger, and hesitation. I take notice to the way his eyebrows draw down-ward, almost in a frown, like he's preparing for my dismissal. The angst-ridden look on his face is a far stretch from the purposeful, sinful illustration he wore seconds ago.

My heart tugs at the thought that this man—this broadly defined, robust man who plays in a rock band—has the self-esteem of a ... battered boy. I rock back on my heels before moving in and place my hand over the depth of his ripped stomach.

"Nothing good will come from this. Mazen already hates me. He worse than hates me. I'm pretty sure if he lost a card game with one of the guys from your road crew, he'd offer me up as payment for his debt."

"Mazen is a far cry from my master." His words cause an exhilarating shudder to reverberate through my small frame.

I remain motionless for a moment, my mind reeling

with a fleet of thoughts. Implications that fucking Cannon may bring. Will Oliver be upset? They share a past, a history that goes far beyond friendship. Would Oliver feel deceived by us both? We're not a couple by a long shot, yet I can't shake off the feeling that I need to seek his permission to screw his bandmate. Will this be the last straw that sends Mazen marching into battle with retaliation fueling his rage? I think we might have forged a cease-fire tonight. At least, I hope so since I so kindly stuck my nose out for him during the little feud with his father.

"What about Oliver?" I give a voice to my internal unease.

Cannon seems to ponder my question. I can't quite grasp the look that seems to flitter across his face. He opens his mouth and then pauses, shutting it. For a split second before, I wonder what he was going to say. Anger gets the best of me. I turn and stalk toward the door. Mind games aren't my jam. The sound of heavy, thundering footsteps echo as he treads into the bedroom.

"Wait," he demands, returning a second later with his cell phone in his hand. He plops down on the red sofa, typing out a message quickly, and then hits Send. Each thump of my heart reminds me of the tick of a clock as I stand, waiting for his phone to ding.

Which it does, repeatedly for a solid minute.

"Read." He gestures by way of tilting the screen of his phone toward me with an outstretched hand.

Me: Are you and Sophia together?

Ollie: Hello from left field. Define together.

Me: Relationship.

Ollie: No. She's not into those.

Me: No claim?

Ollie: Dammit. I like her.

Me: So do I.

Ollie: So does Maz.

Me: The king doesn't get to claim this queen.

Ollie: Can I watch?

Me: Not tonight.

Ollie: Fuck this stupid jellyfish tattoo. She's not replying to my texts. You're with her right now, aren't you?

Me: Yeah.

Ollie: Maz said they had a moment at the wedding.

Me: Now, she's having a moment with me.

Ollie: Be careful with her.

Me: She's safe with me. Don't question my ability to take care of a woman.

Ollie: I'd never question that. Just with her. Don't break her.

Me: She's no flower.

"It's as simple as that?" I suppress a sigh.

Cannon draws an invisible pattern on the armrest of the couch. "I'm a simple man."

I feign surprise, holding a hand to my chest. "You don't say?"

His eyes shift, not meeting mine.

Time dangles between us before he stridently professes, "I'm not Oliver."

Gnashing my teeth, I attempt to suppress a snarl. Oliver is the embodiment of easygoing. He's persistently happy, always trying to make not just me, but everyone around him laugh. He enjoys lifting others up. Oliver glows in neon, bringing attention to him wherever he goes. Cannon is midnight. The pointless assessment of their differences unnerves me.

"I'm not naive." Spite sharpens my tongue. "I came here to meet a stranger to screw my brains out and then send me on my way with nothing more than a sore core and chapped lips. I knew what I was getting into. Hell, I initiated this. I didn't know *you* were HempDaddy. Obviously, that news came as a giant flipping shocker. Pointing out that you're not Oliver is moronic. It's moot and infuriating. Ollie is adorable and sweet and comforting. But I need ... crave—"

"Stop talking. Now. Come here." Crooking his index finger, he commands me toward him. An air of power exudes from his every pore.

The sensuous authority of his gesture has heat emanating from my body. I round the couch, gliding toward him like I'm not in control of my own body.

I'm a puppet, and he's the puppeteer.

Leading with my breasts, I step forward, my hips swaying slightly as my eyes are glued on his. It's easy to see how attractive he is, being this close to him. He's aggressive and rugged and exudes a thick air of masculinity that has my core clenching at just the thought of what he is packing under the black trousers he's still wearing from the wedding.

Merciless lines carve his face as his eyes widen, almost as if he's drinking me up, getting his fill. I use the time to openly access the clear-cut lines of his profile. The icy-blonde hair on top of his head is pulled into a tight braid tonight. The side of his head is shaved, ink sprawling across his skull. I've only seen him with his blond locks down, hitting just under his chin. This look though ... is devastatingly handsome. His dark eyes coil around me, innately holding me captive.

Aside from his weathered exterior, he's mind-bogglingly beautiful. His features are so symmetrical that it almost isn't fair. Pairing his good looks with his natural talent for self-control leaves me wondering if he held a different career that didn't include being a badass, talented drummer, what would he be doing? Cannon is the personification of virile.

I make my way toward him, stopping just short of jumping on his lap. The back of my exposed knees hit the cool wooden coffee table resting directly behind me. Shifting my weight from one foot to the other, I'm curious how this is going to play out. Are we going to kiss? Will there be foreplay?

In a swift motion that causes me to inhale sharply, Cannon stretches both legs out, encasing me in the middle of them before he forcefully shoves the coffee table away from the couch.

"Sit." He leans back against the couch, no trace of pleasantry on his tongue.

I lower my body onto his lap in a loud act of submission. My eyes rake over his assertive broad shoulders as I lower myself on the audacious swell in his pants. He's a towering spruce, and I know he said I wasn't a flower, but his intimidating build and bulge have me cowering inward. My stomach drops as I remember Oliver's warning—*Don't break her*.

I'm not made of glass.

I'm certainly not made of steel either, and by the feel of his already-swollen shaft, I might fold by his touch alone.

26

DIAMONDS DON'T BREAK

CANNON

THERE'S something innate about a sexual partner handing themselves over to you wholly. It's the ultimate display of trust that I seek out in my lovers. The only attribute that is absolute. I need to know that he or she trusts me. Even if what I crave pushes them to their limits, I need them to submit to me that confidence.

Inconsequential specifics, like sex, race, and body type, are far second on my list of must-haves in a partner.

I'm an equal opportunity fuck.

Carnal thoughts creep to the forefront of my mind as Sophia positions herself on top of me, gliding her core across my lap. The minx knows good and well what she's doing. There's no amount of lash batting that can tell me otherwise.

She's here because we met off an app ... to fuck ... as strangers. Sophia lured me in with her sassy, fuckable mouth, banter, and adorable-as-hell plant jokes with no idea that it was me ... a bunk away from her, boring holes into my cell phone, begging it to chime with another message from TattooKitten.

The hardness of my cock, pinned beneath my dress pants, strains against its tight cloth. Her eyes are poised in expectation as she looks up at me through hooded lashes. I take a steadying breath, swallowing down my need to be buried in what I can only hope is her sweet little pussy. My eyes never drift from her stare as electricity sparks between us, thickening the air. Hot and heady breath flows from the tight line of my mouth. I'm not the least bit fearful for the woman seated before me, as if her body was carved, molded specifically to fit my hold. I'm man enough to admit that I'm afraid for myself. I'm beyond fucking terrified because there isn't an ounce of trepidation etched onto her gracefully carved features.

She declared her little fantasy, and here she sits, willing me to deliver.

A metaphorical grip on my balls, like a reality check, rings clear, telling me that she's too good for me. Too beautiful to be tarnished by my darkness. I want to bend her into positions that could break her fucking spine. Ruthlessly edge her until my body quivers over and over before it refuses to produce more cum. My need to be buried in her sweet little cunt is almost overbearing.

Sophia is a diamond. Rare, unique of her own accord, hidden under the deception of the purity she hides behind. I can see it in the glint of her eyes, an unspoken desire burning in her core. She wants to push herself from society's boundaries and explore the real world. One with shattered rainbows and sex swings. Giving society the middle finger, she longs to choose her own happiness. Letting herself explore her sexual cravings without judgment. That's true liberation.

Isn't that all that any of us wants? The confidence to screw whoever we want without labels, or condemnation. To embrace our inner cravings by giving them life, dousing the notion of being judged by society in acid and watching it burn into something magnificent.

My longing to break Sophia, the restrained version of her, to mold her into my perfect little whore, has me grinding my jaw on a level that might require a dental appointment. I'm on the verge of spiraling, sending us into the depths of hell together.

Her melodic voice jars me from my temptation.

"Why do I feel like I'm a shiny, new toy and you're a stray dog, sizing me up? You're all but salivating."

Her virtue is a vise grip on my damn sack, its hold deterring my decision to give in to what we want ... need.

She's too pure. You'll fucking break her. I'll like it. She ... will like it.

Sophia's spine is rigid, her breath held as she waits for my reply, nestled on top of my lap. She hasn't attempted to touch me, run her hands over my body, to take charge. Make no mistake—she's on edge, dancing with desire leading the way. This woman is dripping wet for me. The warmth of her core pressed into mine is a clear indication of how turned on she is by the prospect of being my shiny, new toy. She's blind as a bat if she can't see me salivating. I'm about to pant, growl, and smother her in more ways than one.

It's easy to get lost in her gaze, I think to myself as our eyes hold a conversation that she desperately wants to have.

She's undoubtedly one of the most beautiful people I've ever met, both inside and out. I haven't spent nearly as much time with her as Oliver has. Often, late at night, before I go to the bus to sleep, I hear them in his or her room. They're usually laughing, watching a movie, bonding.

As much shit as Oliver gave Murphy when he and Vanna decided to go full throttle into their relationship, you'd think that Ollie would notice the signs that he's embarking on the same terrain. I shove thoughts of him to the back of my mind. Now is not the time or place. My hands find her flesh. Her skin is silky against my rough palms as I run them up her legs, noticing the small intake of breath she tries to hide.

In the serene moments during my tattoo sessions post concerts, I've come to know Sophia on a deeper level. Passing back and forth my cell phone like an arcade game, we've mastered the art of talking without words. The method in which we've learned to conversate in is deep and raw, undiluted by actual words. Music arouses us; it's a reminiscent connection to a moment, place, or feeling. Changing songs, listening together, and sharing those musing times have allowed us to forge a connection that far exceeds physical attraction. Rhythmic ravishment is etched into our fleshes.

Don't get me twisted; Sophia is exquisite on the outside. With soft waves of red hair, ivory skin that glows in a radiant luminosity, no matter the weather, and a smile so earnest that it almost hurts to be on the receiving end of it. I understand the hushed whispers and craned necks from our stage and road crew staff when she walks by. They eat up her beauty in quick flashes, knowing that they'd be fired on the spot if Oliver witnessed them eyeballing her like she's the only thing that can quench their thirst.

Despite her outward appearance, it's her intellect that pulls me in and keeps me sated during our long tattoo sessions. Sometimes, she talks, giving voice to her dreams. Expanding her business and opening a second tattoo studio is why she's even here, on tour with us in the first place. I can say with certainty that I've come to know her on another level, one that is untainted by just my physical fascination to her. Oliver might have claimed her body. I aim to claim her mind.

Some call it sapiosexual. Although I personally loathe conversing, opening myself up and sharing my thoughts, I love sitting and listening to her do it. The thrill of her voice when she details the spaces architecture and color palette that she envisions to the musing of installing a new scheduling system. Her dazzling determination sets me on fire inside. Like her grit is a match and my soul goes ablaze, just by listening to her well-thought-out plans weaving themselves into existence.

I'd be a moron to ignore her immeasurable outward beauty. It just isn't all that draws me toward her. The more time I've spent with her, the more attracted I've become to her ... charisma, humanity, disposition. I don't see gender. I just see people, and she's the most exquisite human being on this earth. The lure she has on me has happened gradually, and now, here she is, with the creamy expanse of her exposed thighs resting on either side of my body, wrapped around me, prime for the taking.

"Cannon."

The sound of my name rolling off her tongue suffocates my willpower like a plastic bag over my head. There's no fighting it now. My cock juts against the zipper of my pants, trying to free itself.

The weight of her pleading glare cuts me like a knife, slicing into my resolve. It's an odd feeling. Restraint isn't something I lack. I can edge myself, delaying my own gratification like it's a part-time job and I'm a seasoned employee. I could earn a degree from taking myself down, reining in my orgasm. A sudden swerve of her hips pulls me from my thoughts, stationing me right back with her in the now dimly lit room.

"I came here to be ... taken ... roughly. Against my will." Her voice is almost a whisper, cutting through the substantial silence, sexy as hell. Offering only a nod, she inhales, and on exhale, courage bellows from her lungs as if they were made of iron. "If you're the stray, *I'm* animal control. I want you to feel cornered. I want you to viciously fight back just as much as I want to fight and pretend to ward you off. I *need* it, Cannon."

My eyes dip toward her neck as she swallows forcefully.

"Don't go easy just because you know me and I'm not some random woman from the app anymore. This doesn't change anything unless you let it. We decide our fate, and right now, I want you to fuck me like I'm the air you need to survive."

"Your metaphors won't do you any good here," I lie through gritted teeth. *Fuck.* Fuck. "You've mistaken me for Oliver again if you think words have some kind of effect on me. If you haven't noticed, I'm not fond of talking much. That includes your little performance. I do applaud you for using filthy ones though. *That* I do appreciate."

Her brows furrow before she closes the gap between us, her hot breath dancing across my mouth. Squaring her shoulders, the vixen comes out to play. "If you want me to shut up, make me. You know my fantasies. All of them. The ones that should never see the light of day, and yet here you are, sitting on your fucking hands like you're the terrified one. I signed up for this. If you're not man enough to shut me up, Cannon, tell me now. I'm sure there are other men on the app available tonight who won't give a second thought about throwing me around a little."

"Goddamn it."

I fist a handful of soft red waves around my hand, seething and yank her head backward forcefully. She's begging to be brutally fucked. That I can deliver on. My mouth crashes into hers in a show of dominance. It's sloppy. Needy. Everything that I expected it to be. A flash of wild heat races from my spine. All rational thoughts eliminate in my mind when her teeth bite down on my lower lip enough to draw blood.

The metallic consequence of her unsated desire lingers in our kiss as our tongues forcefully tango, both of us fighting to lead.

Panting through each word, in a rush, I say, "If I break you ... it's your fault. You asked for this. I don't want to hear any shit from Oliver when you crawl into his bed tonight, freshly fucked, bruised by my hand and full of my nut."

Sophia's lashes stand tall when she pulls back, retreating from my assault on her mouth. "I'm not mistaking you for Oliver or anyone else." Her hefty breath is laced in truth, ready to break down my resolve. "You have this notion in your head for whatever reason that I'm comparing you both or some crap. I want *you*, Cannon. The man I've been chatting with, getting to know on the app. Oliver's not here, so stop bringing him up."

I raise my brow, dead serious. "He asked to watch. Would you let him?"

"Enough. If you're not going to take me, use me, bend me, break me, I'm leaving. I'm at your mercy in the four walls of this hotel room and yours only. No one else matters right now, and if it did, if Oliver and I even admitted to having something between us ... he gave you his permission, remember?"

My feeble attempt to hide the effect Oliver still holds on to me falls flat.

"To answer your question ... yes. If you wanted that, I wouldn't care if he watched."

Her words grasp my heart as they lance it open, sending the thrashing organ that hasn't beaten the same since my best friend ... and former lover obliterated it into a commotion of genuine delight.

This is all kinds of fucked up. I know it's wrong before the words even leave my mouth. "Say his name again." A plea escapes my lips softer than I meant it to. Pressing my mouth to the curve of her ear, I command her, using a stern voice, "Say it, Sophia. Say *his* name."

"Oliver," she pants, need laced in every syllable as his name dives off the ledge of her lips. She's as aroused as I am at the idea of him watching us.

The tinge of sorrow his name brings as it rolls off her sharp tongue is a reminder of the misery of our past. A history I can't forget despite my best efforts. I've tried booze, drugs, and countless partners. Sleeping with both men and women to rid him from my system. It's been over a decade since we were ... experimenting. Enough time has passed. Memories of him linger, embedded in my mind. Every one of my escapades has been a futile attempt to purge his memory. He slayed me years ago and still has a hold on me.

My fingers splay over her delicately carved hips, and I urgently grind her against my hard-as-steel cock.

When I throw my head back against the couch, she whispers his name again, driving me mad. "Oliver."

My dick throbs, blazing past rock hard and turning into something destructive. Something that only he's been able to elicit from me and something I've longed for, for years. She must feel the twitch in my pants because she presses her hips down, a slight friction forming between us as she rides my clothed lap.

Dainty fingers that have danced over my skin countless times now due to her profession and reason for being on tour with us feel like feathers against my skin. Her hand moves, trailing my skin. Leaning forward, Sophia shocks the hell out of me as she takes my pebbled nipple in her mouth and bites down softly. Thoughts escape me as her almost-unbearable touch tents my pants.

As the drummer for a mainstream band, I've grown accustomed to the wolves, better known as the media, and perfected being invisible. Inconspicuously, I've hidden my wants, needs, desires and hide behind the asshole persona the media has painted me as. I couldn't give a flying fuck what the tabloids say about *me* specifically. It's my family and the legacy that they've built that have me scouring apps, searching for lovers in private, away from prying eyes. Privacy isn't something I'm given a lot of. Except in the bedroom, where I demand it. I'll do anything to keep my personal life off the front pages of magazines and from being televised at all costs.

The devious drummer with a chip on his shoulder is as good as a tagline as they're going to get. Because the part of me I hide—the real me, the side that craves giving in to the innermost, darkest desires of both my partner and me—is the only thing that truly makes sense.

I own the truth.

I revel in it.

And only one person in my inner circle knows about it.

Keeping the bedroom a sacred place to do whatever the hell I want is almost as important as ... music ... or breathing. My sexual appetite shouldn't be anyone's concern. Except it's everyone's. Which is why I refuse to allow my interest and unorthodox sexual needs reflect poorly on my parents and the reputation they've built in our tight-knit community. I'll be damned before I let those secrets spill.

Clenching my teeth, I can feel the pang in my chest beat against my rib cage, attempting to break free from the confinement I keep this part of me locked away in. Like a monster in the night, my cock stirs at the sound of *his* name, my biggest trigger. The soft, delicate way she naively whined it cuts through me like a flame to a torch. Sophia is lighting me on fire, and I'm ready to be burned.

She licks her way from my chest in a path that sets my already-warm skin ablaze, and her mouth finds my other nipple. She places a series of savage kisses around my chest, and her tongue trails meticulously upward, like she's committing the peak of my collarbone to memory, before gliding up my neck in a tantalizing stroke. Landing at the shell of my ear, she takes my lobe into her mouth and offers a gentle suck before outlining my ear with her serpent tongue.

On a hoarse, hot breath, her lips part once more. "Do you want to know how good it felt when he claimed me in my tattoo studio? How he ate my pussy and drank my cum like it was his first sip of water after a drought? I have a feeling that you know just what I'm talking about though. Don't you?"

My gaze—no doubt riddled with clouds of realization, mingled with lust—meet hers. The wide-eyed look she holds me with tells me enough. Sophia knows our secret. A history that has been buried six feet under for years. A secret that we swore would never see the light of day. Yet has haunted my dreams for years. Sophia doesn't cower; she doesn't even question why I want her panting his name in a manner that *should* have her scurrying down the hallway in repulsion. Instead, a vague tenderness passes between us, second to a forceful, heart-jolting buoyancy. Sophia is getting turned on just as much as I am, thinking about *him*.

Oliver is going to be the reason we both come tonight, and the bastard doesn't even know it.

I perish at the forceful domination of her words. I'm convinced that I've never been as hard or turned on as I am right now, being fully clothed. My body aches at the memory of his touch, the roughness of his fingers from years of strumming his guitar. I welcome her touch, admiring the softness of her hands as they dance across my shoulders. The faint dusting of her fingertips should feel like a consolation to his absent touch, yet it doesn't. It feels ... maddening in the best way. I crave him without remorse, but I have Sophia, and I don't plan to let her slip through my fingers as easily as I did him. There's an air of efficiency that radiates off her, drawing me in like a magnet. I'd be lying through my gritted teeth if I said I was in charge tonight. She's holding the microphone, and I'm praying for a cameo in her show.

I'm aroused by her soft caress, the bold yet assertive scan of my facial features and the dizzying beam of approval when her mouth opens, and more vile words flood the air around us.

"His cock was warm, thick, and filled to the hilt until I felt like I was going to explode. Oliver bit his bottom lip and groaned so deeply when he came inside me. The sound coated my body, wrapped around me like a blanket. I've been messaging you, HempDaddy"—she says my screen-name with a coy smile—"and thinking about how I rode him so hard and fast. I've come on my fingers more times than I'd like to admit. Unbeknownst to me, I was in a bunk across from you the entire time. Did you hear me panting while I came? I bet you didn't. You'll be listening now though, won't you? You'll be begging to be buried in my cunt because I assure you, it's that good."

Leaning into the darkness, Sophia firmly plants her feet on uncharted territory. The boldness in her taunting shows just how much she has welcomed the disarray that resides within me into her own life. The gesture is clear when she offers me her body like a noble sacrifice. Nothing—and I mean, nothing—but the soaring idea that one day Oliver will come to his senses, banish the idea of what society expects from him, and admit his true feelings for me and music has ever sent waves of elation through me like she is now.

In this moment, enveloped in darkness, I feel truly seen ... exposed, and it doesn't bother me. Because at the end of the day, this is our secret too. The media would have an uproar with this story. *Hired tattoo artist Sophia Lozier of Rose and Lace Ink Emporium bedded by two members of Kings of Jupiter.* She'd be eaten alive, her career ruined by swarms of people putting their two cents into something that involves them no more than the distance between two competing stores.

Instead of tormenting myself over both of our secrets getting out, I get lost in the way she looks at me, in the flicker of her intense glare. In the way that her dirty words fill me with pride, stroking my soul and assuring it that as long as two people consent, nothing is off-limits in the bedroom.

"Cannon," her voice barely above a whisper calls out to me, *not* Oliver.

My body ignites in a parade of tingles, drifting between the image she painted and the one in front of me. Hands roaming, bodies grinding, I rip her dress at the seam. The cloth falling to the sides of her body, the straps dangling from her shoulders.

My callous palms, from years of drumming, palm her ass as I demand truth in a flat, monotone manner. A truth that will shred the last of my resolve. "Did you bounce on his cock until he came in your pussy?"

I don't wait for her answer before I take my own journey, licking up the side of her exposed neck. Salt and desire mix on my taste buds. A full-body shudder is the only appraisal she gives. It entices me to nibble on her flesh. My mouth burns over her skin until I find myself at the pulsing hollow at the base of her throat. I open my mouth and latch on to the expanse of her neck, biting down like I'm a species not my own.

"I want to hear your words. You couldn't shut the fuck up earlier. Don't hold back now."

"Coming from a man who barely speaks himself."

The balls on this one are the size of Texas, as Mazen declared after his little run-in with her sister's Taser. Little does she know, I'd love nothing more than making her eat her sassy words and guzzle them down along with my hot, creamy nut.

"I thoroughly enjoyed your little story. Finish it. Tell me if he came inside of this"—I cup her sex, my hand folded over the wet cloth at her core—"little cunt." With my other hand, I flip down the cups on her strapless bra, exposing the most glorious set of tits I've ever seen. Two mounds, perky and round, take my breath away. "They're real." I don't recognize I've said that out loud until her laugh echoes around us.

"Everything about me is real. And, yes," she admits, leading me to a truth I already knew, but desperately wanted to hear. I'm jealous of her as she elaborates, "Yes, I milked his dick, pulling every drop from it until there was nothing left to offer."

A fury explodes in my chest. This bitch took *my* cum from him. She drained him of what was ... *is* rightfully mine.

Diamonds don't break.

But I'm going to enjoy fucking this one until it cracks.

27

THE RAPTURE

SOPHIA

A JAGGED PALM clutches my neck vehemently.

Cannon's fingers curve around my throat like a necklace, a perfect fit. The action no doubt driven by a mix of anger, arousal, and wanton need. I gasp at the force of his palm held to the front of my throat. He's clasping it so tightly that my air restricts, breath lodging in my esophagus.

Fire hotter than the depths of hell burns in his irises. The moment the words left my mouth, I saw the switch flip within him. The change in his demeanor. The rapture and promise of my one true desire to be fulfilled.

"Cannon." His name is incomprehensible due to my lack of oxygen.

Carried away by darkness, he seems to have forgotten that people need air to breathe.

Evoking a demon and living to tell the tale is almost unheard of. I've watched enough Ouija board movies to know better.

Despite my better judgment, I flipped a coin, and my

pussy called tails, winning over the rational side—my brain. I want to embark on the mission that I set in motion, but seeing him like this ... unhinged with erratic, pulse-pounding breaths has a tingling in the pit of my stomach waving a white flag in surrender. Peering at me in a mixture of madness, tinged with throes of passion, his eyes meet mine in eager affection and an intensity I've never seen in someone's eyes. I know I've pushed him too far.

I'm chasing after the devil's coattail, and if his steady stare is any indication, I'm screwed, both figuratively and literally. Knowing that the possibility of consequences was probable, I pushed and pushed, and my truth led him over the edge, sending him into a rage driven by lust. The reaction to me calling out his friend and forever lover's name pushed him. His reaction was both swift and violent.

As ready as I am to accept my fate and his retribution and burn by his touch, I won't lie and say I'm not shaking in both anticipation and fear. I've imprisoned us in this hotel room, full of desire so thick that I could bottle it up and sell it as an aphrodisiac serum.

I'm equally as aroused by his blatant display of dominance as I am nervous. There's a steady pulse between my legs, making its own tempo. Everything about this moment screams trouble.

Is this what I was after? Is this the part that thrills me—to be void of choice and at someone else's mercy?

I don't know how else to describe the feeling of being restricted the simple element of air. My senses leap to life. My mind floats well above me in a dreamlike state, hazy and disoriented. I don't know where reality starts and where it ends. I hope it's on the bed with my hands held high above my head and my legs wrapped tightly around Cannon's core.

I'm drowning in the sensual experience that has become this dark room. His harsh breath fans my face as his hand circles even tighter around my throat.

Without loosening his command with his hand, his lips part enough for his tongue to dart out and dance across my lips in a hungry sweep. Cannon's eyes stay trained on mine as the heady sensation of his moist tongue traces along my lips. His scent is my new favorite lipliner.

"There are three items on the bed." He pauses his assault, his words urgent.

My attempt at craning my neck over his broad shoulder to look toward the mattress falls short when his hold on my neck intensifies, and then his palm relaxes when he notices the warm tear falling down my cheek. With nostrils flaring, I inhale in a speedy succession in an attempt to get a full breath into my deserted lungs with the reckless abandon of his force.

"You're going to choose your poison. Then, you're going to get what you asked for. Taken ... however *I* want because I'm the narrator tonight. Do you understand?"

I offer a subtle nod, unable to speak. My body burns by his words, thighs quivering.

"You wanted your choices stripped from you. You asked me on the app to push you to your limits. Contrary to what the media thinks, I'm actually a fairly decent man. I'll give you this choice. Choose wisely." He tilts his head, then dips his chin, gesturing me to make my decision as he removes his hand from my body.

My lungs expand, filling with the air I've been deprived of. Like an unquenchable thirst, each breath is bigger than the next. My chest heaves, greedily gulping all while trying to surprise the anxiety that stirs within me. I want to fall to my knees and inhale air for days, but more than I want my next breath, I want to drink in the promise of his threat. As if a shot of a morphine were injected into my vein, I jolt upward and away from Cannon's deviously carved chest.

Space. I need space. To think. To contemplate if being taken against my will is really something I want.

"We don't have all night, Sophia. I'm sure Oliver will be expecting you soon."

"Is that what this is about? *Him?*" I question, high on his threat. "I'm not one to judge. Some of my favorite books are male on male. If that's what this really is about, he didn't sound like he'd mind. He asked to wat—"

"I'd recommend you not finish that sentence. Choose."

Cannon has set the stage. Lifted the metaphorical curtain. Now, it's up to me to choose my fate, as he so eloquently put it, as to how this scene plays out.

Poking the bear has fared me well thus far. I inch forward, clearly delusional and suffering from hypoxia from lack of air. "Fuck you."

I grapple with my bra, tucking my breasts back inside before spinning on my heel. I take one step toward the door before his hand snakes around my wrist, pulling me with my arm bent behind my waist and his chest to my back. Cannon walks us forward until we're at the front door of the hotel room, and he pushes both of our bodies against it. My cheek smashes into the wood, my eyes shooting daggers from their vantage point at him.

"Choose your poison, or I will choose all three. Trust me, you're not ready for all three at one time. It won't hurt me at all. I promise it will hurt you. I'm not going to ask again."

"My choice was pretty clear when I told you to go fuck yourself."

I knew I should have stopped by the apartment first.

Lacey would have never let me leave without a Taser. Especially if she knew how my night was going to end. I don't want to be turned on right now. It's all kinds of wrong. I know this. Rationally, I know how messed up this is. I feign anger in an attempt to sound sane, reminding myself that these feelings are wrong.

"If you choke me again—"

"You'll what? Gush? Squirt? You can lie to yourself all you want, but you'll only be fooling yourself. I can smell how fucking turned on you are."

"Taking tips from Jupiter?" I ask referring to his hound.

"You're just asking to be choked by my cock, aren't you?"

I feel his body press into mine once more.

"It's so hard for you. It's been hard for you. Not Tattoo-Kitten. You. Do you feel that, baby?"

I don't know if I'm more shocked by his term of endearment or the long rod, which seems to never end, that he's rubbing over my ass and thigh.

"You'd choke on just the sight of this. I'd revel in the sound of it and seeing spit drip down your chin." Cannon unclasps my hand and lowers it, wrapping my fingers around the mammoth-sized monster he has in his trousers. "This is what you do to me. Imagine my fucking delight when it was you who pranced through that door."

"Let me see my options," I spit out while cursing myself for not fleeing this situation. I want to get to the encore even if it breaks me. Yielding to the intense need that's been building over the week, I allow myself to explore my unexpressed sexuality.

Backing away, Cannon moves to replace my stance at the door. A smug smile flitters across his deceitfully handsome face. I know I'm a glutton for punishment. Whatever options I have to choose from are going to scare the hell out of me even if they simultaneously bring me pleasure. In a long stride, I'm at the edge of the bed, shell-shocked at the array of items before me.

A red ball gag and leather contraption.

A black butt plug.

And what appears to be a set of both his and hers nipple clamps.

Glancing over my shoulder, I'm startled when Cannon is no longer standing with his back against the door but rather directly behind me.

"I thought we were playing out my fantasy tonight, HempDaddy, not yours."

His large hand brushes my hair from my shoulder, exposing my neck. "You and I both know that you have more than one fantasy. I want to explore them all with you."

"What about our time constraints? You're the one that said that Oliver will be expecting me soon." I toss his words at him like a bomb.

"Fuck Oliver. He could stand to learn some patience." He shrugs calmly. Much too casual for the man who looked like he was going to rip my head off my shoulders with his bare hands because I admitted that Oliver had come inside of me.

Squaring my shoulders, I step into his personal space, attempting to get back the upper hand. "You would," I goad with confidence.

"I did," he states matter-of-factly.

I'm tossed off-kilter by his unashamed response.

"What?" I stammer, backing up to the edge of the mattress, melting into it as I sit.

Did he just admit to screwing Oliver? My ... friend ... boss ... recent lover. Even though, I had already assumed they banged, hearing it being confirmed...is something I can't quiet explain.

"You heard what I said. It's ancient history that you will not repeat."

I watch as he bends down on both knees in front of me and then reaches behind me and grabs the black butt plug.

"What'd you decide?" Rubbing the edge of the plug over the inside of my thigh, he adds, "This one looks like it will fit."

I must have been roofied at the wedding. There is no chance in hell that this is my reality right now. Much less that the man sitting before me, HempDaddy, is really Cannon freaking Rhodes. This has got to be a wild dream brought on by jet lag, copious amounts of free booze, and a drug that I somehow ingested. Maybe the plane crashed, and we never even made it back to Tampa. That thought is more probable than the so-called reality I'm in.

I pinch my arm. It hurts.

I bite the inside of my cheek, which also hurts.

I slide my finger into the hem of my panties and glide them south. Sure enough, I'm wet. Soaked actually. What in the hell is going on?

My voice rises an octave from my normal tone when I ask, "Is this a dream?"

"No. No, it's not." Cannon doesn't seem to catch on to my internal freak-out and stays on course. "We're going to start with the nipple clamps, okay?"

I'm stunned by his question, and my mouth gapes, words on the tip of my tongue, ready to rebut. No words come though, only a whimper, which he takes as a verbal, *Sure, pinch away, sir*, and presses me backward into the mattress with one of his giant hands.

I tease, finally finding my voice, "What if I wanted the plug?"

"If you're not careful, you'll get all three," he says, paying no attention to the genuine smile on my face as he unfastens my bra this time, sliding it off me.

I'm as exposed as I was a birth, except for the skinny material I call underwear hovering over my hips. I'm so fascinated by the thin metal clamps that I fail to notice Cannon's face as he applies them, clamping each nipple until I look up just in time to see his upper teeth covering his entire bottom lip.

"Panties off," he instructs before sliding out a blindfold from what I can assume was his back pocket.

I tuck a loose strand of hair behind my ear. "You're just a bag of tricks this evening, aren't you?"

"You have no idea." He secures a blindfold over my eyes.

My chest rises and falls in anticipation. "There's not a need to blindfold me anymore. I already know who you are. The kink was not knowing and then being taken."

"Run." His voice is sharp, second to the slap on my ass. When I don't move, he adds, "The kink is whatever the hell I say it is tonight. Now, run."

"What? Where?" My head darts around the room, my sense of vision distorted by the cloth tied around my head. "This is stupid."

His voice is distant when he calls out again, "One. Two."

What in the actual hell?

He's counting down like I'm a toddler.

I take a hesitant step forward toward the direction of where I recall the couch being from memory. "Marco," I call out.

When I don't hear *Polo* as a reply, I huff in annoyance. I feel like I'm living that TikTok video that pokes fun at a woman joking around with her captor. Lacey would be hunched over, dying in a fit of laughter, if she could see me right now, prancing around in nipple clamps and a blindfold.

I'm tempted to rip off my mask and send her a selfie, but I don't want to ruin the whole vibe Cannon has set.

"Is the goal here for me to just walk around aimlessly in this hotel room with my hand out, searching for your cock as a prize?"

The creak of a door opening on its hinges pulls my senses to where I think the hotel door is moments before a swish of the door's wood drags against the carpet and closes with a click.

"You did not just leave me in here." Shoving the material off my face, I storm over to the entryway. To do what, I don't exactly know. It's not like I'm dressed and can swing it open, shouting after him down the hallway. "Asshole," I murmur before movement from the corner of my eye catches me off guard.

He storms to me, his presence enough to scare the living shit out of a serial killer.

In a swift move that seems rehearsed, which should terrify me a lot more than it does, he slides something over my head. A pillowcase ... a bag. Whatever it is, it's hot, and immediately, I know I should have listened to my gut earlier. What kind of woman am I to get wet over the pretense of being taken against her will? A fucking psycho —that's what kind.

This is not me. This is not what I want, I tell myself as I start to thrash against the door that I'm pinned to.

His hard body is behind mine, hands securing the bag over my head.

The word *no* is on the tip of my tongue. I should say it. I should claw his arms like a maniac and call out for help. I know this is all kinds of wrong and disgusting. But a part of me gets lost in the madness. The other part is still deciding on what to do next.

"I'm only going to remove this bag so you can suck my dick. Do you understand? Don't make a fucking sound unless you're gagging on your own saliva, and even then, I don't want to hear you mutter a single word."

I'm standing in a puddle of wetness.

Without being told twice, I drop to my knees. My hands immediately go to his belt, opening the clasp in a rush. Then to the button of his dress pants. In one fell swoop, they drop. I inch forward, prepared to lower his boxers, except there's no more material to drag away. Cannon isn't wearing anything under his pants. He went to a wedding, free balling. I don't know why, but the thought makes me squirm a little more.

"The bag," I say loud enough that he hears me through the material.

I sit expectantly, waiting for his grip to loosen. For it to be pulled from my head, but the movement never comes. Instead, he punches through the bag with what I assume is a couple of fingers and makes a hole.

A makeshift fucking glory hole.

The bastard.

The light in the hole dims as the head of his dick and flesh fill the open space. There's no hesitation in his move-ments. He doesn't stop to rub his cock over my lips in a sensual movement. He grabs the back of my head over the bag and impales my mouth with his long shaft.

I take him to the back of my throat. An audible gag earns me a hard twitch of his engorged cock in my mouth. With a slurping sound, I remove him from my mouth and leisurely lick from the hem of his crown down to his base and then back up again.

Gargling and the sound of me choking, fighting for air around his abundant expanse, fill the room. I palm his thighs in a failed attempt to try to push his body away from me. Which only encourages another hard thrust. I bite back a cry but allow the degradation. Welcoming it like a good little whore because nothing in my life has ever set my soul on fire like this moment of being completely at someone else's mercy.

My poor tonsils.

Cannon grunts. It's my only reward to the onslaught of debauchery that's happening. It's enough to calm my breathing. That and the fact that the hole in the bag is widening with each powerful plunge he makes. The bridge of my nose is greeted with fresh air. I should have chosen the ball gag. At least then I could see what was coming next.

The thick vein in his shaft protrudes each time he slides it in my mouth. An odd sensation of a ball rubs the back of the throat. Is his dick pierced? I don't feel anything with my tongue, leading me to believe he has a Prince Albert. I have half a mind to clamp down my teeth, forcing his movement to stop so I can ask him, but think better of it.

With each forceful drive, I feel used, and I brazenly revel in it as he ruthlessly fucks my throat. He sledgehammers into my mouth, and I welcome his assault, crave it. Even with spit running down my chin, dripping onto my exposed thighs. If his severe and vigorous onslaught is an indication of how Cannon fucks ... my *girl* is in big trouble.

In an abrupt halt of his hips, he pulls his dick from my

mouth and rips the bag over my head. Wayward hairs stick to my cheeks, my mascara is undoubtedly pooled under my eyes from the tears that escaped under his ambush, and despite the insanity that rings clear in my head, I want more.

"More." I give voice to my longing, begging him to deliver like he promised he would.

With a swift movement I've only ever seen in movies, Cannon throws me over his shoulder, my exposed ass cheeks bouncing in the night.

"I want to devour your sweet cunt. The pussy that Oliver tore up and marked. But first, I need to smear you, so he knows I was here too."

My insides pulsate at his words, another rewarding threat.

"I'm going to assume that you're clean since he screwed you the night before we left the country and I haven't seen any men wandering into your bedroom."

"Yes," is all I can manage before he tosses me onto the mattress. "Do you have your latest STD results on your cell phone too?" The faint smile haunting his mouth is enough of an answer as any. "I'm on birth control ... I can't get pregnant. Do your worst." I rest my head against the bed, allowing his darkness to overtake me, begging it to.

It starts at my toes. Like a shadow, it slowly lingers up until I'm surrounded. Except it's not a fog that engulfs around me, pulling me into the pits of desire, it's Cannon Rhodes who flips my body over like a rag doll and buries his himself in me to the hilt without a second thought.

Pain courses through my abdomen, clawing at my insides. As hysterical as it sounds, I welcome it and smile through his intrusion. He's so ... long. Thick. I think I might submit his profile to Guinness World Records if I survive the night.

"Take it all. Just like that. Look at you, opening up for me, letting me in like you're a glove made just for me."

There's no disguising my body's response to him. I want to ask who will keep his bed warm and his demons satisfied tomorrow night, but I know better. The answer isn't something that I'm entitled to or I even want to know. I can't shake the feeling as to why he had to resort to chatting with a woman on an app when he's Cannon freaking Rhodes, drummer extraordinaire. It doesn't make sense. This whole night doesn't make sense. I want to pry, and despite my brain screaming through each thrust he offers, I refrain. I'll take this night to my grave—unless he sends me to it first.

I rise to meet him in our frenzied moment of lust. As my body opens up, accepting his girth, each reckless drive morphs into pleasure. I'm being railed. Rode hard, and all I can think about is him doing this to Oliver, or vice versa. I'm so turned on, and my pussy is *so* full that I can't form a coherent sentence.

"Fuck. More. Harder." I pant a string of words as energy sweeps through me.

Cannon rears back and sinks into my opening with such force that I see stars. My body is his drum, and he's pounding me with urgency.

"I'm. Going. To. Come." My stomach muscles coil.

"I want to see you come unglued on my dick."

Pulling out of me, Cannon flips me onto my back. I glance up through hooded eyes to see him resting on his knees, his large cock—which should be labeled as a deadly weapon—juts out from his midline. I take notice of his carved abs and that delectable V. He moves, placing me in a missionary position before him, and slides into me. I feel like my body has been molded specifically for him. When he bottoms out, he places his hands under my shoulder blades and cups my shoulders with his strong hands.

"This is so very romantic. I didn't peg you as a missionary man." I laugh.

Cannon shakes his head, ignoring my fevered banter, before he lifts me off the bed like I weigh less than a down pillow. He sits me on his awaiting shaft once more in the most overpowering angle I've ever been in. Literally impaling my body, and all rational thoughts—including ones that should never be spoken about movies and lovemaking as a famous drummer is fucking you senseless —abandon me.

Flesh meets flesh as he pistons into me. My stomach muscles grow taut as I desperately try to push back into him with just as much force as he is hammering me.

With each drive of his hips, my need to explode with release comes back full force. There's nothing sweet about this moment. It's raw. Carnal. Ravishing. A deep groan bellows from the pits of his lungs, and he throws his head back in ecstasy. Any restraint that Cannon had beforehand is severed. Abandoned hunger replaces his sanity. I can feel his already-thick shaft pulsate and swell inside of me. The grip of his hands on my shoulders tightens, much like they did earlier around my throat, and he fucks me callously like a wild animal that's been caged for far too long.

Our bodies slapping, paired with labored breathing, is the only sound in the hotel room. Throaty moans mix between us, our mouths hanging ajar. Neither of us leans in to kiss the other. Now isn't the time for romantic notions like kissing. My climax is like a bell inside, dangling on by a thread, and he's the only one who can make me chime.

I feel as if I'm going to topple over or wither like a raisin as the buildup of tension coils in my lower abdomen. The profuse need to explode like a balloon right before it pops when it's been blown up too big pushes me to the brink.

"So ... close," I whimper on a convulsion.

Cannon ducks his head, biting the metal dangling between my chest, and pulls with his teeth. My pebbled nipples, now a dark purple, swell. The pain is euphoric. I need more.

"Pull harder," I instruct through a harsh moan. "Almost there."

I look down to see my buds, hard, swollen and abused in the best way imaginable. My vision blurs as pleasure radiates throughout my entire being. He pulls on the metal strand again, as if he just pulled the pin from a grenade and threw it.

I detonate.

My body jerks in his arms, wave after wave of ecstasy flowing from my core onto his lower abdomen. Deep-seated pleasure overcomes me, causing my limbs to weaken, and I go slack in his arms. I'm spent, both my mind and body. He holds me firmer, securing me in his grasp, and then he plunges, deeper, harder. Using me for his own pleasure now, greedily taking what he needs.

"Get ready for me to set the tempo now," Cannon hums huskily before he pushes into me, chasing the same oblivion I just met. His eyes darken and fixate on my blissed-out glare.

"That wasn't you setting the tempo before?" I sleepily ask, my tits now bouncing up and down, causing the clamps to bounce with each thrust. The pleasure almost sending me into another spiral.

If I thought his thrusts were potent before, my orgasm must have set him off like a butterfly effect. Cannon's hips drive into me as I bounce on his harder-than-steel shaft. Thrust after thrust, he digs in, taking me like I'm nothing more than a rag doll of flesh and bone. The steady sound of his flesh hitting mine with every hard stroke as he impales me would be enough to turn any saint into a sinner. The erotic sound fills the room, along with our ragged breathing from our friction.

Our eyes lock. His says, *You feel so good.* Mine reply, *Harder,* egging him on. The silent exchange reverberates, and he loses all sense of reality.

"On your knees," he demands brashly, pulling his shaft out of my opening and standing on the mattress, hovering over me. His head almost brushes the ceiling; he's so tall. "Open." He thumbs my bottom lip with his hand before he strokes his cock, squirting hot cum into my awaiting mouth. "I told you I'd have you swallowing your words and my nut."

"So dreamy," I say, mouth full.

I swallow and use my wrist to wipe at the side of my mouth. Cannon falls to the bed, sprawled out beside me. His penis still erect.

"I thought you said you were going to mark me, like Oliver did?"

I'm far past being a glutton for punishment. He sparked a whirl of indelible passion in me. I'm a junkie for him now, clamoring for another hit.

"Climb on." He motions down toward his hard shaft.

"You're not serious."

His brows furrow. "Do I look like the type of man who jokes around?"

Glancing between his face and his already-lively dick, I mimic his movement, my brows furrowing. "Isn't there like a couple-of-hours refractory period for guys your age?"

I'm utterly baffled.

"I'm thirty, not eighty. Take what you need, Sophia. Ride me."

I hope I didn't get drugged at the wedding because I don't want to forget this night for as long as I live.

28

KISS AND TELL

SOPHIA

"I'M NOT GONNA KISS and tell."

I tug at my shirt that reads, *Plants are my soil-mates*, as I sit on the couch in our apartment. I feel refreshed having awoken in my own bed.

"Fine, one tiny detail." A wide grin spreads across Lacey's face as I cave. "He said he wanted to send me home, full of his seed as a gift to his guitarist...Oliver."

"Holy crap. That's so hot. I'm about to spontaneously squirt, just from thinking about it." Lacey sits on our sofa, mind blown, looking envious as ever. "I mean, I've never ridden a bull before, but, hot damn, what I would give to ride that one. Take my money."

My cheeks redden, and I toss a pillow in her direction.

"Pump the brakes, waterfall girl. Get your own bull ... bulls! No more fantasizing about them. All three of them are mine." I scold.

With an eye roll, I sip my coffee and scroll on my phone. Being back in the States, I feel like I have free rein to scroll through social media. Overseas, I tried to stay off it other than talking to Lacey since the rates for international use are astronomical. As I'm scrolling mindlessly, doing my best to block out Lacey, a ping dings in my hand.

Knox: Hey, baby girl. I miss you.

While I contemplate what to say back, Lacey presses on. "Bulls. Plural. You said it yourself. Finally, you admit to having three members of Kings of Jupiter all vying for a chance to get in them panties!"

Is it bad to admit that I feel a little exhilarated by my moronic sister's commentary? It's like I've suddenly become a walking, talking bottomless pit of satisfaction, knowing that I've piqued the interest of three extraordinarily handsome men.

Music aside, Oliver, Cannon, and Mazen are more mouthwatering than a seared Wagyu that cost more than my first vehicle, and I would know since I ate my weight in it at the Millers' wedding.

The open admiration that both Oliver and Mazen have displayed leaves me feeling powerful, like a woman was made to feel. Throwing Cannon's secret identity and prowess into the mix, and not only are my thighs quivering, but so is my heart.

Three rock stars. One luxurious tour bus. It sounds like a melody made in heaven. Until the pavement cracks and the allure fades. Then, what will I be left with? A broken heart and vagina from being railed by three Greek god lookalikes and then forgotten about as they move onto the next city.

"I'm a groupie and a ho." Defeat pours from my pores.

A hand covers my face, hiding my disgust with myself. Lacey senses my trepidation.

"No, bitch. You're a queen. Own the hell out of that. If three men all want you and, from what you've told me, seem okay with sharing you ... ride that train until the metal rails gives out."

"Enough about *those* men. Check out what this one just texted me." I hold my phone out in front of me for her to read the text from Knox. "It's been years since we've had a casual chat."

"Don't reply. He had his chance to shoot his shot, and he ruined it by being all sexist when you went out on a limb and we opened our shop."

"You're right. I won't reply."

"Back to you being all dodgy about the shenanigans you've partaken in lately. You've told me enough so I can piece this all together. Now, you can either fill in the blanks or sit here and let's work this all out unless your goal is to have a mental breakdown before the crack of dawn."

Sighing in defeat, I give Lacey an intimate rundown of last night with Cannon. I'm on the verge of sparing her the specifics about Cannon and Oliver's passed tryst, but against my better judgment and because she gives me a knowing look, I spill my guts, not leaving any detail left unspoken.

"That's a lot to take in," she offers a brilliant smile. "Your love life is like a melting pot of kinks, and I'm here for it."

I moan, inwardly chastising myself for chasing a dream of the four of us ... together.

"I don't have a love life," I correct my delusional little sister. "A sex life, yes. Love ... not so much. Thankfully."

Tossing a blanket over both of our legs, Lacey reminds

me that she is wiser than her age presents. "The line between intimacy and adoration is almost nonexistent." Tossing in some wit and showing her true colors, she adds, "Just like there's a fine line between pain and pleasure. It's called the cervix."

My shoulders shake as an unearthly shriek leaves my lips. Laughter booms between us for what seems like minutes. By the time we've settled, we both stretch out, feet on the coffee table, and fall into a peaceful slumber.

It doesn't take long for my dream to shift from something that is PG to something that is a little more depraved … and the cast is none other than the Kings of Jupiter, sans the married one.

29

WAKE AND BAKE

MAZEN

"I'M COMING," I shout and then let out a grunt as I climb out of bed, sleep heavy on my lids.

I feel like I'm nearing eighty more than the dirty thirty when my back catches as I bend over, grabbing a pair of sweatpants that I must've discarded sometime in the middle of the night, and slide them on. The unmerciful thud grates on my nerves the closer I get to the front door.

Where is everyone? How can anyone sleep through this?

The floor to our suite is monitored, which tells me a couple of things about whose fist it could be hammering against the door. For starters, whoever is pounding evidently doesn't have a key card to our suite. Not to mention the fact that Ashton and our crew didn't stop the white-knuckled assailant when they got off the elevator. That means they were cleared by our security team beforehand. Which means the persistent knock is coming from one of only a handful of people.

Pound. Pound. Pound.

"Goddamn it. I said I'm coming," I bark, ears burning. "Knock it the fuck off before you lose the hand you're apparently so fond of."

The sound isn't as forceful as it would be if a man's hand was responsible for the annoying knock. A brief thought crosses my mind that it's Sophia. She doesn't have a key because she left after the wedding. Well, not directly after. She was there to aid me with my father. But fled shortly after sending Oliver into a tailspin. He threw a hissy fit like a scorned lover when she announced she had plans that didn't include coming back to the hotel with him.

With a sliver of hope that she'd change her mind, I made plans of my own in an attempt to drown out my need to make her scream my name. Said plans fell flat when Oliver stumbled into the SUV, slamming the door behind him without Sophia on his heels.

A DEEP, "WHAT THE FUCK?" *echoed in the Suburban when he noticed one of Vanna's friends sucking my dick while she sat beside me in the seat, her dress hitched up around her waist.*

"Catching feelings?" I eyed him suspiciously, waiting on his excuse.

It was all he kept giving me, evading a truth he hid, mirroring my own.

She's a talented artist.

She can free-hand anything.

She's fucking gorgeous.

She has a killer pussy.

Begging for mercy, I was gifted a sliver of reprieve by the scowl the size of Times Square on his face, a clear indication that he was indeed catching feelings. When he leaned against the headrest, apparent aggravation was written across his face.

Fuck, I thought. I was pissed that he'd screwed her. I was even more pissed that she seemed to be screwing with him even if it was unintentional on her part.

"Stop." I pushed at the forehead of the woman sucking my cock like she was trying to get to the center of it like a lollipop. "We're leaving. You need to go."

Her eyes widened when they met mine, hair dangling in her face. "Excuse me? You don't want me to get you off?"

"I said, we're leaving. Time to go." I tucked my dick back into my dark pants and slid a twenty-dollar bill from my back pocket toward her chest. "Call a cab or not. You just have to get out of here."

"Fuck you, Mazen." She seethed, ripping down her dress to cover her exposed legs.

I rolled my eyes, annoyed by her juvenile behavior. It wasn't the first or last time some dumb bitch would shout those words at me.

"Fuck you, dude. That was low, even for you," Oliver said as the door slammed, looking disgusted. "That's the crazy one too. Hopefully, she doesn't claim you did something stupid to her in revenge for that bullshit you just pulled. Damn. Remember when she told Vanna that Murphy was hitting on her, and all he'd really said was that he liked her shoes? She's the worst type of crazy."

"She might be batshit crazy, but she can suck-start a Harley."

"What's up with you suddenly having a porn addiction

and only choosing to showcase it when you know Sophia will be around?"

The sudden change of subject sent my alcohol-induced head sloshing.

Oliver's eyes met mine disapprovingly. "I might be tipsy. I'm not blind or stupid, and she told me you tried to kiss her," he added before using his thumb and index finger to pinch the bridge of his nose, like he used to do when we were kids and he was overwhelmed.

Who was he to call me out like that? Shit.

Doubling down on my defenses, I sized him up before my lips twisted in a cynical smile. "Who are you to judge my sexual escapades? And I tried and got shot right the fuck down—I'll admit it. You need to take a beat and worry about your own sexual kinks, not mine."

A minute passed.

Oliver's nose flared.

Anger coiled in frustration at the back of my throat as soon as the words left my lips. There was no way that Oliver was naive enough to think that I was ignorant to the secret that he'd attempted to guard like a national treasure. I peered into his eyes as his recollection faded, dusting away the cobwebs of our past, and his face pulsed into a tight grimace.

In that moment, he knew that I knew. It was something that we never discussed. We didn't need to. His business or where he stuck his dick had never bothered me before. Tit for tat and all that bullshit.

"That's shitty, man."

Didn't I know it?

"You started this conversation."

"There's only so many times you can push me away before I throw in the towel and decide that your friendship isn't worth the uphill battle. Then, what will do you?"

Emotions swirled behind my eyes as the significance of his harsh words registered. I peered at him in a stop-pussy-footing-around glare. I didn't want his momentum to stop now. He might as well lay it all on the line while liquid courage raced through his veins.

"You're railing your way through women, purposely trying to get caught by Sophia. Tell me, are you jealous? I know you want her too."

"I can get my dick wet whenever I want. I think I just made that point. What is there to be jealous of?"

"You're fooling yourself, man. It's clear to everyone else, and if we can see it, so can she."

"What's that mean?" I fumbled with the air-conditioner control knob. Being in the hot seat was tiring. I kept my eyes trained ahead, trying to keep my inner turmoil contained. I didn't want Oliver to see how unhinged this conversation made me.

"It means you won't admit that you're interested in her to yourself, just as much as I won't admit to catching feelings for her. We're too fucked up for that type of honesty. She's a cool chick, Maz. Down-to-earth. Shoots the shit. Funny as hell. Is it so bad to want to have a friend without a penis to talk to every once in a while?"

Pot, meet kettle.

I ran my hand through my hair, eyes finally settling on his. For two people with decades of friendship between us, we really were shit at communicating.

"If you're attracted to her—and I'm fairly certain you are —stop screwing everything with a cunt and tell her that you like her. Don't just blindside her with your mouth, you obnoxious fucker."

"What exactly would I tell her, Ollie? That she's beautiful? I think she knows. That I think she's got raw talent?

Again, she owns a tattoo studio. She knows she has what it takes to be successful. I'm not jealous that you screwed Sophia. I did—" I bit back the last thing that had me hesitating where Sophia was concerned. Our history. A history she didn't even remember. "I didn't mean to have a heart-to-heart tonight, bro. I just wanted to get my dick sucked before going to the hotel. Can we drop this? My head is pounding. I had a run-in with my dad, and I just want to smoke this blunt and forget about the world. That good with you?"

Oliver nodded, pulling his lighter from his pocket before striking it with his thumb. Nothing paired better with bullshit than smoke evaporating in your lungs.

The rest of the ride home, an ominous silence filled the car. Thoughts of him basically giving me his unspoken permission to seek Sophia out rang loudly in my head.

THE PERSISTENT KNOCKING, like the chime of a clock, draws my thoughts back to the present. Its sound teetering between aggravation and blow my brains out. I'm five seconds away from throttling whoever is on the other side. The person pounding isn't a danger to me or the guys. That fact alone has me huffing one last time in annoyance before I swing the door to the hallway open with the twist of my wrist. My one-eyed assessment of Lindsey, our publicist, dies flat as she floats by me, holding a tray of coffee. Not a care in the fucking world that she woke me up at the ass crack of dawn. Her long dirty-blonde hair, dangling down her shoulders, swings with each step.

Jupiter's muffled bark sounds, telling me I'm not alone

in the suite. Cannon usually flees to the bus, and the newly-weds got their own room last night. By process of elimination, Oliver's here as well.

Shutting the door, I trail behind her swaying gait, teeming in anger all the while attempting to hide my morning wood from her.

"This couldn't have been sent in an email?"

As usual, my eyes travel to the swell of her mango-shaped hips, bound in a pair of ripped jeans that look like they've seen better days. Pulling off the starving-artist image is supposed to be our thing, but she nails it perfectly. Lindsey has always been drawn to music. Her dad was a composer back in his prime. She's of medium height, and once upon a time, my dreams were filled with images of her soft, curvy legs, folded tightly around my face. Those dreams were short-lived when she made it clear that she had ambitions in life and fucking her high school lab partner wasn't one of them. I'm not often turned down, but when I am, it's by a fiery woman with morals. That's probably where my resentment toward walking the line between right and wrong started to blur and flourished.

"Probably. What fun would that have been when I dropped this bomb on you? I wanted to see your face," she says, tucking a loose strand of her sandstone hair behind her ear that's lined with piercings, gold glimmering from the light.

Lindsey is the epitome of a smokeshow. Right after graduation, she was offered a modeling contract, before plus-size modeling became all the rage. She could have been the *it* girl in that industry. She eloquently declined the offer, deciding to follow her heart, and came on tour with us. As our work wife, Lindsey's been the only constant in our lives besides each other. From rags to riches, she's been loyal and our band's biggest cheerleader. She helped book us gigs in the beginning and even designed some of our merch early on. We owe a lot of who we are to her, which is why when we started earning money, we all pitched in and covered her tuition. It was the least we could do for all she had done for us. Now, having graduated with a degree in communications and being offered an actual paid position as our publicist, she's here, ready to bust my balls and get paid for doing it.

I sink onto the couch, begging for its cushions to drag me under and smother me. Anything has got to be better than whatever bullshit she's about to spout off with. When nothing happens, I cross my legs and pull a coffee from the tray just as Oliver's door swings open, and he and Jupiter saunter into the living room.

"You sleep harder than the dead." I rub my hand through my hair, not giving a fuck that it's disheveled. Again, Lindsey's seen far worse from all of us.

A grunt is all I get in response, second to Jupiter barreling toward me. "Ashton's coming to get him," he says, motioning to the collar and leash by the front door.

Imagine a life where you can't walk your own dog. Imagination met our reality. He was a stray when Oliver found him on the beach. Malnourished, coat matted, and sand crusted on his nose. I remember the day we brought him back to my house. We gave him a bath and fed him seared filet mignon the chef had left in the microwave for my dad, who was working another late night. Then, the four of us wrote a name on a sliver of paper and picked out of a cup to determine the furball's new identity, just like we had done with our aliases.

Jupiter.

My dad wouldn't let us keep him, claiming he had

severe allergies. I called bullshit, and he busted my lip for disrespecting him. Fortunately, Cannon's mom loved animals and happily accepted our stray into their home.

The rest is history.

Ollie and my conversation from last night plays on rewind in my mind. His lame excuse about longing for female companionship is a total crock of bullshit. Lindsey has been the only female in our lives that none of us have screwed. Not for a lack of trying on my part—several embarrassing times. With ovaries of steel, she turned me down quicker than someone declining gas-station sushi.

I'm usually happy to see her ... but this morning is an exception since it's at the ass crack of dawn. The front door swings wide, revealing Cannon, clad in jeans and a KOJ (Kings of Jupiter) hoodie. Behind him walks in Ashton, who calls out to Jupiter, who happily obliges his command, knowing that freedom and actual grass are in his future.

Cannon takes a seat on the couch opposite to me, leans over, and places a joint in the palm of my hand. For someone who rarely sleeps, he looks as put together this morning as a news anchor. Even his beard appears to be combed and tamed.

What in the actual fuck?

"Linds said she's about to drop a bomb on us. I think we should light this baby up now. I'd rather be high and down than sober and down." I speak to the small group of degenerate friends surrounding me.

An exacerbated breath leaves her lips as she tries and fails to mask the faint smile on her mouth. "Aren't you guys getting too old to wake and bake?"

"Aren't you getting tired of asking us that?" I regard her with amusement.

Cannon and I share a simultaneous smile.

"Get on with it. We have that radio segment you scheduled. I pride myself on being on time."

She rolls her eyes at my bullshit. I'm the habitually late member of this group.

"Cut the shit." Taking a sip from her cup, she holds her thumb and forefinger out, motioning for the joint she just pretended to be offended over. "Thank you for keeping on schedule and making appearances."

"Thank you for the coffee"—I hold up it, then look toward Cannon, who is on his exhale—"and the buzz."

"The floor is yours." Oliver rubs his neck, settling on the floor.

Ignoring him, we watch in silence, smoke filling the air around us as she fires off a string of text messages. Back-to-back chimes echo throughout the suite before she turns her attention back to us.

"The calvary called me."

MAZEN

THE CALVARY.

Nothing good has ever happened following a sentence like that.

The calvary, better known as our label and team of managers. They're the fucktards behind this ... whatever the hell this is. My temper flares, heat over an open flame, knowing that a shit show is brewing.

The front door swings open, and in walks Murphy, sans his new legal shadow. He sulks into the room, looking every bit as pissed off as I know I did five minutes ago.

With a grimace, he barks, "You know I just got married last night, right?" His eyes roam the room, landing on Lindsey.

"You know we decided you'd do the European tour, and *then* you and your beautiful bride could take some time off and have a real honeymoon?" Lindsey adds emphasis to the word *then*, rubbing it into a wound.

She's cutthroat. Her poised appearance is a front for her

ruthless, ballbuster personality. There's no better way to describe her. Which is why bile rises in my throat as we settle into our seats, ready for whatever it is she's here to announce.

"Don't hate me over this, fellas ..."

The door once again widens, and I wonder who else has clearance to be on our floor.

Four sets of eyes freeze on the doorway. To my shock, Sophia timidly slides inside the suite, looking every bit as uneasy as I know I am.

A swarm of dread takes flight in my stomach.

Why the hell is she here?

I know why she's *here*, here. She has a room in this suite. She works for Oliver. What I mean is, why is she here this morning, and why do I get the unmistakable impression, based on her furrowed brows, that she's not here to chitchat with Oliver over coffee? No, she was summoned here, just like the rest of us.

Which is worse. Way worse.

A red mound of hair is piled high on her head and secured with some hair contraption I think women call headbands. It's black with small metal spikes. My breath falters even more when I take in the shirt she's wearing. *Make America Emo Again* is sprayed across her chest. She's wearing our band's merch. It's knotted on her waist, and a cheetah-printed skirt covers her petite legs, hitting mid-calf. Black-and-white checkered slides cover her feet. Her outfit is edgy. It screams grunge princess, and I'm impressed.

Last night at the wedding, she looked like a queen, ready to slay her court.

This morning, she woke up and said *I'm ready to fuck shit up*. Which is exactly what I fear she is here to do.

I try to hide the smile that threatens to form on my face

by a tight-lipped cough. Clearing my throat, I reach toward the ashtray.

I'm not high enough for this conversation. Rectifying that is my new mission.

"Hey, beautiful." Oliver gives Sophia a once-over as he stretches and pulls a cup from the tray of drinks.

Lindsey swats at his hand. "That one's for Sophia. Caramel macchiato with low-fat milk." Her eyes beam at the red-haired intruder, no threat in sight. There's a levity in her tone as she offers a hand. "I'm Lindsey. Thanks for coming on short notice and thanks for the tip about ordering on the app. I love earning free stuff. Even if I use the band's money," she says without taking a breath before her wide eyes scan back to us.

"I invited Sophia here this morning since the information I am about to relay involves her. As you know, coming off the last tour, your numbers were staggering. Lower streaming means—"

"For fuck's sake, there was a national pandemic. Of course the numbers are askew." My temper sparks.

"Streaming went up at the peak of the pandemic. Not down, Maz." Her cool tone cuts me like a knife. "The label thinks it has to do with your image."

Ocean-water eyes find mine, remorse filling them to the brim. Despite her working for the label, she's always been our friend first, publicist second. Oh, how the tides have changed.

"With all the partying that ensued during the pandemic, you got a lot of bad press. Social media is a major driving force nowadays, and what's floating around the web with your name associated with it isn't good right now. We need a fresh start. To revamp your image."

"I don't see you looking at anyone else, Linds. So, I'm

the problem? Is that what I'm hearing? No one else got their dick wet or has hidden secrets in our little soiree?" I avert my eyes from hers, scanning the room.

"I love you, Mazen. You know that ... but ... yes, you are, and the label isn't happy. Luckily for you, because I'm your fairy godmother or some shit, I have a plan. One that you need to get on board with to save face."

Oliver seems to have caught on, sensing that Lindsey's plan to get my name and image back into America's favor will involve his new employee-slash-hookup. His nostrils flare.

"This plan obviously includes Soph. How? And why her? I swear, if you say what you're about to say, I'm going to fuck shit up. In the sense that Maz won't be the only wild king you have to conquer."

Lindsey inhales, glances toward Sophia, and seems to scroll through her camera roll before looking back up, her eyes darting around.

"Spit it out, Linds. Do I need to make another sizable donation somewhere? What's it going to take to get a gamut of good publicity? If it's influencers hating, let's plan an influencer retreat or something. We can do a private show. Maybe do a raffle and pick one from each platform to come out and hang with us for a week. Surely, that will help. I'll do anything—literally anything—you and the godforsaken label want. Do not include Sophia. She's here as our tattoo artist and nothing more. Do you hear me?"

Murphy and Cannon exchange a glance that says, *Mazen is a horrible fucking liar, and we can see right through him,* before they shake their heads at their inside commentary, and then give Lindsey back their full attention.

I pride myself on being a good judge of character. Right

now, her face is unreadable. Which only irritates me all the more.

"Rodney, Nick, and I have been brainstorming how to help the band's image for a while. That whole stunt where you pissed in a flower pot at the White House didn't do you any favors."

Being on blast isn't for the weak.

Especially when there is an audience—and I don't mean the world. No, I mean the petite red-haired goddess who is now privy to my many shortcomings, thanks to Lindsey hurling my bad reputation around like a tetherball.

"An image of you and Sophia from the wedding leaked this morning."

There it is, folks.

The truth as to why she's here and involved in this mess. I painted a target on her back. Both with my scum-of-the-earth father and unintentionally with the media.

Shoving a hand through my hair, I tug the ends in frustration. I was trying to save her from his filth. He was hitting on her, and … I couldn't fucking stand it for a minute longer, so I swooped in. I thought I was helping. Looks like I invited her into the devil's playground and tied a bow around her neck.

"This"—Linds holds up her phone—"started ringing off the hook at three this morning. Everyone is dying to know who your date is—and I mean, everyone. It's the first time you've been pictured with a woman of Sophia's … caliber."

I take note of the hand that tightens around Sophia's shoulder. Oliver feels threatened. It shouldn't make me happy. It shouldn't, but I'd be lying if I said it didn't do something to me. We've always been competitive. From battling on video games, sports, to women … it's ingrained in our friendship. Hell, we were four kids who morphed into men together.

"I've been up brainstorming how we spin this in the band's favor, and then it came to me." She locks eyes with me for the hundredth time this morning. "We can use this to our advantage. It would be good for your overall image and therefore good for the band's sales. I should have thought about this weeks ago," she adds, tossing a wistful look at Sophia.

The unmistakable redness on her face tells me she knows Lindsey is about to involve her in whatever she's scheming. I drink in the deeply maniacal expression on her face, finding satisfaction that she's suffering through this conspiracy as well.

"The world wants to see another side to you, Maz. The side *we* all know and love. Not the king you are onstage. The real you. The one who donates to homeless shelters and buys presents for every child in the local hospital every Christmas. Let's give them what they want." Taking a breath, Lindsey exhales her plan, the reason for the early wake-up call. My worst fear. "I'm proposing we stage a fake relationship between you and Sophia."

Collective gasps fill the room. The most surprised is Sophia as she sits with her legs tucked underneath her on the chaise adjacent to the couch I'm on.

"The media has dragged our name through the mud enough ... and can we really blame them? We can't. KOJ's die-hard fans couldn't give two shits, but we need to attract new listeners. You fucked your way across the globe one groupie at a time on the last US tour. People are ready to take a KOJ hiatus. This is the best solution we have, given the pictures that were leaked."

"Sex sells." My teeth grind. I'm over listening to this

garbage. "Nowhere in my contract does it mention my personal life."

"You're right, Mazen." My whole name should be a clear indicator to how serious Lindsey is taking this. "It does mention sales though, and right now, numbers are dwindling. People want to see more. They want authenticity. They want to see the man behind the microphone. They're over the fuckboy parade. We've been friends for years, and even I'm getting a little bit worried about you. Plus," she adds, ready to justify her stance on the matter, "you're a celeb. People care more about your sex life than they do the national debt crisis." Her eyes finally divert from mine as she looks around the room, urging someone to go against her. "Tell me you guys don't think the same?"

Oliver chimes in, "You really think coming up with a fake dating gimmick will work?"

Sophia's body shifts, and she sets down her coffee cup on the table. With eyes wide in disbelief, she says, "Do I have a say-so in this? You know ... since it affects my life too."

"Of course. That's why I asked you to meet me here." Lindsey inwardly groans. Apparently, she didn't think Sophia had a backbone of her own.

News flash: she's tough as a nail. I've learned the hard way, having already tried to push all her buttons.

"Need I remind everyone that I'm just here as a tattoo artist? Nothing more. I ... I'm not really sure who in their right mind would agree to this. This is crazy. I get the whole being-seen-together thing, but this seems like an internal issue. One that I should not be a part of. I'm sure there are women in droves who would sign up to date Mazen. I'm just not one of them. Sorry that I can't help." There's a subtle hesitancy in Sophia's voice as she stands, her eyes glancing over Oliver first and then Cannon.

I take note that she skips looking in my direction altogether.

"Take me out of the equation, please. I'm leaving." She slowly backs up until her hand is on the door handle of the suite.

Why did she look at Cannon? Are they friends? Did their little tattoo sessions forge a bond between them? Questions rain down like acid to my overthinking mind. I'm acting like a fucking girl. That's what Sophia does to me. She reduces me to nothing more than a heap of questions. The main one being, *Why don't you remember me?*

"You can decline to participate in this ... I don't know what to call this ... offer ... but you should know that the label has agreed to offer you a hundred thousand dollars for your service and, of course, your full disclosure. If you agreed to fake date Mazen, you'd get paid. A lot. They know about your deal with Ollie and are prepared to offer you the same for your help. Think about the money. Only think about the money if you have to." Lindsey dangles a line.

"I'll fake date him for that kind of bread." Vanna's small voice booms from the front door.

It's a fucking party in our suite this morning.

"Baby, we got married yesterday. It's not good for my pride to hear that the morning after our wedding," Murphy jokes as he stands, walks over to his new bride, and wraps himself around her like a spider monkey.

Vanna's eyes twinkle when he kisses her on her forehead.

My pride is deserted in a wasteland. Sophia doesn't remember me and the night that meant ... too much to me and not enough to her, apparently. Now, she's acting like she's too good to fake date me. Refusing a hundred thousand dollars for someone in her position is asinine.

"Sophia's right. I can fuck whoever I want. Whenever I want. Surely, one of them will sign on the dotted line and date me."

"The women you attract aren't the type who scream *serious relationship material.* Sophia is stunning, owns her own business. Has a college degree. We can use those assets to our advantage."

Embarrassment floods over me. The tide of her dismissal drags me out to sea. "Sure, she has assets. So do some models I've screwed. They're not all bimbos, and trust me"—my attention lands directly on Sophia—"she doesn't hold a candle to any of them. Look at her." I gesture, swallowing my rage in an attempt not to get smacked in the face before noon. I want to use my words to hurt her. I just don't want to get a black eye in the process. Not from her or her little boyfriend next to her. "She looks like a washed-up teenage groupie. Do you think anyone would believe I'd date *her?*"

Hurt lingers on Sophia's face as she stares at me for a brief moment and then closes her eyes. An intense jolt of desolation sweeps over me, our faces mirroring one another's. My dad always used his tongue to cut me the hardest. When that didn't work, he started in with his fist. Lorenzo Wilde is smart though. He never left a visible bruise. Knowing that those could gain attention and threaten the perfectly cultivated image he'd forged for the media. Who would vote for a man who beat his son?

The realization that I'm no better than him lingers in the air around me like a blanket of scalding contempt. Under the burn of my sardonic expression, I hide the festering need swelling within me. I want to leap forward, shake Sophia's head, and force her eyes to open. I want to tell her I take back my vicious words and extinguish the pain in her heart that is undoubtedly there because of me and my stupid attempt to hurt someone before they can hurt me. I want her forest-green eyes that flitter open and claw at me like talons to see through my glowering mask of resentment. I want her to see how bad she hurt me and continues to hurt me. I just want *her*.

"I'd date her."

A bitter jealousy twists like a knife in my heart, carving out the little life that's still left beating in it at Cannon's words. The fucker barely speaks, and when he does, he cuts me with an admission like this.

My broad shoulders heave as I draw in a sharp breath. "You too? Is anyone in this room not bedding my new fake girlfriend."

"Mazen, I didn't agree to this. Don't call me that." Sophia's hostile glare cuts through the quietness of the room.

"You see, Sophia, you don't really have a choice. It's cute that you think you do. When you get in bed with the music industry, you sell your soul."

An anger like I've never known mounts in my chest, ready to explode in an almost-uncontrollable thundercloud of indignation. She's still turning me down. No. Fucking. Way.

I forge on, my voice low, strained with rage. "You've already bedded one member of my band, that I know of, which means you've already sold your soul. Why not make another hundred thousand? Isn't that why you're here in the first place—for money?" My breath comes out ragged. "Take Lindsey's offer, and let's get this spit roast started.

That's what you like to read about anyway. Let's make it a reality."

Murphy, the mediator, intervenes. "Let's can this conversation. Lindsey, maybe you should come back later. Everyone needs to take a beat. Regroup. Chill the hell out."

His words, like ice assailing my frenzy, bring me back down to reality.

"I don't need to take a beat." Sophia's expression verges on torment and disgust. Determination replaces the hurt in the green abyss of her eyes. "I'll fake date you. Despite how much I ... hate you. Because I do need the money. Mark my words: this is only about the money. You ... your opinion of me ... it means nothing. I wouldn't spit on you if you were on fire, and you're going to have to deal with me screwing your *friends*. Because it's going to keep happening, *boyfriend,* and you are never ever going to partake. Let that reality sink in."

I fucking want to throttle her ... then bend her over and punish her for threatening me. I want Sophia Rose Lozier, and it seems my whole motherfucking band does too. *Hell.* The kicker is that she wouldn't even consider fake dating me until I goaded her into it. That's the hardest punch to the gut I've ever received.

Lorenzo should be proud of my new *girlfriend.* She hits just as hard as he does.

STUFFED FRENCH TOAST

OLIVER

"HOW WAS LAST NIGHT?" I ask, my attention glued to the frying pan I'm hovering over.

I hear a deep grunt, a plea to keep my curiosity reeled in. Cannon knows me better than that though.

"That good, huh?"

His lack of response is enough to confirm my suspicions. It was *that* good. I want to be mad, but, hell, I know first-hand how good Soph is. I can still hear the soft purrs that left her lips when she moaned from passion as she unabashedly took her fill of my cock. I remember how she felt when her thighs gripped the sides of my body as waves of ecstasy throbbed through her in an explosive release. And the peace that tethered us together after we both floated back down to reality, too stunned to speak.

I should be pissed that he, too, has experienced her at the peak of climax, quivering in a masterful hysteria of delight. I'm not. I'm more frustrated by the fact that they were together, and I wasn't there to witness them soaring jointly and then vibrating together, burning with liquid fire.

Realization hits me like a punch to my fucking gut as I watch him attempt to eat and scroll through her studio's social media page. Cannon wants Soph for more than a meaningless hookup. The proof is in the stalking. I can tell in the way that he offers quick but purposeful glances when he thinks she isn't looking. After all, I've been on the receiving end of his arousing gaze before. I know those stolen glances all too well.

Cannon is very private when it comes to his sex life. He always has been. He's not the kiss-and-tell type. It's something I can appreciate. Can I even blame him for falling under her spell? For being enamored by her beauty and brains?

Fuck no. Not when I'm equally as enamored by the little Fireball.

I turn to face him, spatula in hand, diverting my wandering thoughts. Armor back in place, I ask, "Stuffed French toast?"

He shakes his head, nodding to the avocado toast resting on the plate in front of him. It still amazes me that this brute of a dude eats that shit and has enough dignity not to hide it. If I didn't know what he was packing under his belt and how he could deliver, I'd call him a cupcake.

"Suit yourself." Shrugging at the fact that he turned down a morning delicacy, I glance out the window of our high-rise, waiting to flip my breakfast.

The cream cheese and strawberry inside gushes out from the two slices of bread, and my mouth waters. The first bite may elicit a moan or induce a coma from its sugar overload. Most likely both.

The sizzle on the pan beckons my attention, cooking is a

good distraction. I attempt to block out Cannon's presence and focus solely on preparing my meal. It's short-lived. The sound of him biting into his toast grates on my nerves. It's most likely not even his presence that has me on high alert; it's the damn sounds he's making as he devours his breakfast.

I have a love-hate relationship with both Cannon Rhodes and food. I grew up as impoverished as one could get while still sleeping indoors, and warm meals were hard to come by.

Starving is a different kind of torture. One that we're never intended to feel. It's been years since I opened a refrigerator and it was empty. But I can still remember the way an empty stomach felt like it was yesterday. The hollow sounds it makes, the cramps that come after days of being vacant. A simple whiff of food from a neighbor's backyard made my mouth salivate when I walked home from school on more occasions than even I can recall. Nothing says you're poor like being jealous of the neighborhood stray, knowing that he at least got scraps or could dig through the trash and satisfy his hunger at the end of the day.

Despite the harsh reality that everyone isn't blessed with being provided simple necessities like food, I've come to terms with my upbringing. I've faced the demons of my past and accepted that I was dealt a shit hand. I remember the first time we got paid. I mean, *really* paid. I ordered over a thousand dollars in groceries. Stocked two deep freezers and ate my weight in food.

Cooking hasn't always been a hobby. For the majority of my life, it was a chore. I'd make my own concoctions with the ingredients I had. Which wasn't much. But I survived. I remember finding a fifty-dollar bill in the parking lot of the grocery store once. The simple bill, adorned by the face of

Ulysses S. Grant, was like winning the lottery to me. I recall looking around sharply and pocketing the bill. That morning, before school, I whipped up a batch of stuffed French toast. It was the fullest I ever recall feeling at school—at least on days I didn't stop by Cannon's house first. His mom was always cooking, trying new recipes with herbs from her garden. I attribute a lot of the meals I know how to prepare to her.

Flipping my meal for the last time, I place my French toast on my plate. With the shake of my wrist, I sprinkle a dusting of powdered sugar on top and drizzle a layer of maple syrup. The silence lingering thick in the air is killing me.

Was it just sex? Are feelings brewing between them? Am I a total dickwad for feeling inferior? Yes. Why, yes, I am.

My mind reels, question after question dangling on the tip of my tongue as we sit at the island side by side. A smidgen of possession comes over me as I think about them. Individually and together.

Filled with a bleak clarity, I break the silence hanging between us. "Are we going to talk about the elephant in the room?"

"What's there to say?"

Disdain is laced in my tone as I run my hand through my unruly bedhead. "Oh, I don't know. How about the fact that you met my girl on an app and arranged a meet and fuck and then casually offered to date her in front of our friends like some sort of ... lovestruck kitten?"

After Mazen stormed off, Murphy swept his new bride into his arms, and they excused themselves for a few hours. Cannon retreated to the bus, his odd sanctuary of sorts, and Sophia said she needed some air. With nothing better to do, I decided to cook and eat my sorrows. Two of my best friends are now tied to Soph. Mazen is her fake boyfriend, and Cannon apparently wants to start dating her too. My heart thuds louder because of the latter, and I wonder how I can persuade them both ...

Don't even go there, Ollie.

When Cannon doesn't respond, rather bites into his disgusting green-covered toast, I decide to go with another tactic. Goading always works.

"You don't date. Anyone."

The look that Cannon nails me with screams infuriation. His body language says, *Fuck off*, but his mouth remains motionless.

I press harder. "As long as we've been friends, I've never seen you with an actual girlfriend ... or boyfriend." I cringe at the word. Not because of the meaning, but because I know he has this weird obsession with keeping that part of him locked up tight. "It's the twenty-first century. People are gay. Teachers, police officers, football players."

He has this delusional thought that the world will treat him differently if he comes out as bisexual.

Fuck the world's opinion.

Saying it out loud, recognizing that side of him, seems to do the trick.

Something must've clicked.

He leans back, arms crossed in a defensive manner. "You don't know shit. Not anymore."

Now, who's goading who?

Ardently, I retort, "I think we both know that's a damn lie. I know *you*. The version you keep hidden. Better than anyone else. Except maybe Soph now." The metal of my fork clangs against my plate as I set it down, giving him my full attention. "I ... shit ... this isn't easy to say—"

"Then, don't say it," he grits out, seeming satisfied, and then takes another bite of his toast.

I lose the fight with my own restraint. "I want to be there the next time you're *with her*, with her. It just makes sense."

Faltering just a morsel, he gives me a side-eye. There's a potency in his glare, a warning that I'm treading on thin ice.

"You're out of your fucking mind."

I take note of the way his chest reddens.

I inch closer. "I'm not. I want her. You want her. Even Mazen wants her even though he's fighting tooth and nail not to admit it. Why can't we all have her together? Think of how good it would be. Don't you remember—"

"Don't go there with me."

"I remember. I can't forget. Even though I've fucking tried. So hard."

"Try harder."

"Don't be a dick. Let's move forward—together. We don't have to fight over her when we can share her."

Timidly, Cannon runs his hand through his hair. "Share her," he says as if he's thinking through the scene I painted for him.

When he finds his voice, it's huskier than normal. Need etched in every syllable. "Talk to Maz. You and I both know something is going on there too. If he's in, I'm in."

That was almost too easy.

"But don't for one fucking second think this is about you and me. That ship sailed a long time ago. This is only about Sophia."

I smother a groan, and it's not from the delicious French toast I'm chewing. It's the memory of the times Cannon and I rolled in his bed together a lifetime ago. Twisted in sheets and limbs. We dove headfirst into bi-land. Only he accepted his desires fully and didn't fight them like I did.

Fuck fighting fate. I'm ready to chase him and her both into the bedroom. He's delusional if he thinks this isn't also about us.

THE SIZE OF RAISINS

SOPHIA

THE CRUELEST OF punishment comes in the form of fake dating Mazen Wilde. Sure, any woman with a set of eyes would claw mine out at the chance to date him. I understand the magnitude of this offer.

It's not lost on me.

Which is why I feel like I'm going to hurl. Because I want to throat-punch him and then lick his wounds right after. I'm indebted to Kings of Jupiter, sinking further into metaphorical bed with them. Knowing this isn't going to end well, I excused myself, needing some much-needed air and advice from my baby sister.

Standing in our kitchen, I lean against our counter, coffee mug in hand ready to word vomit as Lacey walks into the room. I fill her in before taking a sip of my now cold coffee and await her response.

"Why does God love you so much?" she says with a significant raise of her brow. "This is such bullshit. The only good thing that happens to me is not getting charged extra for sauce for the nuggets I already bought. Corporate America can fuck herself. I mean, I already bought the nuggets, and I only get one packet of sauce for ten. Do the math, idiots."

My mood shifts significantly. "You're so dumb." I can't conceal my amusement. "You act like I'm lucky or something." I tuck my legs under my legging-clothed rear. "Not only is he America's playboy, but now, he's my fake boyfriend. I don't see how you can be envious of any of this, and you own a business. Every sale counts."

"Are you delusional or just fucking stupid?" Lacey all but snaps in my face. "You screwed the band's guitarist, drummer, and now, you're being paid a hundred thousand dollars to date the singer. Where in that little brain of yours are you hiding your excitement?"

"Yay me." I feign elation. "You basically just called me a prostitute, making you just as debauched as Mazen."

"No, Julia Roberts wannabe. You're getting paid to date him publicly, not screw his brains out. Besides"—she smothers a smile—"if you ever wanted to reenact one of those scenes from those books you devour, now is your one shot at a harem."

"I. Cannot. With. You. Seriously. Please go away. I'm going to shower and get ready." I walk away, leaving her on the couch with the shred of dignity I have left.

"Wear something slutty!"

AN HOUR LATER, Lacey heartily slaps me on the ass before sending me off with an amused wink.

"It's not every day you get a date with one of the Kings." Her grin of hilarity is palpable as I swing open the door and come face-to-face with the leader of sin himself.

Paying no attention to Mazen, I give Lacey a tight hug, knowing that after our date tonight, we're headed straight to the airport with Belgium as our next destination.

"Love you, sis," I whisper into her thick pink waves. "We're leaving after our date. So, I'll text you when we land."

Tenderly, she replies, "Not more than I love you. Go on. Your date looks like he's going to throttle me."

An icy contempt flashes in Mazen's deep gunmetal eyes. "She's right, Rosella. Let's go before my patience thins, and ... I don't know ... I give her a taste of her own medicine and Tase her back."

"You wouldn't." She flashes a steady display of challenge.

"*Mettimi alla prova.*" Try me. "I almost bought a little Taser necklace. I figured I could wear it like a rape whistle when you're around," he sneers at my sister.

My eyes narrow in alarm. This feud is ... justifiable ... but annoying. Without notice, Mazen raises the back of his shirt, just enough to show the Taser he has stored in the waistband of his black jeans.

"Retribution is my middle name."

"Mazen Wilde!" I yell, chastising him while holding in my laughter.

"Come on." He gestures down the vacant hallway with his hand. "I have no intention of hurting your precious little sister. This is just protection in case she gets all crazy again."

Stealing a glance at his large hand, I spy the jellyfish tattoo on full display. Pride wells in my chest. I'm not conceited enough to believe I'm the best tattoo artist in the world, but I unashamedly smile inside, knowing that every time Mazen grips his microphone, my art is on full display.

"Let's get this over with then." I look over my shoulder, stepping into the hallway. I say to Lacey, "I'll text you when we land."

The schedule to get them back on tour is set. The wedding weekend was just a small detour.

With his hand on the small of my back, Mazen leads me down the hallway.

"Such a romantic. I can't wait to see what's in store for me tonight." I shoot him a twisted smile.

Making our way down the flight of steps that lead to the alleyway of my building, I see Ashton standing outside of the black SUV I've grown accustomed to. Jupiter is sitting next to him, tail wagging.

"Hi, buddy." I bend to his level and rub my nose with his. "Nosy, nosy." My lips soften into a warm smile. What can I say? The husky and I have grown close. Suppressing a giggle as Jupiter licks my cheek, I say, "It's a good thing I'm not like your daddy's other dates, caked in makeup, huh?"

"Get in," Mazen demands. "*Affrettarsi.*" Hurry up. "*Muoviti.*" Move.

"Me or the dog?"

The deep chuckle coming from Ashton soothes my nerves as I climb inside the vehicle without waiting on a response from my jackass of a date.

Jupiter sits in between his owner and me. The space is a nice reprieve. I don't know if it's my abhorrence of the lead singer or the unmistakable pull I feel whenever he's around that has me keeping an expansive distance from him.

The giant husky makes a great buffer.

When the SUV comes to a stop, I glance out the

window, noticing the ocean in all its magnificence staring back at me.

"The boardwalk?"

"Lindsey planned this shit. Not me. Let's go." He slides out the door that Ashton opened for him and takes Jupiter by the leash. Leaning back in the back seat, he says, "There're paparazzi. Linds tipped them off so we'd be sure photographers were here to get our picture. Ready or not, welcome to my world."

He drags his hand through his midnight-colored hair, and I'm envious of its shine. I'm half tempted to ask who his beautician is. There's probably a Facebook group dedicated solely to Mazen's luscious locks.

Hesitantly, I swallow down the large lump in my throat and take his extended hand. When I slide out of the back seat, Mazen pulls me toward his embrace. With the cool metal from the SUV behind me and the warmth radiating from his body in front of me, my thoughts descend in a tailspin. I don't have time to process the ambush of snapping noises that stir around us when he pins me to the vehicle, boxing me in with his hands.

I raise a hand to stop him from leaning forward.

Mazen side steps, pressing into me harder, on a mission. My palm meets his taut stomach. Fingers splaying over the ridge of each defined muscle hidden under his shirt. With one hand, he circles my waist, our bodies molded tightly in an intimate embrace.

My mind reels.

My body ignites.

There's a fine line between fact and fiction, and we're treading the line dangerously.

Finding my voice, I mutter, "What are you doing?"

A flash of laughter flickers in his eyes before he dips his

chin, using it to brush my hair away from my cheek and then leans closer toward my ear and whispers, "Giving the media what they want."

"Which is?" I ask breathlessly.

Ringed with black lashes, his eyes land on mine, capturing me like a tide.

"The declaration of a love so pure that it can be felt in every photograph they capture tonight." The humor in his tone is gone. Even his eyes seem to harden.

Dammit if that isn't the most perfect sentence a man has ever muttered in my presence. Clearly, I'm delusional or have a contact buzz from the copious amounts of marijuana that's been smoked around me because the man before me doesn't usually make my knees weak.

No, usually, he makes me want to offer him a Clorox wipe to wash his face with. I am not prepared to deal with this...him.

"Is it only what the media wants?" my mouth implores despite the protest from my brain.

Tucking his bottom lip in his mouth, he seems to ponder on my question before settling on his answer. "If I didn't want it, I wouldn't do it. I don't know if you've noticed or not, but I don't like being forced to do anything."

"Says the man on a date because his label wanted to tidy up his rogue image."

Without missing a beat, he counters, "Says the woman who's going to cash a hefty paycheck once the world is sold that we're in love."

Point taken.

Impatiently, I gather my thoughts. Thoughts that should be banned. Thoughts that pertain to how soft his lips would feel against my own.

With Oliver, I know what I get. He's a constant. Even

though his tattoo isn't healed, and we haven't had sex again, he's there. Whether we're watching a scary movie on the bus together or playing a game to kill time. He is always making a point to be present. He's about as loyal as Jupiter and equally as cuddly.

Then, there's Cannon, the mysterious drummer with a scowl the size of Texas on his beautiful face and a heart of gold, hidden under mounds of muscle and flesh. Though he's not as talkative by a long shot, he's been making strides by continuing to text me, forgoing his alias of HempDaddy. We talk about plants and his love for the ocean. I feel like I know Cannon better than anyone on tour, which is hysterical, considering our conversations are mostly kept on our devices.

That leaves Mazen Wilde. The heartthrob of the band and my new boyfriend. I can't decipher what his intentions are as he watches me with thundering gray eyes. Eyes that seem to hold me captive in place like a magnet.

My vow not to fall for another musician in my lifetime is shattered when he leans down, a hairbreadth away, and whispers, "Oliver said you wear mint lip balm that tingles his lips. I've been dying for a taste myself."

Holy. Hell. I'm royally fucked because, as it seems, I'm falling for three musicians.

If I had ovaries, they'd be the size of a raisin right now. He's so suave. So charming. I have to remind myself that his words are hollow. He's a musician, for Christ's sake. Lyrics are his forte. A tool used to elicit emotion from his fans. Hell, he's written songs that have been played in movies. I cannot let this ... moment ... faze me.

Hold on to your hate for him, stupid fucking girl.

For an instant, he does nothing but watch me with an

observant eye. Trying to gauge my reaction for his foolish avowal no doubt.

Reaching upward, I cup his chiseled cheek. My resolve dwindles. Two can play this game.

"There's something else he's tasted that I can promise is more mouthwatering than my mint lip balm."

"*Che cazzo.*" What the fuck.

I swear, for a split second, he closes his eyes, leans into my embrace, and loses himself in the image I painted. But as soon as his eyes open, his back becomes ramrod straight, like he came to his senses and remembered that I was enemy number one.

Taking him off guard again, I press my lips onto his, refusing to allow him to claim me in front of the cameras.

This arrangement will be on my terms.

Mazen doesn't get the satisfaction of looking like a doting boyfriend.

He hasn't earned the right to kiss me, for the media or not. So, I take matters into my own hands and smother his mouth against mine with a savage intensity that surprises even myself.

We stand, wrapped in a dreamy intimacy as our mouths find a harmony of their own. Mazen is devastatingly handsome. It makes me wonder if he's truly even mortal. If I hadn't tattooed him myself and seen him bleed red, I would really push that fact more. The guttural way his lips trace mine should be illegal. He should be wrapped in yellow caution tape.

I don't know how much time elapses when Jupiter nudges my leg with his head, breaking our trance. On instinct, I pull away forcefully. I need to put some distance between us. I need a cold shower. I push his chest again, this time demanding his body to move. Mazen doesn't though.

Instead, he leans forward, his mouth grazing my earlobe before he says, "Don't start something you're not prepared to finish."

His words are as challenging as they are frightening.

I brush by him, one hand now holding Jupiter's leash and the other stretched back, waiting for him to grab it.

We walk in tandem around the boardwalk. Playing games, eating fair food, and playing catch with Jupiter on the beach. With sand in my sandals and confusion written across my heart, I'm ready for the night to come to an end. I don't know how many more nauseating smiles I have in me when I see photographers squatting behind buildings or palm trees.

I'm thankful when the sky darkens and the crowd thins. It's been a whirlwind of a couple of hours. Not to mention that the kiss we shared cannot be undone now. The implication of the kiss flashing brighter than the neon lights flickering up and down the boardwalk in my mind.

The security detail must be exhausted from controlling the swarms of fans that have been chanting Mazen's name for hours. It's taxing, and I'm just a fake girlfriend. I can't imagine how he feels.

"This is so crazy. Is your life ever calm?" I ask playfully as I kneel in front of Jupiter, letting him lap my strawberry ice cream cone.

"Not anymore," he replies in a strained tone. "Let's find a seat."

Mazen intertwines our fingers and gently tugs me behind him. He leads me toward the water's edge, and my body complies with his command.

My spirit sinks like my toes in the sand when Mazen

takes off his shirt, uses it like a makeshift towel, and gestures for me to sit down on it.

"Haven't we given them enough tonight?" I whine, my eyes shifting, trying to spy the cameramen who trailed us. "I'm getting tired of fake smiling and—"

"Being around me?" His question comes out quick, his tone wounded.

As much as I loathe Mazen and simultaneously want to ride him like a wave, the despair in his voice pulls at my heart. I reward him with an earnest smile while I join him on the sand, sitting on his shirt.

"No. I'm actually tired. If you remember, we got a rather early wake-up call by your publicist, and I had been out fairly late."

"What were you out doing?" It's a real question, not laced with accusations. As if he's trying to draw a response, his eyes lock on to mine, making it difficult for me to think clearly. "You don't have to share anything. Just forget I asked."

"I was meeting up with a friend."

This is a new side to Mazen that I haven't met yet. He seems unsure of himself. Like asking a question that isn't laced with venom is so out of his character that he, too, has to sit back and wonder what's gotten into himself.

A twinge of vulnerability lingers between us as I sit, motionless and unnerved by his sudden change in demeanor. Playing off on his own need for answers, I give him a half-hearted one and probe into his personal life. With his guard seemingly down, this might be my only opportunity to get to know him.

Here goes nothing.

"I noticed that both of your pinkie fingernails are always

painted hot pink. Is that a part of the tortured artist starter pack?"

Mazen leans back on his elbows, undeterred by the sand as my question registers. For a split second, his chiseled face grimaces, and it looks like he's going to verbally hurl me into the ocean before us until Jupiter nudges Mazen's calf, seemingly offering a bounty of courage to his master. The mutt's coziness seems to seep into Mazen. His slight hesitation evaporates, and his truth leaves me breathless.

"My sister, Bethany, died in a car crash. That I'd caused."

Words fail me.

I'm more than baffled by his truth. It shatters me.

With a mask hiding my swirling emotions, I offer him a sincere apology for digging into something that I had no right to do. Sure, I didn't know his answer would be so ... profound. I still feel like a jerk for grudging up something that is so apparently painful to him.

"I'm so sorry I asked. I'm even more sorry for your loss, Mazen. I know how difficult it is to lose someone you love."

I bite back my own anguish, the gaping hole in my heart caused by deaths of two people I loved most in this world.

A rumble of laughter falls from his lips. "She always had her nails painted hot pink. For some reason beyond me, all of her other nails always chipped first, but her pinkie ones. When she died ... I just remember both pinkie nails were painted pink. *Mi manca.*" I miss her.

"You do it to commemorate her memory," I murmur.

When he offers a simple nod of his head, I reach across the sand and cover his hand with my own, bathing him in admiration for his honesty. It takes a strong person to admit something like that to someone else. Vulnerability doesn't seem like a part of his usual arsenal of armor.

"You never talk about her."

"When's a good time to bring up a dead relative in conversation?"

"When you put it like that? Never. I'm sure talking about her would help." My inquisitiveness trudges on. "I'm here if you ever need an ear."

"If I talk about her, I'll break, and I'm scared I won't ever be able to stop fucking crying then."

A dullness in my chest feels like I'm being swallowed whole. The declaration and rawness in his truth, it's like a boulder on the edge of free-falling down a cliff. The magnitude of his honesty leaves me feeling breathless.

"I ... I don't know what to say. I just can't imagine. I'm sorry."

"Don't be. You didn't kill her. I did."

"Mazen, I ..."

"I don't want your pity." He looks off into the distance with glossy eyes.

"I don't pity you. I ... it's just if you never give yourself time to grieve properly and the grace to forgive yourself, the pain will eat you alive. Until memory lane is a deserted highway and all you have left is anger."

"Sounds like you're speaking from experience. Who did you lose?"

I'm taken off guard by his question. Feeling like the spotlight has been turned toward me and it's shining brightly waiting on my response. This therapy session isn't about me, though, so I redirect the conversation. "I think she'd be very proud of you for not only honoring her memory, but also for *her* song. 'Dearest Bethany.' It makes sense now."

His eyes, as dark as the sky, survey me thoughtfully. "You listened to our album?"

I flush with my cards on the table.

"Why did you listen to it, Rosella?"

Keeping my face deceptively composed, it takes me several long seconds to contemplate my answer. I could lie and tell him that I listened to it to make sure Kings of Jupiter wasn't cringeworthy, claiming that I could never have taken Oliver up on his proposition if their music was garbage. I could tell him that Lacey, my sister, sent the music video to me and raved about it, so I finally caved and listened. Or I could tell him the truth.

"I listened to it because when you sing, I feel like you're talking directly to me." A flush of crimson tide races across my cheeks like a fever. I cannot believe I just told him that.

The slight stubble on his jaw holds me captive when he says, "If you listen to the right track, you might find something that is directed toward you."

His countenance has my mouth curving into a radiant smile.

I scoff. "All music resonates with people in different ways, right?" I nonchalantly ask, contradicting the wild, erratic beats of my heart.

It's Mazen's turn to break into a leisurely smile.

"Yeah. Right."

ALTER EGO

SOPHIA

A TEXT MESSAGE disturbs my reading haze, a Sunday tradition, especially since the band dubbed Sundays as Sober Sundays. While they partake in their ritual of snoozing, I partake in my e-reader's dim glow.

> HempDaddy: Meet me in the kitchen in twenty.

> TattooKitten: You don't have any bags with you, do you?

> HempDaddy: Not for the purpose you're thinking.

His quick wit is both impressive and depressing. Since we shared our bodies, Cannon hasn't touched me, aside from an innocent brushing of our bodies in the crowded hallway of the tour bus.

My inquisitiveness gets the better of me when I find

myself sauntering into the kitchen like Jupiter's doppel-gänger. So obedient.

As I round the wall from the hallway, the sight in front of me leaves me dumbstruck. In the kitchen is an array of plants, pots, and gardening tools, littered on the marble countertop. Cannon Rhodes looks like sin wrapped in a pair of gray sweatpants.

My mouth hangs ajar. "If you had a hankering to get dirty, all you had to do was ask. What's all this?"

The look that he nails me with says, *What's it look like?* He digs, elbow deep, into a bag of soil, diverting his attention back to his task.

"We both like plants. I figured you'd wouldn't mind wanting to help." A gleam of interest flitters across his downcast face.

He wants to hang out with me. I cheer inside, but my face remains a mask of coolness.

Turning on my heel, I stride forward with a springy bounce in my step and blink, taking him in as my pulse skyrockets once again. Cannon continues digging in the large bag, scooping soil into several small, colorful pots. I imagine dipping my hand underneath his sweatpants, and my palms start to itch.

"My mom opened a nursery when I was ten. When Oliver turned sixteen, she gave him a job. He used to help me re-plant."

"I'm sure he's around here somewhere if you want me to fetch him." I plant my hand on the cool countertop, holding my breath.

I hear a faint smothering of a groan before he says, "If I wanted his help, I'd have texted him."

"Point made." I stand next to him, our pants rubbing

against one another. "Well, what are we waiting for? Dole out a task."

Forty minutes later, the small plants that he needed replanted are back in their places, lining the windowsill of the tour bus. We remained excruciatingly quiet as we moved in tandem, nails thick with soil and hearts full. Unlike Oliver, whose words coat my heart like honey, Cannon's presence is enough to calm my soul.

TERRA-COTTA ROOFTOPS and pastel-colored buildings sweep by my window in a haze of striking architecture. I can feel my cheeks growing wider when my eyes land on the rich background that encompasses the capital of Portugal.

Lisbon is breathtaking with its terraces, vibrant and cultural feel, and easy access to the coast. My heart swells when the Atlantic Ocean comes into view. A reminder of home. Although I wasn't born or raised in Florida.

Like its arms, vast and wide as the ocean, Florida accepted us and made roots quickly. I shouldn't be homesick yet. It's only been a day since we embarked on this leg of the tour, but it feels like forever ago. Before my life was turned upside down by a proposition that I couldn't refuse. I don't regret accepting Oliver's offer to follow him and his friends on tour as their personal tattoo artist. Not one bit. It's just been a whirlwind ... overwhelming. To add flame to the fire, I'm now fake-dating Mazen, and oddly enough, our first public appearance—because I have a hard time calling it an actual date—was ... dare I say it ... nice.

Seeing a different version of him has done something within me. As much as I don't want to admit it, and I haven't out loud, it's thawed my aversion to him by an inch or two.

Knowing that his sister died wasn't a groundbreaking discovery. I had known that from scrolling online. It was more hearing the dip in his voice as he talked about her. You can tell that his heart misses her, and in turn, his vulnerability has made my heart pitter-patter in a way that shocks me. Because I never thought there'd be a day where I didn't want to throat-punch him or cut holes into all of his fancy, stupid boxer briefs he leaves scattered on the bus.

I'm a tattooist, not a maid.

Seeing the ocean as it passes by my window is like seeing an old friend. Belgium was nice, but this view is ... magical.

The ocean is like the moon in a sense. Separated from civilization by thousands of miles, yet both the moon and ocean helps tether people together. Out of all the creatures in the sea, Oliver chose a jellyfish to get permanently carved into his flesh. It didn't resonate with me then. I was too awestruck by both of his propositions to have sex with him and go on tour as the band's personal tattoo artist, that I didn't see the tattoo for what it was.

It's a reminder of *home*. Granted his tattoo is wrapped around his junk, I understand the sentiment in his choice of art a little more now.

As an outsider, it's easy to look at musicians or celebrities and forget that they're real people. That they wake up with the same rancid morning breath as the rest of us.

They're gypsies in a sense. Traveling the open roads, led by nothing more than a will to create, and the thrill of sharing their art. It's humbling when you sit back and think about it and a little sad to be honest. Think about how many holidays, birthdays, and special occasions celebrities miss because they're on a movie set or touring the country. Sure, most are richer than sin and can make up for their absence with lavish gifts. But what kind of life is that? The everyday chaos and the grit of the day-to-day are what make life worth living.

If there's anything I've learned from the past three weeks of tattooing and touring with the members of Kings of Jupiter, it's that they're just existing. They eat, breathe, and live to make music. If they're not in the studio, they're sitting in the shared living room of the suites they rent, playing, writing, practicing. The only time they've had off to just be was for the wedding, which was all of two seconds, and now, they're right back to work. There's a certain level of admiration I have for anyone who uses art as an outlet. It's fascinating. I remember when I started sketching. It was nothing more than a meaningless venture to escape my thoughts, my mind. I never in a million years thought it would go from a hobby of mine into a lucrative profession.

Second to tattooing, I love music. I can appreciate the allure of fulfilling a dream. Traveling the globe on a tour demanded by your fans has to be almost as exhilarating as free-falling from a plane. It's a rush, as Oliver explained it. To me, just a lover of music, no matter what genre, I know how I feel when I listen to a good song. Mind, body, and soul, I love getting wrapped up in a melody. Being here on tour and seeing firsthand how Oliver, Cannon, Murphy, and even my douchecanoe, growing-on-me fake boyfriend, Mazen, get lost as they perform is like a small glimpse into their souls. I won't admit this to anyone because I've really been struggling to admit it even to myself: once or twice, I've caught myself glued to the lead singer, spellbound as he gets lost in his performance and I get lost in him.

It's ironic how much I love music since I can't hold a tune to save my life. I can tattoo a mean keyboard though. That should count for something.

My feet itch to hit the pavement with Jupiter and Vanna at my side as the bus comes to a halt in front of a building built for an army. I've grown accustomed to our little trio. While the band rehearses, we explore.

At first, I felt a little ashamed by the freedom I had. Vanna helped me overcome that by reminding me that this is who the Kings of Jupiter are, that it's what they live for. Although I've already established in my mind that they're not truly living, that's my own biases, and it's a moot point since my opinion doesn't matter anyway. They're merely passengers along for the ride, never stopping to enjoy it themselves.

Either way, despite the bustle of their lives as they forge ahead in their careers, I'm here, and I'll be damned if I let this once-in-a-lifetime opportunity pass me by. Which is my mindset as the door opens and we all scurry to our feet.

Before I exit the bus, I look over my shoulder, feeling an odd sensation skirt down my spine. Sure enough, I'm met with three sets of eyes boring into me.

A fluttering feeling stirs in my stomach as I hold the cool metal handrail, my glare dancing between each watchful man's stare. It's not lost on me that I've caught the attention of both Oliver and Cannon, and as awful as it makes me sound ... I sort of enjoy the flirtatious teasing that we've embarked on. Since my night spent with Hemp-Daddy and his startling statement about dating me the morning we were all blindsided by Lindsey—the band's tough-as-nails publicist—there's been a rift in their casual banter. Well, as casual as any encounter with Cannon Rhodes can be. That part I don't enjoy. Not in the slightest. I feel like a wedge between them.

Taylor Swift's "Anti-Hero" plays in my mind as my eyes continue their doting hop, landing on each member of the band in a questioning glower.

It's the attention I've gained from the one and only Mazen Wilde that has my chest constricting and my hand held firmly on the rail. Since our boardwalk heart-to-heart, he's been ... unusually nice.

As the founding member of the don't fuck people in front of Sophia crew, I'm trying to wrap my head around the sudden change in his demeanor. I almost got used to walking into a room and seeing him railing a runway model. One even told me I was pretty. So, there's that.

Diverting my attention, I settle my eyes on Oliver's chestnut stare. He's holding his guitar in his hand in an almost-possessive manner. I'm fearful that the wood is going to splinter his hand under his forceful grip. The change between the four of us is almost palpable. I'm not sure if the scowl on his face is directed at me or the prospect that he's no longer the only man on my radar. *Or in my heart.* Just admitting that makes me feel grimy. I don't want to play the martyr, but I am the reason that Oliver looks like he's either going to smash his instrument into nothing more than a pile of ash or kiss me into next week.

Rolling my eyes, I find my stare drifting in Cannon's direction. He's holding Jupiter's leash tightly in his hand, like a lifeline. As the self-proclaimed least popular band member, he takes it upon himself to care for their sweet dog. The reason being, he can easily walk the streets without being bombarded by a swarm of fans, like Mazen and Oliver seem to do—his words, not mine.

It hurts my heart that he thinks so low of himself and doesn't recognize his importance to the band he helped create. Oliver told me that it was mostly his basement that they practiced in until his parents soundproofed the garage for them all as a gift on his sixteenth birthday. It's funny to think about Cannon being the dark horse of the bunch when he grew up in a home that was pouring love out of the windows.

He's more than quiet and reserved. He's a ... wallflower. In the weeks I've been tattooing the band, I've noticed that Cannon usually remains on the sidelines, where anything social is entailed, and shies from crowds, including the band's fans.

From my one night with HempDaddy, I know how hard and unyielding he can be once he has his eyes set on something. It's like he and his alter ego can't find themselves on common ground. I'm not ashamed to admit that I like HempDaddy a lot more than the man standing only feet away from me. At least with his alter ago, he talked to me. Whether through text or in person, he felt more like a human than the shell of the burly, tattooed man stalking toward me right now.

"He's got to piss." Cannon dips his chin to his four-legged friend at his feet.

That's the only *excuse me* I get before he shuffles down the steps.

Mazen is next to break eye contact, excusing himself and quickly waddling by me down the steps. For some reason, he's also oddly mute when he passes me. As he's the most outspoken man of the group, his behavior has my head spinning like a hamster on a wheel.

It's Oliver, my trusty partner in crime, who is fighting his own battle with how to navigate our new normal for the duration of the tour, that remains a perfect gentleman. "Come on, Fireball. Let's go check out our new digs for the week." Gesturing me off the bus with one hand, he places the other firmly around my waist before we climb off the bus together and are welcomed into the bustling city around us.

With each city we visit, it's becoming harder to keep my life pre-tour in perspective. I can't lose sight that this is just a job. An obligation. Once my eight weeks are over and I get my paycheck, I'll be forced back into reality. And as bad as I don't want to admit it, I enjoy seeing not only the world, but the three men who were staring at me with wonder and possibility in their eyes.

This make-believe world we've been in will surely implode because all good songs do come to an end.

For right now ... I just want to explore the men of Kings of Jupiter, sans Murphy, almost as much as I want to explore this city.

CANNON

ASHTON HANGS BACK WITH ME, standing mere feet away while Jup fertilizes the yard.

"Anything I should be concerned about?" His vape dangles from his mouth, and he has a curious look in his eye.

I shake my head in a what-the-hell-are-you-talking-about gesture.

"Just because you don't say much doesn't mean how you feel isn't written across your face," he clarifies on an exhale.

This earns him a scowl.

"She's breathtaking, talented as hell. I get the allure. She was bored the other night and started this badass wolf." He pulls his shirt up, revealing his biceps covered in fresh ink. "Anyway, just be careful, man. You know she's with—"

"Oliver," I cut him off, offering the truth before he has a chance to cut me with it. The reminder that while they haven't been sexually active since the night they met, they're together in all other aspects. They drink their coffee together in the mornings either on the bus or in our suite. They FaceTime her sister, Lacey, together and talk about stupid fucking reality shows they all binge-watch like a bunch of college kids with nothing better to do. They play board games and end the night cuddling—Oliver's always the big spoon.

They're as shacked up as two people can be without intercourse. I know Ollie is just biding his time before he's buried once again in Sophia's sweet cunt. As soon as his six week expires and his tattoo is healed, they'll be reunited, and I'll be fucked. Back to being the outcast. Horny, alone, and out of luck.

I'm not a moron. I know the only reason she turned to the app was for sex, and I know that it wasn't even her idea. Her sister had made her that profile. While she chose to log in, it was just an outlet, an easy lay. I'm delusional to think that we could have more. That I could fill a void in her, like Oliver has.

I'm a man of few words. I know this. There are things that I'll never be able to give her. Conversations about art, both hers and mine. Cuddling. Something I detest for no reason other than it shows weakness. He's the better man ... fit for her. Oliver is the total package. He's the handsomest man on the fucking planet, he's funny as hell, and he's about as compassionate as a saint. It's odd since he had a horrible upbringing. It might be his way for putting good juju back into the world. Whatever his reason, he's ... better than me. Even knowing this, knowing that Sophia is out of my league, it doesn't stop my dick from twitching when she's near or my stupid fucking heart from galloping like a crazed horse on the loose at just the sight of her beautiful face. Add Oliver's olive body into the mix, and I'm a glutton for punishment.

"She's with the label now"—Ashton's deep timbre pulls me back to reality—"is what I was going to say. Yes, she has that agreement with Ollie or whatever. But as soon as she signed the contract with your label to fake date Maz, the little tryst you all have been partaking in became an issue."

"I don't have any stake in the game," I deflect, attempting to conceal my involvement with Sophia.

"You might play the big, stupid drummer boy. But you're not as big of a dipshit as that statement makes you out to be. You and I both know it, and we both know that you all just eye-fucked each other from the airport to here."

As much as it pains me to admit it, he's right. I laid my claim on Sophia the moment I got my fill of her and marked her with my seed. There's no coming back from something like that, and the truth is ... I don't want to come back from it. Ever. I want her, and I want to let her know just how bad. If I have to compete with Ollie, so be it.

We'll be as mismatched as a couple can get. The beautiful, red-haired siren and the fucked-up blond who's been too scared to come out of the closet for thirty years.

I want Sophia Rose Lozier.

I want her to look at me with those big green globes that make me want to melt and know that her heart beats as fast as mine does when she's around. I want to sit in silence and admire her drawings, praising her natural, gifted talent. I want to give her my sticks after a show, no one else. Not anymore.

The realization of my attraction to her flows from a want to a need faster than an explosion of lava from a volcano.

Which means I need to man up and make my intentions clear. I want to win Sophia's heart. I want to be worthy enough to be called hers. Even if I get just a small piece of her in return. I know that she's already given a sliver of it away to Oliver. I can deal with that.

Let's face it. The fucker has a piece of my heart too.

35

LOCAL PLAYBOY

MAZEN

IT'S standard that the suite is swept by our security team prior to our arrival. What catches me off guard is the blatant presence of an intruder sitting on the couch when I saunter into the living room.

"Don't look so excited to see me." Lindsey beams from ear to ear. She's wearing a black—her favorite color—sundress and sandals, looking leisurely as hell. Like she didn't force me into a relationship not too long ago against my will.

She should run for president.

We've been on the outs since she started playing matchmaker and conned Sophia into dating me, so I speak the truth when I say, "I'm not."

The kitchen is fully stocked, per usual. It's a nice perk that comes with the territory. If your publicist comes by unannounced, with our history, it translates into needing to be buzzed to deal with her demands. Pulling out a bottle of tequila from the freezer—my demand—I open it and take a rich swig, preparing my mind for whatever bullshit is about to happen.

The front door swings wide, welcoming a handholding Oliver and Sophia into the room next.

Another swig.

I don't miss the quizzical look on Lindsey's face as she eyeballs me gulping down my pride.

Yep. You paired her with the wrong heartthrob.

A witty joke is on the tip of my tongue. I swallow it, along with another swig of liquid straight from the bottle. The pun I intended to say sloshes in my stomach.

The gang's all here when Murphy and Vanna, followed by Cannon and Jupiter, meander into the room.

In unison, everyone's head spins to face Lindsey without being asked. Again. If your publicist is in the room, it means business is about to be had.

"I have some good news," she croons before holding up a magazine.

My spine stiffens at the image on the cover. It's a picture of Sophia lying back in my lap, her back pressed against my front, as she sits in between my legs in the sand.

"It seems like my brilliant idea is paying off. Not only is the media talking about you"—her eyes connect with mine —"in a good context for once, but streams have already increased since TaylorTalks wrote this article."

Openly curious, Sophia asks, "What article?"

Lindsey hands her a copy of the magazine before she starts to read a duplicate copy out loud, "*Local playboy Mazen Wilde of the notorious rock band Kings of Jupiter has finally met his match. Both in style and creativeness, the fiery redhead he's been captured with on a couple of occasions now is Sophia Rose Lozier, local tattoo artist of Rose and Lace Ink*

Emporium. Sources ..." There's a hefty pause. "It's me. I'm the source." Lindsey lets out a cunning laugh before continuing, "*Sources say that the duo's promising future blossomed when Mazen booked an appointment at her thriving tattoo studio. It's as if fate has been tattooed on their hearts! Is this the encore for America's most desired musician? If so, my money is on the fiery temptress to slay the devil of rock.*"

An inferno of emotions swirls in my chest. Even knowing this was coming—with our staged dates and photo shoots leading to this very moment—it's as if my head has been submerged in water and I'm fighting a useless battle. It was bad enough having to hide my past with Sophia from my band ... my friends. I've had to wear a mask, concealing my true feelings for our tattooist. Now, the entire world knows about our whirlwind romance, and once again, I'm caged, having to hide my true feelings and intentions. But maybe—oh, this is good—instead of looking at this little charade as another hurdle, a wall blocking her out ... what if I use it as a stepping stone?

I've pushed my feelings down. I've pleaded with my cock and heart to forget her memory like she forgot mine.

Swig.

Maybe it's time to stop fighting against her and start fighting for her. For the ghost I've loved and chased for ten goddamn years.

Swig.

Oliver has made it seem easy enough to accomplish. Cannon, too, although it can't be confirmed. I've witnessed enough stolen glances between the three of them to know something is going on and I'm not invited into their inner circle.

I wasn't drunk or high enough to ignore the budding

tension on the bus when we all got caught gawking at her like a trophy just out of reach.

Swig.

The only problem now is ... me. I'm suddenly the outsider of a band I created. Once the tether, I've now been replaced with a temptress hidden in plain sight.

Rosella detests me.

Can I even blame her?

Swig.

For fuck's sake, I goaded her into hating me with my cruel commentary and screwing women in front of her as a way to push her away. For what reason? Because I was hurt. Scorned even because she forgot me. The man I was ten years ago. It sounds stupid. It sounds fucking insane that a one-night stand compared to all the meaningless sex I've had over the years would have such a hold on me. But it did ... it does. All I've done in return is hand Sophia a lighter and planted myself in front of her, covered in gasoline, ready to be torched.

My plan backfired like an eager exhaust because, now, all I want to do is be on her radar. To show her that I'm not the dickwad the media claims me to be. I want her to see me, Mazen Wilde, the man who met her at a tattoo convention years ago and left a piece of his soul with her. The man who claimed her in ways he's never claimed a woman since. The fame and fortune didn't change me. Nothing *has* changed me, like she did.

Sophia is our muse. Our collective heartbeats turned into a melody.

"Awesome. I guess I can add heart-taming extraordinaire to my résumé now," Sophia mumbles under her breath.

She's a smart-ass, and she speaks her mind. It's something I admire. Right now though, her fucking words pierce through my armor, wounding me like only she can. By the curling of her lip, she not only looks, but also sounds pleased with herself. I know her sarcastic stab really meant nothing more than defeat. A realization that she's now roped to me in more ways than just a contract. Much to my satisfaction and advantage, the world now associates her with me. As mine.

She doesn't know it yet, but that's exactly what she is. What she's been all along.

Even when miles and states separated us, Sophia was my Rosella. My harness of normalcy.

She will be again even if I have to go up against my bandmates to win her affection.

36

FASTER THAN A MINNOW

OLIVER

THERE'S a look in Mazen's eyes as he stares in an intense glare at Sophia that is almost visceral.

It's as if the air in the room has shifted. We're caught in a vortex of his unyielding disposition. I can't decipher what's going on. Hell, I haven't been able to decipher why he loathes her in the first place. Unless ... he doesn't actually loathe her at all.

Like an adolescent boy on the playground, what if Mazen actually likes Sophia too?

My mind bounces through the encounters they've had the past couple of weeks, starting with their initial confrontation at her tattoo studio. Something definitely transpired between them prior to her sister and me storming into the room. What? I don't know. Neither of them has spoken of that night. Even after Cannon and him stormed off, Sophia didn't speak another word about it. We just sat on her couch in the reception area for hours, talking until we were both delirious and called it a night.

While Maz and I both have gotten our fill of beautiful women, he only started making his conquests known when Sophia joined us on tour. That, paired with his infatuation of getting tattooed in a different studio after every show, might mean ... hate doesn't mean hate; it means something else altogether.

Do they have a past we don't know about?

I've always been fond of puzzles. They're the only games—and I use that term loosely—that you could rent from the library for free. I'm an expert at piecing things together. This will be no different.

I swallow down my strong urge to detour into their past, trying to determine if there's more connecting them than this tour, and direct my attention back to the moment. Giving myself carte blanche to say whatever I want, I lead with, "What I just heard is that the label is happy with an increase in streams. Am I right?" I avert my gaze to Lindsey, who is scrolling on her phone, not offering eye contact but clearly listening, which is confirmed by a nod. "Since we don't have a show for two days, I say we take the day to chill. You know what that means?"

"Beach day!" the clan shouts in unison, excitement in their voices echoing off the walls.

Even Jupiter lets out an excited howl. Our mutt loves the water.

It's almost comical, seeing a slightly weighty husky with thick fur splashing around at the water's edge. "I know, buddy. I can't wait either," I squeal dramatically in his direction, earning myself a rather animated tail wag.

Lindsey, with her tight schedule of press releases and prim-and-proper outward persona, is beaming from ear to ear as she says, "We can all benefit from some fun."

"But?" It's Mazen who asks, leaning against the opposite wall, ending our thrill.

"But we still need to sell this whole fake-dating ploy. So," she says drawing out the O sound, "I'm gonna bring my camera, and I'll take some candid shots. No paparazzi. Just me. Are you cool with that?"

Avoiding confrontation, Mazen says, "Don't ask me. I'm used to my life being on display. Ask her." He tilts his chin toward where Sophia is standing, looking seemingly perplexed by this whole conversation.

"I, um ..." It's not like her to be at a loss for words. The only time she fumbles her words is when she's around *him*. That should have been my first clue that I'm not the only fish on her radar. "I guess that's cool. I mean, we need the media to believe it's true in order for streams to increase, so, yeah, whatever needs to be done."

"So, you can collect that check, right?" Mazen's cheeks heat, right along with his temper.

"Perfect." Lindsey beams, ignoring his remark. "Let's get settled. I'll arrange for the team to sweep the private beach and set up a perimeter. We'll meet back in an hour."

Sixty minutes fly by faster than a minnow swimming a dipper. By the time Murphy, Vanna, Cannon, Mazen, and Lindsey pack into the living room, my eyes scan the lot of them, and I notice that one very important person is missing.

Soph.

37

HUNGRY HYENAS

SOPHIA

"WHAT AM I GOING TO DO?" I sigh dejectedly, sinking onto the cool tiled floor of my bathroom.

On the verge of a breakdown, I called my sister, my sounding board. Ignoring the warnings from my phone carrier about the cost of making a call while abroad, I hit her name on the screen with a fervor I'd only experienced a handful of times in my life.

After hearing a quick recap about the band having downtime for a day and declaring it a beach day, she lethargically wiped sleep from her eyes and then sat upright in her bed, giving me her undivided attention. Now that she's up to speed, I wrap my arm around my knees and wait for advice.

"I vote you put on that sexy black thong bikini you just showed me and go roll around in the sand with three beautiful men." Lacey ties her pink locks back in a high ponytail.

Instantly, my throat dries, and my chest feels dull and

heavy. I regret calling her the moment fear creeps up my spine in a slow, methodical gait.

The nonchalant response she gave grates on my nerves.

I want to cuss her out. But I'm about a nanosecond away from spontaneously combusting and think better to use my energy on focusing my breathing rather than screaming what an idiot she is.

Any willpower I have left goes straight out the window when she adds, "You've slept with two of them already. Show the third what he's missing."

There's a rigid, accusatory bite in my tone when I hush-scream into my cell phone, "My scar, Lacey! I don't want those three beautiful men you mentioned to see my fucking scar. For Christ's sake, you know this, and you know why. It's been easy to stay fully clothed, for the most part, until now."

"Sis"—she quiets—"I'm sorry. I wasn't thinking."

"Well, I was. It's all I can think about right now. They'll know ... they'll all see it and know, and it's not anyone's business. I don't want their pity, and I sure as hell don't want the questions that will follow after they see it." Dread fills my gut. "My life is already on display. Hell, I live in their space. I eat their food. I follow them around like another dog. I'm pretending to date the *king* of the band himself. The world has a magnifying glass on my life. I freaking gained over two hundred thousand followers the morning after my boardwalk date with Mazen. Imagine if someone found out about *him* ... my ... shit."

A croak escapes me at the same time a lone tear falls down my cheek.

"My past is mine to bear and mine alone. I don't want them to know about it and look at me differently. I sure as hell don't want their publicist—who is *so* nice, by the way, and you'd really vibe with her—to get a shot of my giant scar in one of these stupid candid photos she's itching to capture."

The faint, extended line of skin that lingers across my lower abdomen is the only visible scar of the day my life changed forever. The emotional scars, they're etched deep into my very being, unable to be healed with anything but time—or so people say. My breathing is rushed, and I can feel the sorrow I attempt bury every single day as my eyes close, trying to escape a full-blown panic attack.

Taking a full breath, I force air out through my nostrils before I inhale with a practiced breath.

The line is silent once more. Lacey knows what I'm doing. This isn't her first time seeing me like this. Once I open my eyes and see her reaction to my mini freak-out, she's going to say something that's going to make me cry harder. Seconds pass before I seal the door shut on my raging emotions and risk opening my eyes. I take a look at my sister's face on my screen. It's evident she's more concerned than she's letting on.

She's as white as a ghost.

How fitting.

"I don't want to talk about it. It's all I did for years. I put my time in. I saw the shrink. I. Am. Fine." I bite out every word, knowing that they're all lies.

Lacey bites her upper lip, and her eyes gloss over. "You're not fine, Sophia Rose. Look at me," she demands. Her command is a lost cause. "It's okay to not be fine. You lost your so—"

"Don't. Please, Lacey. I'm begging you. Don't say it. I am literally holding on by a thread. I'm on the fucking bathroom floor in Portugal, crying my eyes out over wearing a bathing suit. I called you for a solution, not to be reminded that I lost the only thing ... person ... that mattered. Just tell me what to do right now."

I watch as understanding dances over my sister's face on the small screen, and heeding my plea, she regroups.

"Okay. I say you wear the bathing suit and just tie something around your waist. Since you're in the public eye now, I bet you'll start a trend or some shit."

"I don't have a personal stylist here. I only have what I brought, and I obviously did not think ahead to bring a one-piece."

"Ask your new bestie, Vanna." Animosity drips from Lacey's tongue.

This is not the time or place to unpack that jealousy-laced statement.

"Seriously, I'm not asking to borrow a swimsuit cover. You're no help."

"I'm on a different freaking continent, sissy. It's not like I can make a Target run and solve your problem for you. I wish I could. I hate this as much as you do."

Feeling defeated, I pull myself off the floor and pad over to the bed, where my black bikini rests on my bed. With the silky material sliding through my fingertips, I draw in a breath and then release it. "I just won't swim. I'll leave my shorts on and say I'm on my period."

Holding off another full-blown anxiety attack, I focus on the white lie that will keep the question about swimming at bay. That is, until Oliver asks if he needs to send someone out to purchase some coochie plugs—aka tampons.

BY THE TIME the sun starts to set, it is blatantly evident that you can take the men out of Florida, but not the Florida out of the men. Oliver and Murphy chase Vanna around like a pack of hungry hyenas. Cannon is being a loner, as usual, spending his day walking Jupiter up and down the shoreline, stopping every so often to check in on me by way of a smoldering eye-fuck.

If freezing time was my superpower, I'd wield it right now. In this very moment. Where chaos isn't on the horizon and everyone is enjoying themselves. I relish the faint breeze as it dances across my body, the sun beating down and the undiluted laughter that surrounds us. It's nice to just relax and to get the scoop on the men, outside of their artist counterparts.

I've been posted up in a chair under an umbrella, with Mazen sitting next to Lindsey. They're talking about all the times they used to sneak onto houseboats at the marina by their childhood homes. I almost forget that they're famous. Stories about impressive senior pranks or when Oliver broke his foot, trying to skateboard, and didn't have health insurance, so he went to the hospital and claimed to be Cannon, only for Cannon's aunt to be the nurse, totally blowing his cover fill the air around us. Their tales remind me that they're more than musicians, they're people with embarrassing stories and quirks too.

The faint sound of a phone clicking grabs my attention. I turn to face the direction the sound came from, half expecting Lindsey to be the person behind the camera. Much to my surprise, it's Mazen.

"Ahem." I clear my throat. "What do you think you're doing?"

"What's it look like? Taking a picture of my girlfriend.

You have this epic sun flare behind your chair right now. Hold still." He clicks again.

"Should I smile?"

Mazen playfully wags his index finger in my direction. "No smiling. Your serious face has this edge to it. I like it."

"Okay," I whisper, observing the ocean instead of the handsome man lying beside me on top of a towel. It takes every morsel of willpower in my bikini-clad body to keep my eyes glued on the waves.

"Do I have your permission to post this?" he asks quickly before thrusting his cell phone toward my face. I don't have time to process before he asks again, "Do you mind?"

There seems to be a disconnect. My mind is short-circuiting because for the life of me, I can't comprehend why Mazen Wilde is asking if it's okay that he posts a picture of me on his social media. A man who has millions of followers wants to post a picture of me.

A faint tingle sweeps up the back up my neck. I try to laugh at my unease.

"Why would you post that? I'm so confused. I thought Lindsey was doing all the convincing in this little white lie we're partaking in."

A beat passes. Mazen looks like he's thinking intently, searching for a solution or a response.

"We're dating ... and we're on the beach ... together, in this awesome fucking place. Why wouldn't I want the world to see how lucky I am with you by my side, Rosella?"

Muddled thoughts are replaced with a swarm of gooey delight as I grasp his question. A wide smile lines my face. With each passing day and fake date, the line between contract and crush is blurring.

"You're right." I suck in a quick breath before pulling

out my own phone and hitting the camera icon. "Let's see who gets the most likes. My money is on me."

Asserting confidence is usually my strong suit. *Go, girl. Go.* I give myself a mental pep talk before grabbing Mazen by the horns—or in this case, shoulders.

I lean forward, closing the gap between our lounge chairs, and gently place a kiss on his warm mouth.

A sharp intake of breath, like a bolt of surprise, strikes between us when our lips meet. My heart races like a herd of cyclists pedaling toward their finish line as I close my eyes, blocking out the world and solely living in this moment.

Our tongues battle for dominance within the confines of our locked mouths. War has never tasted *so* good.

Mazen's hands gently cup the sides of my face as I hover over him on his lounger. He deepens the kiss, pulling me onto him and nudging my body as close as possible. Nothing else matters as unbridled passion sweeps over us. Not the contract or the fact that Lindsey is most definitely capturing this moment or that his friends—our friends—are most likely watching us. The past and the present—*everything*—disappear as we explore each other's mouth in a dance of wanton need and unadulterated passion.

I forget about the hateful comments we've thrown at one another like stones. All the times I've walked into a room and he was fucking some bitch just to get my attention. Everything that *was* fades into the air around us. Our mouths part only for a few fleeting seconds to catch our panting breaths before we collide again, like fiends looking for their next fix.

Time stills as we live in the moment.

The warmth of Mazen's skin against my palm as I caress his broad shoulders, sun-kissed from the afternoon rays. I quiver under his touch as he explores the skin of my back, my waist, my hips. Finally, our lips part after what seems like an eternity has elapsed. Something unsaid passes between us before Mazen's eyes smolder once more in a lust-arousing, unsated pulse.

"You taste just like I remember," he murmurs as he plants a plethora of kisses along my neckline.

Like he remembers?

"There's so much that I want to say, *Rosella*." He lets out a low hum as delicate as a summer breeze before he grazes my earlobe with his mouth. "Not now though. We have company."

"What in the actual fuck?"

Instinctively, my body goes rigid at Oliver's cold tone.

"You couldn't keep your greedy fucking paws off her, could you?"

There's a deceptive calmness to his demeanor that has me tearing myself from Mazen's embrace. Stirring the pot has finally caught up with me. It's boiling over, and only I'm to blame.

I've fallen into a dick trap, and I can't get up.

"Please don't." I hold my hands up as I stand, and I press them into Oliver's defined chest. "I kissed him. It wasn't the other way around. If you're going to be mad at anyone, be mad at me." There's an air of finality in my voice.

Succumbing to the fact that I like ... that I'm attracted to them all, I know I need to come clean. There's no time like the present to admit that you're a secret cum dumpster. Even if it means having to lose out on the money from both of my contracts because there's no way in hell that this can go any way other than south. It's time I own up to what I want—or think I want—and stop hiding like a coward. I'll accept the consequences as they come.

"Ollie, I like you," I say, my palms still pressed up against his chest. Small droplets of water from a recent dip in the ocean slide down, pooling in the crease of my fingers. "I like Cannon too."

He gives me a slow smile but doesn't say anything.

"And I think I also like Mazen."

The deep sound of a masculine laugh bellows from behind the three of us as Cannon walks toward me with a grin of amusement written on his face. Long strands of wavy blond hair are piled on top of his head. The sun has been good to him today.

"He's not mad, Sophia," he says, mere inches from us.

I smile in earnest at his nearness, forgetting whatever it is he's talking about.

Cannon draws closer, encasing me in his strong arms. With his mouth to my ear, loud enough for both Mazen and Oliver to hear, he says, "He wasn't trying to be a dick. It was more an accusation. We both knew it was only a matter of time before Mazen made his move too."

I'm dumbstruck.

Swept away in astonishment that Cannon, the brooding blond, is the one spelling it out for me. His usual melancholy scowl has vanished without a trace.

"What's gotten into you?" I ask swiftly without thinking.

Cannon's glum-faced expression has been miraculously replaced with a tentative grin that is irresistibly devastating. Satisfaction is etched onto his face when he croons, "You, Sophia."

It's a matter-of-fact statement. One that steals my breath.

"Jupiter and I—obviously, Ollie too—watched you climb on top of Maz. You were claiming him, and he almost let you take the reins until the very end. That's what Oliver was implying. He couldn't keep his paws off you. Not in a bad way."

My eyes skirt over to where Oliver is standing with his hands tucked into his boardshorts pockets. He's grinning at me with zero trace of animosity toward the singer in his gaze. Oliver opens his mouth, and a deep chuckle escapes.

"Now that you've told us how you feel, that you want us ... all of us, what are you going to do about it?" Oliver's bronze eyes beckon me.

Lindsey makes her presence known. "For starters, I'm going to dip out on this little ..." She waves her free hand around in the air while the other holds her camera bag and cell phone.

I all but forgot about their sandy-blonde publicist. Add it to the list of embarrassing things that have happened today. Getting caught with my hand in the cookie jar is one of them.

"Whatever the fuck is going on here, I don't have the energy to deal with it today. My one word of advice: 'discretion.'" She air-quotes the word. "Keep this out of the media for now. That means not only behind closed doors, but where no one—and I freaking mean, no one—is privy to whatever is going on here. When this"—she adds a dramatic flip of her wrist—"becomes something that warrants my attention, let me know. Until then, get behind closed doors."

At the end of her compelling commentary, Lindsey walks away, leaving the three of us with Jupiter. Who I swear is silently judging me.

I give him a you-love-them-all-too gawk back.

Love. Eww. That is not remotely close to what this is.

This is nothing more than wanting to be worshipped and filled to the brim with an ecstasy that only they can deliver.

Murphy and Vanna must have fled to their suite already.

Damn lovebirds.

It's hard to ignore the ember that illuminates from Mazen's usually icy stare as it deepens, fading into a shade that lingers on paranormal. He tilts his head to the side, angling his chin. "You heard her. Let's move this"—he dips his chin toward his friends, who all seem to be on the same page—"inside."

High on hope that tonight will be the night of giving voices to our guilty pleasures, I blurt out a secret, a desire that I've suppressed for days. "This sounds like the start of my dream."

Three sets of eyes deadpan.

"Crap. Did I say that out loud?"

"Yes, the fuck you did." Ollie's voice is stiff and unnatural.

Like a man who won't be satisfied with a simple explanation, Cannon hurls me over his shoulder like I'm a rag doll. With Jupiter flouncing beside us, we storm back to the house. Each step wider than the next.

In the distance, I see Oliver and Mazen abandon our towels and beach supplies, both scurrying to catch up with us.

There's nothing but wanton need and inquisitiveness about my dream etched onto their collective expressions as they jog behind us.

38

PLEASURE AND PAIN

CANNON

A SUFFOCATING sensation eats away at me from the inside as the door to our suite swings open. The woman standing before me, looking like nothing more than a delicious snack waiting to be devoured, isn't Sophia Lozier, the innocent tattoo gun–wielding woman who has slowly become a fixture in our lives. She's the vixen I met off the app. A flash of desire edges her bright green eyes.

My shoulders heave as we stand toe to toe in silence, desire mounting between us like two nations on the brink of war.

Nostalgia pricks at my throat and grips my already-erect shaft, hidden below my boardshorts. It's been too long since I've been buried in TattooKitten's tight cunt.

The need to spear her on my already-throbbing dick is crippling. I stagger to the patio door, fling it open, before doing the same with the lid to the hot tub. Each step I take is painful. There's a fire gnawing in my gut that borders insanity. That's what Sophia fucking makes me. Insane. I think about her perfect tits, slender body, and bouncy little ass all the goddamn time.

It's a sickness that I never want to be cured of.

Her mouth parts like she's going to say something before she closes it, biting her bottom lip and offering a resigned shrug, like she's accepted the beast inside of me for who he is. And she has without question. There hasn't been any persistent doubt about the night we shared our bodies and souls. Sophia gets *me,* both inside and out. She doesn't push for more. For an explanation about Oliver and me or why I'm as closed off as a deranged child. I can tell by her lingering stares that she yearns to know why I am the way I am, but despite her prolonged torment, she hasn't inquired.

It's for the best.

The truth is barbed with a history that won't ever be repeated anyway.

A flash of remorse is engraved onto her delicate face when she asks, "Shouldn't we wait on the others?"

I nod my head, regretfully, and then think better of it. Oliver had her first. It's time I put my own needs ahead of the band's. Especially where Sophia is concerned. I climb into the hot tub and extend my hand toward her. Lightning flashes in the pools of her forest eyes as she climbs in the water with her jean shorts on and laughs.

"This is so warm. It feels amazing."

A male voice echoes around us like a blanket. "You know what else feels amazing, Fireball?"

I bite my cheek forcefully in an attempt to not admit a truth I keep buried. *Oliver.*

The two of them climb into the water with us, relaxing into their respective spots. We each have a corner. Before Mazen speaks up, his eyes flash with a display of impatience.

"Tell us about your dream, Rosella."

"Is he always this demanding?" she asks, cupping water and letting it drizzle down her chest.

Streams of hot liquid meander over her skin, dipping into the cups of her black bathing suit. I fight the urge to end this insufferable game of foreplay and dive right into the promise land of a foursome.

Looking up from cagy brows, Oliver gives her a simple, "Yes," as an answer.

"The dream. Please tell us." Mazen's eyes are nothing but pools of appeal. If he's resorted to using manners, it means the bastard is just as desperate as the rest of us to hear about it.

Sophia smiles, sparking a glint of eroticism before she nails my coffin shut. "It's not a big deal or anything." Another arresting smile graces us. "I had a dream that we were all together. At the same time."

Her nonchalant performance is maddening, and she knows it.

Playing on her aloofness, I swiftly slide her weightless body in front of mine, water sloshing with my sudden movement. A tsunami-sized gamut of interest helps urge me on as I wrap my arms around her smooth stomach, holding her body snugly against mine. I'm rewarded with a quick intake of her breath and her body as it eases against mine.

"Use your words. Tell us what happened in the dream," I command, trying to coax her into painting the picture the three of us are dying to see.

"I ... we ... we had sex. Like I said."

It's Oliver who slithers like a snake through the water now with a wild calmness. Taking her feet and legs into his lap, he turns her body so that she's now floating on top of both of us.

"How did it start? You're an artist. Paint me the picture and don't fucking spare one miniscule detail, baby."

The delicious sensation of his demand causes goose bumps to dance alongside my spine.

It's hard not to relive the hunger we once shared for one another with Sophia on my lap, her ass perched directly on my raging hard-on. She swallows, and her eyes connect with Mazen's. Except he doesn't budge or move an inch. He leans back, arms wide along the edge of the hot tub.

"I don't remember how it started. I just remember the deed itself."

I nuzzle her ear, my eyelashes dancing above her lobe. "Tell us how you felt being worshipped like a queen by the three of us. How were we positioned?"

She succumbs to our gentle coaxing, and a floodgate of information comes out.

"We were all there ... together ... with one another, limbs intertwined. Cannon was lying on the edge of the bed." She pauses, her eyes meeting mine, flickering with amusement. "I was sitting on your lap, riding you. It felt so good, rocking back and forth on your hard cock. Like in the hotel. Do you remember?"

My dick twitches at her question. "I'll never fucking forget it."

I know she feels as needy as I do in this sweltering moment when she leans over her shoulder towards me, her mouth burning with fire, and sucks my bottom lip into her mouth.

Against my better judgment, I ignore the aching need in my pants and rest my chin on her shoulder. "Where was everyone else?" I probe, eager to see what positions my bandmates played in her little wet dream.

We all notice the shiver that ripples over her body as her

lips purse. "Mazen was fucking me too. He was"—her pupil's flare—"in my ass. You were both taking me at the same time. Sharing me, claiming me. I was so wet for you both. You barely even needed to use lube."

I glance across the water to find Mazen seemingly staring off into space. If it wasn't for the corner of his mouth pulled into a slight smile, I would think he wasn't even listening.

"Where was I?" Oliver asks from beside me, a smile perched on his mouth.

There's an unmistakable jolt of electricity in my body when his outer thigh brushes against mine in what I know is an intentional movement. The thing about Ollie is that he's deliberate in everything he does.

Sorry, he mouths almost apologetically as his large hand grabs ahold of my thigh that he just ground against with his own. With his palm draped over my thigh underneath Sophia's leg, mere inches from my throbbing cock in my pants, we're both at his mercy.

The vein in my shaft thickens like an awakened river has been opened, blood coursing at the excitement her little play-by-play brings and the fearful clarity that Oliver just awakened within me. It's like the veil he's kept over his beautiful fucking eyes for years has been lifted. The realization of his deliberate movement coats my throat like a wine from Miller's Winery. I desperately need more from her and him.

I feel as if my world has careened off its axis ... because it has.

I'm about to dive off the edge of insanity when Sophia adds, "You were in my mouth, Ollie. Your jellyfish tattoo was healed—thank fuck—and I was sucking you off. You tasted so good. I can still taste you on my tongue. You were on the brink of release, and when I felt your balls tighten, I took your dick from my mouth and let your seed fall in waves right into Cannon's open, waiting mouth. It was the hottest thing I'd ever seen in my life."

"Fuck. That sounds..." The wealth of Ollie's dyed blond hair moves in the breeze when he quicky turns to face me. "Like it's happened before."

A beat of time freezes as his words ... his confession ... his acknowledgment resonates somewhere deep in my chest. Passion pounds, forcing blood through my heart toward my agonizingly hard dick.

Those words bring both pleasure and pain. A memory and foreshadow of what's to come.

A gentle moan pulls my attention back to the bodies filling the warm water with me. I was too preoccupied with the onslaught of appeal Sophia painted that I momentarily forgot that I still existed alongside everyone else.

Another moan is pulled from Sophia's parted mouth and swallowed by Mazen's as he forcefully grips her by her hair, tilts her head to meet his, and slides his fingers into her awaiting mouth. The tentacles of his jellyfish tattoo line down the fingertips that dip into her warm opening as they slide past her teeth.

She's sitting on my lap, grinding against my dick with her legs and feet dangling on Oliver's lap, all the while sucking on Mazen's fingers with her sultry mouth that just weaved the best daydream I've ever heard.

With slack jaws, both Oliver and I watch the scene before us unfold. A scene that has been destined to happen since she stepped onto our tour bus.

Mazen's tongue replaces his fingers, and Sophia succumbs to the forceful domination, her chest rising and falling at a rapid pace. Our siren is loving her reward for telling us about her dream. She's at our mercy in this hot tub. But make no mistake; she's the skilled lover harboring a savage mastery of power.

Sophia has morphed into our queen in a matter of weeks. The thought both excites and scares the shit out of me.

I turn my head to the side, trying not to pry on their moment, only to find Oliver watching me intently. Sweeping his lashes up and down, he looks my face over with a renewed sense of appreciation, like it's the first time he's seeing me again or allowing himself to notice.

Detecting an inferno of wanton need mirroring my own, I allow my eyes to roam. Traveling from his eyes to his plump mouth to the spot right below his ear that he used to love for me to kiss. Under his steady gaze, I lean forward. Oliver's eyes widen in approval. I press an open kiss to the warm hollow of his neck. Leaving his skin scorched by my touch, I look, savoring the approval in his irises. Approval I've chased like the tide for years, only to be turned down, made into a fool by his repeated dismissal. Instinctively, I prepare myself for the hurt that's to come when he comes to his senses.

Oliver Collins is the reason for my seclusion.

Because the one time I spoke my truth, he made me feel like it was one-sided.

By the look in his eye right now, I know that it's not. He's fought a good fight though.

"Ahem." Sophia clears her throat. No doubt taking in the exchange in front of her. "Would you two like some privacy?"

Her question isn't laced in disgust or accusation. It's inspired by a history that she's been privy to without it being spelled out for her. Mazen's facial expression, on the other hand, is off-putting.

"Don't answer that." Mazen jumps out of the hot tub. "I'm not really into group escapades so I'm going to bounce and give this little trio"—he flicks his wrist—"the green light to do whatever the hell you want. Without me."

"Mazen"—Sophia pouts—"nothing is happening. It was just a dream I had. Just hang out with us. I don't want this to be … weird."

Weird.

That's exactly what this whole day has been.

39

LITTLE SCAR

OLIVER

MEMORIES CLOUD my vision like a thick fog.

After we ate dinner, mostly in silence, with haunting looks from Lindsey, Murphy, and Vanna, everyone decided to go their separate ways.

Mazen retreated to his suite to open fan mail. It's his thing. He claims he never wants to forget where we came from, and being able to read cards and letters from our fans keeps him humble.

Lindsey fled to her room, claiming that she had a headache. Which I know is a lie because I saw her sneak outside with Ashton.

Filthy little publicist.

Murphy and Vanna decided to take Jupiter on a walk with a couple of members of security since Ashton was otherwise preoccupied.

That leaves Cannon and Sophia. Except I don't know where either of them is. A sinking suspicion guides my feet outside toward our tour bus.

Years ago, before our first number one hit, Cannon and I had a fallout of epic proportions. An argument about expanding our … relationship … and becoming official. Cannon told me he loved me, and I told him that I wasn't worth loving and that we needed to cool the jets on our explorations with one another.

I always assumed he fled to the bus like a sanctuary in order to put distance between us. Our break in rolling in the bedsheets turned into spending countless hours in the studio together while attempting to keep up our charade. Hiding our indifferences was exhausting. The bus was his safe haven. I could understand that. He needed space to process the unwanted space that my denial gave him.

It's why it's the first place I think to go.

This conversation has been neglected for far too long.

In the hot tub … we shared a moment. A split fucking second where I allowed my mind to drift back to a decade ago. I hate to admit it, but it felt … good.

Right. It felt right to have his lips on my mouth again. I wanted them somewhere further south.

The mind-blowing thought of Cannon's mouth on my skin is short-lived when I walk up the three steps into our tour bus and find Cannon's hips thrusting.

"Such a good fucking girl," he hums. "Swallow every drop."

The dominance in both his stance and the appraisal he showcases is new. As big, broad, and burly as Cannon is, you'd be surprised to know that he's a bottom. Well, apparently, a switch. But when we were … whatever the fuck we were … exploring our sexualities, he was always the bottom. He likes to be dominated, demeaned. Yet the assertive tone he praises Soph with as she listens to his command is like a cock ring to my shaft.

My dick is as hard as a rock when I make my presence known.

"How's it feel to be in charge?" I ask, my words solely meant for the drummer's ear. "Do you like it, Cannon? Does it make you feel powerful?"

At a loss for words, Cannon straightens his back before helping a scrambling Soph to her feet. There's a calmness that wafts off him in waves that I haven't seen before. It's been years since I allowed us to be together … intimately. It's apparent that time has changed him in more ways than one. I remember him being a jittery mess the first few times we fooled around. We were nothing but horny teenage boys with time to kill in his parents' basement.

The first time he nutted by my hand, he didn't talk to me for a week. I won't lie and say that it didn't feel wrong to me either. I wasn't as embarrassed as he was, and even though society told me one thing, my body told me another. He couldn't look me in the eye, even at band practice after that.

One could claim that I introduced him to this way of living. Even though he forged on to experiment in ways that I only ever have with him. His dick is the only one I've ever sucked. His ass is the only male ass I've ever sunk into. The second time I made Cannon Rhodes come, I sucked him off in the locker room after his football practice.

Unlike Cannon though, I made my intentions clear from our first kiss. There was no room for emotions in the sheets. I didn't know what love was.

To me, back then, that pesky emotion was shown through sex. Things were fine until he said those three little words and ruined everything. Then, we left to tour, Mazen came back from a trip to Chicago with a chip on his shoulder, Murphy started meditating, and the rest is history.

Well, aside from the little fact that I made him feel guilty about his desires, after the lines of sex and lust blurred and I pushed him away. I'm the one at fault for shattering his heart, the real reason for our drummer's wayward behavior.

I ruined him in all the ways one could by succeeding in pushing someone away. It wasn't until years later, by watching Murphy and Vanna have a successful, healthy relationship, that I learned people were capable of love. That I, too, was capable of love if I let myself feel it.

Cannon threw me into a tailspin before I was ready to believe in hope or anything remotely close to love. I had grown up alone, without a lick of supervision or compassion, and the fleeting feeling scared the shit out of me. I did what any confused new adult would do. I deflected and immediately extinguished my own fears by making Cannon out to be the bad guy.

In reality, he's the one who got away, and I fucking shoved him and his memory into a box so tight that it'd need a crowbar to open it. Until tonight ...

The thud of my shoes echoes in the crammed space and guides my thoughts back to reality, grounding me with each scuff of my heel. Cannon dwarfs me in height, a solid four inches taller than my frame as he hovers above me. Regardless of our size difference, I'm in charge. I'll never give up control. Not after growing up without any.

"I asked you a question."

"It feels good." The deep timbre of his voice echoes off the walls of the bus. "I like it."

"Do you remember how good it felt when I was in charge?" I press into his space, ignoring Soph's gawking eyes.

A beat passes before Cannon nods, answering in a way

that I knew he would. As much as he fights to control, reining in his true self, he savors the thought of giving it all up. Handing over the power and relishing in the struggle of it all. Unleashing his inhibitions to give into the desires that he was ashamed of as a kid, he now seeks them out as an adult. His desire to be controlled is almost palpable. I'm not as oblivious to his kinks and secret sex meetups as he likes to think I am. He might as well be sporting a *Verified Kinkster* T-shirt.

Little does he know that this little power exchange is like gasoline, setting my own kinks ablaze.

I've gotten off on this knowledge more than once. That he's out there fucking men and women, but not getting fucked himself. At least I hope he hasn't given anyone else that part of him that only belonged to me.

Soph appears openly amused by the power relinquishment happening in front of her.

I shock her further by padding the glint of moisture left over from Cannon's release that glistens at the corner of her mouth with my index finger.

A hint of disbelief hangs in the air around the three of us as I methodically bring my finger toward my mouth and suck the wetness off. The act is registered by the sharp inhales of breath around me.

"Did you just ..."

Ignoring Soph's question, I divert my attention, roughly grabbing Cannon's face. Crushing his cheeks in my grasp. If he wants to be dominated, I'll gladly fulfill that wish.

"Did you nut before her?" My voice is stern, domineering, as I tighten my fingers on his jaw. "Don't make me ask twice." Finality rings in my tone.

"Yes. I did. She wanted to suck me off."

Disgust plagues my every thought. "Make it right. For your one release, she gets two."

I step back, giving Cannon room to right his wrongs. He grabs Soph by the hand and quietly guides her to the master bedroom in the rear of our bus. I follow along, eyes burning into their backs, my cock growing harder and harder from the power dynamic shifting in the small space between the three of us.

It's always the quiet ones, the funny ones, who swing the hardest dick.

Without words, Cannon kneels before Soph, removing her shoes before he starts on her shorts. He was always a good listener. Even as kids. He never was one who wanted to get in trouble, go against the grain. It's a wonder he's not a full-fledged drag queen due to how hard he's tried to suppress his true self.

"Can we turn off the light?" Color drains from Soph's face.

The blatant nerves that hang from her question are very off vibe for her. She's let me eat her out several times over the past couple of weeks. In hindsight, I guess she has kept her shirt on every time. That ends tonight. I don't want any more barriers between the three of us. Not them partaking in fun without me and not us being denied the right to see her delicious, naked body.

"No." I drop down, taking a knee in front of her, alongside Cannon. "I want to watch you come apart by his tongue. The light stays on."

"I, um ... shit. I need to tell you both something then." There's a hesitation intwined with her plea. Scooting back on the bed, she drags her legs underneath her and sits crosslegged. Apprehension twists on her face, and her shoulders tense when she says, "I had a hysterectomy."

"And I've had a dick in my mouth. What's the purpose of telling us this?"

She swallows a couple of times, having difficulty finding her voice. "My mom died of cervical cancer. Lacey and I both had genetic testing done." A small quiver escapes her beautiful mouth. "I tested positive. I carry the gene. When I was old enough, I elected to have my ovaries and uterus removed as a safeguard. I lied when I said I was on my period earlier. I just didn't want anyone to see my scar." Her fingers splay against her core, fidgeting with unease.

The discomfort she's displaying tells me that there's more to the story than just a precautionary surgery. As the seconds pass, her dismay grows. I lean in, pressing a soft kiss to her temple before settling on the bed next to her.

"Why are you telling us this now, Soph?"

"Because you're about to take off my pants, have your wicked ways with me, and I don't have a shirt on. Just this bathing suit top. So, you'll see my scar. It's ugly, so ugly and repulsive, and I wanted to give you a warning. I ... I just feel more comfortable telling you before you see it and jump to whatever conclusion men usually do when I'm with them."

"Do we look like the regular fuckboys you toy with?"

There's a substantial weight in her heady glare. "No. Of course you both don't."

"I've seen it, Sophia. Remember?" Cannon asks while climbing up to sit next to her on the bed.

"It was a lapse in judgment and in the heat of the moment. I wasn't thinking clearly when you saw it, Cannon."

"Nothing about you is ugly. Scars and all. Trust me, mine run deep. Nothing about you can scare me away. Not now. Not ever." He glowers before saying, "And you were thinking clearly. You just didn't care in the moment. Just like you shouldn't now. We all have scars, visible or not. Don't be ashamed. I'm not."

I get it. I hurt him in ways I can't begin to think of. If I could turn back time...

"Show me the defining scar," I instruct, rolling my eyes. "I want you. All of you. A little battle wound won't deter me."

Soph doesn't move. It's Cannon who gently palms her chest, pushes her back against the mattress, and ever so slowly unbuttons her shorts. He leisurely slides them down her legs and then moves on to her bathing suit bottoms.

The expanse of her body is breathtaking, just like I recall.

The faint white scar lining her lower abdomen isn't anything to be embarrassed about.

"It's barely noticeable," I admit.

"Thanks. Trust me, it's noticeable. A reminder of what could have been." She glances up toward the ceiling before closing her eyes.

"Let Cannon take your mind off the scar. He owes you two orgasms." Grabbing his chin, I pull his head down, lowering it until he's hovering over Soph's exposed core. "Lick her clit so she'll forget about her demons."

It only takes seconds for her body to break out in a chorus of purrs as he laps her center like a deranged pussy connoisseur. His nearness is like a thrilling current running through my body. My senses are heightened. Every hair follicle on my body stands at attention, like he's directing the show. It's an illusion, I know. I'm powerless right now. That much is discernible.

Oblivious to the way my body is reacting to him, Cannon makes out with Soph's opening with expert strokes of his skilled tongue. With each sinful lap, I fall deeper into the abyss of this moment. It feels like time ceases when guttural sobs of wanton need explode from Soph's parted lips. Her greedy cunt pulses in a ferocity that has her splashing Cannon's chest with her release.

Wet liquid coats his chin, cheeks, and mouth.

My palms itch. I so badly want to lean forward and lick her release off his face. This isn't about me though. It's about her. I refocus my attention.

Through each convulsion, Cannon drinks her in as she continues riding out her wave.

Finally breaking from her core, he sits back a little on his heels. His hooded eyes find mine, and we share a knowing look.

His eyes saying, *I know you want me, too, you fucking bastard,* although his lips never move.

Desire ripples through me and I'm a goner when he leans toward me, lips coated with Soph's cum. A mixture of lust and agony somersault in my stomach. Thoughts I haven't given attention to in years pound in my chest like a drum.

I want *him.*

Again.

Without warning, Cannon leans forward, a look of burning hunger in his eyes as he claims my mouth. There's no pause, no second-guessing. Just him declaring a cease-fire on the war we waged eons ago.

Our mouths collide in a hungry power surge as his lips send me a soul-reaching message. There's nothing pretty or romantic about our kiss. It's messy. Fueled by repressed longings and wasted time. This kiss is as much challenging as it is gratifying.

Time ceases to exist as our mouths make up for the years we lost. The scruff of his face rubs against mine. We part on a tormented groan. I don't know if it's him or me that makes the sound, to be honest. I just know that I want ... need more. I stroke his cheek in a manner that gives off far too much emotion than I'm ready to admit to.

"You kissed him with your eyes open." Sophia's chest rises and falls in rapid succession. She looks as turned on as I feel.

"I've wasted too much time pretending not to see him. I don't want to waste another second," I admit before my hands travel down Cannon's chest and stop at the waistband of his shorts.

My dormant sexuality rouses at the peak of passion, and for the life of me, I don't know how we can go back to normal when the sun comes up tomorrow, knowing that this euphoria exists between the three of us now.

40

CAN'T SUCK IT MYSELF

SOPHIA

CLOTHES GO FIRST.

Followed by our inhibitions.

All I can think about is the burning desire to be filled to the brink by these two men. It'd be better than Christmas morning if Mazen were here too. I saw the contempt in his eyes. The warning in his tone when he claimed he didn't do group activities.

It's his loss then because group activities might be my favorite pastime now.

"I want to watch Cannon suck your dick."

Oliver's eyes dart from mine to his drummer's. "Fuck. That was forward."

"How much more forward can one get when you just licked his cum off my lip?"

"Point made. I want him, too, but my tat isn't healed. It's only been three weeks."

"Good thing you have a tattoo artist on standby," I say calmly.

His eyes grow dark, wild, darting between the two of us as Cannon and I sit on the bed, Oliver standing at its foot, commanding the room.

"Do you want to taste me?" His tone is predacious, sending a shiver of desire down my spine.

A gulp comes from beside me before Cannon answers with a quick, "Yep."

The smolder of Oliver's eyes burns into me a second before his resolve fades. "You told me six weeks."

"It's recommended. If you'd like my professional opinion, let me see how it's healed first. I can touch it up if need be, in a couple of days. No biggie."

Featherlike crinkles form around his eyes, and he laughs. "I've been suffering for three weeks for you to just now offer this up as an alternative."

A hefty amount of humor lingers in my tone. "I wanted to see how much willpower you had in you."

"Zero." A smile tugs at the corners of his mouth. "What are you waiting for?" He turns toward Cannon. "I sure as shit can't suck it myself."

"You so would, wouldn't you?" I offer an eye roll.

"Most fucking definitely."

A predatory scene unfolds before me. Cannon tugs down Oliver's pants in one fluid motion. His hard shaft springs to life. My artwork is on full display.

There's no hesitation as Cannon drops to his knees from the mattress, taking Oliver's erect shaft into his mouth. I contemplate getting a notebook out and taking notes because, man, can this dude suck a cock like it's no one's business. Using both hands, he jerks the base while sucking the tip. His tongue trailing around the head.

I'm lost in a sea of gurgles until Ollie's voice cuts

through the air in a tremulous whisper. "Oh fuck. Just like that. You remember, don't you, baby?"

Cannon's answer is muffled by the flesh he's swallowing like a champ.

Team No Gag Reflex is in the house.

I make use of my free time by lying back and enjoying the show.

With each confident dive of Cannon's mouth, I watch in awe and appreciation by the tenderness of Oliver's gaze from above.

The praise that he sighs, "Right there. You're such a good fucking boy." Followed a few minutes later by a, "Let me feel the back of your throat. That's it. Take me deeper," has me clenching my legs together.

Burying his hands in the blond hair on top of Cannon's head, I watch as Oliver drives his veined shaft into the back of Cannon's mouth with a forcefulness that makes Cannon cry out. Not from pain. Not in the slightest. Rather with unleashed desire for the man standing before both of us.

A man I had pegged as a joker. A soft soul. I must be a horrible judge of character because Oliver Collins is a fucking powerhouse of demands and praise.

I'm defenseless as I boldly stare, assessing the intoxicating scene before me. I peer at the two men intently, eager for my turn to be commanded and sandwiched between them. My knees quiver as my core starts to tingle, demanding its own attention.

With each maddening piston of Oliver's hips, my breathing becomes wilder.

An explosive current races through me as I forcefully shout, begging, "Stop. Please stop."

I want...need to be the center of all of this masculine

attention. Call me needy. I don't even care. I've been called much worse.

"I was wondering when you'd have enough. Don't be jealous, baby."

My cheeks heat under the intensity of Oliver's gaze as he pulls his shaft from Cannon's mouth, then leans down, eyes still locked on mine, and claims the mouth that created his pleasure.

Oliver parts their kiss a fraction, giving just enough space to spit. He fucking spits into Cannon's open mouth, and, hot damn, I melt. The harsh breath that leaves my mouth has me sounding like Jupiter, panting.

"So hot," I admit, giddy like a schoolgirl.

"Like I was saying"—Oliver tilts his neck to the side—"don't be jealous. We're here because of you, baby. You're a fucking Lamborghini in a room full of Teslas."

Wrenching my gaze from his, I scoot toward the end of the bed and thrust my hand into Cannon's hair and then pull backward. My slapdash movement is unexpected. It causes Cannon's broad shoulders to heave as he catches his breath, his wayward eyes locking on mine.

"I want some."

I wait patiently for my request to register. When it does, Cannon mimics Ollie's movement and spits their mixed saliva into my mouth.

We're all high on endorphins and the smell of sex in the air.

I dive in, my mouth crushing his. Fueled by the ravenous need to be included in this moment. There's nothing sweet about the series of kisses we share. Our teeth nip; our tongues dance. With his head tilted at an angle, I pause my assault on his mouth.

"Are you going to sit on your knees this whole night, or

are you going to get up and fuck me?" Oliver isn't the only director here. "Boss Daddy over there said you'd pay your debt. Two orgasms, remember? I'm ready to collect."

Cannon's callous hands from years of holding his drumsticks slide down my stomach. His warm fingers dance over my scar as he looks up, peering into my soul.

"So beautiful," he says. His gentle words send a current of adoration through my veins.

A part of me revels in his exclaim. The other part, the hungry, more deprived part doesn't have time for romantic notions. Especially not by the man who chased me around his hotel room, put a bag over my head, and used me in the best possible way the last time we were together.

My deep-seated need to be filled hangs thick between the three of us as Cannon moves his hands to my breasts, pulling both of my pink nipples with his fingers.

"Ahh," I gasp, my body melting into the mattress.

He leans forward and skims his mouth, warm breath on my crested peaks before he sucks one in his mouth and releases it with a popping noise.

I'm drowned in a flood tide of fiery sensations. My body aching, ready to soar until my peak is reached once again.

"Fill me up, Cannon. I want to milk your dick. Both of your dicks. Swapping spit isn't enough for me."

"Say less."

I moan aloud with an outcry of satisfaction when he enters me in one solid thrust of his wide hips as I lie on my back, perched on the edge of the bed. Legs spread wide for both men's viewing pleasure. Our eager response to one another's touch is evident in our roaming hands, and surrendering moans that radiate through the room, echoing our throes of pleasure.

"How long has it been?" I hear Oliver ask.

I was so hypnotized by Cannon that I forgot about Oliver standing behind him.

"Cannon, I'm going to fuck this tight little hole while you fuck our girl," I hear him say from his stance behind the man driving into me with force. "But I need to know how long it's been for you. Do we need to prep?"

"There's lube on my bunk." He grunts, his flesh hitting mine.

"A little presumptuous, were we?"

Shuddering, Cannon lifts my calve and drapes it over his shoulder. "Hopeful. I was hopeful you'd come to your fucking senses."

41

NO COPS

SOPHIA

THE SHRILL RASP of a phone pulls me from my sex-induced coma. When Oliver, Cannon, and I broached the line of foreplay, a frenzy between the three of us was awoken. One thing led to another, and pretty soon, we became a heap of limbs and panted breaths.

Somehow, we managed to make it back to the suite—Oliver's room, to be exact. The full-size bed in the bus had not allowed for the room that was needed to fully explore the moment we were all eager to embark on.

Keeping my eyes closed, I wait for Ollie to stir and grab his phone. Its insistent, demanding momentum keeps up a steady ring when I realize that his phone is on the charger next to him, plugged into the port and silent.

Eager to end the incessant hum, I untangle our limbs, toss on a T-shirt found at the foot of his bed, and climb from it in search of my cell phone. It's no surprise that Cannon is nowhere to be found. Despite our threesome last night, as perfect as it was in the bubble we built, reality always comes in the morning. We're not a throuple. Although the title alone sounds sexy and endearing. We're just acquaintances ... friends, who shared a naked evening.

Nothing more.

I find my shorts, my phone tucked into the back pocket, and alarm bells ring as I see the name on the screen.

Lacey.

"Soph," my sister says as soon as I yawn a hello.

"Yeah." I let out a yawn, not knowing the time.

"He found us." A sob escapes her.

An eerie chill hits me like a punch in the stomach moment the words resonate. Worry and uncertainty erupt within the cave of my chest. I hesitate to ask who, already knowing the answer in the pit of my stomach. My lip twists, my teeth biting their flesh.

My heart constricts.

My lungs deflate.

My soul leaves my body as thoughts scamper all at once in my mind, disorderly. A million questions swarming. *How? When? Why?*

It's been a decade since we fled Chicago. Why is he coming to collect now? So much time has passed. I let my guard down. I became comfortable. It wasn't enough to put thousands of miles between us. It'll never be enough until my dad's debt is paid in full, either with the money he owes *him* or my life.

"Sophia." A plea leaves her lips. Long gone is the professional-body-piercing, Taser-wielding badass.

The pink-haired woman whispering my name like a plea is the barely eighteen-year-old sister that clung to me like a lifeline so many years ago. The one who refused to leave my side, the girl who morphed into a woman right in front of me, my shadow. I told her then that I'd go to the ends of the earth to protect her, and I will until I take my last breath. Our father's shortcomings, his failures, are not her cross to bear. They're mine. I gladly accepted them so that my baby sister didn't have to.

"How do you know?" My voice, although stiff, is just earnest enough to coax the details from my panicked sibling. It's blanketed in a calmness that I've mastered over the years. One that says, *I'm not afraid of anything*, while simultaneously begging for a ray of hope to settle upon us.

"A brick. I was in the shower when I heard the glass shatter downstairs. Devon said he'd check it out. When he came upstairs, he was holding a brick."

A long pause.

I want to ask her why Devon, our tattoo studio's hired security guard, was in our apartment while she was in the shower, but now is not the time or place. I pocket that information away for later. I only have enough energy right now to solve one emergency at a time.

"There was a note tied to the brick, Soph. It's him. He's come to collect." Her voice quivers. "He found us."

Old fears flounder as I move hastily around the room, gathering my belongings. I catch myself glancing over my shoulder to the bed where Ollie lies. I don't want to wake him. With his knight-in-shining-armor complex, I know that telling him, involving him, will only bring danger to his doorstep. I refuse to do that. My heart beats frantically in my chest, each wallop a reminder that Lacey's well-being is my only concern right now.

I'm not naive enough to believe that we just popped up on *his* radar overnight. My name and our tattoo studio have been featured on television, commercials, and several popular ink magazines over the years. He's known where to find us. Anyone with half a brain could if they knew where to look. It's the *why now* that has me second-guessing myself in quick assessment.

No one—other than the guys, the label, our security detail, and my sister—knows about my arrangement with the Kings of Jupiter. Somehow, although I don't know how yet, he must've caught wind that I'm working for the band and not just dating a member. Knowing that I'll be receiving a lump sum of money at the end of my arrangement must've lured him out of hiding. He's a scorned fugitive, having been robbed blind by my dad. No doubt the reason my dad was later framed for murder and put behind bars. We fled before his arraignment. Now, our manhunt comes to an end.

We've been found. My sister has been threatened.

It wasn't enough that our dad abandoned us after our mom's death and buried his sorrows in the bottle. It wasn't long after Mom passed that his morals and willpower started to slip. First came the alcohol. Then the hard drugs. Then the gambling, no doubt to afford said drugs. Now, even behind bars, the bastard is still finding ways to ruin our lives. The debt he owes was passed on to us.

Lucky us.

If I was given the ultimatum of his life or ours, his soul would be damned before I could even blink. I'm far past hatred though. I don't even loathe him. He's nothing to me, to us. Just a dark part of our past. One we haven't been able to outrun. Trust me, we've tried.

Running from the conniving owner of the gambling ring my father had outwitted cost me my child.

My sweet, sweet boy. Roman, I named him.

Roman Forest Lozier.

History always has a way of catching up with people. I can't evade him this time. I don't want to if I'm being honest. I want to murder him with my bare hands for everything he stole from me. His goons pushed me down those steps. I'm not a fool. They were his orders. A message received loud and clear. He wanted his money and wouldn't stop until he received it.

After my body recuperated enough to be discharged from the hospital, Lacey and I left Chicago with one bag each and an empty car seat. I didn't know where we'd go. I just knew we had to get away. My fragile heart couldn't handle staying in the city with the memory of my mom ... and my deceased child looming over me. I remember we drove and drove and drove. Until the ocean line welcomed us with a long-awaited embrace.

I speak almost in a gagged whisper. "Tell me what the note said, Lacey. Every word. Don't skip anything. Wait." I'm sliding on a pair of shorts when I pause. "Is Devon still there?"

"Yes," she hiccups through tears. "He's right here."

Knowing that I want to speak with him, she hands him the phone without a prompt.

"What's going on? Lacey said she knows who did this. Do I need to call the cops? The whole front window of your shop is shattered." He breathes out loud enough for me to hear the panic in his hissing exhale.

"No cops. Do you know where we keep our gun downstairs?" When he doesn't respond right away, I add, "This isn't the time to play dumb. Lace told me about it. I need you to go downstairs and get it. This person ... those men who did this to the shop, they want something from us. Something we don't have, but they won't stop until they get it. This was a warning that his patience is running thin. I just need you to protect her until I get there."

He sighs, "With my life."

Something is definitely going on between them. At this point, I don't honestly care. If it means he'll shoot first and ask questions later just to shield her from impending danger, I'm sold on whatever is going on with them.

"I'm leaving Portugal shortly. It takes almost eight hours to get there. Stay at our apartment. Have Lacey, calmly, call the staff and tell them that we're closed and to take a personal day. Then have her make a post on social media, too, so that no one walks in," I instruct. "She's my ... everything." My voice is shaky, and tears are on the verge of falling. "Please don't let anything happen to her."

"I won't. It seems like we have some things in common." His truth lingers in the air. "I'm going to need some answers when you get here though, boss."

"It's been Lacey and me battling the world alone for so long. I don't know ... I'll do my best to answer what I can. Thanks, Devon. I'll owe you big time. Please give the phone back to Lace."

"Don't be upset with Devon. It just happened," Lacey confesses, her voice stammering, in fear of the repercussion of getting caught sleeping with an employee.

News flash: I'm the epitome of bad decisions. Last night's escapades were a clear indication of that.

"That's the least of my worries." I redirect her. "I'm glad he was there with you when it happened and that you're not alone. I need to know what the note says."

I know I need to wake Oliver up. I need to tell him that I'm leaving. He deserves to know what's going on, but I don't have the courage to tell him the truth, and I'm not good at goodbyes. I take one last glance over my shoulder, casting my eyes over the softness of his slumbering body, and tiptoe out of his room.

Making a beeline for my bedroom, I braid my hair and

brush my teeth in the span of two minutes. Then hastily pack a small bag of my clothes, before stringing it over my shoulder before walking into the hallway.

Inching closer to the front door, I whisper, "Lacey, tell me."

Her voice creaks as she chokes on the words. "It says, *I've been counting your breaths like I've been counting my money. Both don't exist to me. Give me what I'm owed, or prepare for your shop and your sister to catch fire.*"

"Dammit," I mutter under my breath. "Listen, I'm on my way. It's going to take a while to get there though. I will figure this out. I will keep you safe. I've never broken that promise, have I?"

"No," she answers quickly.

"I'm not about to start now. Devon's going to stay with you until I get there. I love you, Lacey Monroe Lozier. More than anything in this entire universe. I won't let him hurt you."

"It's not me he wants to hurt. It's you, and you know it. He proved that when he—"

The pain in her shaky voice throws me off-kilter.

Interrupting her, I say, "I'm resilient," and swing open the door to our hotel room.

Shock fills my core like a vehicle submerged underwater when I realize Mazen is standing in the hallway, holding an envelope and Jupiter's leash with a joint between his lips. The furry mutt dances in excitement at his owner's side.

Thoughts falter as I peer into Mazen's burning eyes as they implore me. A fragment of time passes as he assesses me like I'm ... a stranger. I don't have time to analyze his glower as I turn my attention back to the receiver.

"Lacey, I'll be there soon. I love you." I disconnect the

line, my attention now pleading with the scowling man in front of me.

The rich outline of his chest strains against his jacket. I gulp down my approval for Mazen fucking Wilde. Even if his look is edging on the side of murder and not lust.

"I need a favor." I bounce on my feet, nerves threatening to win the battle waging inside of me. "A big one." When his jaw thrusts forward, I continue, "I need to fly home. Right now. I need to go, and I..." Hot tears scold my lids, threatening to fall. "It's Lacey. My sister. She's in trouble. Can you take me to the airport? That's stupid. You can't take me. Can you call Ashton?"

With a taut mouth, Mazen's eyes dart across my pleading features. I don't even want to consider how I look, freshly fucked without an ounce of makeup on and worried beyond words.

Mazen remains wordless but offers a nod with a quick dip of his chin. Is he upset that Oliver, Cannon, and I officially were *together*? Surely, that can't be the reason for his strange standoffishness. He was there in the hot tub, too. He just made his inclination to not partake in our group fun known. He slings my bag over his broad shoulder without warning, and I notice the sharp line of his mouth. A mouth I kissed so passionately, that felt so right, pressed tightly against mine, that I forgot all the reasons why I'd refused to kiss him weeks ago.

Something's wrong.

Off.

It doesn't sit well in my stomach. Between Lacey's call and Mazen's stuffiness, my nerves begin to fray. I can feel the tears pooling in my eyes, on the verge of tipping over my lids. I can't focus on him. I pull my thoughts back to my sister, knowing that there isn't enough capacity in me to decipher what his deal is right now.

The only thought consuming me is getting back to the States, to my sister.

A BRIEF TRIP LATER, our driver parks us on the private tarmac. I'm hesitant to bid Mazen farewell. This car ride tops the one when he retrieved me like a gallon of forgotten milk the day after I slapped him. A whirlwind of three weeks it's been.

The silence that lingers between us is thick, smog-like, threatening to suffocate us both.

He shows me enough decency by opening my door and setting my bag at our feet. I reach forward, wrapping my arms around his middle, and press our bodies together.

What the heck? I think for a moment of suspended time when he doesn't hug me back.

Less than twelve hours ago, we were bordering the line between getting jiggy and letting our smoldering glares cut one another in half. I frown and shake my head, throwing in the towel on whatever this awkwardness between us is about. He probably regrets our kiss. Knowing that Lindsey is going to have a conniption fit if word gets out that we're all ... together. It makes sense. He's doing the logical thing by pulling back. I don't blame him. I can't blame him. Even if his dismissive glare cuts worse than it should.

It would be *his* image and career on the line.

I vowed not to fall for a musician, much less three of them.

I don't have time to deal with his doubts, eager to get back to my sister and figure out what the hell is going on. I give up on reading Mazen, turning my attention to Jupiter instead, and fall to my knees to bid the adorable pooch I've grown to love goodbye.

My future is bleak, much like the lack of conversation going on. When I stand up, my expression hardens. I don't know what's going to happen when I get back to Tampa. I do know that I don't have time to explain what's going on. Even if I'll forever be grateful to him for bringing me here and arranging the flight crew for a quick departure on short notice. If he can't give me more than a couple of flutters of his thick black lashes, then I'm ready to go.

Reluctantly, I smother a cry while I smooth my hand over my hair in a nervous motion. I shift indignantly from shoe to shoe before taking a deep, shaky breath and stepping backward toward the plane.

"Tell Oliver I'll call him when I land. He should be up and caffeinated by then." I force a smile over my thundering heart.

Two things happen, movements in succession.

Mazen unhinges his jaw, and my feet plant firmly on the concrete beneath them. For a moment, I think he's going to say something, give me an inkling as to why he's surveying my face like he's looking for a crack in my exterior.

A beat passes.

And then another, until he regains some sense and closes his hard-lined jaw.

I manage to offer a small, forgiving smile before I turn and make my way toward the plane. A rapid string of footsteps thud behind, causing me to turn. Mazen jogs behind me with the faint line of pain clouding his luminous eyes. I take notice of the same manila envelope he had in his hand earlier.

"Mazen, I have to go. It's urgent. Whatever this is"—I reach out and grab his hand, intertwining our fingers—"we can sort it out later. Okay?"

I place another featherily light kiss on his cheek before walking to the door, thankful that the flight attendant who greets me isn't the one that he screwed in front of me on a previous flight.

I care about him. Each of them. For different reasons and in different ways. My heart is divided in three ways. Yet, as I stare into the smoky gray eyes of Mazen Wilde, I know that he has the power to destroy me the most.

Call it intuition.

Mazen's love is lethal, and it will either break me beyond repair or help piece together the already broken parts of my soul if I let it.

With my hand on the rail and feet planted firmly in the plane, I hear his raspy voice call out to me from a few feet away.

"Rosella." He beckons my attention. When his eyes lock onto mine, despite the distance, they're darker than they were moments ago. Bitterness burns in the center of them. "Where's your son?"

His question plunders into my chest, slicing through me at the exact same time the flight attendant seals the door shut in front of me.

42

JULIAN

SLEEP DOESN'T COME easy when your mind is racing. I'm confused by his question and the pain echoed in his features, and my mind wanders restlessly. Each attempt at sleep is more futile than the last. Questions fly through my head quicker than pelts of rain in a thunderstorm.

I finally succumb to the numbness that only sleep will allow as it pulls me under like an anchor in the sea.

I'm disoriented for a split second when I awake. Realization hammering into my chest. I'm stateside. *Home.*

My mouth pulls into an irritated line as the pilot takes his sweet time coming to a halt. I listen for his instruction, my mind still trying to grasp the look on Mazen's face when he asked me where my son was.

Hurt people hurt people.

It's the mantra I've had for weeks where Mazen and I are concerned. It's like we've constantly been walking a tightrope of feelings. After we kissed in the hot tub, I really thought we'd found some sort of balance.

That semblance was shattered by one quick query.

White-hot anger courses through my veins as my mind tries to weave together a practical reason as to why he would ask me where my son was. Had Oliver and Cannon's knowledge about my scar tipped him off? *No.* They both believed my story about my hysterectomy. Which wasn't all a fabrication. I did have a hysterectomy. It just wasn't because of my mom's cancer diagnosis. It was in a futile attempt to save *his* life.

My *son's* life.

Because of what those bastards had done to me. The same men who undoubtedly threw a brick into my shop's window.

A nightmare I haven't been able to wake from is knocking on my front door again.

There's no logical explanation as to why Mazen asked me about my son. Unless ... *he knows.*

How would Mazen have found out I had a child? My medical records are in Chicago. What is it to him anyway?

It all comes back to his reputation and our fake-dating contract. I guess if his new girlfriend had an estranged child, the media would have a freaking frenzy with that kind of news.

That's it. He's just worried about his image.

My thoughts move frantically from one problem to the next as my chest aches as I remember Lacey's call, her hysterical voice, and the fear tethering us despite her being a continent away. The plane starts its descend, and my stomach dips. Frantic beats of my heart thud against my rib cage like a bird that's ready to break free and take flight as I sit and weigh how I'm going to navigate the royally fucked-up situation I'm faced with.

I settle on selling a kidney on the black market. It seems

like the only reasonable solution. I need cash—a lot of it—and I don't have time to wait. My head swirls with doubts as the stewardess finally opens the door. I grab my bag, stand, and fall into the night.

With each step, I grow closer to my sister. There's a tortured ache in my chest that only her well-being can dull. I *need* to see that she's safe with my own eyes.

It seems like yesterday that I climbed these same stairs and left the country for the first time. High on excitement and the adventure of the journey ahead. It's been a whirlwind of a couple of weeks. Between bickering with Mazen, getting lost in my art show after show, and exploring awoken desires with Oliver and Cannon, there's a pang in my chest knowing that this chapter of my life has come to an abrupt end.

It's for the best though, I try to tell myself as thoughts swirl, emotions as out of control as a rogue hurricane in the summer.

Who gets to say they traveled with a rock band?

This experience will forever be embedded in my soul. Just like the three of them.

An unmarked black SUV is parked in front of the steps. Thinking that Mazen arranged for transportation to take me home, I approach it without worry. I only slightly hesitate before deciding to open my own door or waiting for the driver to notice my arrival and get out and do it for me. It's not that I've grown accustomed to being catered to; it's just that it's what always seems to happen. Maybe flying alone is different. The band's hired workers only give a damn when the band is near or something like that.

Pushing down my confusion and disquieting thoughts, I open the back door of the vehicle. I push my bag inside and then climb in. Taking a moment to gather myself, I rest my head against the headrest and exhale a pent-up breath.

The material is warm, as if the vehicle has been on for a while, waiting my arrival.

I nod toward the driver. "I'm ready. Please take me to ..." I ramble off my address to the shadowy figure in the driver's seat.

There's a shift in the air of the compact vehicle. Causing an evanescent feeling of apprehension to quake in my stomach. I glide my hand across the leather seat and snake it up the door, gently tugging on the handle.

Shit. It's locked.

A quiver of panic slithers down my spine. I don't know how I know something is wrong, but I do.

"I think I dropped my keys to my house outside when I climbed in. Do you mind unlocking the door so I can check? It'll just take a second," I say coyly, an innocent grin on my face. A mask to the frightened feeling coursing through my veins.

"I don't like being ignored." An oddly familiar voice rasps from the driver's seat. "Do you love him?"

Thoughts race through my mind as the driver's voice dizzies my senses, and I try to place the voice with a face. A thread of hysteria holds me captive in its grasp as the sound of the familiar voice finally registers.

"Knox?" I ask, my voice shaking. *It can't be him.* Surely, it can't, right?

The moment our eyes lock in the rearview mirror, icy fear twists in my hollow stomach.

"Why are you here? How did you find me? Do *I* love who?"

Images build in my mind, like a puzzle piecing together

before my very eyes. A minute ticks and then two, a thick silence fills the vehicle.

"I'm here to collect you for—"

Julian Caddell. He doesn't need to call him by name for me to know exactly who he's talking about. It's the only explanation for Knox's presence.

I've been lured out of the band's protection by Caddell. He knew I'd flee, to save my sister and is using Knox to do his bidding.

A man from my past is my biggest enemy's accomplice.

I clench my hand tightly, until my nails dig into my palm.

"My uncle ... Julian. You remember him, don't you?"

A riptide of panic sweeps over me, consuming me whole—mind, body, and spirit. Images of my mentor and me spending countless hours tattooing, getting to know one another, being intimate surge through my mind in rapid succession. It all makes sense—the random text message, his interest in my life years ago. He was keeping tabs on me all along.

My heart palpitates in fear. "Your uncle? I don't understand. Did you know who I was when we met?"

"You will. At least you took his warning seriously and flew home before things got messy. He'll be pleased that you're ready to square up."

Questions fog my mind.

"Either by payment or death. For your sake, I hope you stopped at the ATM," Knox adds with a smirk on his face.

A face I used to have memorized. Lips that I kissed hundreds of times, eyes that roamed every inch of my body.

I gulp, all but wheezing at the realization that I've been played, like a fool. Just like my father who fell into Caddell's trap.

I was Knox's apprentice. His lover for a brief time. I know this man. At least, I thought at one time that I knew him. His presence gnaws away at my confidence. I've been one step ahead, for years, and now...it's over.

I pant in terror. The comprehension that Knox fooled me hits ... hard. He's been hiding in plain sight this entire time. He's had to have known I was on tour all along. How else would he know that I'd be on *this* plane tonight? Fuck. I don't want Mazen and the guys to be dragged into this mess ... my mess.

Wake up. You're dreaming. This can't be happening.

"I can see the wheels spinning in that pretty little head of yours. You were always so smart. It's a shame that things have to end this way. You should have taken me up on my offer and married me when I asked you years ago. Julian said he would have forgiven your debt. You only have yourself to be mad at, baby. You dug this grave on your own. Are your arms sore?"

TO BE CONTINUED...

Book 2, *Queen of Jupiter*, in the Ink & Lyrics Duet can be pre-ordered **here.**

Need a support group to discuss the end of Kings of Jupiter?

Join the discussion group on Facebook where you can chat with other readers **here** and join my newsletter **here** for exclusive excerpts, giveaways and other bookish news.

ACKNOWLEDGMENTS

Inspiration comes in many forms, and my biggest one is music. The ultimate muse. It speaks to my soul, and honest to God, it doesn't matter what the genre, I can get lost in it. Between the queen, Taylor Swift, and Machine Gun Kelly's last album, I was in harmony heaven. Can we talk about the sexy skater-boy punk era that Daddy Colson is in? I. Am. Here. For. It. If I could personally thank him, I would. Alas, this public declaration will do.

As always, I'd like to give praise to my beta team—Kerri Elizabeth, Elle King, Sarah Larson, Courtney DeLollis, Kayla Harper, Jennifer Foor, and Michelle Valentine. Words truly cannot express how much I appreciate the time away from your families that you dedicate to helping me hone my craft. Even when your criticism cuts me like a knife, I welcome the pain because I know my stories will flow better as a result of it.

The Author Agency PR deserves a round of applause for all of their hard work in getting my novel and social media platforms in front of people who love to read!

A sincere thank you to my agent, Savannah Greenwell of Two Daisy Media. Your friendship and guidance are a gift in my life.

I'd also like to give a special shout-out to my readers for taking a chance on every story I weave together. I know that Kings of Jupiter is spicier than my previous novels. I know that it might not be everyone's cup of tea, but in the end, isn't fiction supposed to be just that—fiction? A make-believe realm for us to emerge ourselves in. An escape from the mundane lives that we live. Thank you for allowing me to create this safe space for my heroine to be loved by three men without societal shamming. Thank you for one-clicking and giving KOJ a chance. Thank you for allowing my wild imagination to soar and for supporting my art.

Last and certainly not least, thank you to my real-life book boyfriend, aka Mr. Stayton. You might not be a billionaire, rock star, or a member of a harem ... but you're my world.

Nacole Stayton is thirty-something years young and resides in the Bourbon Capital of the World with her husband and son. Her debut novel, The Upside of Letting Go is an Amazon top 100 bestseller. She spends her days working in healthcare as a practice administrator and her evenings pinning away on her next novel. She can usually be found playing with monster trucks and dodging Nerf gun darts or enjoying an iced coffee poolside.

www.ingramcontent.com/pod-product-compliance
Lightning Source LLC
Chambersburg PA
CBHW060608300726

48975CB00005B/1494